Worlds Apart

Ber Carroll

First published in 2014 by Killard Publishing

Copyright © Ber Carroll 2014
Layout by www.formatting4U.com

The moral right of the author has been asserted.

National Library of Australia
Cataloguing-in-Publication data:
Carroll, Ber, 1971–
Worlds Apart / Ber Carroll
ISBN 978-0-9924721-0-8
Font: Garamond 12.5

The characters and events in this book are fictitious and any
resemblance to real persons, living or dead, is purely
coincidental.

Other titles by Ber Carroll

For Michael and John

Paris
March 1975

Dearest Cathy,

Bonjour ma sœur chérie! How are you, baby sister? And how are Mam and Dad, and Gerry and Paddy? Even though I miss you all very much, Joe and I are having a fantastic time. How can I describe it here? Fun. Sophisticated. Deliciously foreign.

We are settling in well and making a new circle of friends. You should see the other embassy wives with their glitzy dresses and glittering jewels – they sparkle from a mile away and I feel like Cinderella by comparison! I've already told Joe that I need a bigger shopping allowance. You should visit us, Cathy, and help me upgrade my wardrobe – you have such a good eye for fashion. We have plenty of rooms in the house; so many, in fact, that the entire family could stay and we'd hardly notice! Did I mention that we have a maid? Anna is Polish, and has adequate English (when she chooses to speak!). She lives in – which seems to be de rigueur in Paris – and she is so quiet and mousey that I sometimes forget she's in the house. Last week I was walking up the stairs when she appeared out of the shadows on the landing above me and I screamed, frightening the wits out of the both of us.

I have some news, Cathy, really good news, but you must promise to keep it to yourself for now. I'm pregnant! Isn't that wonderful? Moving here was clearly the right thing to do. Both of us were so jaded from the disappointments and stress, a change was just what we needed. I'm quite certain that I'm having a little girl. So certain that I've already picked out a name, something Irish, of course, but I'm not going to tell you what it is, not until I'm cradling my baby in my arms and I can see her precious little face for myself and whisper her name to her. In a few weeks, I'll announce the

1

news to Mam and the boys and whoever cares to listen. By then the baby will be bigger and stronger, and I'll want the world to know that she's here to stay.

I'm writing this letter in one of the many local cafés. The smell of croissants and freshly brewed coffee makes me feel inordinately content and happy within myself. Dublin seems very far away, worlds apart from here, not just in miles but in every possible way. The food, the people, the frantically fast traffic on the street outside, the overall vibe and beat of the city – everything is so different. We both feel a strange sense of belonging in this city, as though this is where we are meant to be. Our pale skin and Dublin accents are irrelevant, because belonging is something you feel in your heart, and I've realised it has nothing to do with what you look like, or where you are born and raised. Don't tell Mam and Dad that I can't see us coming home. I know they'll be devastated, but Joe and I have to do what's right for us. There are any number of positions that Joe can apply for when his term at the embassy is over. He's so happy here. We both are.

Do consider coming over, Cathy, and not just for a few days. The city is thriving, and there are so many jobs for typists you could have your pick. As I've said, you are more than welcome to stay with us. We'd be there for you if you needed us (including Anna – imagine, a maid at your beck and call!) but you could have your independence, too.

Write back soon and tell me all about the family, your work and, of course, the latest man on the scene. One of the few things I miss is being able to hear firsthand about my baby sister's escapades!

Lots of love always,

Moira

Chapter 1

Dublin, February 2010

Erin gazed at the narrow, jagged lines streaked across the window panes. The rain had ice in it. All day it had been coming in short, bitter bursts, whipping sideways against the glass. It felt reassuring to be inside, and to imagine, rather than experience, how cold and sharp it would feel against her bare head. The room was artificially warm and bright, the oil heaters lending a slight stuffiness to the air, the electric lights overcompensating for the gloominess outside. It would be dark by the time she left school at four o'clock and, if the weather forecast was to be believed, it would be freezing by early evening.

'Tristan Keary, stop that right now!'

'Sorry, Miss.'

'It's Mademoiselle, not Miss.'

'Sorry, Mademoiselle Donovan.'

'Sorry? I thought we were in a French class here.'

Tristan looked blank, an expression he had practised and

perfected since the day he'd started secondary school, in fact maybe since the moment he'd been born. Erin emitted a long-suffering, very teacher-like sigh.

'Emily, please tell Tristan how to apologise en français.'

'Pardonnez-moi.'

'Merci, Emily. Tristan?'

'Pardonnez-moi, Miss – I mean, Mademoiselle.'

'Lucky for you, Tristan, that an apology somehow sounds far more genuine when it's said in French! Now, everyone, continue with your work, please.'

Erin stared at her students until one by one they succumbed, heads swooping towards exercise books, pens twirling in thought, and silence – beautiful, rare silence – crept across the classroom and into the recesses of her head. Not pure silence, of course. Sighs, sniffs, shuffles and position-changing in chairs, rulers clattering against desks, the rain thrashing against the glass, thwarted in its attempts to get in, the sound of paper being torn – coming from Tristan's direction? – all removed the possibility of complete quiet. Nevertheless, it was as close to silence as Erin would get in the remaining twenty minutes of this forty-minute class and it was to be enjoyed.

In these rare moments of quiet, she often paused to consider how fond she was of them, her students, and this class of third years in particular. Each of them, in their own unique way, had a special place in her heart: Emily, bright, earnest, a question always hovering on the tip of her tongue waiting to be asked – its answer, when provided, promptly analysed and catalogued for future use; Tom, awkward, self-conscious, far too serious; sweet little Aoife, always so eager to please; Darragh, accident-prone, writing clumsily with his left hand, his right in plaster after tripping over in the school yard last week, his second broken bone since Erin had known him; Aaron, looking achingly more adult than his classmates, downy hair on his upper lip, his long legs folded under the desk, towering over Erin and most of the other teachers in the school; Lisha, originally from Nigeria, who had arrived in Ireland and into this class two years ago but who remained on the outer and unsure of her place amongst these teenagers who were the same age as her but with so little else in common. Even Tristan, with all his bravado and clowning around, was special. Erin hadn't told them yet that she was leaving, that this was her second-last week at St Patrick's Community School. She would tell them next week. She smiled to herself as she imagined the outcry at her news.

'But, Miss, I mean Mademoiselle, it's the middle of the school year!'

'And this is our Junior Cert year. The most important year of our *lives*!'

'Why are you going? Is it something we did? Is it Tristan?'

'Of course it's not me, knuckle-head!'

'Who will we get now? Don't say Grouchy Gallas! Not her, please. *Anyone* but her!'

Erin would miss them – more than she could ever tell them. She felt guilty for leaving like this, in the middle of the academic year, the Junior Cert exams looming on the horizon. She wished that she had it in her to stay, that she could hold it together for another few months and guide them through the mock exams and then the real thing.

'Is it your health, Mademoiselle? Is it because of your heart?'

She imagined that Aoife, trying harder than the others, would hit closest to home. Yes, it was her health, and in many ways it was her heart, too. Despite the guilt, the worry that they might do badly in their exams because of her untimely departure, the suspicion that Madame Gallas would be too stern with them and ruin their enjoyment of the language, Erin felt sheer and utter relief that she only had the bones of one more week to get through. She was hanging on by a thread, the thinnest thread imaginable. Part of her, the part that felt a week was interminably long, wanted to stand up right now and walk without explanation from the classroom, through the grid of corridors that led to the main door, outside into the stinging rain, breaking into a run halfway down the drive, no longer able to disguise or control how desperately she needed to get away. In light of thoughts like this, and the disruption they'd already suffered in term one due to her 'heart' trouble (which had in fact been a severe – not to say, excruciatingly embarrassing – panic attack), it was much better that her students had someone more steady to guide them over the coming months.

The sounds of fidgeting increased in volume, a sign that some of the students had finished their assignment. Erin's attention was required, to control those students who were finished and allow the slower ones to complete their work in some degree of peace and quiet.

'Tom, avez-vous terminé?'

'Oui, Mademoiselle.'

'Apportez-le ici.'

Tom gathered his book and pencil and, looking as though the weight of the world were on his shoulders, loped towards her desk. Erin quickly marked his work, keeping one eye on the classroom, particularly Darragh and Tristan, who looked as if they were up to no good.

'Super, Tom, c'est très bien.' He blushed at her praise. She hoped Madame Gallas would see how well he responded to positive feedback. Maybe she should leave notes on each child, a document outlining their strengths and weaknesses and how to get the best out of them. Would Madame Gallas be affronted by such a document? Surely she would take it in the spirit in which it was intended.

Madame Gallas – a native of France – had lived in Ireland for more than twenty years, but acted as though she had only just arrived. She had excellent linguistic skills along with a dogged determination to turn the flat Dublin accent of the students into a beautiful French accent like her own, but her rather irritable disposition and poor opinion of the students got in the way of her success. 'The pupils, they speak out of turn and in rude tones of voice! They have *zero* respect. Irish children need lessons in good manners *much* more than lessons in French.'

Her nickname – Grouchy Gallas – was rather deserved, in Erin's opinion, not that she would ever let on to the students that she agreed with them on this matter.

'Lisha, venez ici!'

Lisha pushed back her seat. She came forward, her body strangely still even in movement, her eyes fixed ahead, no sideways glances at would-be friends, no smothered giggles at being singled out like this.

Erin smiled as she took the exercise book from Lisha's outstretched hand.

'Merci, Lisha.'

Lisha returned her smile with a slight upward movement of her lips. Of all the children in the class, Erin hated leaving her the most.

'That's a reflexive verb, Lisha,' she said, making a small correction.

Lisha nodded gravely, and returned to her desk in the same autonomous manner in which she had left it. Erin watched, a lump in her throat. She'd been on the outer at school too, and even as an adult – a teacher, no less – her chronically awkward schoolgirl self was never far beneath the surface. Lisha had an obvious air of displacement which Erin recognised and worried about. She hoped that Madame Gallas would go out of her way to make Lisha feel included, and that she wouldn't mistake Lisha's reticence for the rudeness she so abhorred.

'Aargh. Did you see that, Miss?'

'Mademoiselle!'

'Mademoiselle. I'm being bullied, Mademoiselle.'

'Well, you might as well learn how to say it in French, Darragh. Il m'embête!'

'Il m'embête!'

'Excellent. Now, Tristan, pick up the paper you threw at Darragh, please.'

The next class was her fifth years, then first years, then lunch, and then sixth years. She'd had the sixth years all the way through their secondary education. She'd seen them morph from children to teenagers to young adults. They were confident, her sixth year students, confident in a way she'd never been. And polished, so polished and accomplished in how they spoke and dressed and carried themselves. Poised on the precipice of their adult lives, anything was possible and they knew it. She was tempted, very tempted, to take them aside and whisper a word of advice in their ears: 'Jump at every opportunity that comes your way, travel as far and for as long as you possibly can, and don't *ever* make the mistake of thinking your dreams will keep until later.' Her confident, accomplished sixth year students would think she were a nutcase if she did such a thing, though. She'd been doing this job for too long, almost twelve years, and to be honest, she was a little crazy from it. How many students had she seen through? She was too exhausted to count. Physically, mentally, spiritually exhausted.

'Clodagh, the classroom is not the place to be changing your hairstyle! Now leave your hair alone and collect the rest of the finished assignments for me, s'il vous plaît.'

'No, Nicole, you cannot go to the toilet. You can hold on for the ten minutes that are left of class.'

'Courtney, please don't sneeze all over Caroline. You know where the tissues are ...'

'Tristan, this is your last warning! You will be laughing on the other side of your face if you have to spend your lunch break doing lines. Vous comprenez?'

Yes, she was exhausted from them. From the sheer effort

it took to control them in class, in transit in the corridors, in the playground at lunchtime, not to mention the school tour to Paris last year. This job, this environment, was a bad place to be if one wasn't feeling strong. The noise, the constant demands, the relentless visibility, the perceptiveness of the students and their ability to sense weakness and vulnerability from a mile away.

She wasn't being fair. Yes, she was tired and weary beyond description, but that was as much due to things happening outside the classroom as to things happening within. There had been many good times, times when she'd laughed until tears ran down her face, times when she'd thought she'd burst with pride, and those precious moments when she could tell that she'd made a difference, a lasting impact on a student's life. The time Darragh back-answered her in French, making her want to congratulate rather than scold him. The time Tristan used his initiative to learn as many French swear words as humanly possible. Courtney, Caroline and Nicole, inseparable at school and even more so on the school tour, exclaiming over the fashion in Paris and how 'chic' everything was! The sixth years learning a rap version of the French National Anthem for the Christmas concert last year. Yes, there had been many good times. To be honest, the problem wasn't the students, the school, or even the job. The problem was her.

'Okay, everyone, take out your homework books, please.'

'Lisha, can you please hand out these audio discs? Merci.'

'Nicole, don't you have a homework book today?'

'Attention tout le monde! Is everyone paying attention? Your homework is to listen to the disc and answer the related questions on page trente-deux.'

Erin tuned out from the groans and sighs and exaggerated dismay. How would they react if they knew that this was the last homework they would receive from her? She had already decided that next week would be homework free – to soften the news of her departure. She could hardly believe that she was going, *finally* going. For so long she'd been stagnant, trapped and unable to move. Leaving still wasn't easy – in fact, it was extremely complicated – but she had everyone's blessing and that had been the tipping point: that and the mini-crisis she'd had last year.

'Mademoiselle, why are you choosing to go so far away?'

Erin imagined that it would be Lisha who would ask the million-dollar question: Lisha who knew all about travelling and getting away from things and the harsh truth of how difficult it was to start a new life. Australia *was* far away, too far away to return from on a whim or, more likely, in a rush of guilt, the same guilt that had trapped her until now. She had a friend in Australia, Melissa, and a job – if she wanted it – in the school where Melissa worked. Secondary school teachers were apparently in short supply, and the visa process had been disconcertingly swift (only a few months from start to end). More poignantly, Australia had been the next country on her itinerary when she'd had to cut short her travels twelve years ago. It felt like unfinished business, as though she couldn't go forward with her life until she revisited the point at which it had gone so irrevocably off the rails. Australia made sense on so many levels, but it also made no sense at all. She vacillated between believing it was absolutely the right thing to do and thinking it was crazy, irresponsible and utterly self-indulgent. In fact, the only constant feeling she had about her upcoming trip was fear. Even at those moments when she was unwavering and convinced, she still managed to feel quite consistently petrified.

'Mademoiselle, what will I do without you?'

Of course Lisha would not say this out loud, but her eyes would say it, her dark, expressive eyes flashing with panic, abandonment and betrayal. Lisha had the most to lose. Of all of them, she was the most vulnerable. She needed a figure of authority on her side, to keep the cruelty of the other girls in check, to involve her in the class and help make her less of a sitting target. She needed a friendly face, someone who smiled rather than sneered at her. Erin decided that she would speak to Madame Gallas at least about Lisha, if not about any of the others.

'Hey, Miss, we should have a going-away party for you!'

She could imagine Tristan's input, too: a party, the perfect excuse to slack off in class. Erin was in fact planning a class party, involving chocolate croissants and pains au chocolat, and some word games and music, all with a French theme, of course. She was having an adult going-away party, too – next weekend – a gathering of family, friends and a few work colleagues to send her off. She hadn't wanted a big fuss and would have preferred to slip away unnoticed, but Laura had insisted.

'This is a big move for you, Erin – and it should be marked and celebrated in a *big* way.'

Laura had been amazing. On a practical level, she'd organised a roster of family members to care for Moira – Erin's mother, Laura's aunt – and on a psychological level, she'd countered all the reasons why Erin couldn't go with reasons why she could, and must.

'Your own health is at risk here, Erin. Your body has given you a warning.'

'Don't worry about your mum. She won't be alone. There's a big family of us here to help.'

'It's only for a year. Remember that. You owe yourself this. A change of scene.'

'You're not being selfish, silly. This time out is life-saving and non-negotiable. Got it?'

Though Laura was her first cousin, they hadn't always been close. As children, the three-year age difference had seemed vast. Erin was at playschool by the time Laura was born, and well established in primary school when her cousin, an extraordinarily self-possessed little girl, started in Junior

Infants. The same had applied to secondary school and university, Erin always a stage ahead in her life and consequently out of reach. The birth of Olivia, Laura's daughter, had changed things, for once putting Laura a step ahead. Olivia's dimpled face, cherubic arms and legs and surprisingly hearty laugh drew Erin to cuddle and play with her at family gatherings. Spending time with the baby meant spending time with Laura, and it was often the two of them taking turns at rocking the pram in a quiet room of the house while the party raged on next door. Laura had accepted Erin's help so gratefully and humbly that Erin soon extended an offer to babysit anytime she was needed. And so, through Olivia, they'd transitioned from a rather distant relationship to something much closer, providing support and advice to each other, becoming friends and allies amidst the boisterous, male-dominated family of which they were part.

Erin glanced at the clock. One minute to go until the bell. She released her hold on the class and allowed them to talk amongst themselves, or in the case of Tristan and Darragh, fling-shot each other with balls of scrunched-up paper. She allowed herself the same leniency, letting her thoughts drift to Australia, imagining herself teaching French at Macquarie Grammar School (where Melissa worked), her students co-operative and inspiring, with eye-pleasing tans and sun-streaked hair, an unrelenting blue sky visible through the windows, warm air waiting to caress her face and skin when she went outside.

The bell rang, its sound harsh and intrusive against the soft tones of her daydream. Her students jumped to their feet, suddenly in an extraordinary rush.

'Push your chairs in after you, please.'

'One at a time through the door.'

'Tristan, please keep your hands – and legs – to yourself.'

As Erin continued to talk, her words falling on deaf ears, she was struck with a terrible thought. What if the Australian students were just a better-looking version of the students here? Had she kidded herself by believing they would be different, easier to handle, less draining by the end of the day? Did doing the *exact* same job, coaching, chastising and coaxing another set of teenagers, qualify as a 'live-saving' change? When the initial glow of being in another country faded, and the day-to-day realities of her job reasserted themselves, would she feel trapped and panicky and frightened all over again?

'Tristan! I am blue in the face from telling you to behave!'

And what if there was another Tristan waiting for her in Macquarie Grammar School? Or a kid worse than Tristan, without any interest in French at all – not even the swear words – and without that 'loveable rogue' smile that made it so hard to stay cross with Tristan?

A tanned, more evil version of Tristan Keary. Now *that* was a truly scary thought!

Chapter 2

Laura consulted her list of questions, not to remind herself what she wanted to ask but to centre her thoughts and her sense of being. She liked lists – rather a lot, really – and at any one time she had a number of them on the go: work lists, home lists, shopping lists; lists for Esteban and Olivia; short-term lists that could be satisfyingly scrunched into a ball once each task was ticked; longer-term ones which attempted to pin down and overlay some goals on the slippery future. The lists gave her a sense of structure, an illusion of control, and she hung onto them for dear life.

Finally, Laura raised her head to assess the young woman sitting on the other side of her desk. According to her CV, Kasia Kaminski came from a small village outside Legnica, in south-west Poland. She didn't look particularly Polish, Laura thought. Her skin was pallid, almost unhealthily so, and her hair had a long fringe cut at an angle to her face, making it difficult to see her eyes. She wore a black skirt and jacket, the fabric shiny under the spotlights in the ceiling. An off-white shirt, faux-pearl earrings and pink lipstick, too bright for her skin tone, completed the image.

'How long have you been in Ireland, Kasia?'

'Five months.'

'And have you been working during that time?'

'I babysit for my cousin, who I stay with.'

'Any other work?'

'No. It has not been easy to get a job with the economy as it is.'

Each of the five candidates Laura had interviewed so far had mentioned the economy, implying that they would not be interviewing for this role had the job market been stronger and other work opportunities available.

'What kind of work would you seek if you had the choice?' Laura asked in a casual tone, hoping to draw out an honest answer.

'I would like to work in an office – like this one.' Kasia lifted one hand from her lap to motion to the hub of workstations visible through the floor-to-ceiling window. Her gesture drew Laura's attention to her long, bony fingers. She tried to imagine those fleshless fingers curled around Olivia's plump little hand, and had to swallow a sudden lump in her throat.

'I started this company with my husband five years ago,' she said quietly, redirecting her gaze from Kasia's hands to the workstations on the other side of the glass. Dressed casually in jeans and T-shirts and busily tapping their keyboards, the staff within the cubicles managed to look both relaxed and energetic. Most wore headphones, which made them appear younger than they were, and their eyes were trained on huge, state-of-the-art computer screens.

'So you own all of this?' Kasia looked impressed.

'Yes.'

'What does the business do?'

'We're a translation services centre.' Laura was aware that her voice held more disillusionment than pride, and this caused another – harder – lump in her throat. 'We translate brochures, manuals and websites for businesses and government departments, both here in Ireland and overseas. We have twenty people working for us now, all different nationalities.'

Kasia smiled, for the first time in the interview, and nodded approvingly. 'I noticed that it was very multicultural when I walked in. Yes, when the economy gets better I want to work somewhere like this!'

At least she was honest, Laura thought, unlike others who had tried to persuade her that being a nanny was their first choice when it clearly wasn't.

'Running this business with my husband is very demanding, which is why I need someone to help care for my daughter, Olivia. Someone to bring her to and from playschool, to ballet classes, swimming lessons and other activities, as well as perform some other chores around the house.'

'You mean cleaning?'

Laura had to stifle a sigh. *Here we go again.* 'Yes,' she said firmly. 'Some basic cooking and cleaning, unloading the dishwasher, hanging out the washing, everyday things like that – secondary, of course, to minding Olivia. Would the household duties present a problem for you?'

Kasia took a moment to think, and then raised her thin shoulders in a shrug. 'It is not my preference, but I will do it if it is part of the job … What age is your daughter?'

'Olivia's four-and-a half.'

Laura couldn't help but smile as she pictured Olivia as she'd left her this morning: upside-down in her bed, one of her cuddly toys serving as a pillow, and sound asleep in the pure and absolute manner she approached everything in her life. Laura had manoeuvred some blankets over the curled-up body, smoothed wisps of her fairy-floss hair from her small, perfect face, kissed the warm curve of her cheek and tip-toed from the room so as not to wake her. Downstairs, Cathy, grandmother and reluctant fill-in nanny, was making herself a bolstering cup of coffee for the ordeal ahead.

'This is an ungodly hour to start the day!'

'It's seven-thirty, Mum, hardly the middle of the night.'

'By your standards, maybe.'

Her mother was not at her best in the mornings; for that matter, she was not at her best with young children either.

'Olivia's lunch is in the fridge – just remember to put it in her bag before you go. And I've laid out her clothes on the chair in her room. There are two outfits to choose from – you know how she likes to have a choice in these matters!'

'Don't we all!' Cathy retorted, making it quite clear that minding Olivia was not *her* choice. She wasn't even dressed for the job at hand – her frilled white shirt, skin-tight leggings and high-heeled boots were decidedly impractical.

'Don't be late when you pick her up from playschool – the staff get cranky even if it's only a few minutes.'

Cathy, who was always late, and much more than a few minutes, too, looked affronted. Whether it was by the request for her punctuality or the perceived inflexibility of the playschool staff, Laura wasn't sure.

'I'm interviewing someone today, Mum. A Polish girl.'

'I don't care where she comes from once I'm off the hook!'

Though Cathy's tone was more dry than sarcastic, Laura couldn't help feeling a stab of hurt. She went out of her way not to ask too much of her mother, and wouldn't have asked her to help out this week if she hadn't been totally desperate. Cathy had very clear limits on what she was and wasn't prepared to do. She liked to buy Olivia gifts and clothes, and take her into town to see pantomimes and other shows, but she didn't wish to be involved in her granddaughter's day-to-day routine – the one area where she could be, if she made herself available, infinitely useful.

'And Olivia will start school in September?' Kasia was asking now.

'Yes.'

'And what will that mean for her nanny?'

18

'I don't know just yet,' Laura replied truthfully. 'Olivia will still need someone to drop her to and from school, and there will be the usual household chores, so we will need help of some sort, but I'm not sure if it will be full-time help or not.'

'So I may need to find new accommodation and a new job in six months' time?'

'In the worst case, yes. It should become clearer what's needed as the time comes closer and we can plan accordingly.'

Laura still maintained a faint hope that her mum and dad would help out when Olivia – who was, after all, their only grandchild – started school, perhaps picking her up a few days a week and keeping her until Laura or Esteban got home from work. Yet she knew that Cathy would baulk at the idea of such structured assistance, and her father, Ian, would look apologetic and uncomfortable but would defer to his wife.

'The child is your responsibility, Laura, not mine or your father's or anyone else's.'

Cathy liked to say this frequently, and Laura fully agreed with her mother. It wasn't as though she expected a lot of help from Cathy. Not at all. Just *a little* help would be nice.

Cathy had set her boundaries right from the beginning, from the moment Laura announced she was pregnant. Laura unconsciously grimaced as she recalled her mother's less-than-enthusiastic response to her big news.

'*What? Why?* You're only twenty-six – you could have waited at least another few years.'

'Esteban and I want to have our family while we're young.'

'*Esteban* and *you* have absolutely no idea what you're talking about!'

'Mum, you had *me* when you were young. You were only twenty-four, remember?'

'That's what we did back then. We got married and immediately had children; it was expected. But nowadays girls can wait, and figure out what they *really* want from life before jumping into motherhood.'

'Esteban and I *really* want this baby.'

'Who's going to take care of the child when you go back to work?'

'I don't know.'

'Well, don't look at me.'

'I'm not looking at you!'

Thus Cathy had exempted herself from Olivia's care even before Olivia came into the world. Over the years Laura had tried and tested every form of childcare there was, and by now she was, unfortunately, intimate with the pitfalls of each: long day care (a breeding ground for childhood illnesses), family day care (long waiting lists and restrictive hours), au pairs (high turnover rates), and nannies (expensive, and generally unwilling to work longer than the standard nine-to-five).

Cathy changing her mind and helping when Olivia went to school was an ideal world, the same ideal world in which she was a doting mother and granny who couldn't do enough for her family. In the *real* world, Laura would probably have to keep Kasia, or whoever it was who got the job, in a complicated, part-time and unnecessarily expensive arrangement.

A knock sounded on the door and jolted Laura from her thoughts. Esteban popped his head inside. He smiled at Kasia first, and then Laura.

'All going well in here?'

The question came across as friendly, casual even. Only Laura knew the desperation, the same as her own, running beneath Esteban's question. They needed Kasia to be the one; they were at domestic breaking point.

'Kasia, this is Esteban, my husband.'

Kasia stood up and extended her hand. Laura noticed again how thin she was – not just her hands and shoulders, *all* of her. Of course her weight didn't have anything to do with her suitability for the job, unless she had an eating disorder or some other serious health problem. Was there a polite way of asking about her weight, or lack thereof? No, no, of course there wasn't.

Esteban, undeterred by the long fringe, looked Kasia in the eye. His gaze was deep and probing, and often disconcerting to those who didn't know him very well. Laura could vividly remember the first time he'd turned that gaze on her, more than ten years ago now, in the café-bar of University of Granada where she'd been an international student.

'You are Laura?'

'Yes.'

'I am Esteban.'

'Yes.'

'It is nice to meet you.'

'Yes.'

'Ah, lovely Laura, if we are to practise linguistic interaction you will have to manage more than just the one word. And perhaps you should consider saying it in Spanish, sí?'

She'd laughed and returned his intense gaze with a rather brazen one of her own, knowing straight away that she wanted more than just language practice with him.

'My wife tells me you are from Poland,' Esteban was saying to Kasia now.

'Yes.'

'How are you finding Ireland?'

'Good.'

'Good?' Esteban raised both eyebrows, making it clear that he expected a more comprehensive response.

Kasia blushed, and the colour that seeped into her face suited her, made her seem less aloof, more pretty. 'The food is good, very nice and fresh, no taste of chemicals like home. And the people here are good – most of the time. But I am finding it difficult to get on my feet and start working. Ireland would be *excellent* if I could get a job!'

Again, Laura was struck by her honesty, and by how competent her English was: she seemed to have no trouble understanding what was being asked, and expressing her feelings in reply.

Esteban rewarded Kasia's more detailed response with another smile, his teeth white and even against the tan of his face, his almost-black eyes shining, inviting a reciprocal smile. A little below average height, he had a slim and boyish physique, and dark-brown hair that suited him best when it was slightly long, like now. Despite the ups and downs of the last ten years, and the stresses and demands of the business and family life, he still looked remarkably like the self-possessed young man she'd met in the café that day. She wished she could say the same for herself. Where was the flirtatious, adventurous girl who had sat across from him? The girl who'd made love with him that very afternoon, trusting her instincts and living wholly for the moment? That carefree girl *never* made lists, and didn't know how to be cynical or disillusioned. Where had she gone? Who had taken her away and replaced her with this older, weighed-down, second-rate version?

'You are a foreigner too,' Kasia stated.

'Yes, I come from Spain. My wife came to Granada to learn Spanish. She promptly fell in love with me and decided to stay. Now I am trying out her country.'

Esteban made it sound awfully romantic, and it had been. Five warm wonderful years in Granada before starting another new life together in Dublin. In fact, Olivia, born exactly nine months after the move to Ireland, could have been conceived in either country. That didn't stop Esteban from claiming her as Spanish, and Laura as Irish. They both adored her.

'I found it hard to get started over here, too,' Esteban said to Kasia, 'and I understand how frustrated you must feel. But I'm certain that you'll find someone to take you on, and I know you'll be very loyal and hardworking to repay your employer for giving you a chance.'

Laura could see that her husband had struck a chord with Kasia: the girl looked willing to clean the house from top to bottom and do anything humanly possible to demonstrate her loyalty, if only she were offered the job. Esteban had a way with people, always empathising with their particular circumstances before gently challenging them to work harder or think outside the box. All of a sudden, Laura saw herself and Esteban through Kasia's eyes: Esteban with his exotic dark looks, genuine smile and inbuilt charisma; Laura with coffee-coloured hair, clear grey-blue eyes, winter-pale skin and a smile and manner that felt so forced these days. Did Kasia find them an odd couple? Ill-matched in personality and in looks?

Esteban, his mini-interview over, turned to his wife.

'I brought my flight forward to eleven. It gets me into London in time for lunch. I have meetings all afternoon but I'm still hoping to make the seven o'clock home.'

Esteban did all the travelling for the business, which meant regular flights to London, Berlin, Paris and Madrid, and frequent jaunts to other more far-flung cities, too. In fact, a great deal of their conversations were centred around the minutiae of his travel itinerary.

'Will you need dinner tonight?'

A wry smile pulled at the corners of his mouth. 'Save me a few scraps if you can!'

Had Kasia not been present, he would have fondly yet somewhat absently brushed his lips against Laura's forehead as goodbye. Instead, he turned graciously to the Polish girl and she received the tail end of his smile and attention. 'It was a pleasure to meet you, Kasia. I wish you the very best of luck with everything.'

The atmosphere in the room changed once Esteban had left, and Laura felt as though she were getting a view into the future, a time when Kasia was living in her house and had observed – and formed opinions on – Esteban and her as parents, and as individual people and a couple.

Laura stared down at her list, trying to regain a sense of purpose, of authority even, from the printed questions. Where had she left off? Did it matter? Interviews were such an unreliable way of establishing someone's suitability: if the candidate had any degree of intelligence, motivation or creativity, they could easily fool you into believing they were something they were not.

'Do you smoke?'

'Yes, but not around children.'

Not the answer Laura had been hoping for.

'And have you got any references?'

'My cousin. I can give you her phone number.'

'Do you have anyone else? Any employer back in Poland?'

'I can ask my teacher, if you wish.'

Again far from ideal, but explainable, as Kasia's CV claimed that she'd left her home country straight after completing a degree in marketing and management, and without any work experience. Of course, that was presuming her CV could be relied on – Laura had heard some horror stories about fabricated experience and qualifications. It almost didn't matter that neither marketing nor management were of much use when it came to minding a four-and-a-half-year-old child. All that mattered was that Kasia had some level of education and intelligence, and that she was honest.

'Yes, I would like your teacher's phone number, please.'

Laura paused to think of what else she should ask this girl before she entrusted Olivia to her care. But instead of channelling another few relevant questions, her mind began to fly through all the things she had to do after this interview: a conference call with India, a team meeting on the new immigration services website, a Spanish brochure she wanted to translate herself in order to keep her skills up to speed, and then lunchtime, when she hoped to duck out to buy a going-away present for Erin. She couldn't believe that Erin was leaving in just a week's time. Even though Laura had played an active role in persuading Erin to go in the first place, she really didn't know what she was going to do without her cousin. Erin was her main babysitter, sounding board and friend. Only Erin understood Laura's frustrations with her mother, with Esteban, with work and everything else. She was going to miss her. Terribly.

'Well, thanks for coming in, Kasia. I'll be in touch over the next few days.'

Laura went through the motions of shaking Kasia's hand and giving her a brief tour of the premises before seeing her out. Later on today, when she had a spare moment, she would phone Kasia's cousin and ex-teacher, and provided they said nothing too drastically negative she would call the girl back and offer her the job. It was clear that Kasia didn't really want to be a nanny and that she had no direct experience with children other than her cousin's brood, whom, it now occurred to Laura, she should have quizzed her more closely about. Other things that were clear: Kasia smoked, didn't like cleaning, had no proper references, and in fact did not meet most of the criteria on Laura's list. The bottom line was that Kasia was a compromise, like everything else these days.

Back in her office, staring blindly through the glass wall as though it was a portal into her own thoughts and not into the business she and her husband had built from scratch, Laura frittered away a few minutes of precious time daydreaming about jetting off on a plane, leaving the nanny problem and other drudgeries far behind, seeing new places, meeting new people and returning to a fresh, more impulsive way of life. She suddenly realised that she was jealous of Erin, jealous to such an extent that she felt rather overwhelmed, and utterly ashamed of herself. A tear trickled down her face, startling her before she roughly wiped it away. What was *wrong* with her today? She loved Olivia, Esteban and her job, absolutely, unquestionably. So why this sudden, *mad* yearning to get away from them?

Chapter 3

Erin applied a fresh coat of lip-gloss, dabbed her face with powder, and then, because she felt silly and excited and out-of-this-world happy, did an impromptu imitation of a plane taking off with her hand: up, up, up, whoosh and away. When her hand came back down to earth, she leant in closer to the mirror to examine her reflection. Her eyes were shining, excitement virtually glowing through their deep brown, and her cheeks were slightly flushed, the effects of the champagne everyone seemed so intent on forcing her to drink. The rest of her skin looked paler than its usual olive tone, probably due to the harsh lighting in the restrooms. Her hair still looked great, though, dark and sleek with lots of badly needed volume, thanks to a visit to the hairdresser that afternoon. If she could have hair like this every day, she could achieve great, great things. She giggled. That was the champagne talking … or thinking, more like.

'Ah, so this is where the girl of the moment is hiding out!' Her Aunt Cathy's reflection appeared next to her in the mirror. 'Everything all right, love?'

'Never better,' Erin responded and meant it.

On that reassurance, Cathy set about fixing her own lipstick, her mouth slightly apart as she applied a deep-red colour which complemented her stylishly cut blonde hair. Her knit dress was extremely flattering to her gym-toned figure, as were her very fashionable, very new, high-heeled boots. High heels were Cathy's signature fashion item: Erin had never seen her aunt in a pair of flats. Cathy was in her mid-fifties, but could quite easily pass as a woman ten years younger.

'Cathy, you're my "fun" auntie. You know that, don't you?'

'I'm your only auntie, you goose!'

As a child, Erin had loved going to visit her aunt. Cathy still lived in the same detached house on the corner of a tree-lined street, the house having the same hint of glamour as its owner. It was a big house, capable of accommodating more people than it did – Cathy, Ian and Laura – and Erin used to fantasise about sleeping over in one of the light, airy guest rooms. Though such an invitation had not been forthcoming, Cathy had always made her feel extraordinarily welcome, laying out chocolate biscuits and fizzy drinks and, as Erin got older, supplying cast-off lipsticks, nail-polish and costume jewellery for her to take as she wished. Erin had been ambivalent about Laura back then; it was her aunt she'd looked forward to seeing. It was funny how she and Laura had become close in the long run.

'I'm going to miss you, Cathy,' she stated, swallowing a hiccup. She must remember to go easy on the champagne.

Cathy stopped rearranging her hair and turned to give Erin a quick hug. 'I'll miss you too, pet. But let's not dwell on it – it'll only make us both upset. Go out there and enjoy the rest of your night. Go on. Out you go.'

Erin did as she was told, thinking, as she swayed back into the party, *her* party, that Laura was far too harsh on her mother. Yes, Cathy was a little frivolous and not your stereotypical grandmother, but she was fun and had great zest for life, and that had to count for something, didn't it? Life without fun was very, very dull. Sadly, Erin knew this fact firsthand.

* * * * *

Laura took a sip from her glass of wine and surveyed the party she'd organised in Erin's honour. Family, friends and colleagues were squashed into the small function room upstairs at O'Donoghue's pub, and everyone seemed to be mingling well and having a good time. The finger food had come out on cue, and the music was just the right volume and mix to appeal to the wide range of ages. Later on there would be cake and a speech, which would probably embarrass Erin but would be entirely appropriate for the occasion. Laura had organised it all – invitations, food, music and cake – right down to the very last detail. It had just involved making another list – a party-for-Erin list – and it had got done, just like that.

Speaking of Erin, where had she gone? Laura scanned the room, taking in the clusters of people close to the bar, some perched on stools, others standing, drinks in hand, heads bent in conversation. She swept her eyes along the rear of the function room, to the staid bench seating and low tables, but couldn't spot her cousin. Her roving gaze caught her Uncle Gerry, who beamed a smile at her and made in her direction.

'Ah, Laura, there you are!' Gerry hung a friendly arm around her shoulders and planted a stubbly kiss on her cheek. 'And where's the better half tonight?'

'He's at home minding Olivia,' Laura explained, not for the first time. Why was it so hard to go somewhere alone without fielding a thousand questions about her husband's whereabouts? 'We have a babysitter crisis now that Erin is leaving!'

'Ah, you should have said something earlier,' her uncle exclaimed. 'Aidan could have come over ... Don't be afraid to ask him the next time you need someone to mind the little one.'

Aidan was the youngest of Gerry's boys and, in Laura's opinion, more irresponsible than his three brothers put together, which was quite an achievement. Olivia would be safer taking care of herself than being 'minded' by Aidan.

'I'm sure Aidan is busy with his social life at college,' she muttered as diplomatically as she could.

'Of course, there's Colm too.' Gerry cupped his chin as he pondered his eldest boy's suitability for the job. 'Colm has a steady girlfriend now and I'm sure the two of them wouldn't mind staying in the odd Saturday night to look after Olivia.'

Yes, Laura was sure that Colm and his new girlfriend would be quite keen to have a house practically all to themselves. Laura suddenly had a picture of her cousin making out with his girlfriend on her modular couch. She gulped some wine to obliterate the picture from her mind.

'Don't worry, Gerry. We have a new nanny starting next week and I'm sure that she'll do a bit of babysitting here and there.'

'Ah, that's good news. Your mother will be happy – she was feeling the strain.'

Laura felt a flash of hurt, followed by a more enduring frustration. Strain? Cathy didn't know the meaning of strain! She had an idyllic life, constantly going for coffee with her friends, scouring the internet for discount airfares and jetting off for romantic getaways with her husband every other weekend, shopping for clothes and accessories as though shopping were an Olympic sport. To think that lending a helping hand with her granddaughter for one *measly* week was a strain the whole family had to hear about!

Though Laura didn't verbalise her thoughts, Gerry was perceptive enough to read her expression. 'Sorry, love, I didn't mean it like that. Of course, minding Olivia is a delight for your mother.'

Gerry looked so troubled that Laura had no option but to try to shrug it off. Her uncle brimmed with good intentions, always wanting to help, to solve whatever the problem there was, and the mere thought that he may have caused friction between Laura and Cathy was enough to keep him awake at night. Laura had always felt especially fond of her Uncle Gerry, and knew that he felt the same way about her. Some of her earliest memories were of riding high on her uncle's sturdy shoulders, squealing with laughter as he held her upside-down by the ankles, and how important and special she'd felt when he'd asked her to be a flower girl at his wedding. Gerry had married late and his boys were a good few years younger than her. He maintained that Laura had broken him in and thanks to her he'd had the requisite qualifications by the time his own children came along.

Laura's thoughts were interrupted by a loud guffaw, and she didn't need to turn her head to identify from whom it had originated. Yes, there was Uncle Paddy bumbling towards them, and it was too late for her to discreetly slip away. If Gerry was her favourite of her mother's siblings, Paddy was her least favourite. Paddy saw himself as the joker of the family, the problem being that his jokes were more like insults and were always at someone's expense. Gerry's earnestness made him an easy target for Paddy, and when it came to Laura his cracks invariably adopted a Spanish flavour.

'Ah, Laura, where's the Spaniard tonight? Did ye have an argumento?'

The problem with Paddy was that there was often a grain of truth in his remarks, and for that reason they stung. She *had* argued with Esteban tonight. She had wanted to ask one of the mums from playschool to mind Olivia, but Esteban had been adamant that he didn't want to leave his daughter with someone they hardly knew. She had accused him of using Olivia as an excuse to get out of going to the party, and he responded that he was doing nothing of the sort, but admitted that he was tired and didn't mind staying at home. She followed by shouting that he couldn't be more tired than she was. The argument had ended the same way all their arguments ended: her screaming like a fishwife, and Esteban saying nothing at all, his shutters down, making her want to scream all the harder.

'You're looking a bit more cuddly than the last time I saw you, Laura. Must be having a few too many tapas and paellas, eh?'

Paddy had absolutely no sensitivity to people's feelings, and had a booming voice that everyone in the vicinity could hear. He always, *always* commented on Laura's weight. It was true that she had put on some extra pounds. With the mood she was in, if he said another word she would not be responsible for what she would do.

Paddy had a brood of boys too, most of whom were here tonight. They stood as a group, talking earnestly amongst themselves. In fact, Paddy's boys were more of Gerry's temperament, and Gerry's unruly lot were more like Paddy. Maybe in the same way that Laura was the complete opposite to her own mother. Had the genes got mixed up somewhere, or did children consciously try to be different from their parents?

Ah, there was Erin, coming out of the toilets, slightly unsteady on her feet. She looked amazing in her black cocktail dress, her skin glowing, her hair shining; it was though she was lit up from the inside. Laura had always envied Erin her beautiful olive skin and glossy hair, so different from her own paler skin tones and, in her opinion, nondescript hair.

As Laura watched, Erin almost lost her balance and had to hold on to someone's arm to steady herself. Mmm … The guest of honour was decidedly tipsy. Laura gulped back the rest of her drink, deciding that if her cousin was going to get drunk, she would keep her company. It was the least she could do.

* * * * *

Erin, her fingers curled around the stem of a fresh flute of champagne, instinctively sought out her mother with her eyes, and seeing that she was alone, made in her direction. If Cathy looked ten years younger than her age, Erin's mother – Moira – looked ten years older. She sat in one of the far corners of the room, detached from the party in much the same way she was detached from life.

'Hi, Mum. Are you enjoying yourself?'

'Yes,' Moira smiled. 'Though I don't think this place is as good as it used to be.'

An interesting observation, Erin thought, given that Moira had never set foot in O'Donoghue's pub before tonight.

'It's a good crowd, isn't it, Mum?'

'Moira, Gerard, Patrick and baby Cathy,' Moira recited in reply.

'Yes, Mum, all your brothers and sisters are here tonight.'

'Moira, Gerard, Patrick and baby Cathy,' Moira repeated, before her gaze focused on the small dance floor. 'Has Cathy gone out dancing yet? She loves to dance, you know!'

'Yes, Mum, I know.'

Moira cupped a hand over her mouth. 'Oh, that Cathy! She's so naughty,' she giggled. 'I don't know what we'll do with her.'

Erin smiled as though she was in full agreement.

'We spoil her, all of us,' Moira continued fondly. 'She's the youngest, the baby of the family, and we just dote on her. Oh, but she's as bold as brass … I have to be the sensible one, being the eldest … Let me tell you, it's very tiresome being sensible all the time.'

'Yes, Mum, I'm sure it is.'

'Moira, Gerard, Patrick and baby Cathy.'

Moira recited the names of her siblings a few hundred

times a day. It was her mantra, her mainstay. After all, her brothers and sisters were the only thing that had remained constant in her life. Everything else had disintegrated beyond recognition.

Erin felt a sudden urge to cry. She was overwhelmed by the sheer unfairness, the hopelessness and the sadness of it all. Her mother was only sixty-seven. Until the onset of her illness she'd been an intelligent, well-read, well-travelled woman, a loving mother and a devoted wife. She should have had many more good years to look forward to. If her younger self had known that this was coming, a time when she couldn't hold a conversation without reciting the same phrase over and over again, a time when she was living more in the past than the present, a time when a roster would determine whose turn it was to mind her, she would have been truly horrified.

Laura appeared by Erin's side, as though by some sixth sense.

'I'll sit here with Moira for a minute.'

'You don't have to. I —'

'Go away, Erin. Spend some time with your guests.'

Erin blinked her eyes to clear away the tears that had formed. 'God, you're not half bossy!'

'I was bossy,' Moira chirped in. 'I was the eldest, you see.'

Laura shared a rueful grin with Erin. 'Yes, Auntie Moira.'

Moira leant closer to Laura. 'And who are you again, dear?'

'I'm Laura, Cathy's girl.'

'Oh, yes. Of course you are.'

Moira was finding it harder and harder to keep track of who was who in the family, particularly the faces she didn't see every day. She always knew Erin, though she sometimes got mixed up as to what age her daughter was, occasionally packing a lunch for her in the mornings and enquiring why she wasn't wearing her school uniform.

'Go, Erin. Go back to the party,' Laura commanded.

'Okay. I'm gone, I'm gone!'

Erin left her mother in Laura's care – in effect, what she was about to do for the coming year – and made her way back to the thick of the crowd. The champagne had lost some of its glow, as had the party and the crazy notion that it was okay to go away and leave her mother. How long would it take for Moira to completely forget her face or, worse still, that she had a daughter at all? When Erin eventually came back from Australia, would her mother lean close and ask ever so politely, 'And who are you again, dear?'

* * * * *

Laura turned on the light in the landing. It cast a soft glow into Olivia's bedroom, over the rumpled bedclothes and her upside-down silhouette. Laura turned her daughter the right way up, her body much heavier in sleep than awake, tucked the duvet back in place, kissed Olivia's forehead and then, for good measure, planted a second kiss on her button nose.

'Night, night, Floss.'

In her own bedroom on the other end of the landing, she used the borrowed light to get undressed, allowing her clothes to spool on the carpet at her feet, a carelessness she wouldn't usually allow herself. As she got into bed, Esteban stirred and his arm snaked around her waist to pull her close. She felt like wriggling free, pushing him away, but the heaviness of his arm held her captive for long enough to melt some of the resentment she'd harboured from earlier.

'I am sorry.' His voice, thick with sleep, whispered in her ear. 'I do not like it when we argue.'

'I'm sorry, too,' she returned automatically.

'Let's not fight about little, insignificant matters.'

'Yes,' she said wryly. 'Let's keep our arguments for the big stuff.'

Her Spanish husband, contrary to popular perception, did

not thrive on spectacular arguments and passionate making-up afterwards. At heart, Esteban was a gentle soul and hated discord of any kind. Laura knew he would sleep easier now that they had both apologised.

'How was the night?' he enquired, pressing his cheek deeper into the pillow.

'It was good. Everything went off perfectly. I tried to get drunk, but it didn't work.'

Esteban chuckled. 'And Erin?'

'Erin was in top form.'

For a while they said nothing. The silence felt like an extra blanket on the bed, warm and comforting. For a few minutes, Laura floated on the verge of sleep, pondering it, trying it out for size, but then her thoughts woke her up, rattling inside her head and rousing the rest of her body.

'Esteban?'

'Mmm ...'

'Maybe I shouldn't have encouraged Erin to do this ...'

'Huh?'

'What if something happens to Moira while she's away? She'll never forgive me if it does!'

'I don't think ...'

'Or what if Erin has another attack? Like the one last year, but this time with strangers around and no family to help her through.'

Esteban tightened his arm around her waist, restraining her as one might restrain a toddler who was spiralling out of control.

'Relax, lovely Laura. It is time to sleep. Let go. Relax.'

Under his command and the confinement of his arm, she did let go and finally fell asleep.

* * * * *

Erin stared at herself in the bathroom mirror. If her reflection earlier in the night had been glossy, this was the matt version, the real her. An Alice band held her hair back from her face, all traces of make-up cleansed from her skin, her eyes a little watery with tears she'd struggled to keep at bay at various points throughout the night, including now. The party was over, everyone had said their goodbyes, and in three days' time she was getting on a plane and not returning for a whole year. She felt excited, scared, happy, sad, jittery, nostalgic and guilty, guilty, guilty.

It had been a good party, a great party in fact, and she must thank Laura again for organising it all. Cathy had started the dancing, jiving with Ian on the small dance floor, not minding at all that they were the centre of attention until others came to join in. When the DJ finished for the night, Gerry stepped in to take his place, his baritone voice keeping the music going with a traditional song about immigration that had both Erin and Laura in fits of laughter.

'God love him, Gerry thinks I'm getting on a ship and never coming back again!'

There had been a few lowlights during the night, one when Paddy cornered her and made his usual – not remotely funny – remarks about her single status.

'Ah, it's the girl herself. Where have you been hiding all night?'

'Nowhere, Paddy, I've been right here.'

'Tell me once and tell me no more, are you going to meet the man of your dreams out there and bring him back with you so we can *finally* have a wedding?'

'I have absolutely no idea.'

'Ah now, Erin, you need to be more enthusiastic and committed than that. Sure, Laura brought the Spaniard back with her. And you'll have no language barriers in Australia – it should be very straightforward! Ha, ha!'

For once Erin had struck back at him. 'Jesus, Paddy, will

you just shut up. Believe me, I'm not single by choice, and I'll be as fucking happy as you if I meet a man in Australia!'

Paddy had jumped as though he'd received an electric shock. 'I'm sorry, love. I was only having a joke, that's all.'

'Well, Paddy, it's *not bloody funny.*'

Her uncle had uttered a few more mumbled apologies before making himself scarce. Now Erin found herself smiling at the recollection. Actually, maybe the scene qualified more as a highlight than a lowlight. She'd never really learned how to retaliate or stick up for herself, and cutting comebacks were something she only ever thought of when the opportunity to deliver them had long passed. Now that she thought about it, her bravery hadn't just been spurred by the fact that she was getting on a plane and didn't have to face her uncle for another twelve months. There was also the effect of seeing all her college friends tonight – friends who had, one by one, got married and started families, friends whom she usually caught up with at their homes, playing with their children and having cups of tea at their kitchen counters. Seeing them on a night out, dressed to the nines with wine glasses in their hands and attentive husbands by their sides, made her realise that it had been a long time since she'd seen them at this sort of social event, and for some reason that realisation made her feel distant from them – as well as very single. And how dare Paddy make light of it, how dare he act as if it was something she could change at will.

Enough brain space wasted on Paddy. She had so much else to think about, so much to cram into the next few days. What to pack and what to leave behind. Chores around the house which she wanted to finish, cupboards and drawers that needed cleaning out, that sort of thing. Bills and paperwork for Moira and herself. Not forgetting to print her tickets, pack her passport somewhere safe, and ensure that she had enough of the right currency when she got there. Should she make a list? Just this once? No, she would not.

She and Laura were different in that respect. Tonight her cousin had casually commented that her life would fall apart at the seams if she didn't keep lists. Erin had a different viewpoint. In fact she'd developed a deep mistrust of lists, and tried to conduct her life without them. As far as she was concerned, if you had to write something down in order to remember it, then you had really *forgotten* it. Everything she had read on Alzheimer's and other related diseases advocated mental workouts and memory training as essential for maintaining brain function and health. And so she never gave in to the urge to write things down, always endeavouring to train her brain to remember of its own accord, without prompting or assistance. The downside of not keeping lists was that her mind never felt clear; there were always things whirling round and round in it, like now.

A sound, a click, startled Erin from her thoughts.

She opened the bathroom door. 'Mum?' Her voice sounded small and insecure in the draughty landing. 'Mum?'

Moira's bedroom was empty, the covers on the bed neat and undisturbed. Erin's stomach did a sickening little turn. She ran down the stairs, jumping the last three steps, and did a quick check of the kitchen and living room, though she knew in her heart that the sound, the click, had originated from the front door.

'Mum? Mum?'

The door opened into the bitter cold. Erin's cotton pyjamas and bare feet were totally inadequate for the wintry night that greeted her. Her mother was on the other side of the garden gate, illuminated by the street light overhead as she diligently leant over to close the latch.

'Mum!' Erin rushed down the path, damp, slippy and chillingly cold under her feet. She flung open the gate that Moira had so carefully latched, and grabbed her mother by the arm.

'*Where are you going?*'

Moira looked perplexed. 'I'm meeting Joe outside the cinema.'

She was wearing peach-coloured lipstick and eye-shadow, gold teardrop earrings and her best coat. She really thought she was meeting Joe. How could Erin persuade her that it was 2010 and not 1970? How could she tell her that the cinema – if the one she had in mind still existed – would be closed at this hour of the night? Worst of all, how could she tell Moira that Joe, her beloved husband, had died five years ago, after a long, exhausting battle with cancer?

'I think that's tomorrow night, Mum. Come on inside, you'll need to get your beauty sleep before then.'

Docilely, Moira allowed herself to be led back up the garden path, back into the semi-detached house, out of her clothes and into bed.

Erin tucked her in tightly and kissed the papery skin on her forehead. 'Night, Mum! Straight to sleep now.'

For a long time afterwards, Erin sat on the side of her own bed, shivering after her dash into the freezing night and on alert should her mother get another notion to go out and meet Joe. Her stomach continued to turn, champagne, guilt and frantic worry a sickening mix. On the floor, her suitcase lay open, its lid propped against the wall, like a question.

Are you? Will you? Can you?

Surely tonight's events proved beyond all doubt that she shouldn't get on that plane?

Dare you, replied a familiar, contemptuous voice, that of Rachel Murphy. Once upon a time, Erin's misery and humiliation had been Rachel's sole focus in life. Though Erin hadn't set eyes on her since the day she'd left school, Rachel's sneers and disdain seemed to be permanently etched in her psyche.

Dare you, dare you, dare you.

Chapter 4

'Look at you! You haven't changed a bit. You still look exactly the same as you did in college. Bitch!'

Erin laughed at Mel's exuberant greeting and gave her a warm hug in return. 'I think you need glasses, Mel. But what about you? You're *completely* different.'

Melissa had changed hair colour, body shape, everything. Blonde, tanned, wearing a skimpy top and a very short denim skirt, she looked nothing like the mousey-haired girl who'd been Erin's best friend in college. She seemed taller than Erin remembered, but maybe that was because she was thinner, and she looked remarkably *young* – significantly younger than her thirty-four years.

She seized Erin's arm. 'Come on, come in. Sorry I couldn't meet you at the airport. I had a beginning-of-year staff meeting I couldn't get out of. Blah, blah, blah … it went on forever. Totally bored out of my senses.'

Mel even *sounded* younger than her years, if that was possible. However, the mere mention of a staff meeting, even in such irreverent terms, was enough to make Erin want to gag. Oh dear, if she was going to teach at Melissa's school she would have to start feeling more enthusiastic about it.

'This is lovely, Mel,' she said, looking around the living area of her friend's one-bedroom attic-style apartment. The living space was small, with correspondingly small pieces of furniture, and it was a little dim. The cream walls and sofas had clearly been chosen to introduce more light, and provided a gorgeous contrast to the wooden floorboards, which had a dark, burnished sheen, their age the most striking feature of the room.

'Come on.' Melissa ushered her further into the apartment. 'Fling your bags over there. Now let's have a drink.'

A short while later, Erin was sitting out on Melissa's tiny balcony, a glass of sparkling wine in her hand as she absorbed the vista and the smells and sounds around her. Melissa's apartment was in Balmain, which, she informed Erin, was an old, originally working-class suburb in Sydney's inner west. Dusk shrouded the narrow streets and houses but did not disguise the obvious character and charm of the area. The houses, squashed together in terraces, had minuscule front gardens and ornate cast-iron balustrades on their first floors. Trees dotted the streets; in fact there was a surprising amount of greenery given that the area was so built-up. Cars were bumper-to-bumper along the kerbs: it looked as though finding a park would be a nightmare.

Melissa, who had seen the view thousands of times, was much more interested in being updated on their old circle of friends than in discussing the charms and challenges of living in Balmain. 'How about Orla O'Brien?'

'Married, two children,' Erin replied dutifully.

'Angela Harris?'

'Married, *four* children.'

'Deirdre Flynn?'

'Separated, two kids and another on the way.'

'Didn't you just say she was separated?'

'She is. She has a new fiancé, and he's the father of the new baby.'

'Bitch! How can she get two men to marry her when I can't even get one?'

Erin laughed. 'I must admit, the same thought occurred to me.'

University had been a much happier experience for Erin than her years at school. She and Melissa had been part of an eclectic group of friends: Angela Harris, a plump girl whose raucous laugh could carry for miles; Orla O'Brien, skin and bones next to Angela, with frizzy hair that was the bane of her life; Deirdre Flynn, a self-confessed slapper and party girl; Mel, enthusiastic and always ready for adventure; Erin, still lacking in confidence but happier than she'd ever been. Everyone in the group had a place, their differences accepted and even celebrated. They used to tease each other, roll their eyes on occasion, but they had never ever sneered.

'Bitch,' Melissa repeated, her good-natured grin making the word sound quite harmless, almost affectionate. 'Well, at least you're here now and we can be shamelessly single together. It'll be just like the old days. Remember?'

Though it felt like a lifetime ago, Erin did remember. She pictured herself and Melissa twelve years younger, their faces softer and full of wonder as they travelled through Europe; drinking cold, fizzy beer as they sampled the nightlife of each new city; that sense of invincibility as high-speed trains whizzed them from one country to the next; lugging backpacks and guidebooks and an emergency supply of instant noodles to each new destination. France, Italy, Greece. Then on to Asia: India, Nepal, Vietnam and finally Thailand, where she'd got the call about her father.

'You have to come home,' Moira had sobbed. 'I'm sorry, Erin, but you have to come home.'

And so Erin had gone home, and left Melissa on her own to spend another couple of weeks in Asia before she flew to Australia, the next stop on their itinerary. Melissa fell in love with Australia, so much so that she applied for a permanent visa and stayed on, living a life that could have been Erin's too – if only her father hadn't got cancer.

'How *is* your mother?' Mel asked gently, obviously sensing Erin's disquiet.

'The same,' she replied with a heavy sigh. 'She has good days and bad days, and even on the good days she's liable to do anything … I really shouldn't be here, Mel – Mum's in no state to be left alone.'

'Now, Erin, listen to me,' Mel began in her most formidable teacher's voice. 'You've put your life on hold for twelve years. First for your father, and now your mum. She could live with this Alzheimer's for another five to ten years. Where would you be then? It could be twenty years – twenty of your *best years* – you'll have given up.'

What Mel was saying made sense, and Erin had heard it plenty of times before – from Laura and the rest of the family, and even from her own doctor. It seemed that everyone agreed it was unreasonable to expect a daughter or a son to give up ten or twenty years to care for a sick parent. And it seemed that everyone had some kind of threshold ('I'd sacrifice one or two years, but not five'). But how could one apply a threshold without knowing the full picture? Without knowing at the outset what time period was involved? How long the illness might last? How bad it might get? Without that information, all one could do was make the decision day-by-day – and day-by-day it had been inconceivable to leave her father when he was terminally ill, and just as inconceivable to leave her mother when she began to show signs of memory loss straight after her husband's death. In fact, leaving had been out of the question until Erin's health and own mental state had become a problem.

'Let's not talk about it any more,' she said with forced brightness. 'Top up my glass and tell me everything I need to know about Sydney.'

Much later on, lying on Mel's surprisingly comfortable sofa

bed but not feeling the slightest bit sleepy, Erin put her guilt to one side and allowed herself to feel a sense of accomplishment. She was *here*. She had put the final few bits and pieces into her suitcase, weathered the emotional goodbyes to her mother and Laura, and got on the plane. She was *here*. She had made it. Step one: tick. Step two was to get a job; she was meeting the department head at Mel's school tomorrow. Step three: find somewhere to live; using Mel's tiny living room as digs was obviously not going to be feasible in the long term. And step four, she impulsively decided, was to have a relationship, any kind of relationship, even a dead-end one. It had been far too long.

She still felt scared, and each of the 'steps' she'd just decided on was more frightening than the last. But adrenaline was rushing through her veins, tingling her fingers and toes, and diluting her fear to the point where she hardly even knew that it was there. In fact, the adrenaline was so powerful that it was all she could do not to leap from the bed and rush outside to meet this new life head on.

It's the dead of night, she told herself sternly. Settle down.

Easier said than done. An hour or so later, her throat dry and scratchy, she got up to get a glass of water. Drinking at the kitchen sink, she suddenly remembered that she hadn't taken her vitamins since she'd left Ireland. Her sanity hinged on those vitamins; it was no wonder she couldn't rest tonight. Turning on the lamp in the front room, she moved around the clothes in her suitcase until she located the small plastic container that held all the pills: gingko, Omega-3, Gotu Kola, vitamin C, vitamin E and the all-important vitamin B Complex. She swallowed each tablet with a gulp of water, and returned to bed feeling even more alert. Rummaging in her luggage once again, this time in her cabin bag, she located her book of Sudoku puzzles. On the plane she'd completed eight of the ten medium-difficulty puzzles in the book: long-haul flights were perfect for brain training. Tomorrow she would walk to the closest shops and buy herself a sim card for her phone and another Sudoku book.

She finished the remaining two puzzles, drowsiness creeping over her at last. Switching off the lamp, sinking deep under the soft, cotton duvet, she drifted away into a sound sleep.

* * * * *

Laura stood at the kitchen counter gripping her phone with one hand and her coffee mug with the other, trying to stay calm. Kasia was starting this morning – she would be knocking on the door any minute now – and Laura had planned to take the day off work. She'd wanted to settle Kasia in, show her where she would be sleeping and run through some basic house rules while taking the opportunity to observe how she interacted with Olivia. The only problem was that Johan, one of her staff, was on the line declaring that he was sick. Johan was *never* sick. He was tall and muscular and *German*, a perfectionist in everything, including health.

'I am feeling very ill,' he pronounced in a sad, little-boy voice.

'But today's the deadline for the documentation,' she groaned, forgetting, in her distress, to show him any sympathy. 'They're shipping the product tomorrow. It'll cost thousands if there's a delay.'

'I know, I know. I would go in, you know I would, but it is very possible that I would vomit all over the documentation.'

Though she loved Johan, he had a tendency to be too detailed on occasion, and now he'd managed to make her feel queasy too. What was she going to do? Johan was the only German translator on staff, and though they used a number of freelancers for overflow, would she be able to recruit one at such short notice?

'It's okay, Johan, I'm sure that I'll be able to find someone to fill in,' she said, trying to convince herself as she spoke. 'But I'll have to be able to reach you throughout …'

'I must go,' Johan yelped and dropped the phone before she could finish.

Oh, dear, he really was very ill. Damn, damn and damn! There was no way she could recruit a freelancer from home. She would have to go into the office. And assuming she actually managed to find someone, she'd have to stay to liaise between the freelancer and Johan at home to ensure that the job was completed to the appropriate standard. Damn it, damn it, damn it! Of all days. And she'd never seen Johan with as much as a sniffle.

The doorbell rang. Kasia. Laura put down her barely touched coffee and somehow mustered a welcoming smile as she walked through the hallway to the front door.

Kasia stood outside in the half-light of the morning, flanked by two large backpacks which apparently contained her belongings. She wore a cotton long-sleeved top, and tight faded jeans. Her feet were clad in cheap-looking ballet pumps. She had no socks or jacket, and though she wasn't shivering she looked very cold.

'Welcome, Kasia. Come in. Let me take one of those bags.'

As Laura closed the door behind Kasia, she noticed Olivia standing on the stairs, clutching her teddy in one hand and her baby blanket in the other, her cheeks flushed and warm, her eyes bleary but curious. Her daughter wasn't shy. In a moment she would walk carefully down the stairs and engage her new nanny in very adult-like conversation. But for now, standing on the steps with her halo of tousled hair, Olivia seemed extraordinarily vulnerable.

How can I go into work and leave her with this stranger? What kind of mother am I? If only Esteban were here …

But Esteban was in Prague and wouldn't be back until tomorrow. He was never at home when things went wrong. Laura felt a spurt of anger. How bloody nice for him to be waking up in a comfortable hotel room and not being torn in two between his child and an emergency at work!

Why am I always the one who's being compromised?

'This is your room, Kasia. We'll leave your bags here. Olivia is across the way, and we're over there. You can use this bathroom ...'

Back downstairs, she showed Kasia the layout of the kitchen, how to work the dishwasher and the location of Olivia's colouring books and craft. She moved quickly, Kasia and Olivia trailing mutely behind her.

'I'm sorry, but I'm going to have to leave you to get to know each other without me,' she said a little breathlessly when she felt the basics had been attended to. 'Something has come up in the office.'

Kasia and Olivia looked equally disapproving at her announcement.

'I've written down everything you need to know, Kasia. It's all in this manual.'

Laura indicated the display folder she'd set neatly on the kitchen counter last night in anticipation of this morning. She grinned rather ruefully, acknowledging that a manual was a poor substitute for her presence, but got no response from either of them.

The traffic on the way into the city was appalling. Her stomach clenched with each enforced stop, protesting that a half cup of coffee didn't qualify as breakfast. Esteban would have enjoyed a sumptuous Czech breakfast by now. And his hotel was in the centre of the business district, a quick stroll and he'd be at work. None of this maddening stop-start traffic for him.

Now she wasn't being fair. Esteban worked hard, too. In fact, he was one of the hardest workers she knew. Had she really just begrudged him his breakfast?

Sorry, love. She apologised to him in her head. *I am such a grump these days. Sorry.*

* * * * *

The department head at Melissa's school was not at all what Erin had expected. She'd imagined that the students would be good-looking, but not the staff, and certainly not her potential boss! He was young, only a few years older than her. Tanned, cropped dark-brown hair, a completely different species from her old department head at St Patrick's (Ted, a lovely man, but sixty-odd and overly fond of his grey woollen cardigan).

'Jack Thornton.' Well dressed in dark trousers and a Ralph Lauren blue-and-white striped shirt, he shook her hand with the same conviction in which he'd stated his name.

'Hello, Jack,' she replied, feeling quite self-conscious and underwhelming in her far-from-new charcoal-grey suit. Her hair fell loosely to her shoulders, wisps straying over her face and constantly giving her the urge to gather it up in a ponytail (in fact, it *had* been in a ponytail until Mel had commanded her to take it down). Inside the open collar of her plain white shirt she wore two delicately twisted strings of small black beads, a going-away present from Lisha. Now she worried that the necklace jarred with the rest of her outfit and didn't look professional. No, it was fine – otherwise Mel would have insisted she take it off.

'Sit down, Erin.' Jack gestured to one of the two seats across from him. 'Would you like a tea, or a coffee? A glass of water?'

'I'm fine, thanks,' she said, her voice uneven from this belated attack of nerves.

'Melissa tells me that you went to university together. In Dublin, wasn't it?'

'Yes.'

'And what have you done since then?'

Jack already had a copy of her resumé, and a cursory glance through would have told him that she hadn't 'done' an awful lot.

'I've been teaching – at the same school,' she replied, nerves continuing to play havoc with her voice and causing it to sound raspier than usual. 'St Patrick's is a public school in a working-class suburb of Dublin. I taught French to a variety of year groups.'

'Did you stay so long because you loved the job, or was there another reason?'

Jack asked the question in an open, nonjudgmental tone of voice and in return, Erin tried to be as honest as possible.

'My father had a terminal illness, and soon after he died my mother developed Alzheimer's. It was hard to think about my career development when all that was going on at home.'

Jack nodded, as though her answer resonated with him. 'When we have instability in certain areas of our lives, it's natural to want to keep everything else as constant as we can.'

Was he admitting that he had instability in his life, too? Or was he simply doing his best to be empathetic and put her at ease? Whatever his intentions, her nervousness seemed to be finally abating and a grateful smile pulled at the corners of her mouth.

'In fact, it might shock you to discover that I've been teaching at this school going on ten years now,' he revealed with a rueful shrug. 'So we're similar in that regard.'

He understood. He knew how it felt to get stuck somewhere, in a rut that seemed to get deeper and more entrenched and hopeless with each passing year.

'Okay, I'm shocked.' Her smile, completely of its own volition, turned into a grin. 'But in our defence, I think every teacher should stay long enough to see at least one year of students progress the whole way through. There's a lot to be learnt from seeing how much they grow and develop, and when you see them graduate you get a better appreciation of their journey, and your own part in it.'

'I couldn't agree more.'

Jack used this thread of conversation to talk about the values of the school and what kind of young adults they wanted to release into the world. He was openly passionate about the students and the role of languages and other cultures in their development. Erin added her own opinions and experiences where appropriate, and the more they spoke the less it felt like an interview, and more like a chat – with someone she liked.

'Let me show you around before we finish,' he offered when he had clearly covered all the things he wanted to say. 'I can't expect you to get a feeling for the school when you've been stuck inside my stuffy office.'

His office was far from stuffy. It was bright, relatively new and well organised, but Erin declined to point this out.

Jack walked her around the school, proudly showing off some of the classrooms and facilities, smiling and nodding at students along the way (he was obviously quite popular). Erin asked questions as they went, drew mental comparisons with St Patrick's, and asked him to deposit her at Mel's office when he eventually glanced at his watch and said that he had a meeting to attend.

'Well, that's everything, I think.' Jack smiled as they stood outside Mel's half-open door. His eyes glittered when he smiled, she noticed now that she was close up, and a very attractive dimple appeared at the right side of his mouth. 'I don't see the point in beating around the bush, Erin. I can see you fitting in here, and I hope you feel the same, and as the academic year has already begun, I'm keen to have you on board as soon as possible.'

Erin struggled to find an appropriate reply, both his proximity and his openness catching her off guard.

'I suppose you will need at least a few days to sort out your tax file number and legalities like that.'

She nodded somewhat distractedly. 'Yes, I'll need some time to get organised.'

One last flash of that affable smile. 'Well, give me a call as soon as you're ready.'

'I will.'

Mel was eating her lunch, a box of fresh noodles. 'Well, how did it go?' she demanded, undeterred by her full mouth.

'Really well.' Erin leant against Mel's desk and folded her arms. 'He's nice, very straightforward ... I could see myself working with him. In fact, I think he has pretty much offered me a job. I just have to get my paperwork sorted out.'

'Awesome!' Mel swallowed and grinned. 'We can have lunch together every day, go for power walks during free periods, gang up on students who are mean to us ...'

Erin eyed the box of noodles, her stomach contracting with a jealous pang. 'Speaking of lunch, did those come from the school canteen?'

'Yup. We have a cool canteen. It's a cool school, really. You'll love it here. And I *knew* you'd hit it off with Sir Jack.'

'Did you?' Erin asked, more than a little curiously.

'Yup.'

'How could you be so sure?'

Mel shrugged as though it were obvious. 'Because he's straightforward, as you put it yourself, and he's easy to like – even when he's asking me to stay late for meetings, or do extra lunchtime supervision.'

Erin's lips twitched. 'You could have warned me, you know.'

'Warned you about what?'

'I didn't expect him to be so good-looking, and it sort of put me on the back foot at the start of the interview.'

Mel snorted. 'Oh, come on. It's just Jack. And you can't fall for virtually the first man you meet over here. That's so not allowed.'

'Of course I haven't fallen for him. I was just commenting, that's all ... Anyway, he's probably attached.'

Oh God. She was *unashamedly* fishing for personal details on Jack Thornton. Potentially her new boss and, as Mel had quite rightly pointed out, the first male she had met in Australia. How pathetic!

'Actually, he's *not* attached.' The bell rang, at which Mel shovelled a last fork-full of noodles into her mouth, somehow managing to eat, sigh and speak all at the same time. 'Back to the grindstone. This next class is my worst. They're more like kindergartens than Year 10s.' Year 10s were the equivalent of fourth-years in Ireland – the different numbering system was something Erin would have to get used to.

'Well, I'll leave you to it.' Erin grinned, very glad that it was Mel who had to face a roomful of immature 16-year-olds, not her. 'See you later.'

Erin made her way out of the school, taking her time and trying to visualise herself teaching in the neat, well-appointed classrooms she passed along the way. The facilities were undeniably first-class, and the grounds were impeccable. One of the students, a girl on her own, caught Erin's attention, her head downcast, books clutched to her chest, walking leadenly to her next class. It seemed that no matter what type of school, public or private, religious or secular, or even what country in the world, there was always at least one student like that girl. Erin's thoughts immediately jumped to Lisha. Was Madame Gallas watching out for her? Were the other students any more friendly? Doubting either possibility, Erin resolved to write to the Nigerian girl. A distant support had to be better than none at all, and now that Erin wasn't her teacher and bound by all the restrictions that came with that role, she could be a friend.

Some more students passed – girls – and they cast Erin coy yet friendly glances, proving that, for the most part, this was indeed a nice school. But despite that, and despite the lovely modern buildings and grounds, not to mention the rather gorgeous head of department, Erin still couldn't seem to summon up any excitement or enthusiasm about working in Macquarie Grammar School.

Which left her in somewhat of a dilemma.

* * * * *

Oh God, was that the time already? Six o'clock and the software documentation *still* wasn't complete. Johan was on speakerphone talking through a last-minute glitch with Wolfgang, the freelancer – a highly technical conversation in German that Laura couldn't hope to follow. However, her presence was still required because at some point they would need her opinion – it had been like that all day – and then they would temporarily revert to English. She estimated that they were still two hours from sending the finished file, which meant she wouldn't be home until at least eight-thirty. She hadn't mentioned anything about Olivia's dinner to Kasia – she'd assumed she would be home by then. Neither had she gone through Olivia's bedtime routine. Oh God. She'd better call Kasia. Apologise again for dumping her in it on her first day, and give her some instructions on what to do.

Laura motioned to Wolfgang that she needed to step out for a minute. Clicking her office door softly behind her, she sat down at one of the empty workstations directly outside and dialled home. It rang, once, twice, three times. Had Kasia gone out? Surely she wouldn't have decided to take Olivia for a walk at this time of day, when it was cold and dark and busy with rush-hour traffic?

'Hello?'

Thank God, *thank God* she was at home. 'Hi, Kasia. It's Laura.'

'Yes?'

'I'm sorry. I'm still at the office. At this stage I don't expect to be home until half eight, which is after Olivia's bedtime, but maybe you could keep her up this once so I can see her when I get in?'

'Okay.'

'And would you mind making her something to eat?'

'Okay,' Kasia repeated in the same unimpressed tone.

Laura felt a stab of irritation. Kasia had sounded just as detached and cold at lunchtime, when she'd called to see how things were going. Couldn't she make the effort to inject the slightest bit of warmth into her voice? Wasn't it obvious to her that Laura needed reassurance? Then again, maybe she was pissed off at being abandoned on her first day, and annoyed that she was expected to work overtime without any notice. And Laura could hardly blame her for that.

'Thanks, Kasia. I'll get home as soon as I can.'

Laura put down the phone and for the first time that day she sat completely still, doing absolutely nothing, gazing into space as a strange lethargy paralysed her limbs. At that moment she was simply too tired to get up and return to the conference call. If someone had told her that the software problem had been solved and she was in fact free to go home, she would have been too tired for that too.

'Laura?'

Jadedly, she turned her head to the voice that had called her name. It was Savita, and she was carrying a plastic bag and her usual gentle smile.

'I made this Tandoori chicken last night,' she said, holding out the bag, a container visible through the thin plastic, 'and as usual I have too many leftovers.'

Savita encapsulated everything that Laura loved about her job. Her exotic clothes, jangling jewellery and musical voice coexisted with her ingrained kindness, motherliness and wisdom. She was like a bright star, illuminating the dreariest day, yet it was steady, sustainable light that emanated from her. Her traditional Indian dishes took hours and hours to concoct and she derived great pleasure in divvying them out to her colleagues, just as those on the receiving end derived great pleasure from both her cooking and generosity. Everyone adored Savita. She was like a walking advertisement for all the wonderful aspects of diversity.

'Thank you.' Laura smiled humbly. 'You can't begin to know how much I appreciate having a ready-made dinner tonight.'

Savita's lips lifted in a return smile. 'I think I have some idea. Goodnight, Laura. See you tomorrow.'

'Goodnight, Savita. Thanks again.'

Laura dragged herself to her feet. Suddenly hungry, she reheated the chicken in the kitchenette's microwave and shared it with Wolfgang. The unexpected sustenance seemed to clear the freelancer's brain and soon afterwards he found a solution to the problem that had been causing the delay.

Laura got home at eight, earlier than what she had forecast to Kasia but still appallingly late. As she closed the door behind her, Olivia rushed out to the hallway.

'Mum!'

Was Laura imagining it, or was Olivia's hug extra tight? 'Hello, Floss.' She leant down to kiss her flyaway hair. 'Sorry I'm so late.' Laura looked up to see Kasia standing silently at the kitchen door. 'Thanks for today. I'd better put Floss here straight to bed. I'll be back soon.'

Laura and Olivia, clutching hands, climbed the stairs slowly. They were as tired as each other.

'How was it, Floss?' Laura asked when Olivia was tucked safely in bed. 'Did you like Kasia? Did you get along okay?'

'Yes, Mum.' Olivia's response was uncharacteristically brief. Then again, she was very tired.

'What did you do together?'

'We played and watched some telly and went for a walk.'

'Where did you walk to? The park?'

'No.' Olivia yawned and snuggled deeper into bed. 'Just along the streets to see the houses.'

Of course, Kasia would want to have a look around the immediate area. Tomorrow Laura would tell her how to get to the local shops and the park.

'Was Kasia nice to you?'

'Yes, Mum.'

Was that a slight hesitation that Laura detected in her daughter's voice?

Laura tucked Olivia's blankets a little bit tighter around her and planted a kiss on both cheeks. 'Night night, Floss.' Turning out the light, she paused on her way out. 'What did you have for dinner?'

'Bread and jam,' Olivia replied sleepily.

Bread and jam. For *dinner*.

It was inadequate, *completely inadequate* sustenance for a child.

Just as she was inadequate, completely inadequate as a mother.

Chapter 5

Sydney seemed to have many faces, Erin thought as she walked along George Street. The city centre itself was sophisticated, urbane and very corporate, totally at odds with the character-filled inner suburbs like Balmain and the relaxed, leafy beachside suburbs she'd explored with Mel at the weekend. The streets hummed industriously with cars, taxis, vans, and couriers weaving on their pushbikes. People strode past, busy on their smartphones. The sun was out in full force, and the buildings, streets and commuters were glossy and clean-cut against the azure sky.

Erin stepped out of the sun and bustle into the dim, still interior of the Medicare office. She had applied for her tax file number online, but there was a different process for Medicare. She – along with her passport and a copy of her visa – was required to attend one of the offices, and so here she was. A computerised ticket machine stood directly inside the door of the office. She pressed the appropriate selection, took her ticket and went to sit on one of the few remaining seats.

After a few minutes, she realised that she was in for a

substantial wait. There were six clerks, fifty or so customers, and the transactions at the counter did not appear to be particularly fast. She looked around, studying the other people who were waiting on this Thursday morning. It was an eclectic mix: backpackers, mothers with babies, old people with walking aids, a melting pot of nationalities across all the ages. The couple next to her was speaking to each other in Mandarin, or perhaps some other Chinese dialect. Across the way, a mother of Middle Eastern appearance scolded her young child in a foreign tongue. Two young men – South American? – chose to stand rather than sit, their tight clothing and gold jewellery making a clear, proud statement of their sexuality. Earlier on, as Erin had walked through the streets amongst the people of the city, she had noticed for the first time how multicultural Sydney was. Here in this Medicare office, where everyone was still, rather than in transit, their differences were even more evident.

A mild disturbance at the ticket machine brought Erin out of her reverie. A couple in their sixties with matching grey-peppered hair, dark clothes and swarthy skin stood at the machine, debating with each other in a foreign language. The woman waved her hands with growing agitation, the man shrugged and repeatedly shook his head. Erin assumed they were having a difference of opinion, maybe over what option on the machine suited them best. But the disagreement endured, new arrivals lining up behind the couple and, when it became obvious that they were stagnant, overtaking them in the queue. The woman's face shimmered with sweat. She was clearly beginning to panic, and Erin finally realised that neither of them could understand the instructions on the machine. Everyone in the waiting room was staring, adding to their humiliation.

Erin rose from her seat and approached the couple.

'You need some help?' she enquired with a friendly smile, pointing at the machine. The woman nodded frantically, looking close to tears. As she didn't have the language skills to determine the exact nature of the woman's transaction, Erin took the liberty of selecting a general option, hoping that the clerk would be able to deal with whatever query it was at the counter. But when she handed the ticket to the woman with another smile, the woman glanced at it, and then at the big digital screen behind the counter, and raised her hands helplessly. Quite evidently, she didn't even have the literacy skills to marry the four digits on her ticket to the screen.

'I'll stay.' Erin pointed to herself, and then to the service-calling screen. 'I'll stay until it's your turn. I'll tell you.'

The woman waved from Erin to the screen, and Erin nodded and said yes until she secured a shaky, grateful smile. She stood with the couple, smiling intermittently, until her own number was called. Then she waited another fifteen minutes until the couple's ticket came up, and escorted them both to the nominated booth. Before she left, the woman grasped her wrist and thanked her with a torrent of words Erin could not understand but which seemed profoundly sincere.

Erin left the Medicare office with her temporary Medicare card and the rest of the day to spend exploring the city. She was now another step closer to joining the workforce and becoming a true resident of Sydney. She bought herself a coffee and sipped it leisurely as she strolled towards Circular Quay. Along the way, she glanced at every face that passed her by, noticing and revelling in the different shades of skin and hair and eyes. She listened for accents and snatches of different languages and the sounds of other cultures. She wanted to work here, in the city, in the midst of its wonderful, on-tap diversity, and not in some suburban school where ninety per cent of the population spoke and looked the same. This thought and its sheer definiteness took her by surprise.

As did the fact that by the time she fell into bed that night, after a long, tiring yet extremely enjoyable day of sightseeing, the woman's face and her panicked, helpless eyes were still on her mind, as though they somehow held the answer to her dilemma.

* * * * *

Laura used her own set of keys to unlock the varnished front door of Moira's house.

'Hello,' she called, alerting the older woman to their arrival.

'Hellooooo,' Olivia echoed in her small, sweet voice.

'I'm in the kitchen,' they heard Moira reply in the distance.

Laura shut the door behind them, and hung their coats and scarves on the post at the end of the stairs before leading the way down the narrow hallway to the kitchen.

'Something smells nice,' she smiled.

Moira, stooped over the frying pan, nudged some pieces of bacon with the spatula before looking up. 'Just making a spot of breakfast,' she said brightly. 'For some reason, I fancied a cooked one. I'm sick to my back teeth of cereal.'

'But it's dinnertime, Auntie Moira,' Olivia exclaimed. 'Breakfast was hours and hours ago.'

Moira looked confounded by this. 'Dinnertime? Really?'

Olivia nodded solemnly. 'Yes. When we were in the car, Mummy said it was five o'clock. You did, didn't you, Mummy?'

Laura shrugged as though the time was irrelevant. 'Yes, but it doesn't really matter because bacon and eggs makes a nice dinner as well as breakfast.'

Moira looked confused and quite embarrassed by her mistake. 'I must have had a nap, and assumed it was morning when I woke up. Yes, I think that's what happened. What an eejit I am!'

'Eejit isn't a nice word,' Olivia contributed in a holier-than-thou tone. 'Idiot isn't nice either. Mum says silly is okay to use.'

Moira regarded her gravely. 'You're right, child. I'm silly, very silly indeed. Tell me, have you had your dinner?'

'No. And I'm starving.'

'Maybe you and your mother can have some bacon and eggs with me. Then I won't feel so silly.'

'Can we, Mum?' Olivia asked excitedly, her imagination captured by the notion of eating breakfast at dinnertime.

Laura couldn't think of any reason why they couldn't. In the car on the way over, she'd been racking her brains on what to have for dinner. Esteban was away, so they didn't have him to consider. As for Kasia, so far she tended to take or leave mealtimes with the family.

'Thanks, Moira, it's very kind of you. Let me help with the cooking. Olivia, maybe you can set the table, love.'

The breakfast-cum-dinner was delicious: crispy bacon, runny eggs and French toast, laden with fat and calories, but for once Laura didn't care. The food settled comfortingly in her stomach, and the stream of conversation between Moira and Olivia was nourishing in its own way, too. They seemed to share an honesty and earnestness that transcended the age gap.

'And you've no brothers or sisters?' Moira asked Olivia conversationally.

'No,' Olivia replied, before confiding, 'Every night, after I say my prayers with Mum, I whisper my own special prayer for a new baby. So I think one will be coming soon.'

Laura spluttered on her tea. Good Lord! This was news to her.

'Please God, there will.' Moira nodded in agreement. 'I don't know what I would have done without brothers and sisters. Gerry was such a helpful little boy – he would fetch things for me and deliver notes to my friends. Paddy made me laugh – he always had a new joke. And Cathy was the life of the party. Nothing was dull when Cathy was around …'

'Cathy's *my* grandmother,' Olivia pointed out importantly.

Moira looked momentarily taken aback. 'Yes, I suppose she

is. How silly of me to forget. Now don't tell her I told you, but she was a very naughty little girl, always getting into trouble.'

Olivia was agog. 'Really? What kind of trouble?'

Moira waved a hand dismissively. 'Oh, this and that. But I can tell that *you* are a very *good* little girl.'

'I am,' Olivia assured the older woman. 'Even my new nanny, Kasia, says she's never met anyone as good as me.'

'Kasia, that's an interesting name,' Moira mused.

'She's from Poland,' Olivia said with an informative air.

'Ah, Poland. Our housemaid was Polish, too.' Moira seemed to start at the memory. 'Now what was her name again? I can't believe I've forgotten. I can see her face as clear as day, but her name escapes me … I must ask Cathy when I see her. She'd remember.'

Olivia's eyes widened. 'Did you and Granny Cathy live together?'

'Yes. In Paris. Cathy and me … and Joe.'

'Who's Joe?'

Laura winced at Olivia's perfectly innocent question. She tried to catch her eye, to signal to her to talk about something else, but Olivia's attention was firmly fixed on Moira.

'Joe was my husband,' Moira replied sadly. 'He died before you were born.'

More often than not, Moira referred to Joe as though he were still alive and she expected him to walk in the door at any minute. She seemed exceptionally lucid today – other than mixing up breakfast with dinnertime.

'How did he die?'

'Olivia,' Laura interjected. 'Don't be a nosy parker. You'll upset Moira.'

'It's okay.' Moira shrugged matter-of-factly. 'The child is curious, and that's understandable. He died of cancer, Olivia, which is a horrible disease. It was in his lungs, and so he had trouble breathing. He's in heaven now, and he can draw lovely, deep breaths.'

'How far up is heaven?'

'I would say it's where the sky ends and the universe starts.'

'And is it inside or outside?' Olivia was going off on another tangent, thank goodness.

'Well, that's an interesting question, I suppose it's a bit of both.'

Laura roused herself to clear the table, while Moira and Olivia continued to chatter. Moira had barely spoken throughout Laura's other visits, and it was wonderful to hear her so engaged, and just as wonderful to see the rapt expression on Olivia's heart-shaped face. Laura scraped the plates clean, before sinking them into sudsy water. Rubbing the grease with the scouring pad and listening in on the conversation about heaven going on behind her back, she felt unusually serene. Overall, this had been a really lovely visit. For everyone. She resolved that she would bring Olivia to see Moira more often.

* * * * *

'You've *what?*' Mel exclaimed when she came home from work and Erin broke the news.

'I've decided not to take the job at Macquarie,' Erin repeated calmly from where she was sitting on the sofa.

'But you *told* Jack that you would.' Mel's voice was so incredulous that it quivered.

'No,' Erin corrected her friend, 'I told Jack I would call him once my paperwork was sorted out. I didn't *ever* say that I was accepting the job.'

'You implied it by omission,' Mel argued, coming closer and looming over Erin in her seat.

'Don't be ridiculous, Mel.'

'You're the one who's being ridiculous. You're throwing away a perfectly good job here!'

'It is a perfectly good job, but for someone else, not me,' Erin tried to explain. 'Every fibre of me is screaming in protest.'

'At least one of your "fibres" must understand that Macquarie is one of the most elite schools in the city,' Mel countered sarcastically, 'and that it pays well – you know how rare that is for teaching. You're mad, Erin, stark raving mad to turn this down.'

Erin hadn't expected Mel to be this upset. Of course, she realised that Mel had been looking forward to them working together, but surely Mel could see that particular benefit was incidental to the job being right for Erin in the first place?

'Sit down, Mel.' Erin waved at the spot next to her on the cream sofa. 'I can't explain properly while you're glowering at me like that.'

'I don't want to sit,' Mel retorted, sounding a lot like one of the mutinous teenagers she taught at school. After a few moments, she relented and landed next to Erin with a flop.

Erin rewarded her cooperation with a slight smile. 'Let's start again. I'm *not* taking the job at Macquarie, and maybe I am mad, but that's my decision, okay?' She stared at Mel, who eventually nodded. 'Now, you'll be glad to hear that I have a plan. I've already been online and looked at some other jobs, ones that I'm genuinely interested in. There's one in particular that I'm going to apply for.'

'What is it?' Mel enquired, still sounding very petulant.

'It's teaching English as a second language in an English and Settlement Services College.'

Mel frowned, clearly perplexed. 'But it's still teaching, isn't it? I assumed, from the fact that you're going to turn down a perfectly good job, that you wanted to get away from teaching?'

'Not from teaching: from school. I want to get away from *school*,' Erin clarified, but Mel still looked confused. 'I hated school when I was a student, absolutely *hated* it, and I would have never taken that job in St Patrick's if Dad hadn't been so ill. With him having chemo and going in and out of hospital, I couldn't pass up the flexibility of the shorter work days and the long summer holidays, and I consoled myself that I would get something else eventually, when the time was right. But I got stuck there. Me, who hated school, teaching in the same one for almost *twelve years*. When I went to Macquarie last week, I realised I can't compromise myself like that again, no matter how good the job seems on paper.'

Mel's expression had softened. She looked as though she was beginning to understand. 'I didn't realise you hated school so much. You've never said so before.'

Erin shrugged. 'Well, I'm saying so now.'

'But this job you want to apply for is in a college. Isn't that splitting hairs?'

'The college helps people settle in the country, find childcare and jobs and somewhere to live as well as ensuring that they have functional English,' Erin elaborated, hearing her voice become animated. It seemed that simply reciting the job description was enough to make her feel excited. 'I know I'd really enjoy those broader aspects of the role. And I'd be dealing with adults, Mel, not school kids. So there is a difference. In fact, a *big* difference.'

'What if you don't get it?' Mel was playing devil's advocate now. 'You shouldn't get your hopes up.'

'I phoned the agency before you came in,' Erin admitted with a sheepish grin. 'The pay is lousy, the college is located in a particularly unattractive part of the city, and the position has been vacant for more than a month.'

'I told you that you were stark raving mad!' Mel rolled her eyes, but she was grinning now too. 'But it does sound like you're in with a good chance.'

Erin jumped up, too full of nervous energy to sit for any longer. She would begin work on her application right now. Mel could help. With both of them working on it, it would be perfect. She *had* to get this job. Nothing had felt so important for a long, long time.

* * * * *

'Shit!' Laura stared disbelievingly at the streak on her pants, which had started off as white, the same colour as the bleach, but was turning to orange before her eyes as fabric dye was stripped away. 'Shit, shit, *shit!*'

It had been a stupid idea to start cleaning at this hour of night, and now the satisfaction she craved from having at least achieved something concrete today had been completely eradicated by the fact that she'd spilt bleach on her suit pants. Should she give up? Leave the bathrooms until the weekend? No, she'd continue. At least she'd be able to tick something off her to-do list. Mind you, she'd also have to add something else straight on the end of it: buy a new suit.

She scoured the walls of the shower, her frustration lending extra vigour to each scrub of the nailbrush on the grout. In the distance, she heard the slam of the front door. Kasia was home. Laura scrubbed even harder. She knew she was being unreasonable, but she hated that a virtual stranger could walk in and out of her house at will. The situation wasn't helped by the fact that Kasia was not communicative about her movements. Sometimes she joined the family for dinner, sometimes she didn't. Sometimes she stayed in her room in the evenings, other times she went out. She never announced her plans until she was sitting at the dinner table, or on her way out the door, and the uncertainty of what to expect each evening made Laura constantly ill at ease.

Opening the cabinet above the vanity to stow away a spare bottle of shampoo, she noticed that the lid on one of the other bottles – an expensive perfume – was slightly askew. The scent was not a favourite one, which was why she kept it in the spare bathroom, but nevertheless it was odd. Laura was meticulous about things like that.

'Oh, you are cleaning.' Kasia hovered at the bathroom door, quite obviously startled to see Laura ensconced in there.

'Yes,' Laura replied, looking over her shoulder, aware that she must look ridiculous in her bright yellow rubber gloves and office wear. 'Unfortunately, the only time I have free for cleaning is late at night,' she added pointedly.

'I will clean this,' Kasia indicated the bathroom with an unenthusiastic motion of her hand, 'in the future.'

Given that Kasia was the person who predominantly used the spare bathroom, Laura had been hoping that she would take the hint.

'Thanks.' Closing the cabinet door, Laura removed a tiny streak from the glass mirror. 'Did you have a nice night?' she asked, making a conscious effort to be friendly.

'Yes.'

'Were you catching up with friends?'

Kasia nodded vaguely.

'In town?'

'Yes.' Kasia, clearly not willing to be drawn into a conversation, stepped back from the doorway. 'Goodnight, Laura.'

'Goodnight.'

God, it was so hard to like her. If she had revealed something, *anything* about her night, that she'd been out with girlfriends, or on a date, or seeing her cousin, Laura could have latched onto that one thing and felt that she knew this stranger slightly better than before. But Kasia consistently refused to reveal anything, so she remained a stranger, and Laura couldn't get comfortable with having a stranger in her house and, more importantly, caring for her daughter.

Basin, chrome taps, mirror, Laura scrubbed and scoured until the rest of the bathroom was as clean as the shower. There, she was done. Now she could go to bed feeling at least slightly on top of things. Before she turned out the bathroom light, her eyes returned to the cabinet above the vanity. The perfume might spoil; she should put the lid on properly. No, she would leave it for now. It would be interesting to see if it was still askew the next time she thought to check.

Chapter 6

Erin took a jittery breath. She was wearing the same outfit as she had for the interview at Macquarie Grammar School. In hindsight, this felt like a poor choice, because this job was meant to be something new and different, and how could she feel new and different if she was dressed exactly the same? And it seemed that she was having another spurt of last-minute nerves, too. Deep breath in. Deep breath out. In … Out … In … Out. That was slightly better.

Though the English and Settlement Services college was in a rather rundown part of the inner city, the building itself looked as though it had been recently renovated, its bare brick walls freshly painted white. Inside there were more white walls, dark grey carpet tiles underfoot and an array of multicoloured armchairs to sit on. The reception area was clearly the hub, with streams of students passing through on their way to class, a babble of voices and languages permeating the room – in which Erin was the only person who remained stationary and silent. The receptionist, a young girl of Middle Eastern appearance, called across the noise to her.

'I've told Adam you're here. He'll be right down.'

Adam McKenna, the managing director of the college, had already spoken to Erin on the phone, and she reminded herself now that she wasn't about to meet a complete stranger and there was no need to feel so nervous. In fact, Adam had sounded nice, albeit a little overzealous, on the phone: full of questions about her teaching experience and her exposure, if any, to refugees and migrants; extremely animated when he spoke about the college and the vacancy he was trying to fill.

In her mind, Erin had matched his articulate and mature voice to a man in his fifties with greying hair and a busy smile, so when a much younger man bounded down the stairs at the back of the reception desk, she assumed it was another staff member, or perhaps a student. When that man headed in her direction, extended his hand in greeting and said, 'Hello, you must be Erin', she looked at him in askance.

'I'm Adam,' he prompted, no doubt seeing the confusion on her face.

'Yes, of course.' She blinked in surprise, stood up from her seat and clumsily shook his hand. 'Hello, Adam.'

Now that she was standing, Erin realised that not only was she a couple of years older than him, she was slightly taller, too. But what he may have lacked in height, he made up for in solidness, his white shirt and dark trousers fitting snugly. Fair hair curled at the nape of his neck. Green eyes with golden flecks assessed her. 'Let's start with taking a walk around, Erin. Classes are about to start for the morning – it's a really good time to see the place in full action. Let's go.'

'Okay.' She smiled cautiously. 'Lead the way.'

She followed Adam through some sliding doors that opened onto a long corridor. His pace was quick; in fact he walked as though he might break into a run at any moment, and he spoke as energetically as he moved, offering a steady flow of information as he went. Erin found it took some effort to keep up with him on all fronts, and she was mildly relieved when he stopped outside an office inhabited by a middle-aged woman who was busily tapping on her keyboard.

'Morning, Lydia. This is Erin. Erin is interviewing for a teaching position and I'm just showing her around.'

'Hello, Erin. Very nice to meet you.' Lydia spoke with a crisp British accent that wouldn't have sounded out of place on the BBC World Service. Both the clarity of her voice and her sleek blonde hair, secured in a ballet-type bun, seemed at odds with the haggardness of her face. She smiled welcomingly at Erin, but her smile had the unfortunate effect of making her look even older, with deep grooves extending along her cheeks and around her mouth.

'Lydia is our first stop for the students. She assesses them in reading, writing and speaking English, and then decides how many hours of classes they need. We provide a total of five hundred, six hundred or nine hundred hours, depending on Lydia's assessment.' Adam supplied this information without stopping for a breath.

Lydia turned and indicated some worksheets on the table behind her desk. 'They undergo a number of tests,' she confirmed. 'It's quite a comprehensive process.'

'How long do the tests take?' Erin asked politely.

'It depends.' Lydia shrugged. 'Sometimes their communication is so poor I need to get an interpreter. Other times they're so nervous it takes forever just to put them at ease.'

'Lydia is also responsible for the home tutoring service,' Adam continued. 'We have over a hundred part-time tutors now.'

'Volunteers?' Erin enquired.

Lydia nodded. 'Thank God for people's generosity.'

Adam took a few restless steps towards the door. 'Now, I know you have someone coming shortly so we'd better move along.'

'Goodbye, Erin. And good luck.' Lydia smiled again, and though it was a warm, genuine smile, its effect was somewhat diminished by those deep lines on her face which, now that

Erin had had some time to form an opinion, spoke of hardship and tough times rather than age.

This time Erin was more prepared for Adam's long strides and nonstop commentary, and she was more successful at keeping up. He didn't halt until they reached the computer room, a large rectangular room with about fifty terminals. This morning almost every seat was taken, the students varying from young women in burkas to old men with stooped shoulders and gnarled fingers. Erin and Adam didn't go inside; they watched through the glass panels. The students seemed to have varying levels of ability, with some quite independent, and others looking scared and unsure, and regularly seeking assistance from the supervisor.

'We encourage them to email friends, read newspapers, join online communities, and fill in government forms and job applications online. This room is critical to producing students with functional English and who can fend for themselves in Australian society.' Adam looked at Erin and grimaced. 'An enormous share of our annual budget goes on computer maintenance and upgrades. I'm always being asked to reduce costs, but it's the one area in which I refuse to compromise.'

For the first time, Erin realised that the college wasn't just an extremely important social service, it was in fact a business, with costs and revenues for which Adam was clearly responsible.

They continued on, pausing a short time later at another large room with a variety of prams and strollers lined up outside. Erin assumed it was a classroom, but looking through the window revealed that it was in fact a childcare facility: walls painted in primary colours, children clustered on the playing mats, pieces of art pegged to drying lines strung overhead. Now that Erin thought of it, of course many of the female students would be mothers, and having somewhere safe to put their child while they learned how to communicate and live in this foreign country was fundamental to their success.

'Just like the computer room, this childcare centre is at the very heart of what we do,' said Adam. 'The women and children come as a package, and we do our best to help them both.'

Erin nodded. She was glad that he had begun the interview with this tour: it told her much more than any questions she could have thought of while sitting in his office or some meeting room.

Next, he led the way to one of the classrooms, and introduced Erin to the teacher in charge, Fran, who in turn introduced her to the students, a group of ten.

'This is Erin. She is going to watch for a little while. She is learning, too.'

Fran, a mature, well-groomed woman, continued with her class, the subject of which was an excursion to the shopping mall.

'What kinds of shops do we need to visit?' she prompted, and then turned to the whiteboard to document the answers. 'Yes, the supermarket, for food and groceries. Where else? The butcher, for meat ... The post office, to send a letter home ... Anything else? How about the chemist? Does anyone need to go to the chemist for medicine? How about the ATM? Do we need to get some cash to pay for our shopping?'

'We take a topic and immerse ourselves in it for the hour, talking and writing on the board and in exercise books,' Adam explained sotto voce to Erin. 'We try to group students of equal ability together, but as you can see we still get quite a wide range of abilities in the class.'

'Are the classes always this small?' Erin whispered back.

'Classes generally have fifteen to twenty students. But today is mosque day, so the attendance isn't good.'

Adam and Erin stayed until the class finished, forty

minutes later. Having observed Fran in operation, Erin was beginning to feel quite confident that she would be able to do the job.

'Let's go upstairs,' Adam said, resurrecting the sense of urgency that had abated while he'd been sitting down in the class.

Erin followed him back towards reception. Though it had been less than an hour ago, it felt as though a long time had passed since she'd sat in one of the multicoloured armchairs feeling nervous.

Adam bounced up the stairs with the energy she was beginning to get used to. 'My office is over there.' He pointed to a nondescript room. 'Accounts and payroll are in the offices on the far end, and the other rooms are mainly used for counselling.'

'Counselling?' Erin queried, slightly out of breath from the stairs.

'Some students have experienced trauma and torture in their home countries,' Adam said, 'and mental distress is an impediment to learning. For them, English classes, childcare and computer facilities are simply not enough to facilitate the transition to a new life – they need professional counselling, too. Here, let's sit in my office for a while, and you can ask me as many questions as you can think of.'

Adam's office was cramped and rather dingy, and it was clear that the recent renovations Erin had seen evidence of downstairs had not extended to the second floor of the building. In addition to the worn furniture, threadbare carpet and the odd piece of rugby paraphernalia – a framed orange and black striped jersey on the wall, and what appeared to be a full-sized rugby ball wedged under the desk! – there was mess: papers strewn across the desk, and three mugs of old coffee sitting atop what could be important documents. Drawers were ajar in the filing cabinets, and a few balls of scrunched paper, obviously intended for the bin, were scattered on the floor. Erin sat in one of the visitors' chairs, and tried to act as though she didn't notice. She had to confess to being somewhat intrigued by the man sitting across from her: his obvious dedication and commitment to the college, the energetic – almost hyperactive – manner in which he rushed about, all of which seemed slightly at odds with how relatively young he was for such a senior role, and the disorganisation evident here in his office. He wasn't wearing a wedding ring, but of course that didn't mean he wasn't married or in a relationship. In fact, Erin imagined him with a supportive partner who encouraged his career progression and facilitated the compromises that came with that. Adam's partner would be blonde, pretty, well educated, and so fastidiously tidy that he remained unaware of how much mess he left in his wake.

She was getting sidetracked. Adam's marital status had nothing to do with this job, or with her. All that mattered now was that she liked him and could see herself working for him.

They continued to talk, discussing Erin's Teaching English as a Second Language certificate, which was more than twelve years old, and confirming contact details for Erin's referees. They even went as far as agreeing on a tentative start date – two weeks from today, allowing Adam enough time to complete the reference checks and produce a written employment offer and contract.

'I've got it!' Erin squealed down the phone to Mel as soon as she got outside. 'I'm starting in two weeks.'

'Hip-hip-hooray,' Mel replied dryly. 'It's not every day you bag a low-paying job in a rundown part of the city. Let's pop open the champers when you get home.'

* * * * *

Laura opened the door at the sound of the bell and was surprised to see her mother standing in the misty rain, several shopping bags clutched in each hand.

'Hello, Mum. Been shopping, I see.'

Cathy swept inside, perfectly attired for the weather in a long trench coat, which she took off and hung on the coat rack inside the door. 'I thought you might like to see what bargains I snared – your father is usually totally uninterested.'

'Olivia, surprise for you,' Laura called up the stairs. 'Granny is here with some shopping for us to admire.'

Cathy's wince melded with Olivia's distant squeal of delight. Cathy always took some time to acclimatise to being called 'Granny'.

'Coffee, Mum?' Laura asked, leading the way to the kitchen.

'No thanks, I had one in town.'

Laura filled the kettle, deciding to have a coffee herself anyway. She'd spent the morning working on her laptop, quite a tedious beginning to the weekend, but necessary due to another looming deadline. Some caffeine might perk her up.

'Where's Esteban?' Cathy enquired.

'Gone to get his hair cut.'

'And the nanny?'

Laura put a cautionary finger to her lips. 'Kasia's in the front room watching TV.'

Olivia ran in. 'I didn't know you were coming on a visit, Granny,' she beamed, hugging Cathy's legs.

'I didn't either,' Cathy replied, stooping down to peck her granddaughter's forehead with a kiss. 'My head decided, my body just followed, and here I am!'

Olivia giggled and clambered onto one of the breakfast stools. 'Show us what you buyed.'

'It's bought, not buyed,' Laura corrected automatically.

Cathy extracted a pair of skinny jeans from one of the bags and held them up against herself. 'Aren't these fabulous? I got

78

them half price. Never pay full price for designer clothes, Olivia. You've got to be patient and keep constant watch until they go on sale.'

An interesting piece of grandmotherly advice, Laura mused whilst sipping her coffee.

'And I got this top to match the jeans. It's always best to buy a complete outfit, Olivia, so you're not looking for matching pieces later on.'

Olivia fingered the satin material of the top. 'It feels nice, Granny.'

'That's because it's good quality, Olivia. Look, I bought this necklace and bangle as accessories.'

Olivia donned the bangle and admired it on her wrist. 'What are accessories?'

'Accessories are handbags and shoes and jewellery to make your outfit look special,' Cathy explained. 'Sometimes the accessories are more important than the clothes.'

Olivia eyed the jeans and the top on the counter, and then the bangle that dangled loosely on her tiny wrist. 'What if you run out of money one day, Granny? Will you be able to sell all this back?'

Cathy smiled indulgently. 'Of course, I won't run out of money, darling. Where on earth do you get these notions from?'

'But what if you do?' Olivia's expression was perfectly earnest. 'You're always shopping.'

Laura struggled to disguise a snort of laughter. How very observant Olivia was.

'Sometimes, I think you're too grown up for your age, Olivia.' Cathy's tone was becoming less indulgent by the minute. 'At four-and-three-quarters you don't need to worry about money and adult things like that. You should play and have fun – and that's about the sum of it.'

'What age should I worry about money, Granny?'

'I don't know.' Cathy threw up her hands. 'When you're eighteen, I suppose.'

'Is there money in heaven, Granny?'

'Sorry?'

'When you go to heaven, do you need money to buy things?'

'She's been talking to Moira about heaven,' Laura explained to Cathy before replying to her daughter directly. 'No, Floss, you don't need money in heaven. God gives you everything you need.'

'Even new clothes and accessories?'

'Yes, if you need them. Now, what else has Granny got in those shopping bags?'

Thankfully, Olivia dropped the subject of heaven and was much less judgmental about her grandmother's spending habits as Cathy proceeded to reveal what was in the other bags. In fact, Olivia was so smitten with a pair of stone-coloured wedges she asked politely if she could try them on.

'She's adorable,' Cathy said in an undertone as her granddaughter tottered around in the shoes, 'but she's far too sensible for her age.'

Though Laura felt slightly defensive about this, she had to admit her mother had a point. 'She's around adults too much, I think, and playschool is only a few hours a week. Real school will be good for her – she'll make lots of new friends and she'll use them as role models rather than us.'

Every time Laura thought of Olivia starting school, she felt a swell of panic, and now was no exception. She was still no closer to finding a before and after school care solution. The only thing she'd figured out was that it seemed unlikely Kasia would be part of the plan.

As though on cue, Kasia emerged from the front room. In one sweeping glance she absorbed Olivia in the high heels, Cathy in her designer clothes, and the array of shopping bags and clothes on the kitchen counter. Just as Laura registered Kasia's obvious disapproval, she heard a key turn in the front door. Esteban was home. He strolled into the kitchen, a newspaper tucked under his arm, and was clearly surprised to find it rather crowded.

'Ah, Cathy, I didn't know you were visiting. What a nice surprise!'

He kissed his mother-in-law on each cheek.

'Nice haircut,' Cathy remarked in a flirtatious tone.

It was a nice cut, Laura conceded, though not much hair had been taken off. Laura could imagine Esteban instructing the barber, 'Un poco. Just a little.' Minimal as the trim was, it did have the effect of showing more of his face, and he looked rather drawn and tired today.

Olivia kicked off the shoes to launch herself at her father, his presence almost a novelty these days. The two of them disappeared in the direction of the TV room, Olivia hitching a ride in his arms. Kasia moved towards the fridge, jerking the door open and assessing its contents with that critical sweeping gaze of hers before extracting a bar of chocolate. Chocolate and sweets, several spoons of sugar in her tea, layers of marmalade on her toast – Laura had noticed her nanny's fixation with sugar within the first few days of her moving in. How *on earth* was she so skinny? And how did she manage to stay warm in that thin top she was wearing and those sockless feet? Laura had never seen her wear a cardigan or jumper or even a jacket. Despite the fact that she was obviously warm-blooded, she always looked cold to Laura.

Kasia departed too, pausing at the door of the front room before deciding not to join Esteban and Olivia and heading upstairs instead.

Laura and Cathy were alone.

'Your daughter is too sensible, your nanny seems to have an attitude problem, and your husband is quite obviously exhausted,' Cathy said in a monotone.

Laura nodded, feeling suddenly overwhelmed.

Sounds of a kids' TV show floated from the front room. Some floorboards creaked as Kasia walked around upstairs.

'Mum, what are you doing tonight?'

Cathy looked surprised at the question. 'Well, I'm going out to dinner with your father and some friends. You know, Carol and Tim and the usual gang.'

Laura grimaced. Of course, her mother had plans. She *always* had plans. 'How about tomorrow night? Are you free?' She didn't know why she was bothering to ask.

'We usually go to the cinema on Sunday night. Why?'

Laura shrugged, the sense of being overwhelmed morphing into an altogether darker feeling of defeat. 'I thought it would be nice to go for dinner with Esteban, that's all.'

'Have you asked Kasia to babysit?'

'No, no, I haven't. I don't want to ask anything extra of her right now. Not until we're more used to each other.'

Cathy's mouth tightened. 'I might be able to do it next weekend.'

'Thanks, Mum. What night?'

'Maybe Friday. I'll have to ask your father.' Cathy cast a sharp, questioning look at her daughter. 'Is everything all right with Esteban?'

'Of course. We're just both very busy.'

Cathy began to fold her new clothes, placing them reverently back in their bags. 'I'd better get going. Your father will be wondering where I am. I'll send you a text to confirm Friday night once I've talked to him.'

'Okay, Mum, thanks.'

A short while later, Laura kissed her mother goodbye at the door and watched her stride away, rain speckling her trench coat, bags swinging nonchalantly from each hand. Shopping sprees, coffees in town, dining out with Carol and Tim and 'the usual gang', weekly trips to the cinema. God, it was hard not to feel insanely jealous.

Laura laughed softly. Feeling jealous of her *own mother*?

Quite clearly, she was losing the plot.

Chapter 7

'Jack, it's Erin Donovan.'

'Great to hear from you, Erin. How's Sydney treating you so far?'

Erin winced at his enthusiastic tone. She hated situations like this, hated to let people down. 'Good, thank you.'

'And have you managed to negotiate your way through the bureaucratic side of things?'

'Yes, yes I have.'

'So when can you start with us?'

'I can't – I mean, I'm not –' she stuttered, keenly aware that she sounded every bit as awkward as she felt. 'Actually, I'm calling to say that I've accepted another role, Jack. I'm sorry if I gave you the impression I was definitely going to come and work for you. I like the school, I really do, but I need a change of scene. I hope you understand.'

A pause stretched down the line, and Erin felt even more excruciatingly uncomfortable.

Finally, Jack spoke. 'Well, thank you for calling to let me know.' He sounded stiff and distinctly less enthusiastic.

'I'm sorry, Jack, I really am. I hope you find someone else soon.'

Erin put down the phone with a heavy sigh. Mel, who was marking exam papers on the dining table while listening to music on her iPod, glanced up.

'How was he?' she enquired, popping out one earphone so she could hear Erin's response.

'Very obviously disappointed.'

Mel shrugged matter-of-factly. 'He'll get over it.'

'I feel really terrible.'

'You'll get over it, too.'

Reinserting the earphone, Mel slashed a series of red crosses down an exam paper that evidently wasn't up to standard. Her head bobbed in time to the music on the iPod, and her lips mouthed the words. The song was clearly a favourite.

'I wish I was better at things like this,' Erin commented, more to herself than Mel.

Her friend looked up again. 'What?'

'I wish I was better at situations like this,' Erin repeated more loudly.

Mel yanked out both earphones this time. 'What do you mean?'

'I mean I wish I was better at saying no to things, at confrontation, and that I could say my piece without agonising about what the other person thinks of me now that I've let them down. Without feeling so *guilty* all the time …'

Mel was frowning. 'You said yourself that you made no real commitment to Jack at the interview, so you have no reason to feel guilty.'

'Exactly. But I do.'

'Geez, Erin, jilt the guilt. Life's too short.'

The phone rang, jolting them both.

Erin, the closest to it, answered. 'Hello?'

'Erin?'

'Yes.'

'It's Jack again.'

'Oh hello, Jack.'

What did he want? Was he going to try to convince her to change her mind? Mel shot her a questioning glance, to which Erin shrugged her shoulders while listening as closely as she could.

'Yes, Jack … That would be nice … Yes, okay … Bye.'

'Well?' Mel enquired when Erin hung up for the second time.

'Nothing.' Erin felt colour flooding her face.

'Come on. What was it?'

'Nothing, really.' God, she was absolutely hopeless at lying. Another thing she needed to improve on.

'Erin!' Mel almost growled.

'Look, he asked me out to dinner, that's all.'

Mel looked as taken aback as Erin felt. 'To discuss the job?'

'No. He made a point of saying it wasn't about the job. I think he's asking me out on a date.'

'Awesome.' Mel's grin encompassed her whole face. 'Why didn't you say so straight away?'

'I don't know. Maybe because he's your boss and I thought it might make you feel awkward.' Now Erin was grinning, too. 'And I seem to recall that you *specifically* said I'm not allowed to fall for the first male I meet.'

'Well, if you really like Sir Jack, and he really likes you, then I'm sure we can overlook that.' Mel's expression was perfectly deadpan. 'And I suppose I should be thankful you didn't take up with the taxi driver, or one of the customs officers!'

Erin laughed. 'Why do you call him Sir Jack?'

'Because it suits him.'

'How do you mean?' Erin quizzed. 'Are you saying he looks like a teacher?'

'He *is* a teacher,' Mel pointed out. 'But yes, he does have that air of quiet authority, and the essentially clean-cut looks of a true Sir.'

Erin laughed again. 'You're an idiot, Mel.'

'I'm quite aware of that.'

'And the guilt has been officially jilted …'

'Excellent.' Mel smiled approvingly.

Shortly afterwards, Mel resumed her peculiar brand of multitasking: marking exam papers while listening to music on her beloved iPod.

Erin was free to daydream. Jack. Jack with his dark cropped hair and, to borrow Mel's words, clean-cut looks. *Sir Jack*. No, she must not call him that. It was simply Jack. Erin and Jack. Jack and Erin. She felt the urge to doodle their names together on a piece of paper. That's what came from hanging around with Mel too much. Now she was acting like a teenager, too.

Time for a nice hard Sudoku puzzle, or maybe a crossword. Some brain training was the perfect way to put an end to this juvenile behaviour.

* * * * *

Laura looked around the meeting table and smiled. It was a proud excited smile, because this was one of those moments when she unreservedly loved her job, and the wonderful team of people she worked with.

'Good afternoon, everyone. Thank you for making the effort to be on time – *for once*.' François, who had a well-known contempt for punctuality and at whom Laura's good-natured teasing was directed, snorted quite loudly. 'And welcome to the inaugural meeting for Project Chariot.'

'Project *Chariot*?' François queried in his haughtiest tone.

'Of course Chariot is a code name,' Laura continued, ignoring him. 'Our client's new model four-wheel-drive is expected to cause quite a stir in the market, and their competition would love to get their hands on the operation and maintenance manuals we're contracted to translate. So I don't want the client's name uttered at any stage, at any place, by any person sitting in this room. Understood?'

They all nodded, with the exception of François, who snorted again, an action he used to show his agreement, disagreement or any other response to the matter at hand. Despite his penchant for making noises with his nose, François was a trusted and talented member of staff who had been with Laura and Esteban from the inception of the company. Proficient in both French and Italian, he was a Trojan worker. In the early days Laura and Esteban had been quite daunted by their new employee, but once they'd figured out that his cynicism was nothing but a means of playing out his very dry sense of humour, he had become a close friend to them both.

'All in all, we are responsible for translating the manuals into twenty-eight languages, twelve of which we will translate in-house. The remainder will be sub-contracted out under Savita's management.' Laura paused to give Savita an encouraging smile. It was the Indian woman's first time managing a project of this size, and she had confessed to Laura that she was apprehensive about the scale, complexity and tight deadlines. But Laura was absolutely confident that Savita had the right skills for the job, the most important being her unfaltering calmness in times of stress.

'Any questions?' Laura enquired, looking around the table.

Johan raised his hand.

Laura hid a smile. 'Yes, Johan?'

Despite his enormous height, Johan often seemed like an earnest little boy, particularly in meetings like this, when he tended to raise his hand to seek permission to speak. François' fake cynicism was the perfect foil for Johan's little-boy intensity, and Savita's serenity and sweetness enveloped everyone. Laura felt a wave of wellbeing and happiness wash over her. She was going to enjoy this project immensely, working with her most favourite people, and having the satisfaction of being the one who had courted and eventually signed the contract with one of the fastest-growing motor companies in the world. These days it was usually Esteban who signed the deals, while she concentrated on the delivery side of the business. This deal was all *hers*, from start to finish, and she was determined to enjoy it.

The meeting disbanded and Laura was not long back in her office when her phone rang. Reading through the string of emails that had arrived while she'd been away from her desk, she picked up the handset somewhat distractedly.

'Esteban is on line three,' Polly, the receptionist, announced in her ear.

'Thanks.' Laura pressed the flashing button to pick up the call. 'Hi, love. Where are you?'

'Still at Heathrow. I do not have long to speak. My flight is boarding.'

She sighed. 'I thought you'd be almost home by now.'

'We're forty-five minutes late boarding, and apparently there is a lengthy queue waiting for take-off, so it is realistic to expect further delays . . . Last boarding call now . . . I'll text you when we touch down.'

These days Esteban sounded more like a flight announcer than a husband.

Though it was nothing new and she really had no reason to feel so annoyed, it was some time before Laura could begin reading her email messages again.

Chapter 8

'This is really lovely, Jack.' Erin looked around her once again. The restaurant's well-spaced circular tables, high-backed chairs and white table linen had an elegant, expensive feel. It was an old building, with high ceilings and large arched windows looking out onto a busy corner of Darling Street.

'I aim to please.' Jack smiled and shrugged.

So far, everything had been going amazingly well. Jack had chosen this gorgeous French restaurant, guessing, correctly, that being a French teacher she was likely to be something of a connoisseur of French food. And he was really good company. Conversation had flowed easily right from the beginning, light as he joked self-deprecatingly about his job and lack of social life, and becoming more serious when he revealed a failed marriage and two children who lived with his ex-wife in Melbourne.

'Jessica is twelve, and Talia's nine. They come and stay with me in the holidays and the odd weekend during term.' He looked very vulnerable as he spoke about his daughters, whom he clearly adored. 'My ex-wife remarried a few years ago. Her new husband owns a bistro in Brighton – the girls seem to love it there.'

Jack went on to talk at length about his daughters, revealing that some nights he couldn't sleep for worrying about them. He mainly worried about Jessica's chronic lack of confidence, and he was forever trying to think of ways to boost her self-esteem (which, on a practical level, wasn't easy given that he wasn't on hand to build her up day by day). Talia, the younger one, was outgoing, sporty and much more robust, but he worried about her, too. He suspected that his ex-wife, Andrea, was too lenient and didn't provide the discipline he felt Talia needed to keep her on the straight and narrow. Erin could tell from the set of his face and the slight cracks in his voice, that the end of his marriage and the subsequent relocation of his family to Melbourne had caused him a great deal of hurt, and ongoing anxiety.

'How about you?' he enquired, making an obvious attempt to move the conversation away from himself. 'Any significant exes I should know about?'

Erin grimaced. 'Nope.'

Of course she'd had relationships, but there was absolutely no point in mentioning Dominic, who would have been perfect if he hadn't been so obviously in love with his ex-girlfriend; or Paul, who had been a little bit too much in love with himself; or Luke, an extremely loveable, and ultimately hopeless, alcoholic-in-the-making. She'd much rather obliterate those particular relationships from her mind than dredge them up here.

He shook his head, evidently refusing to believe her. 'A beautiful girl like you? There *must* have been someone.'

Erin blushed. Of course he didn't really mean that she was beautiful, not with her hair, which despite her best styling efforts was still on the flat side tonight, and not with her nose, which had always been too big, and definitely not with her too-long arms and legs and obvious lack of gracefulness. No, Jack was just being nice, and it was this instinctive niceness that made her like him so much.

'Actually, it's been great to hook back up with Mel,' she digressed after taking a quick drink of water to cool down her face. 'To have a friend who's single, too, and to have a proper social life again.'

Jack smirked. 'We hear about Mel's escapades in the staff room every Monday morning – it's one of the highlights of the week.'

'I can imagine.' Erin smiled affectionately. 'Mel just refuses to grow up. She thinks like a teenager, talks like one. Must be because she's around them so much at school.'

Jack grimaced. 'Teenage kids seem to age me rather than make me feel younger.'

'Me too.' Erin laughed.

'Actually, Mel's one of the few teachers the students truly respect,' Jack revealed, becoming temporarily serious. 'She talks their language, likes the same things as them – Facebook, Twitter, iTunes. She's our authority on Gen Z.'

'It's not just social networking that she embraces,' Erin added dryly. 'Last week she asked me if I wanted to go *skateboarding*.'

Jack raised his eyebrows. 'And you turned her down?'

Erin laughed a little bit too loudly, attracting some curious glances from nearby patrons. 'I can hardly keep my balance on my own two feet!'

'Are you and Mel going to continue as flatmates?'

'Unfortunately, there isn't enough room in her apartment for two people.' Erin shrugged ruefully. She was not looking forward to moving out, but no matter how neatly she folded up the sofa bed each morning, Mel's living area had been taken over by her suitcase and other possessions and now looked very bedroom-like, not to mention awfully cramped. 'I'm officially flat hunting, so if you come across anywhere suitable ...'

'I'll keep a watch out,' Jack promised.

Their main course arrived, the food rich and extremely filling.

'Dessert?' Jack asked as the waiter hovered with menus in hand.

Erin groaned. 'I don't think I can fit in another morsel.'

Jack asked for the bill, and shortly afterwards they left. Outside the restaurant, on the bustling street corner heavy with pedestrians and passing traffic, he kissed her. Actually, it barely qualified as a kiss. His lips did nothing more than brush against hers, but the sensation lingered long after it was over, and the impulsiveness seemed to have surprised him as much as her.

'Do you want to go on somewhere for a drink?' he asked, looking slightly abashed.

'Yes.'

Holding her hand firmly in his, he led her across the road to one of Balmain's most popular pubs, music and voices wrapping around them as soon as they set foot inside.

Jack ordered two beers and they stood in the noisy, pulsating crowd, smiling a little inanely at each other.

'I'm really enjoying tonight. We must do this again. Soon.'

Jack was a good conversationalist, clearly intelligent, evidently a good father to his girls, and so good-looking it was hard to believe that he really was single. Now he was talking as though it was obvious they would see each other again. To all intents and purposes, this night seemed to be the start of a relationship.

Had it really been that easy?

Jack bent his head and kissed her again, a deeper, more daring kiss that sparked an immediate tingle of response within her. Erin moved closer, hooking her arms around his neck, kissing him back.

Whatever this turned out to be – a short-lived fling or lasting relationship – she was determined to enjoy every moment of it.

* * * * *

'Well, this is nice, isn't it?' Laura smiled brightly across the candle-lit table.

'Yes.' Esteban returned her smile with a soft one of his own.

'I was lucky to get a table. This place books out weeks in advance, but they had a cancellation.'

'Yes.' He smiled again. 'You were lucky.'

Laura bit her lip. 'I hope Olivia will be good for Mum.'

'Of course she will.'

'I mean, I *know* she'll be good, but you know how Mum isn't that keen on babysitting, so I hope it goes extra smoothly …' Laura's voice trailed away. She was prattling, talking rubbish. Here she was – on a rare date with her husband – and she couldn't think of anything interesting, or even slightly meaningful, to say to him.

She picked up her wine glass and took a long, fortifying drink from it. The wine was too heavy and sweet for her taste, but she decided it wasn't worth the time or effort to order something else. The leather-bound menu lay open on the table in front of her. She'd already glanced through it without making a decision on what to order. It might be easier to ask the waiter and simply order whatever he recommended. They shouldn't waste time – Cathy had specifically asked them to be home before eleven. God, what was wrong with her? Why couldn't she relax?

'Are you happy, Esteban?' she heard herself asking.

'What do you mean?'

'I want to know if you're happy.' Her voice sounded squeaky, a few octaves above its usual pitch. 'With your life here. With me.'

He didn't answer straight away. Laura became aware of an ache deep inside her that seemed to get stronger with each moment of silence.

'I am happy with some things,' he said eventually. 'With our home and our beautiful daughter. With how successful our business is.'

'What about everything else?' she asked, wanting to say

'What about me?', but not daring because she was too scared of what the answer might be.

'Everything else seems to be a little hard right now.' He sighed, looking weary and very ill at ease.

Silence descended again. Laura drank more wine, her mouth dry and slightly numb. Esteban refilled her glass. Where was the waiter? They really needed to order their food.

'Are *you* happy, cariño?'

His question penetrated like a dart. She flinched. Then admitted, 'No.'

God, her answer was even more bleak than his had been. This was turning out to be the dinner date from hell. They would have been better off staying at home, working independently on their respective laptops, distant but at least not analysing how unhappy they both were.

'Do you know *why* you're unhappy?' he asked softly.

'No ... Yes ... I have too much to do ... I feel constantly overwhelmed and I don't seem to know how to relax any more. I don't like Kasia living in our house, but at the same time I realise I need her there in order to make things work. I'm proud of our business too, and some days I can't wait to go into the office. But I hate it almost as much as I love it, especially the demands it makes on *you*. I wish you didn't travel so much. I wish Mum would help more. I think I'm jealous of Mum's lifestyle, which is totally pathetic ...' Laura ran out of breath. Tears burned behind her eyes. She mustn't cry. There would be no salvaging this 'date' if she did.

Esteban's fingers interlaced with hers. 'This is just a stage. What do you call it? A rough patch.'

'Is it?' she asked, swallowing a sob.

'Yes. It will pass.'

Laura tightened her fingers around his. She really wanted to believe him.

Finally, the waiter came. They ordered their meals and another bottle of wine, a lighter variety of red at Laura's request. She didn't know if it was the effect of the alcohol or of Esteban's hand holding hers, but her tension eventually eased away. They started to talk. About Esteban's family and the possibility of his mother coming to visit later in the year. Laughing over Olivia's recent fascination with heaven and all things ethereal. Reminiscing about a carefree holiday they'd had in Tenerife before she was born.

It was eleven-thirty before they got home, giggling guiltily as they struggled with the key in the lock.

The door whipped open and Cathy regarded them with an unimpressed expression. 'You're late!'

'Sorry, Mum. The restaurant was really slow.' Laura tried, unsuccessfully, to contain a hiccup.

'Well, at least you look like you've enjoyed yourselves,' Cathy commented tartly before going to wake Ian, who was asleep on one of the armchairs.

'Bye, Mum. Bye, Dad.' Laura hugged her parents in turn. She really was very grateful to them. 'Thanks again. Sorry we were late ...'

Laura closed the door softly. Her eyes met Esteban's and suddenly she was in his arms, kissing him as frantically as he was kissing her, the way they used to kiss when they first met. His hands slid under her top, unhooking her bra in a smooth, practised movement, cupping her breasts. She heard herself moan, and the sound seemed amplified in the silent, sleeping house.

'We can't ...' she mumbled against his lips. 'Not here ... Olivia ... Kasia ...'

Taking her hand, he led her upstairs. The bedroom door firmly shut behind them, he peeled her clothes from her body, sweeping her bare, tingling skin with his coolish hands. She met his urgency with her own, roughly removing his clothes, pulling him backwards onto the bed, wrapping her legs around him. His weight pressed down on her, and every muscle in her body contracted with anticipation and desire.

God, this was good, so good. Nothing mattered right now, nothing other than his body and hers. She let go of all her conscious thoughts, fully surrendering to the moment, and cried out as she climaxed around him.

Afterwards, cocooned in his arms, she came back to reality. God, she hoped Kasia hadn't heard them. That would be so embarrassing. And she hoped Cathy wouldn't decline future babysitting requests because they'd come home late. She shouldn't have drunk so much wine; she would have a terrible hangover in the morning.

Esteban stirred against her. Tonight he had more or less admitted that he wasn't happy. She had said the same, but if she had her time over again she'd have chosen her words more carefully, and said that she was stressed and over-tired rather than unhappy. Right now, she really didn't care about herself and how she felt, all she cared about was him. Her husband was finding their life together 'hard'. *He wasn't happy.* How could she ever fall asleep knowing this?

Chapter 9

To: Lisha.Mbah@stpatricks.ie

From: Erin <Erin.Donovan@yahoo.com>

Dear Lisha,

Hello all the way from Australia! Sydney's a beautiful, vibrant city, and I'm very much enjoying exploring it and getting used to the way of life. I've also found a job which I'm very excited about. I'll be working in an English and Settlement Services College, teaching immigrants and refugees from places like Syria, Afghanistan and Algeria. Maybe some of my new students will be from Nigeria, too.

I hope that school is going well for you. Please don't feel you have to respond to this message – I've been thinking about you over the past few weeks and just wanted to say hello.

Warmest wishes,

Erin (aka Mademoiselle Donovan)

PS: Thank you again for the beautiful necklace. People comment every time I wear it.

To: *Erin* <Erin.Donovan@yahoo.com>
From: *Laura* <Laura.Torres@globaltranslation.com>
Hi Erin,

I had no idea that you were planning a career change on top of everything else. It sounds like a brilliant job, perfect for you. Nothing half as exciting happening here. Your mother is well enough. I never really know what to expect from her on any given day, and in a strange way it's a nice break from the rest of my life where I know only too well what to expect and end up feeling depressed ☹. A rather lovely development is that Olivia and your mother seem to be fascinated with each other. Olivia doesn't mind at all when Moira repeats herself, and Moira seems unfazed by Olivia's relentless questions. It's really sweet.

Everyone else has been great, too. Gerry fixed the bathroom tap, which had been annoying Moira for years (or so she claims!). Mum changed the curtains and bought some new cushions for the living room, and the transformation is quite remarkable.

Congratulations on the job again and talk soon,

XX Laura

Dear Mum,

I've found my own apartment, and knew you would want to see it so I've enclosed some photos. Obviously, I have a lot of furnishing to do, but hopefully you can see the same potential as I do. The outlook sold me – I can see myself gazing at the city skyline for hours on end – as well as the location, just a few streets away from Mel.

I've popped in some other photos, too. There's Mel and me in a pub in Balmain, and Sydney Harbour on a sunny afternoon (I took that one from the Manly ferry. Isn't it stunning?)

Hope the photos help you visualise what it's like here, Mum. I'll send on some more in a few weeks.

Miss you,

Xx Erin

To: *Erin* <Erin.Donovan@yahoo.com>

From: *Lisha.Mbah@stpatricks.ie*

Dear Mademoiselle Donovan,

Thank you for writing to me. I am glad that you are settling in well to your new life. I don't think you will come across Nigerian students in your college. According to the newspapers, many countries are looking at deporting us, as they believe there is no longer political oppression in Nigeria. But mother and father have heard that the Islamic Laws are becoming more strict, and Christians like us risk punishment (the military are very violent). Even though our family does not enjoy living in Dublin, at least we are safe here. We pray every night that we won't be sent back.

School is the same as ever, I still have nothing in common with the other girls and I miss your friendly smile. I was surprised but very happy to get your email. Reading the words made me feel like you were here. I am also happy that you like the necklace. Maybe I will make more jewellery in my spare time.

Please write again. I check my messages twice a week at computer class.

Kindest regards,

Lisha

To: *Laura* <Laura.Torres@globaltranslation.com>

From: *Erin* <Erin.Donovan@yahoo.com>

A small piece of news I forgot to mention when I last emailed. Okay, I didn't exactly forget to mention it, more that I didn't want to make it into a big deal. I'm seeing someone. His name is Jack, and he's really lovely. He works at Mel's school. Actually, he was almost my boss, but luckily for me I turned down the job — otherwise he says he would not have asked me out to dinner.

This is classified information for now. Please do not tell anyone, ESPECIALLY NOT PADDY. We've been on three dates — dinner and movies, standard stuff – so it's early days yet and I don't want the family to get overexcited and jinx me.

Gotta go. It's my first day at work tomorrow. Feel quite sick at the thought, excitement and the usual nerves. Hope I can sleep.

XX Erin

Chapter 10

Erin surveyed her new students, and fifteen pairs of dark, curious eyes returned her gaze. The class was made up entirely of women, most of them young, and about half wearing veils of some kind. According to Adam, this female-only class had been formed because many of the students had either a husband or father at home who did not wish for them to learn in the presence of other males.

'Good morning. I'm Miss Erin, and I'm a newcomer to this country, too.'

Her brief introduction was met with silence. Not even a smile was proffered in return.

'I'll be your teacher for the next six months. You probably don't understand a lot of what I'm saying now, but in six months' time you will be able to speak to me in English. You will be able to ask me questions, you will offer information about your family and your weekend, and you will be able to converse with shopkeepers, your children's teachers at school and whoever else you need to communicate with …'

Erin paused, searching once again for a response of some sort. Her students remained mute, their faces uniformly blank. They clearly didn't understand *a word* of what she had just said to them. Oh God, this was going to be hard.

'Let's start with our names.' She pointed to herself. 'Erin.' Then, picking up a blue marker, she wrote on the whiteboard.

My name is Erin.

One by one, she asked each woman to stand and say her name. They did as she asked, their heads bowed with what seemed to be a combination of humility and slight embarrassment. Their accents were difficult to decipher, and Erin had to discreetly consult the class list to establish how each name was spelt and pronounced. Adam had given her the list this morning (along with the syllabus and teaching notes), informing her at the same time that many of the students had a low level of literacy in their native language, let alone English.

'Thank you,' Erin smiled when all the names had been supplied and correctly transcribed onto the board. 'It is nice to meet you all. Now, please turn to the person on either side of you and tell them that it is nice to meet them.'

Fifteen uncomprehending faces looked back at her.

Erin demonstrated by walking over to the closest student and holding out her hand. 'Fila.' Erin remembered the name mainly because it had been one of the simpler ones she had written on the board. 'Fila, it is very nice to meet you.'

Soft brown eyes blinked amid a plump, caramel face.

'Fila, it is nice to meet you,' Erin repeated patiently.

Fila's hair, ears and neck were concealed by her veil, but a smile played on her lips, as though she found this class, and what was presently being requested of her, mildly amusing. Finally, she spoke, her voice timid and girlish. 'Fila, it is nice to meet you.'

'No. You say, "Erin, it is nice to meet you." And you shake my hand like this.'

'Erin, it is nice to meet you.'

It had taken twenty minutes to get a student to smile and say a short sentence in English.

Erin forged on with her first class, pretending that she

knew exactly what she was doing and that she fully believed these students would have functional English in six months' time. She even managed to coax a few more halting sentences from them before the bell went for recess.

As they filed past her desk, she smiled determinedly and kept up a chirpy monologue.

'See you after the break.'

'Goodbye for now.'

'Enjoy your coffee.'

But as soon as she was on her own, no amount of determination could hold her smile in place. Quite clearly, she was way out of her depth with this job. Maybe she would cope better as time went on – this was only her first day, after all. Then again, maybe today was indicative of the future, and this impulsive career change been nothing but a huge, excruciating mistake.

* * * * *

'Hello?' Laura called. 'Hello? Moira? Are you there?'

Olivia looped through the front room to the kitchen, and back out to the hallway. 'Where is she, Mum?'

'Maybe she's upstairs.' Laura ascended the first few steps, calling out as she went. 'Moira? Moira?'

Floorboards creaked overhead. Moira appeared, looming over the banister. She was holding something in her hand. A book? 'I'll be down in a minute.'

'What are you doing?' Laura asked suspiciously.

'I'm having a bit of a clean out.'

'But you have a cleaner,' Laura pointed out. 'She comes in on Fridays, remember?'

Moira arched her brows. 'That one? She's completely useless!'

Laura smothered a laugh. 'Let us help you, then. We like to clean, don't we, Olivia?'

'*You* like to clean, Mum. Dad says you're a clean freak.'

'Does he now?' Now Laura was the one arching her brows. 'Come on, Floss, let's go and help Moira.'

The upstairs of Moira's house was more compact than Laura remembered: three bedrooms, the smallest of which used to be Erin's, one bathroom, and a landing so narrow it gave Laura a sense of vertigo as she walked along it. The air up here smelt dusty: maybe Moira was right about the cleaner.

'You've been going through your wardrobe?' Laura surveyed the clothes and shoeboxes strewn across her aunt's bed. Moira put down the book she was holding. It was a photo album, its cover made of shiny dark-blue plastic.

Moira bit her lip as she looked at the mess. 'I couldn't find the dress I was looking for, and before I knew it I had taken the lot out.'

Olivia gravitated to the photo album and opened the cover. 'Are these photos of you when you were young?'

Moira nodded. 'Yes. When I was in Paris. With Joe and Cathy.'

Olivia turned a page, studying the smiling faces and yellow-tinged colours.

'Which one is you, and which one is Granny Cathy?'

Laura answered. 'Moira, why don't you sit down next to Olivia while I sort out these clothes?'

Moira looked relieved to sit. The energy that had caused her to purge the contents of her wardrobe seemed to have dissipated as suddenly as it had come upon her.

'Cathy is the prettier one of us,' she answered Olivia matter-of-factly. 'Moira, Gerard, Patrick and pretty baby Cathy.'

'And where's Joe?'

Moira turned a few pages. 'Here's Joe.' Her voice had a catch.

'He looks nice,' Olivia commented in a very grown-up tone. 'Very friendly, you know.'

Laura mentally shook her head. How did Olivia come up with these things? It was as though she'd been around a lot longer than her not-quite five years. Still listening in on their conversation, Laura began to sift through the clothes. She was surprised by how many outfits she remembered, clothes she hadn't seen Moira wear for years and years. They triggered disjointed memories. Eating cake in Moira's kitchen, her aunt wearing beige slacks and this matching cashmere polo-neck. Her aunt pressing a ten-pound note into the palm of her hand for her birthday, her royal-blue blouse at Laura's eye level. Sipping a fizzy drink in the local pub, Moira in that black and red patterned dress. Moira, like Cathy, used to have a lovely figure, trim, but not too skinny. Sadly, none of these clothes fitted her now. Though Moira might sometimes have more than one breakfast, she was far more likely to forget meals than repeat them. Her arms and legs were stick thin, and as she turned the pages of the album with Olivia, she looked frail and insubstantial, a shadow of the woman in the photographs.

'And who's that woman there?' Olivia enquired inquisitively.

'Oh, that's the maid.'

'You mean Anna,' Olivia clarified. Then, on seeing Moira's confusion and her mother's surprise, explained, 'You couldn't remember her name the last time, Auntie Moira, so I asked Granny Cathy.'

Moira nodded, distracted. 'Anna. Yes, of course.'

'And here's Joe again.' Olivia had turned the page. 'He looks like my daddy when he's going to work.'

Moira glanced down. 'He had to be smart for his job at the embassy,' she said in a wistful tone.

'I wonder if Joe can get his cancer medicine in heaven,' Olivia mused.

'I don't think he's sick any more,' Moira replied, a smile plumping her face, giving it an injection of youth.

'How did he get better?'

'God makes sure that everyone in heaven is healthy and happy.'

'That's good.' Olivia nodded in approval. 'It would be horrible if poor Joe had to die all over again.'

Laura eavesdropped, caught between horror and amusement. Were other little girls of Olivia's age like this? Obsessed with mortality and the afterlife? Thank God Moira didn't find it upsetting to have Joe's passing dissected in such detail! It was funny how Olivia seemed to provide instant clarification for the older woman. Maybe the rules were simpler: Moira was clearly the adult, Olivia the child, and it was Moira's job to answer Olivia's questions as accurately and correctly as possible. Whatever it was, Moira was noticeably less confused when she was around Olivia.

Laura stowed Moira's old clothes in the far corners of the wardrobe: glamorous frocks that had been worn to embassy cocktail parties, woollen coats with brooches on their lapels, chic skirts and blouses purchased for other special occasions. Clothes of a different era, a different woman, really. Laura then arranged Moira's current clothes, plain, colourless, a lot of them shapeless, directly inside the door where her aunt could easily find them. A few items, cardigans and sweaters with holes, a blouse with a large stain down the front, she rolled into a ball and tucked under her arm. She'd put them into her own rubbish bin at home: Moira was likely to fish them out if she put them in the bin downstairs. On the weekend, she would pick up a few new things for her aunt to wear. Practical things, but at least a little more stylish and colourful, and more reminiscent of the woman she used to be.

On her way across the landing, totally on impulse, Laura opened the door to Erin's bedroom. Pillows and cushions in varying shades of pink were tumbled at the head of the bed. On the dressing table, a hairbrush and some cosmetics lay in wait. One of the doors of the built-in robe stood ever so slightly ajar, as though asking for someone to press it shut.

'It looks like Auntie Erin still lives here,' Olivia commented by her side.

'Yes, it does,' Laura replied, missing Erin in that instant more than she had at any point since her cousin – her best friend – had left.

Moira came up behind them as Laura closed the door. She reached out and pulled Olivia close, kissing the wispy hair on the top of her head. 'Children are precious. So very precious. We should never forget that.'

Laura felt her eyes well up. She didn't know if it was all the memories she'd stumbled across while sorting through her aunt's clothes, or seeing Erin's bedroom so empty and aching for her return, or witnessing Moira's surprisingly deep affection for Olivia, but suddenly it was all she could do not to cry.

Chapter 11

Erin's new apartment had one very modest bedroom, an open-plan kitchen and living room, a bathroom so minuscule it could be mistaken for a closet, and a balcony that barely fitted a small table and two matching chairs. But had the apartment been any bigger it wouldn't have felt so cosy and intimate, and Erin wouldn't have loved it as much as she did. Jack had found it for her. It belonged to the friend of a student's aunt, who wanted to rent it out while she went gallivanting across Europe – or something like that. It had the same period features as Mel's place, dark wooden floors, corniced ceilings, gorgeous wrought-iron on the balcony, and was only a short walk away. It was so perfect that Erin could have kissed Jack. Well, actually, kissing Jack was something that was occurring with more and more frequency. It was what came after kissing that had become more relevant, and if she was ready for that step.

A firm, commanding knock reverberated from the front door through the apartment. Mascara brush in hand, Erin paused. The bathroom mirror reflected her slight frown of confusion. Her watch confirmed that it was only six-thirty. She'd said seven to Jack, hadn't she? Oh God, she hadn't even begun to prepare the home-made pizzas she'd invited him around for. Well, at least she was dressed – five minutes ago that hadn't been the case – and given how fast things were progressing with him, opening the door in a state of semi-dress would have been asking for trouble.

She quickly finished applying the mascara, then ran her fingers through her hair one more time. The last thing she saw before turning away from the mirror was the question in her eyes. *Are you going to sleep with him tonight?* She didn't know the answer, and suspected she wouldn't until the very last moment.

'Oh, Fizz. It's you.'

Erin was rather relieved to find that it was her elderly neighbour who had knocked so resolutely on the door. Not that she wouldn't have been happy to see Jack, she just wasn't ready for him yet. Fizz lived in the lower half of the house, and had introduced herself with a freshly baked apple tart and a bottle of champagne the day after Erin moved in. Once invited inside, Fizz had proceeded to consume two large glasses of the champagne while making Erin's acquaintance. Her real name, she had revealed, was Phyllis. Her lifelong appreciation of French champagne – the real stuff, not those 'sparkling wines' which were apparently substandard – had brought about the nickname Fizz, which was so much more fun and interesting than Phyllis, wasn't it? Since that first visit, she'd dropped in several times, and Erin enjoyed her company, the impromptu glasses of champagne (or cups of tea, depending on the time of day), and the bubbly conversation that always ensued.

'Hello Erin, dear. I wasn't sure if you'd be home. A young girl like you would be out on a Saturday night, I told myself. I got a notion to go baking again this afternoon, and I'm trying to find a home for these chocolate brownies.'

Fizz held out a plastic container, which Erin accepted gratefully. She'd tasted Fizz's baking a few times now, and her stomach rumbled in anticipation. 'That's really kind of you, Fizz. Thank you.'

Fizz smiled, then looked at Erin more closely. 'You do look all dressed up, my dear. Are you on your way out somewhere?'

'No,' Erin replied, shrugging a little self-consciously. 'But I am expecting someone over for dinner.'

'A man, is it?' The older woman enquired.

'Well, yes.'

'Oh, isn't that nice for you! Well, I'd better leave you to it.' At the top of the stairs, she paused with some last words of advice. 'Don't do anything I wouldn't do.' Her titter echoed down the stairwell.

Erin laughed as she closed the door, suspecting that Fizz had been far from a saint in her day. Fizz claimed that she was seventy-four, but Erin found this hard to believe. For a start, she was remarkably sprightly, and Erin had seen her climb the stairs with the nimbleness of a much younger woman. Her hair was dyed pale blonde, she wore comfortable yet stylish clothes, and her face was always made up, even when Erin had met her taking out the rubbish in the early hours of the morning. Fizz was a funny mix of quaint and modern, demure and naughty. And she clearly didn't believe in the concept of neighbours keeping to themselves.

Erin set the brownies down on the counter, and resisted the temptation to sample one. She had twenty minutes before Jack was due, barely enough time to roll out the dough she'd made earlier and slice some capsicum, olives and pepperoni. She worked deftly, enjoying the experience of cooking in her own kitchen, not Mel's, or her mother's. In fact, she would like to do some cooking classes one day to improve her skills and culinary repertoire. Maybe when she was more settled at work. Rather ironically, of all the changes in her life, it was her new job – which she had wanted so vehemently – that was proving the hardest one to get used to. Though the staff at the college were friendly and Adam extremely supportive, ultimately Erin was on her own for long stretches of time with groups of students who had little idea of what she was saying, and whose hopes and dreams of a new life in a new country started and potentially ended right there in her classroom. Her students didn't speak unless spoken to directly, they were as cocooned from each other as they were from her, and she felt their isolation as though it were her own. Erin had always viewed language as an enabler, a positive, but in her classroom she saw how it could be a barrier, an all-powerful and sometimes excruciating impediment in every aspect of daily life. And so, despite how much she would love to do a course in Italian or Asian cooking, she felt unable to take on any more challenges until she had her job under control and felt more certain that in six months' time her students would be at least be semi-functional in English.

At precisely 7:01, another knock sounded on the door. Jack. Exactly on time, or as close to it as humanly possible. She should have known it wasn't him earlier. Smiling to herself, Erin rinsed her hands under the kitchen tap and went to answer the door.

'Oh, are those for me?'

Jack, holding a large bunch of lilies in his hand, grinned. 'I thought I'd give them to the old lady downstairs.'

'Ssh ... Don't let Fizz overhear you calling her old.'

'Of course they're for you!'

'Thank you, Jack, they're lovely.'

She took the lilies from his outstretched hand, and raised her face to meet his kiss, which was slow and comprehensive and evoked a response in her that was quite inappropriate for the communal landing.

'You'd better come inside,' she croaked.

Closing the door behind him, she put the lilies on the hall table and turned back into his arms. His hands buried in her hair, pulling her mouth closer, and his kiss resumed with a heightened level of urgency, as though he sensed, somehow, the decision she'd come to mere moments ago.

Slipping her hands across his shoulders, she eased off his

jacket. It tumbled, unheeded, onto the mat inside the door. Walking backwards, still kissing, she managed to unbutton and discard his shirt, somewhere near her new sofa. His jeans, the last to go, spooled on her bedroom floor.

By the time Erin made it to bed with Jack Thornton, by the time he undressed her and made love to her in that thorough manner of his, there were parts of him scattered all over her apartment, and, indeed, all over her brand-new life.

* * * * *

Laura's eyes felt heavy. It was getting harder and harder to concentrate on the report she was reading, and it was probably not a good idea to be engaging in something so mentally demanding at bedtime anyway. The phone rang, and she answered it with an involuntary yawn.

'Hola, cariño. You sound tired.'

'I am.' She stretched, put the report aside until the morning, and sank further under the covers. 'It's been a long, long day.'

'A good one, though?'

'Yes … *no* …' As busy days went, today had ranked as fairly normal – until she'd got home from work. Confronted with an untidy kitchen, a cold house, an inadequately clothed child and a surly uncommunicative nanny, her day had taken a distinct turn for the worse. Now, something snapped in her, unleashing a negativity that had been building steadily despite her efforts to rein it in. 'It's Kasia, Esteban … she … she …'

'She what?' Esteban enquired warily.

Laura picked just one of the many things that were wrong. 'I've told her *three* times where the park is, but it seems that she would much rather march Olivia around busy, fume-clogged streets than take her to the bloody playground.'

'Sssh, cariño. She might hear.'

'As a matter of fact, she's out tonight. A free house. Hip-hip-hooray.'

Esteban released an audible, disenchanted sigh. He did not like sarcasm. A few moments later, enough time for him to summon a conciliatory tone in reply, he said, 'I am sure Kasia is just trying to find her bearings. There will be plenty of opportunity to go to the park later on, when she is more settled in.'

'She's had over a month to settle in, Esteban, and no amount of time will change the fact that she's a cold fish. As soon as I walk in the door, she disappears to her room. She doesn't like to talk about the day and what they've done together – it's as if she can't wait to be away from Olivia and me.'

'I'm sure it's not like that at all, cariño. She spends all day long with Olivia. You know how demanding that can be. Of course she must want some space and time to herself at the end of the day.'

'Esteban, you're not listening to me. We've made a mistake. Kasia is not right for Olivia, or for *us*. We should let her go now, before Olivia forms a bond ...'

'Laura, you are not listening to *me*. You are making judgments too quickly. You are not giving her a chance.'

'How would you know?' Laura heard herself shout – *really* shout – and felt an immediate sense of relief. Too often in the last few weeks she'd had to moderate herself, for fear Kasia would overhear. 'You've hardly been home. How would you *bloody well* know anything about it?'

As always, the louder and angrier she got, the quieter Esteban's voice became in response. 'I don't need to be there to understand what is happening. No one is good enough for our darling Olivia, and in some ways I agree with you on this. But we must not let our guilt taint how we view this situation. Kasia is doing fine. Olivia seems to like her. These things, these problems you have with her, they are small, insignificant –'

It was lucky for him that he was at the end of the phone, lucky that he was staying in some nondescript hotel in Belgium, because if he'd been standing here she could have slapped him. 'These problems are not small and insignificant, and I resent you trivialising them like this, not to even mention the fact that you clearly don't respect my judgment ...'

She had more to say, much more, but she suddenly couldn't utter another word. She was too angry, too upset and simply too disappointed – in Kasia and in him.

Tears that felt weary and defeated trickled down her face. She shouldn't have yelled – Esteban hated it when she shouted.

'Laura? Are you still there?' she heard him ask cautiously. 'Laura? Talk to me.'

It was a few moments before she could gather herself to respond.

'Esteban, she gives Olivia bread and jam for breakfast, lunch and tea.'

In Laura's opinion, Kasia's approach to meals and nutrition seemed to sum up this untenable situation in its entirety.

'We will talk properly when I get home,' he promised.

'Okay,' she replied, even though it wasn't okay at all.

Kasia was not okay. Laura would never warm to her.

Olivia was not okay. She was destined to come second to the all-consuming demands of the family business.

Laura and Esteban were not okay. Laura had never felt so distant from her husband, or so misunderstood.

And this would be another night when she couldn't sleep, even though she was so tired she could hardly summon enough energy to turn out the light.

Chapter 12

Quite suddenly, Jack had become part of every aspect of Erin's existence. Sprawled on the lounge in her apartment, lying naked under the sheets in her bed, shaving in her bathroom as though it were his own, and constantly in her head when she wasn't with him. Every morning, she dressed with him in mind, choosing clothes that were smarter, more fashionable, and accessorising with belts, bangles and bags. Even when she didn't have plans to meet him, she imagined him waiting for her outside work. 'Surprise,' he'd say, and lead her in her nice clothes to a nearby bar for an impromptu drink. While teaching, she laughed and smiled and spoke with an extra sparkle, as though he were in the room amongst the students, listening to every word, appraising every gesture she made.

'Well, is this love?' Mel enquired, keeping a tight hold of her glass of wine as the crowd around her swayed.

Erin grinned sheepishly. 'More like obsession. I can't stop thinking about him.'

The pub was Saturday-night full, bodies jammed together, music drowning out their voices. It was Mel's choice of venue, and Erin felt quite old in the mostly twenty-something crowd.

'It's been so long since I've had a boyfriend, I'd forgotten how intense it is at the start,' Erin explained further, her voice hoarse from trying to talk over the music.

'Well, here's to you and Jack.' Mel raised her glass theatrically. 'Intense, obsessed, in love, or whatever you happen to be!'

Giggling, Erin clinked her glass with Mel's. 'Now all we have to do is to find you a man.'

'Stop right there.' Mel gulped some of her drink. 'Despite the obvious lack of success, I prefer to rely on my own resources when it comes to men ...'

Over the past few weeks Mel had been on a number of dates, men she'd hooked up with in dark hazy bars and clubs but who consistently failed to impress when she met them again in the cold light of day.

She sighed. 'They're all too boring and set in their ways, or the other extreme – immature and self-obsessed. Why can't I find someone who's grown-up and responsible, but fun and young-at-heart as well? Is that asking too much?'

'Maybe we should go somewhere with a slightly older crowd?' Erin suggested.

'But I like it here,' Mel replied stubbornly. 'I like the music, the vibe ...'

'The men are virtually babies,' Erin pointed out.

'So?'

'Come on,' Erin coaxed. 'Let's try somewhere else.'

Mel shrugged and threw back the rest of her drink, which Erin took as her acquiescence.

They left the bar, arms hooked, Mel slightly unsteady on her feet.

'Thanks for coming out with me tonight,' she said suddenly.

'What? Why are you thanking me, you twit?'

'Because I know Jack would have asked you to do something with him.'

Mel was right. Jack had asked Erin to go out tonight, but despite the fact that she was somewhat obsessed with him and wanted to be with him as much as possible, she had no intention of doing so at Mel's expense. Memories of depressing, achingly lonely weekends – pre Australia – hovered in Erin's consciousness. Her parents' illnesses had stunted not only her career, but also her social life. She had hardly noticed it happening, the years slipping away, her friends becoming more and more domestically tied down, until on the few occasions when Erin *could* go out, she had nobody to go out *with*. No one was free on Saturday night, or any part of the weekend: it was family time, for husbands and children – not for friends. And everyone had mortgages and bills to pay, and no money for even a midweek girls' night out. And so, regardless of what happened with Jack, regardless of how serious or even domesticated they might get down the line, some of Erin's weekend time would always stay firmly on reserve for her closest friend.

'Let's try here.' Erin pulled Mel into a sophisticated-looking wine bar. 'This looks like the sort of place that would attract a more mature and responsible clientele.'

'Don't forget fun and young-at-heart,' Mel added.

'Got it. Mature, responsible, fun, young-at-heart ...'

Just like Adam, Erin thought, suddenly struck by the obvious compatibility of her boss and her best friend. Fun, energetic, passionate, they were *perfect* for each other. The only problem was that Adam had a girlfriend (Lydia had mentioned something about her at lunch one day.) Oh, well, so much for that. Back to the drawing board – or rather establishments like this – to find Mel's perfect man.

'What are you looking so thoughtful about?' Mel asked suspiciously.

'Nothing.' After a quick scout of the crowd, Erin caught the barman's eye. 'Two glasses of Sauvignon Blanc, please.'

* * * * *

Kasia was out again, Olivia was sound asleep in bed, and Esteban was not due home for another couple of hours. Laura worked swiftly and methodically in the silence, pressing shirts, tops and sheets with the hissing iron, and then folding them into neat, satisfying piles. She actually liked ironing. She found it peaceful, therapeutic. Sometimes she'd hold a warm, freshly ironed garment to her face, and it would comfort her more effectively than a hug from Olivia or Esteban. The laundry room was small and square and like a sanctuary from the rest of the house. It was mainly Laura's domain, and she liked this too, the seclusion and privacy it offered.

Switching off the iron, she gathered piles of clean laundry to her chest for distribution around the house. She put away Esteban's and her clothes in their respective closets, and left Olivia's outside her door – she didn't want to risk waking her daughter by opening and shutting drawers. In the guest bathroom, she put warm, clean towels on the rack, and caught her reflection in the mirrored doors of the cabinet. God, she looked tired, her eyes and skin so dull. When had she started looking so worn out? Her skin used to glow, her hair used to shine. She had photographs, somewhere in the house, to prove it. And Esteban used to tell her how beautiful she was, his hands buried in her hair, his mouth dropping little kisses along the curve of her neck. Laura closed her eyes and tried to conjure up an image of her younger self, hoping that by doing so she could tap into that girl, take some of her radiance and zest and optimism and use it to get through her life today. It was useless. The girl was too elusive, and when Laura finally opened her eyes she felt even older, and more weary and weighed down than ever.

Feeling suddenly and quite irrationally piqued, she slid back the doors of the bathroom cabinet. There was the perfume, the lid still slightly askew. She assessed it with narrowed eyes. Had the level gone down? She thought so, but couldn't be sure. Taking the bottle in her hand, she opened the drawers of the vanity, rifling through the contents. She found an old eyeliner, and put a small, inconspicuous line at the level where the liquid stopped before returning the bottle to its place on the shelf and shutting the doors.

Before leaving the bathroom, she gave the tired, cynical woman in the mirror a hard, contemptuous stare.

Chapter 13

'Hey, Erin.' Adam popped his head inside the door of the classroom. 'Fancy a midmorning coffee? I'm making.'

Erin, sitting at her desk and trying to recover from the class that had just finished, summoned a tremulous smile. Adam had this uncanny habit of appearing whenever she was having a bad moment, doubting her decision to take this job and her value-add in the classroom. He'd perch on the side of her desk and recount funny anecdotes collated over his five years with the college, always succeeding in cheering her up.

'How can I refuse such a chivalrous offer?' she replied with fake brightness.

This morning's class had been a nightmare, the students sullen and uncommunicative, showing no progress at all. Maybe a strong coffee and some of Adam's funny stories would ease the feeling of inadequacy that had overcome her as soon as the students had filed out for morning tea.

Following Adam to the communal kitchen, she sat at one of the small, square tables while he, true to promise, made the coffee. He bounced around the kitchen, filling cups with boiling water, coffee granules and milk, and raiding the cupboards for biscuits.

'Thanks.' She smiled gratefully, cupping the coffee mug with her hands. 'This is really excellent service.'

'I aim to please.' He grinned. 'So, how's it going?'

She bit her lip. 'Not so good.'

'Tell me about it.'

She sipped the coffee, and almost spluttered. It was far too strong. Maybe she should offer to make it in the future. Still, it had been a nice gesture on his part. 'I feel like I'm getting nowhere, Adam, that my students are learning absolutely nothing at all ...'

He responded with a lopsided smile. 'It's a steep learning curve for them.'

'I know, but I thought I'd be able to see small improvements each day.' She sighed deeply. 'I can't detect any progress at all. It's almost like they're impenetrable – my teaching is not getting through.'

'They're not just learning to speak another language, Erin. Some are learning to *write* for the first time, as well as to interact socially in a completely different manner from what they're used to.'

'I know.' Erin sighed again. 'It must be overwhelming for them. But I'm equally overwhelmed – by the sheer extent of what they don't know, what they *need* to know to survive.'

'Have you finished that?' Adam nodded at her half-empty cup.

'Yes.'

'Come with me.'

Somewhat bemused, Erin followed him from the kitchen, and down the maze of corridors that led to the childcare centre. Why was he taking her here? As soon as Adam unlatched the safety gate and stepped inside, there was a universal squeal of delight and a stampede of little legs in his direction. He cast Erin a slightly embarrassed glance before crouching down to greet his pint-sized fan club, ruffling hair and tickling under arms.

'Adam!' Thu, a diminutive Vietnamese woman whom Erin had chatted to a few times in the canteen, sat with a picture book held aloft but nobody there to listen. 'You're interrupting story time.' Her resigned, half-amused tone indicated that interruptions of this kind happened on a regular basis.

'Sorry,' he grinned. 'Where are the others, Thu?'

'Maria is settling the babies, and Zelda is in the kitchen preparing morning tea.'

Adam straightened, and holding a small hand on each side, led the flock back to their teacher, who resumed the story.

'I love story time,' he admitted to Erin in an undertone. 'Sometimes I escape down here when things get too much in the office.'

'The children obviously adore you.' Erin smiled.

'I've an assortment of nieces and nephews who climb all over me at any given opportunity, so I'm quite used to small children.'

Watching the rapt faces of the children as they listened to the story, Erin felt her anxiety ease, and her sense of hope return.

'This is the reason why we do what we do,' Adam spoke quietly by her side, without taking his eyes off the children. 'The next generation. If their parents have integrated well, then they will too. They will get good jobs and benefit the community in many ways. If their parents haven't integrated, and don't speak the language, these children will stay on the outer of society, struggling with limited education and ultimately low incomes. If you ever have any doubts, Erin, come down here. Thu is always pleased to see visitors.'

Adam and Erin stayed to the end of the story, and then waved the children goodbye. Clicking the safety gate behind him, Adam immediately became more serious, the man who had ruffled hair and distributed tickles turning back into the executive who strode around the college at high speed and was responsible for everything.

'Gotta run. I'm late for a meeting with the Department of Immigration. Catch you later.'

And with that, he was gone. Slowly, thoughtfully and a lot more optimistically, Erin made her way back to the classroom.

* * * * *

Laura began the week purposefully, with a brand-new list. It was an all-encompassing list, including both work and home tasks, because the two sides of her life were intricately and unavoidably intertwined. Just writing the list felt good, putting an order to the jumble in her head. Deeply engrossed, she resented the knock that sounded on her office door.

'Yes?'

Savita poked her head inside. 'It's just me. Can I come in?'

Laura smiled, her resentment melting away as soon as she saw who it was. 'Of course.'

Savita glided into the room in loose trousers and a long, embroidered top, her usually serene face marred with a frown.

'Is something wrong?' Laura asked, immediately concerned.

'This new project is making me very busy,' Savita stated in her soft, sing-song voice.

Laura put down her pen and gave the Indian woman her full attention. 'Yes, I imagine it would be. It's very demanding, co-ordinating all the different aspects of a big project like this. But you're doing very well, Savita. Even François says so, and you know how cynical he is!'

Laura knew that François wouldn't mind a small joke at his expense, but Savita didn't even smile.

'Last night I did not get home until 9pm. My son was already in bed, and my husband was not happy.'

Laura nodded. She knew only too well how Savita felt. 'Are

126

you saying it's too much for you? That you want to hand over the reins?'

Savita looked thoughtful. 'No. Not yet. I like being the boss of the project, but I need to come to terms with the cost of it. I'm letting you know how I feel, that is all. I am not looking to hand it over to someone else. Not yet, anyway.'

'Thanks, Savita. Please do put your hand up if it gets too much.'

Laura sat in thought for some time after Savita left. It was interesting how the Indian woman had referred to the 'cost' of her new role. It struck a chord with Laura. Everything had a cost. The question was, what should one do when the cost became too high?

Seeing movement out of the corner of her eye, she looked through the glass wall of her office to see Esteban walking among the workstations, stopping to chat and offer the odd word of advice as he went. His tie was slightly askew, and she could tell from the droop of his shoulders that he was tired. Her heart ached as she watched him.

Was this business of theirs, this thriving, profitable but infinitely demanding enterprise, worth the personal cost? The cost to them as a couple, and as a family unit? Was it worth the separations, the misunderstandings, and the constant stress?

Laura had been questioning this for a few months now, but she was no closer to finding an answer. All she knew was that the solution wasn't as easy as hiring someone to lighten the workload. The business was deeply dependent on both her and Esteban, and it was hard to imagine it running successfully without both of them being fully involved and committed, as they were now. To that extent, they were both pretty much irreplaceable. To have any hope at all, they would need to hire at the executive level, and executives didn't come cheap. Global Translations was growing solidly, but they still had to be very careful with money.

Even though there was no question in Laura's mind that the personal cost had crept too high, she still had no idea how to bring it back down to an acceptable level. Savita's situation was more clear-cut. She, at least, had the option of stepping back. And just having the option, even if one did nothing with it, could in itself ease some of the stress.

Laura looked down at her half-completed list. What she had written suddenly seemed trivial and unimportant. She picked up her pen.

Be a better mother and wife.

She glanced up and watched her husband for another few clandestine moments, before writing,

Make Esteban happy again.

Chapter 14

Dear Mum,

Three months already! Where is the time going? Winter in Sydney is sunny and dry, and it's quite amusing to see the locals wearing hats and scarves and mittens when it's really not that cold! My apartment is fully furnished now and I feel very much at home in it, largely due to my neighbour, Fizz, who makes it her business to ensure I'm not lonely (or hungry, for that matter).

I've enclosed some more photos. I thought you might like to see where I work, so there's one of my students, and another of my colleagues (the guy with the fair hair is Adam, my boss, and the woman with him is Lydia). And you're probably already wondering about the photo at the beach, and who it is I'm with! That's Jack, my boyfriend. You'd like him, Mum. He's a teacher, too.

Laura tells me that everything at home is going well.

Give Gerry, Paddy and Cathy all my love,

XX Erin

To: Erin <Erin.Donovan@yahoo.com>

From: Laura <Laura.Torres@globaltranslation.com>

Moira showed me the photo of Jack. He's gorgeous, Erin. The two of you look perfect together, and the beach looked stunning. I must admit to a very strong pang of jealousy. Moira's positively thrilled that you have a boyfriend. She's showing the photo to everyone — Paddy, Gerry, Mum, the cleaner. I think she really wants to see you settle down, but obviously not in Australia. She believes it's only a matter of weeks before you come home, the poor love. I know it's selfish to say so, but I wish you were coming home soon too. Work is spiralling out of control. If it weren't my own business, I'd be thinking of leaving. But you can't exactly resign from your own company, can you?

To add to the overall stress, it's becoming more and more evident that we've made a mistake with our nanny. She's cold and very aloof, and she only half-listens when I give her instructions on Olivia. Esteban says I'm being picky and hard to please. What would he know? He's hardly home these days, and Kasia is just one of many things we disagree on.

Wish you here so we could talk. Forget I said that. I'm delighted that you're in love and having such a wonderful time.

XX Laura

To: Laura <Laura.Torres@globaltranslation.com>

From: Erin <Erin.Donovan@yahoo.com>

Oh, Laura. Both you and Esteban sound like you're working yourselves into the ground. Can't someone hold the fort while you both take a hard-earned break?

Don't write Kasia off just yet. I've been quietly despairing over my students, who've been totally unresponsive to me, but yesterday I finally had a breakthrough. An Afghan girl called Fila, said, 'Good morning, Miss Erin. How was your weekend?' I was so ecstatic, I wanted to kiss her. I see now what Adam meant, how there are all sorts of cultural differences at play, not just the language, and how time itself is the single most important factor.

Do something with Kasia that isn't work-related – you might see her in another light. And please, please consider a holiday.

XX Erin

To: Erin <Erin.Donovan@yahoo.com>

From: Fila Azizi <Fila.Azizi@gmail.com>

Hello, I send you an email. Fila.

To: Fila Azizi <Fila.Azizi@gmail.com>

From: Erin <Erin.Donovan@yahoo.com>

Hello Fila,

I am very happy to see that you are online. You are progressing as well with your computer lessons as you are with your language classes. I will see you back in class in one hour.

Kind regards,

Erin

Dear Erin,

I received your letter, and enjoyed looking at the photographs. I've always liked the name Jack, and everyone here thinks he's very handsome – particularly Cathy, and she's somewhat of an authority on these matters. Gerry thought you looked very suited to each other, and Paddy remarked that teachers are good husband material.

Laura found me a pen and some notepaper so I could write to you. Olivia is here, too. She is such a dear little child. And she has so many questions. She even asked me if there are televisions in heaven. I certainly hope so, I said.

Well, that's all from me, my dear. I look forward to your next letter and hearing more about Jack,

Love always,

Mum

To: Erin <Erin.Donovan@yahoo.com>

From: Lisha.Mbah@stpatricks.ie

Dear Erin,

I'm writing this on the eve of the Junior Cert exams. I should be studying but I'm finding it really hard to concentrate. I've made a decision about something, and I need to tell someone or I'll burst. I'm leaving school. There, I've said it! I can almost hear your gasp of disapproval. Before you make judgments, listen to my reasons. I am not happy at school, and because I'm not happy it's hard to stay motivated. If I have a job and pay taxes, Immigration Services will see that I'm contributing to the country, and take this into account when reviewing our family's situation. If the worst case transpires and we're sent back to Nigeria, my earnings will be needed to fund the move and the cost of re-establishing ourselves there. Despite these good reasons, Mother and Father will be furious. Leaving Certificate, university degree, post-graduate qualifications, they want it all for me. They're obsessed with education. In my opinion, experience is what counts.

My mind does feel clearer now that I've told you. Hopefully, I can revise for tomorrow's English paper now.

I will be back in touch after the exams.

Regards,

Lisha

PS: I made some jewellery to sell at the school fair. The girls picked up the beads with the tips of their fingers, as if they might get dirty from them. It was then I realised how badly I need to leave this school.

Chapter 15

'Good morning, Miss Erin. It is a nice morning, yes? Bright and sunny.'

Fila's smile was as bright as the winter morning outside. Now that she had found her voice, she shyly but consistently sought conversation with both Erin and her classmates. As her reserve dissipated, her personality – curious, girlish, mischievous – began to shine through.

'Good morning, Fila, and my lovely class.' Erin set down her books on the desk and beamed at her students. 'How are you all today?'

They greeted her in chorus, some of them adding an answer to her question about how they were: well, good, happy – not the most exciting set of adjectives in the world, but a genuine response nonetheless. Erin smiled at them again, happiness bubbling inside her. At last she was getting somewhere with these students. She could see and hear their progress – she could even *feel* it. The classroom felt more optimistic, more relaxed, and was definitely more interactive. It was easier to gather momentum, and to digress and explore as they went along. Thus, her days were pleasantly unpredictable and flew past.

'Today, we are going to do some preparation work for Refugee Day,' Erin announced, snapping out of her brief reverie. 'We are going to discuss the purpose of the day and how we will celebrate. Now, tell me what the day means to you, and I will write your thoughts on the whiteboard.'

'Freedom,' one of the older women said immediately, and Erin wrote it down on the board.

'Peace,' offered one of the younger girls.

'Respect.'

'Choice.'

'Safety.'

'Human rights.'

Erin rushed to keep up, her handwriting suffering. This was a topic her students understood well; these words were familiar to them. The words on the board had had a fundamental impact on their lives, and were part of their decision to leave their homes, families and countries behind in favour of a new, safer, more prosperous life in Australia. Three-quarters of the class were refugees. They'd run away from injustice, hatred and violence, and ended up here in Erin's classroom. English was the currency they needed to embark on their new lives, and it was her job to teach it to them. The responsibility remained both daunting and thrilling.

'What are the things you miss about your home country?' Erin asked when replies to her previous question had run dry.

'My house.'

'My mother and father.'

'My aunts and uncles and cousins.'

'Our belongings.'

Their answers resonated with Erin. She, too, missed her mother and the rest of her family, particularly Laura and Olivia. She missed her old bedroom, and the clothes and shoes and knick-knacks she hadn't been able to cram into her suitcase. When she went to bed at night, she thought of everything that she missed, and sometimes it took hours to fall asleep. But when she woke the next morning she would see the blue sky in the crack between the curtains, and she was always glad to be where she was. She loved winter in Sydney. The crisp skies, the fresh cold mornings that morphed into perfect sunny days. This is my new start, she told herself each morning, and the day that greeted her outside seemed to reflect the clarity and brightness inside her.

'And what do you want from your new life in Australia?' she asked next.

'A good job.'

'A house all to ourselves.'

'Education for my children.'

'Success.'

Other than missing home and worrying from afar about her mother, everything else in Erin's life seemed remarkably aligned. She thoroughly enjoyed her tiny apartment, and her rather busy social life. Her relationship with Jack was speeding ahead. His girls were coming up from Melbourne for the school holidays, and Jack was planning numerous activities with them.

'I can't wait for you to meet them.' He had looked proud and excited as he announced all the plans.

Erin was slightly wary of meeting Jack's daughters. She was experienced enough with children to realise that the girls liking their father's new girlfriend was not a foregone conclusion. Still, meeting Jack's family was a natural progression in their relationship, and she was prepared to go forward as bravely and resolutely as he was.

'Thank you.' Erin turned from the board to face the class. 'That was excellent. Now, I would like you to copy all these words and phrases into your notebooks so that you can practise them at home.'

Class-wide groans met her request. Though the women were slowly progressing with their verbal skills, their writing abilities were still very far behind. Because of the level of correction needed, they wrote in pencil, awkwardly forming the letters and words, frequently rubbing out and trying again. Fila was the exception. The Afghan girl had accelerated past everyone else, and was proving to be a gifted student with a genuine talent for languages. Erin was delighted with Fila's progress, but she found it saddening that the girl's intelligence had been unutilised until this point in her life.

The rest of the class, however, had a long, long way to go, and only three months left to get there. Erin was determined to do everything in her power – extra classes, one-on-one tuition, whatever it took – to give these students the new start they deserved. In the meantime, she was looking forward to the Refugee Day celebrations next week, and interacting with her students in a more relaxed, informal environment.

* * * * *

Laura was not having a good day and, evidently, neither was Moira. Laura found her aunt in the living room, gazing vacantly at the TV, the volume so loud that Laura felt the threat of an instant headache.

'Goodness that's loud.' Laura picked up the remote control from Moira's armrest and turned the volume down considerably. 'That's better. How are you, Moira?'

Moira seemed confused by Laura's sudden appearance in her front room. 'How did you get in?' she asked in a puzzled tone.

'I have a key, remember?'

'No. No, I don't remember.'

Laura sat down on the two-seater couch, and for a few minutes the sounds from the television substituted for conversation.

'Why did you come again?' Moira asked, turning her head abruptly to scrutinise Laura.

'I just popped in on my way home from work,' Laura replied lightly.

Moira fixed her eyes back on the television. 'Moira, Gerard, Patrick and baby Cathy,' she muttered under her breath.

Laura said nothing.

'Moira, Gerard, Patrick and baby Cathy.'

After repeating the mantra a few more times, Moira pointed the remote control at the TV, turning it off. 'I'm bored, Cathy,' she announced.

'I'm not Cathy,' Laura pointed out gently. Her aunt seemed very agitated tonight. 'Would you like a cup of tea, Moira?' she asked, hoping that some caffeine would have a calming effect.

Moira rolled her eyes, and then giggled. 'Never mind tea, let's have a sherry.'

Laura thought quickly. Was there any reason why Moira shouldn't have a sherry if she wanted one? Laura couldn't think of any, so she got to her feet and looked through the glass cabinet next to the fireplace. Amidst the dusty contents, she found an unopened bottle of sherry. Taking two upturned wineglasses in her other hand, she closed the cabinet door with her elbow.

'I've never tasted sherry before,' she commented.

Moira laughed derisively. 'Don't be so silly. Of course you have.'

Laura decided not to argue the point. She poured two glasses and handed one to Moira in her armchair. 'Well, cheers.'

'À la tienne.' Moira, rather surprisingly, responded in French.

As she sipped from her glass, Laura felt the sweetness of the sherry dissolve the edges and frustrations from her day. She didn't usually call to see Moira on her way home from work. Olivia was having an evening out with her grandmother, a rare occurrence, and Esteban was away again, so there had been no pressing reason to rush home. Work had been particularly crazy today, with lots of blips with Project Chariot and an uncharacteristically disgruntled Savita. Home promised to be just as demanding, with laundry and cleaning and paperwork all to be dealt with before she could call an end to the day. This visit to Moira was a respite in the middle of all the craziness.

'This is nice, Moira. Very relaxing.'

'It's nice to have some time alone.' Moira seemed to be in agreement, but then revealed that her mind was in a completely different time and place. 'Joe's at the embassy, and for once Anna isn't skulking around.'

'Moira, we're not –' Laura began.

'Ssh, Cathy. I'm glad we're alone, because I need to talk to you ...'

'I'm not Cath –'

'Now, I want you to be honest with me ...'

'But, I –'

'Just hear me out,' Moira insisted. 'For once.'

'Moira, I –'

'Tell me.' Moira leant across and took Laura firmly by the arm. 'Are you on the pill?'

Laura felt Moira's fingers pinch her arm, and saw the determination in her aunt's eyes. It was best to give in, she decided, and play the part, because it didn't look like Moira would let go otherwise.

'Yes,' she improvised. 'I'm on the pill.'

Apparently satisfied, Moira nodded, let go her grip, and sank back into her chair. Silence followed. Moira seemed deep in thought, but in a matter of minutes, her eyes closed. Bemused, Laura extracted the glass from her aunt's hand and found a soft blanket to tuck around her legs. She poured herself another glass of sherry, sat back down on the couch, and wondered what the hell that had been all about.

Chapter 16

'Welcome, everyone, to our Refugee Day celebrations. It is our honour and privilege to celebrate this day with you all, and we have a very special evening ahead – stories to listen to, music and dance, a wonderful variety of food ...'

Adam seemed even more animated than usual, and Erin found herself smiling fondly as she listened to the rest of his opening speech. The room buzzed with anticipation. Brightly coloured helium balloons floated overhead, a different country name written on each one. Flags adorned the walls. At the back of the room, behind the rows of chairs, tables of food lay in wait. When the speaking and other performances were finished, the tasting and more informal celebrations could begin.

'Now, it is my pleasure to welcome Padma, who is going to perform a Sri Lankan dance for us.'

Adam stood to the side and Padma, dressed in a peach-coloured shimmery top and matching sarong, took centre stage. A lotus tucked into her dark upswept hair, she nodded shyly at Adam, whose duties apparently included being the sound technician for this event. After he pressed some buttons and turned a few dials, the music, a strong rhythm of drums and cymbals, filled the room and Padma moved her elegant arms upwards. As the rhythm took hold, she turned and swayed and teased the audience, who began to clap in time.

'Isn't she great?' Erin whispered to Lydia, who was sitting next to her.

Lydia nodded. 'She's wonderful. Actually, it's hard to equate this beautiful young woman with the mute, withdrawn girl I assessed last year. You know, Padma and her family spent ten months in a detention centre after trying to come into the country without visas. It was a very harsh introduction to Australian life. But look at her now!'

After Padma's dance, Adam introduced Abdullah, who sang an Iranian pop song. Abdullah danced enthusiastically as he sang, and the crowd applauded uproariously when he bowed breathlessly at the end.

'He has no family here,' Lydia commented sotto voce to Erin. 'We have so many young men like him who are here all on their own. Without their families, it falls to us to help keep them on the straight and narrow, and out of trouble.'

The longer Erin worked at the college, the more she came to realise Lydia's pivotal role in it. While Erin had contact with only a fraction of the students, Lydia assessed each and every one of them, and it seemed that she never forgot their names, or their stories.

Adam was back at the podium.

'Thanks, Abdullah. That was very entertaining. Now, we have a change of pace. Fila is going speak for us, and tell us her story.'

'Fila?' Erin frowned in confusion. 'My Fila?'

'Yes,' Lydia confirmed.

And it was indeed Erin's Fila who was making her way to the podium, wearing her veil and a bashful smile.

'Hello,' she announced, her mouth too close to the microphone. Adam moved her back a little. 'Hello,' she repeated after a small, self-conscious giggle. 'My name is Fila

... I am from Afghanistan, and I am proud of my heritage – but I do not want to live in my home country ... After the fall of the Taliban, laws were passed to give Afghan women rights, and to protect us from violence. But in many parts of Afghanistan, these laws are ignored and women cannot work, or go to school. They cannot seek medical help from a male doctor, and they are often beaten and abused ... Because of these reasons, I am glad to be in Australia. I am learning to read and write and use the computer ... I am very excited about my future here.'

'I had no idea she had prepared this,' Erin exclaimed, feeling rather emotional as she clapped at the conclusion of Fila's very short but nevertheless remarkably clear and well-rehearsed speech.

'She wanted to surprise you,' Lydia revealed.

'Well, she certainly succeeded!' Erin brushed away the tears that had sprung to her eyes.

Following Fila, a woman from Sierra Leone recited a poem in her lyrical native tongue. Next came a teenage boy who treated the audience to an energetic performance on his hand drums. A father, who had left his wife and daughters behind in Burma, finished with a heartbreaking speech about families split apart and the terrible conflict, guilt and loneliness he felt every day. Then Adam declared the formal part of the proceedings to be over, and put on some background music. Chairs scraped back, and people drifted towards the tables of food, filling their paper plates with a selection of delicacies and traditional fare.

Erin sought out Fila, congratulated her on her speech, and pretended to be outraged by her secrecy. Then she conscientiously worked her way around to each one of her students, encouraging them to converse with her about the event.

After the food, someone turned up the music, and suddenly there was dancing, a medley of different styles erupting and causing much laughter and clapping. Of course Adam was in the midst of the chaos, linking arms and twirling around like a child who had eaten too many lollies.

Erin rolled her eyes to Lydia, who was next to her again. 'He's completely mad.'

'Completely,' Lydia agreed gravely.

Adam was doing some sort of Iranian dance routine with Abdullah, both men shaking their torsos and clapping their hands above their heads.

'His girlfriend must be a saint to put up with him,' Erin mused.

Out of the corner of her eye, she caught Lydia's questioning glance.

'He doesn't have a girlfriend,' said the older woman.

'Oh, but you said …'

'There was someone a few months ago, but from what I know it's over now,' Lydia divulged. 'And what about you? Who's the nice man I spotted waiting outside work for you last week?'

Despite herself, Erin blushed. 'That's Jack.'

To hide her sudden embarrassment, she concentrated on the makeshift dance floor. What was Adam doing now? It looked suspiciously as if he was demonstrating how to break-dance.

'Good Lord.' Lydia bent over laughing, clutching Erin's arm to balance herself. 'Oh, there's not a day when that man doesn't make me laugh out loud.' She snorted, and then, with some effort, regained her composure. 'Come on, you and I have to be the party poopers, I'm afraid. Those young men should get back to their lodgings before they get it into their heads to take the party elsewhere. And the girls will be in trouble with their families if they come home late.'

'You're always thinking of the students, Lydia,' Erin marvelled. 'You obviously care about them a great deal.'

A smile folded across Lydia's face. 'While they're here at

the college, they're like family to me. I worry over them. I pray for them at night. When I see how much they've learnt, it makes me proud and happy. I could not ask for a more fulfilling job than this.'

Erin felt humble listening to her.

The song finished, and Lydia turned off the sound system before another one could begin. At the silence Adam looked momentarily confused, but then he spotted Lydia at the helm and registered the party-is-over expression on her face. Quite suddenly, he switched from break-dancing to shaking hands and sending people on their way. Thu, from the childcare centre, foisted wrapped leftover food onto the departing students. Erin and Lydia began to stack away the chairs. Food and dirt littered the floor, and serving platters and cups and cutlery were piled up in the kitchen sink. Cleaning it all up was going to take some time.

Adam clapped his hands together. 'Where do you need my services the most?' he enquired of Lydia.

'The sink, my dear,' she replied dryly.

Obediently, he bounced off towards the kitchen, and Lydia sniggered in his wake.

'I always put him on wash up. I know he's a darling, but there's something very gratifying about seeing the boss with suds up to his elbows.'

Erin swept the floor while Lydia scooped paper plates into a black garbage bag. Thu helped Adam in the kitchen.

An hour later, Lydia nodded with satisfaction. 'It's cleaner now than before the celebrations!'

Adam emerged from the kitchen brandishing a bottle of wine in one hand, and some glasses in the other. 'I think we deserve a quiet drink after all our hard work.'

Erin sank into one of the plastic chairs. It had been a hard day, but an extremely rewarding one. She still couldn't believe that Fila had stood up and spoken in front of everyone.

Adam handed her a glass of wine and she smiled at him

gratefully. 'I didn't know you were such a talented dancer.'

He grinned sheepishly. 'Neither did I.'

Lydia sniffed. 'You'll be stiff and sore tomorrow.'

Adam rubbed one of his elbows. 'I already am ... How come you didn't dance today, Lydia?'

The older woman shrugged. 'I was too busy talking.'

Adam blinked his green-gold eyes at Erin. 'Lydia can *really* dance. She used to be a professional.'

Erin regarded Lydia with widened eyes. 'You were?'

'Yes ... until my charming ex-husband bashed me against a wall and shattered my collarbone and my jaw.'

Erin gasped in horror.

Lydia reached out and took Erin's hand in hers. 'Sorry, darling, you didn't need to know that detail. It happened a long time ago.'

Though Erin was horrified, she wasn't surprised. Right from the first moment she'd set eyes on Lydia, she had instinctively known that something like this was part of her history. Lydia's story was written in the lines on her face.

'That's awful, Lydia. Your wonderful career destroyed ...'

'I found another wonderful career,' Lydia stated, 'and that was my revenge. He was a bully, my ex-husband, a horrible, mean, spiteful man. The only good thing I'll say about him is that he taught me how to fight my corner, how to be truly *brave* ... and I've discovered that life is much more exciting when one approaches it courageously.'

Erin wanted to ask her more, how she had broken away from her bullying husband, if he had been charged by the police for injuring her so badly, but Adam seemed to think that enough had been said.

'How about you, Thu?' he turned his attention to the tiny Vietnamese woman. 'How do you fare on the dance floor?'

Thu giggled. 'Not good. I stand on my poor husband's toes whenever we dance.'

'Erin?' Adam enquired. 'Any talent on your end?'

'Absolutely none.' She grinned. 'Categorically clumsy and uncoordinated, I'm afraid.'

After establishing everyone's prowess on the dance floor, Adam went on to investigate who could hold a tune.

'Not me.' Lydia rolled her eyes. 'I can't sing to save my life.'

'Thu?'

'Sing?' Thu raised her thin eyebrows. 'Yes. My family tell me I have a nice voice.'

'Erin?'

'No. Not a good singer, I'm afraid.'

'So we have Lydia who can dance but cannot sing,' Adam summarised. 'Thu who can sing but can't dance. Erin who claims she can neither sing nor dance, which I doubt, but will accept at face value … for now. And me – not very talented at either singing or dancing, but unable to stop myself whenever the opportunity to perform arises.'

They all laughed, and Adam, spurred on by their response, went to put on some more music.

'It's Padma's music,' Lydia cried, recognising it from earlier. 'Come on, Adam, show us your best Sri Lankan moves.'

Adam raised his arms over his head, crossing them at the wrist, and jiggled his hips as he endeavoured to imitate Padma. He had the wrong physique – he was too stocky – and he looked hilarious. Determined to win their praise, he threw in some belly-dancing and some Greek-inspired stamping, while his audience howled with laughter.

'Come on, you lazy lot, get up and join me.'

And they did, laughing even harder, tears rolling down Erin's face as she made a feeble attempt to move to the rhythm.

She accidentally bumped up against Thu. 'Sorry, Thu.'

'Concentrate,' Adam commanded in a mock prima donna tone.

Once she had controlled her giggles, Erin tried to emulate Lydia, who was incredibly graceful and versatile even when she was mucking around.

A long time ago, when Erin was about fifteen, Rachel Murphy had sidled up to her at the school disco and sneered in her ear, 'You look ridiculous.' Rachel disappeared into the crowd without specifying what it was about Erin she found so ludicrous: her style of dancing; her new black and white dress, which Erin loved but was already beginning to doubt; her hair, which was pulled back into a high ponytail and didn't look so different from everyone else's ... at least Erin hadn't thought so. Rachel didn't come near her for the rest of the night. She didn't need to, as she'd already achieved exactly what she'd set out to do. Moira picked up Erin afterwards, driving home through the quiet, suburban streets and casually enquiring if her daughter had enjoyed herself. Amazed by her own acting ability, Erin assured her mother that the disco had been the best night ever and that she'd had a wonderful time. Alone in her bedroom, the act was over and she had cried herself to sleep.

Funny that she was remembering this now. Maybe Lydia's reference to her bullying husband had jarred her mind. Maybe it was just the dancing.

Thu, like Erin, was an awkward but willing dancer, grinning good-naturedly as Adam twirled her around and around and around. At one stage, Adam deserted Thu mid-twirl, disappearing into the kitchen before returning with a mask, fashioned from a paper plate with two holes cut out for his eyes. Lydia was thrilled with the mask, and she and Adam improvised with it, swiping if off each other, strutting and preening, Erin and Thu collapsing with helpless laughter.

Shortly after midnight, Thu noticed the time and exclaimed in horror. 'My husband will think I have been kidnapped.'

'And my cat will think I've deserted him,' Lydia added in agreement.

Everyone was suddenly exhausted. The impromptu dancing fest was over.

Outside, they walked towards the main road, where they stood in a huddle. Taxis were evidently scarce, and it was ten minutes before a free one coasted along. Lydia and Thu, heading roughly in the same direction, shared it.

Erin burrowed into her jacket. 'Gosh, it's cold.'

Adam grinned. 'You're becoming acclimatised, I see.'

He wasn't wearing a coat, and his shirt sleeves were pushed halfway up his arms.

'Don't you feel it?' she asked, shaking her head at him.

'Nope.' He shrugged. 'I've always been warm-blooded.'

Warm-blooded. Yes, that was Adam in a nutshell, passionate about everything he did, from his work and the serious business of running the college, to dancing and singing and throwing himself wholeheartedly into the moment. There was nothing cold about him at all: not his eyes, with their hint of gold, nor his slightly dishevelled hair.

A taxi appeared in the distance, its yellow light indicating it was free.

'Great!' Erin waved at it wildly. 'Do you want me to drop you off somewhere?'

'No, thanks. I'm in the opposite direction.' Gallantly, he opened the taxi door for her. 'Safe home, Erin. See you tomorrow.'

The taxi sped away, and Erin's last impression of Adam was of him standing by the side of the road, his arm raised as he waved her off. He was really quite lovely, she decided. Hyperactive, yes, but never, ever boring. Tonight she felt that she'd got to know him a little bit better. And Lydia and Thu, too. All her colleagues were lovely. She was lucky to work with them.

The house was in darkness when Erin got home. She turned the key as quietly as she could on the main door, and crept up the stairs, being careful not to disturb Fizz.

Inside her apartment, the message light flashed on her phone. It was Jack, a few hours ago, wondering if she was home yet. He'd also left a message on her mobile, a message she hadn't noticed until now, she had been so busy dancing and laughing and having fun. Suddenly, for some inexplicable reason, she felt guilty.

Climbing into bed and snuggling under the covers, Erin closed her eyes and processed everything that had happened. Though utterly exhausted, she was still on some kind of strange high. What a wonderful, special day it had been! The performances and speeches, and the atmosphere as all the nationalities had come together to celebrate. If she'd had any remaining doubts about her job, they had been categorically wiped out today. Everything about her role and the mission of the college had been so gratifyingly validated, even down to the fact that her colleagues were becoming more like friends.

At last, Erin felt herself relax and sleepiness take hold. There was something, something she had meant to mull over and analyse, but it evaded her now. Something about Adam.

Oh, yes. He didn't have a girlfriend.

That's if Lydia's information was up to date.

Strange that he didn't have a girlfriend.

This was her last thought before she succumbed to sleep.

Chapter 17

Kasia was waiting in the hallway when Laura came home.

'I think Olivia is sick,' she stated matter-of-factly.

'Sick?' Laura frowned in surprise. 'What do you mean?'

Kasia shrugged. 'She doesn't seem to have much energy, and she did not eat her dinner.'

'Where is she?'

'Watching telly.'

Laura hurried into the front room where she found Olivia huddled on the couch.

'What's up, Floss?' Laura crouched down and took Olivia's small hand in hers.

Olivia transferred her bleary eyes from the TV to her mother. 'I feel tired. And my head is sore.'

Laura felt her daughter's forehead, and then her tummy. Her skin was burning.

'Let's get you some Panadol, Floss, and then up to bed, okay?'

Laura strode past Kasia, who was hovering by the doorway. The girl followed her to the kitchen and watched mutely while she extracted the Panadol from the medicine cabinet and poured some into a measuring cup.

'You should have rung me at work.' Laura's voice came out harsh and accusing.

'I am sorry.'

'If you had rung me, I would have told you to give her medicine to bring her temperature down, and she wouldn't be feeling so bad now.'

'I am sorry.'

'Do you not know these things?' Laura demanded, suddenly incensed. Kasia was obviously contrite, but her general offhandedness and lack of emotion, as well as common sense, was infuriating. 'Do you not know how to tell when a child has a temperature? When you should call her mother?'

'Not exactly. But I will know next time.'

Shaking her head furiously, Laura left the Polish girl in the kitchen and went to tend to Olivia. This morning, as she'd been leaving for work, she had thought that Olivia looked pale. She'd intended to phone Kasia during the day to check on her daughter, but something had come up every time the thought entered her head and she had ended up forgetting. Laura was guilty too, and this irrefutable fact, irrationally, just made her feel angrier.

Within minutes, Laura had Olivia tucked up in bed.

'Will I be better tomorrow, Mum?'

'I hope so, Floss.'

'What if I'm not? Will you stay at home to mind me?'

Laura felt her chest tighten with guilt. 'Mummy has to go to work. Kasia will mind you. She'll read you stories and let you watch lots of princess movies, okay?'

'Okay.' Olivia nodded sleepily. 'Mum, I've been thinking …'

'Yes?'

'You know how people get buried when they die?'

'Yes,' Laura replied hesitantly. Olivia's current obsession with life and death had resulted in many curly questions.

'Well, how can they be buried on earth, but still be up in heaven?'

'Well …' Good Lord. How was one supposed to come up

– without any warning or preparation – with intelligent, age-appropriate answers to such questions? 'You see, your body stays on earth, but your soul goes to heaven.'

'What's your soul?'

'Your soul is the real you. It's what you are on the inside, how you think and feel.'

'Can you see it?'

'No.'

'And how does it get up to heaven?'

'The angels come down and take it up in their wings.' Laura planted a kiss on Olivia's hot forehead. 'Now, *my angel*, it's time for sleep, okay?'

'Okay ... night, Mum.'

'Night night, Floss.'

As Laura half-closed the door of Olivia's room, she became aware of Kasia loitering on the landing. The Polish girl usually made herself scarce as soon as Laura got home from work. She seemed to be abnormally present tonight.

'Why do you call her Floss?' she asked, her eyes blinking beneath her too-long fringe.

For a moment, Laura felt too disheartened to reply. Her daughter was sick. She had been sick *all day* without anyone taking proper care of her. In all likelihood she would be sick tomorrow too, and even though Laura knew this now, it didn't alter the fact that she simply couldn't stay at home and care for Olivia.

This was not the kind of mother she wanted to be.

'Because of her hair,' she answered Kasia tiredly. 'It reminds me of candy floss.'

Was it possible to lose one's soul without dying and going to heaven? To lose one's essence? One's beliefs and spirit and sense of self?

While Laura had been preoccupied with the business and trying to run a household at the same time, had someone, unbeknownst to her, come along and stolen her soul?

* * * * *

The next morning, Olivia's fever was less extreme, but she was lethargic and complaining of a sore throat.

'It hurts when I swallow ...'

'Where does it hurt exactly? Up high in your throat, or down low?'

'Down low. It's like I have a lump there.'

'Open wide, and let Mum have a look.'

Obediently, Olivia opened her mouth.

'Say ah ...'

'Ahhhhh ... Do I need to go to the doctor?'

'I don't think so. I can't see any sign of an infection.' Laura hoped she was right. 'Now, try to rest, okay? I'll call you later.'

Downstairs, she found Kasia standing at the counter, eating from a cereal bowl.

'Keep Olivia in bed as long as you can,' Laura instructed her. 'Give her Panadol every four to six hours, and lots of water. Ring me if anything changes – if the Panadol doesn't bring her temperature down, or you think she's getting worse.'

Kasia nodded, her expression apprehensive at the level of responsibility being required of her.

Her stomach churning with guilt, Laura left the house, walking through a light sun shower to get to her car.

As usual, the traffic was horrendous, with North Circular Road at a complete standstill. Laura drummed her fingers on the steering wheel as she waited while a set of lights changed from red to green and back to red again, all without a single car progressing through the intersection. On impulse, she decided to call her mother.

'Cathy,' she called out, using the voice recognition feature on her phone.

'Cathy,' it echoed in a warped voice, and proceeded to dial the number. The ring tone filled the car just as the traffic moved forward a smidgeon.

'Hello?' Her mother's voice was husky.

'It's me, Mum.'

'What time is it?'

'Early.'

Cathy yawned, and Laura's mind conjured up an image of her: tousled hair, sleepy eyes, stretching in her warm bed.

'Sorry for ringing so early.' Her apology, with its undercurrents of envy, sounded a little brusque. 'Olivia's sick … and I wanted to ask if you could call in and check on her today – that's if you have any spare time …'

As usual, her mother's response was less than enthusiastic. 'I suppose I could change my plans this afternoon.'

What plans? Going to the hairdresser? Having coffee with her friends? *More* shopping?

'Thanks, Mum. I really appreciate you doing this.'

The traffic moved an almost indiscernible distance. In truth, these small movements forward disguised the fact that the drivers were getting nowhere. The situation seemed to reflect the state of Laura's life: a great deal of effort, but no real progress.

At least Esteban was coming back tonight. Just the thought of him walking through the door, his suitcase gripped in one hand, his laptop case in the other, was enough to make her feel better. Immediately, he would immerse himself with Olivia, telling her anecdotes about his trip, reading her stories and, hopefully, coaxing some food into her. When Olivia was asleep, he would turn his attention to Laura, listen to all her worries and guilt, and reassure her that they were doing the right thing.

Altogether more positive by now, Laura turned up the music on the radio, and hummed along to the song that was playing until, at long last, she got through the problematic set of traffic lights.

* * * * *

At lunchtime, Esteban called from Rome to inform Laura that his flight was delayed. Apparently, the incoming flight was late arriving from Dublin, and there had been a knock-on effect on its departure time out of Rome. For some reason, Esteban always found it necessary to explain the specific reasons why his flights were running late.

'Two hours, cariño, that's all.'

Just enough to miss Olivia's bedtime.

Despite back-to-back meetings, Laura managed to squeeze in a few phone calls home to check on Olivia. Kasia and Cathy, who was visiting during one of Laura's calls, both assured her that Olivia appeared to be improving. Olivia herself, when she came on the phone, sounded as though she was in good spirits, despite a croaky voice and frequent bouts of coughing.

Despite all their assurances, Laura was not at ease until she got home from work and saw her daughter for herself.

'Have you been eating?'

'Granny gave me some biscuits.'

'And how do you feel?'

'Very bored. Where's Daddy? I thought he was coming home.'

'Daddy is late, Floss.' Laura tried to mask her own disappointment. 'You won't see him until the morning. Okay?'

Olivia stuck out her bottom lip. 'I haven't seen him in ten whole days.'

'I know. This trip has been a long one, hasn't it? Tell you what, I'll send him in when he gets home to give you a secret kiss. But you'll be so fast asleep, you won't even feel it.'

'I will.'

'Nope. I bet you won't. Night night, Floss.'

Downstairs, Laura paused. There was so much to do, she didn't know where to start. She should make dinner. Yes, it made sense to do that first so that she and Esteban could eat together as soon as he got home.

A half-hour later, a curry simmered on the stove while Laura carried out her next task: a quick tidy of the kitchen and the living room. She gathered abandoned shoes, toys and books, returning them to their rightful places. Fifteen minutes of effort made a startling difference. If only Kasia would contemplate a similar tidy-up before Laura came home each day. It would be so nice to come home to a neat, orderly house.

Next, Laura tackled the ironing. It was a good thing that this was a chore she didn't mind, because it seemed to pile up at a relentless pace even when Esteban was away. Methodically, scrupulously, Laura pressed Olivia's jeans, tops and vests. She might not be with her daughter for much of the day, but at least Olivia's clothes were soft and smooth, and proof of Laura's love. With Olivia's clothes folded neatly into piles, Laura moved to her own skirts, trousers and shirts. The hiss from the iron punctuated the silence. Kasia was out. For the first time all day, Laura felt at peace.

While pressing fresh sheets for Olivia's bed, Laura heard Esteban's key in the lock.

'In here,' she called out.

'Where else?' he grinned wryly, leaning down to plant a cold kiss on her lips. Beads of rain glistened in his dark hair. 'I come home to find you with your secret addiction: the iron.'

Every now and then, Esteban would urge Laura to get a cleaner, to take the pressure off and erase at least one duty from her busy life. She would shake her head before explaining, yet again, that she actually enjoyed doing it herself and that she was very reluctant to have another 'stranger' in her home.

She smiled at him. 'I didn't know it was raining outside.'

'Just a light drizzle.' He shrugged. For someone who had grown up in a relatively arid part of the world, he was very accepting of the Irish climate. He had once told Laura that rain was his novelty, in the same way that the sun was hers. 'How are you, cariño? Have you missed me?'

'Of course I have,' Laura replied, adding a smile because she hadn't meant to sound so perfunctory. 'Olivia is sick.'

Esteban's expression darkened with concern. 'You never told me this.'

Laura shrugged. 'You had to rush when we spoke earlier, and I didn't have enough time to slip it in. Actually, she's been sick since yesterday. Kasia didn't think to phone me at work, or to give her Panadol. Thank God, she seems a lot better today. Despite the neglect.'

'I will go and check on her,' Esteban declared. He adored his daughter and, just like Laura, would be feeling guilty now that he hadn't been there when she needed him.

A few minutes later, he returned, looking a little sheepish. 'I'm sorry, cariño, I woke her up. I know it was selfish of me, but I wanted to let her know I was back ... and how very much I love her.'

Laura smiled. She understood. She had often done the same thing: woken Olivia up to let her know that she was home, and that she loved her. 'How was she?'

'She seemed well enough.'

'The worst of it has passed. Last night I was really worried about her. And this morning too. I felt totally heartless going into work.'

Esteban raised his hand, his cool fingers lightly touching her cheek. 'You should not worry yourself so much.'

'If you had been here, you would have been as bad,' she told him.

'Yes, you are probably right.'

More often than not, he missed out on it: the worrying. Parents worried about their children when they saw them hurt, or sad, or disappointed. Stealing into their bedrooms late at night to feast on their tiny faces, or talking to them on the phone, was a kind of removed contact, and did not stir up a fraction of the worry a parent felt when they were there on the ground, a firsthand witness to whatever had gone wrong. In Laura's opinion, distance diluted worry, and Esteban, because of all his travelling, had never been more distant from his family.

He sniffed, smells from the kitchen finding their way to his nostrils. 'Something smells delicious.'

'I made a curry.' Laura switched off the iron. 'Come on. Let's eat.'

He kissed the top of her head. 'Despite your addiction to ironing and worrying, you are nevertheless an excellent and caring wife.'

She laughed. 'Such flattery! I think you must have missed me, too.'

Dinner was unexpectedly romantic: muted lighting, the best part of a bottle of wine, and so much to talk about. Afterwards, in bed, Esteban took her into his arms and proceeded to demonstrate exactly how much he had missed her.

Laura fell asleep happier than she'd been in a long time. Her last thought was the hope that Esteban was happier too.

Chapter 18

Erin's mind was busy as she caught the bus to work. It was an unusually cold morning, and the bus was packed with hat, scarf and mitten-wearing commuters. Unable to secure a seat, Erin hung onto one of the straps. As the bus stopped, started, and hurtled around corners, she thought about Jack. His girls had arrived in Sydney for the school holidays, and tonight Erin would meet them. Jessica and Talia, both with the same dark-brown hair and clear, guileless faces. Jack had photos of them all over his house, and from the photos and Jack's descriptions, Erin felt she knew the girls at some level already. Meeting them was different, though. It was a significant occasion, not just in relation to Erin and the girls, but because it marked a new, more official milestone in her relationship with Jack.

Jumping off at her stop, Erin nestled deeper into her jacket and walked the remaining distance to work at a leisurely pace. This kind of morning made her feel happy. The pure air and flawless blue sky. Bare, naked trees alongside fat, luxurious evergreens. Her cool face and hands contrasting with the warmth of her body beneath her heavy jacket.

'Excuse me.' A man, wearing a turban and a winter coat

over a white tunic and loose pants, stopped her as she was about to enter the college.

'Yes?' She gave him a friendly smile, assuming that he was a new student and not confident enough to proceed inside. His dark beard had flecks of grey and his eyes had tell-tale crinkles at their corners, but other than that he had a relatively youthful appearance.

'You are Miss Erin?'

Erin smiled more cautiously. How did he know her name? 'Yes, that's me.'

'Fila's teacher?' he asked next.

'You know Fila?'

'I am her father.'

'Oh, nice to meet you.' Erin automatically extended her hand.

He glanced disdainfully at it. 'I am not here for pleasantries.'

Stung, she recoiled her hand. 'How can I help you?' she enquired in her most professional tone.

'You,' he pointed accusingly at her, 'are a bad, wicked influence on my daughter.'

With some effort, Erin dismissed the urge to step backwards from his threatening stance. 'Excuse me?'

'You give her unlimited access to computers, and all the revolting material on them ...'

'As a matter of fact, we have security blocks on our computers, the same as –'

He cut her off. 'Last week, I found out that you had a party here, men and women dancing together.'

'It was not a party,' Erin corrected. 'It was a celebration of –'

'*My daughter did not get home until very late,*' he spat, drowning out her response.

'The celebration ended at eight,' she reasoned, but her voice was quivery instead of firm. 'We were very mindful of our students getting home at a reasonable hour.'

'You are not mindful of anything but your own warped values.' He stepped forward. As she backed up against the wall, Erin's anxiety levels skyrocketed. He was far too close. She had no space to breathe. The hatred in his eyes, the cruel set to his mouth, trapped her every bit as effectively as his physical proximity. Her chest tingled with suggested pain. Oh God, not now, not here.

'You ... *disgust* ... me.'

Don't answer. Don't even listen. Just breathe. The pain isn't *real*.

'What's going on here?' Adam's voice penetrated her terror.

Fila's father stepped away from her.

Adam glanced questioningly at Erin. She couldn't speak. Focus. Name each student, slowly, first names and last names. And breathe ... *breathe* ...

Now Adam was speaking to the Afghan man. 'I will not tolerate you intimidating my staff in this manner.'

'She is the teacher,' Fila's father argued. 'She is the one responsible for filling my daughter's head with inappropriate things.'

Erin should have responded. After all, he was referring to her, unfairly accusing her of leading his daughter astray. But her throat felt choked and full, and she had a horrible feeling that she would cry if she tried to speak. At least the tingling sensation seemed to have eased; whether this was due to Adam's timely arrival or her coping strategies, she wasn't sure.

Adam took Erin's arm and linked it firmly through his own. He had no jacket on, she thought distractedly. He had to be freezing.

'Erin is responsible for teaching a curriculum that has been approved by the Department of Immigration, in consultation with members of your community. In the future, if you have issues with what your daughter is being taught in class, please make an appointment with me.'

The Afghan man snorted. 'An appointment is not necessary. I have said all I need to say. My daughter will not be returning to this college.'

'I'm disappointed to hear that. Fila is a bright and committed student.' Adam ushered Erin towards the door. 'Please wish her the very best of luck for the future.'

Inside the college, Adam guided Erin up the stairs and into his office.

'Sit,' he ordered. 'I'll get you a strong cup of tea.'

Erin did as he instructed, embarrassed that her hands and knees were visibly shaking. Adam squeezed her hand before scurrying away. In his absence, she fought back the tears that were filling up her throat and the backs of her eyes. She would not give that dreadful man the satisfaction of crying. Replaying the scene in her mind, she berated herself for not responding differently, for not suggesting at the outset that he come inside to air his grievances, for not insistently fighting her corner instead of yielding to his louder voice.

Adam returned with two steaming mugs of tea.

'Thanks,' she mumbled without meeting his eyes, mortified that she was still shaking and on the verge of tears, a grown woman who fell to pieces at the slightest confrontation.

Rolling a seat over from the other side of the desk, Adam sat down next to her. 'I know it was upsetting, but try not to let it get to you. Fila's father is feeling threatened, and what happened was because of him, not you.'

'It *was* because of me,' she disputed in a stronger voice, still keeping her eyes down. 'There's something about me that makes people behave like that, something *weak and pathetic* ...'

His hand reached out, raising her chin so he could look her straight in the eye. 'Now listen to me ... There's something gentle and intrinsically kind about you, Erin ... Something that makes your friends and co-workers and students feel warm and valued and lucky to have you in their lives ... Something I would personally like *never* to see changed ...'

Erin shook her head. Adam had no idea that she was the girl who had spent most of her school days trying to make herself invisible. The girl who used to cower against the schoolyard wall at recess, cornered by mockery and jeering. The girl who could never think of a cutting response when she needed one, but came up with dozens of retorts in bed at night, hours too late. It didn't matter that the girl was now a woman, that she was a teacher, a supposed figure of authority instead of a hapless student, or even that she was living in a different country and continent. There would always be something about her, a weakness, an air of displacement, or perhaps inferiority, that stronger individuals could instinctively detect and attack.

'I'm easily frightened,' she tried to explain. 'People sense it.'

'Nonsense,' he replied, refusing to believe her.

Dear Adam. He was the kind and warm one, such a good boss, and becoming a close friend, too. He was committed and scatty, serious and fun, all in one quirky package. And he was consistently obliging and caring, making her tea like this and allowing her to recover in his office when he must have had a thousand pressing matters to attend to.

She sipped the tea and almost gagged. Adam's tea was as awful as his coffee. She really must remember to decline the next time he offered to make her a cup of anything.

This, for some reason, made her smile.

* * * * *

'Are you all right?' Jack whispered in her ear. 'You don't seem to be yourself tonight.'

'Sorry.' She smiled apologetically. 'Something happened at work today, and I just can't seem to get it out of my head.'

'Your turn.' Jack gallantly handed her a luminous pink bowling ball. 'Take your frustrations out on the pins.'

Erin laughed as she slotted her fingers into the holes. 'I haven't played in years.' She ran and released the ball down the lane. It promptly rolled into the channel on the side. 'And clearly I haven't improved at all since I last played!'

Jessica, who was close enough to hear, smiled faintly at Erin's self-deprecating comments. Talia seemed to be more interested in what was going on in the other lanes. Both girls had been polite but reserved over dinner – a shared family-sized pizza in the bowling centre's restaurant. Since emerging into the loud music and noise of the lanes, they seemed slightly more at ease, but still far from enthusiastic about making Erin's acquaintance. Erin didn't want to foist herself upon them, so she maintained a friendly distance. But despite her frequent smiles and gentle attempts at conversation, she was finding the evening quite excruciating. Shaken by what had happened with Fila's father, she would have much preferred to lick her wounds in private than go out. Still, she knew how much this meant to Jack, and hadn't the heart to cancel on him. Poor Jack, he seemed to be the only one who was truly enjoying himself tonight.

With zero points showing next to her name on the board, she sat down next to Jessica and mustered another friendly smile. 'See how hopeless I am? I bet you I'll come last.'

'Usually it's me who comes last,' Jessica revealed, kicking her toe against the ground. 'Talia always beats me. At everything.'

There it was: the lack of confidence that worried Jack so much. Blatant not just in the words she had spoken, but in the hang of her head, the sag of her shoulders, even in the loose, unconvincing way her arms fell by her sides. And though it really wasn't any of Erin's business, she couldn't help feeling an instant affinity with Jack's older daughter. Because everything in life had a pecking order: school, work, families. Jessica, like Erin, felt that she was low down on the pecking order within her own family, and possibly at school too. Instinctively, and with an illogical fierceness, Erin wanted to protect Jack's daughter and build up her self-esteem. Was Jessica happy at school? Did she have enough friends? Was she shrewd enough to float under the radar of the inevitable schoolyard bullies?

Of course it wasn't her place to ask any of these questions.

'What other things do you do when you visit your dad?' she asked instead.

'We go to the city to see the museums and parks,' Jessica replied without enthusiasm.

Jessica got up to take her turn. Though taller and more sturdy than Talia, she was significantly less coordinated. She ran and rolled the ball awkwardly, and both of her attempts ended up in the channel.

'I think we should have our own separate contest to see which of us is worse,' Erin commented when the girl returned to her seat looking disheartened.

Jessica looked away, focusing on something in the far distance. 'Are you going to marry my dad?'

Erin's mouth gaped in surprise. She closed it, and promptly checked Jack's exact whereabouts. He was coaching Talia on how to curve the ball. It seemed she had to field this question without his assistance.

'I don't know him well enough to marry him,' she explained as tactfully as she could. 'Getting to know both of you is part of getting to know him.'

'Does that mean you'll marry him one day?'

'No … I mean, I don't really know …'

'Talia says you're getting married. He's never introduced us to a special friend before.'

Well, that was a rather interesting fact, and went a long way to explaining how ill at ease the girls were feeling.

'I promise you that we have no plans to get married.'

Jessica was visibly reassured.

As the game neared its end, everyone paid particular attention to the results screen.

'Daddy first, me second, Jessica third, Erin last,' Talia announced. 'Erin, your go, but it won't change the overall result.'

Erin rolled the last ball and managed to knock five pins, her best effort of the night.

'Just as I'm starting to get into the swing of it,' she protested, as though the result would have been different if they had played on.

The atmosphere in the car was distinctly lighter as Jack dropped Erin home.

'Thanks,' he murmured, squeezing her hand before she jumped out of the car. 'You were great.'

'No worries. I enjoyed it.'

And she had, at least by the end of the night.

In bed, she had lots to think about before she could fall asleep. Poor Fila, dictated to by her domineering father. Then Jessica: awkward, insecure, forever in Talia's shadow. The two girls had resurrected Erin's own shallowly buried memories of feeling inadequate and second-rate.

A few months into secondary school, Erin had found herself sitting in front of Rachel Murphy in assembly. Still finding her feet at the school, and getting used to the timetable, the teachers and the other girls, when Rachel leant forward to whisper in her ear, Erin assumed she was about to hear something amusing or friendly.

'I hate you,' Rachel had hissed.

Her face burning, Erin sat mutely for the rest of assembly, feeling Rachel's unfathomable contempt envelop her from behind, frantically trying to work out what she'd done to evoke such strong feelings in someone who didn't know her, and until now had not even spoken to her.

The problem with Jessica was that she had a blatant vulnerability that some nasty girl like Rachel could exploit. Lisha, back in St Patrick's, was also beset by that same terrible vulnerability. Erin wanted to shield them both, and every other young girl like them. Because when someone like Rachel Murphy told you that they hated you, those shocking, demeaning words, which took only a couple of moments to utter, could stay in your head forever.

'Jessica and Lisha are young,' mocked an alert, all-too-familiar voice in Erin's head. 'They're still forming their personalities, and they can change. It's too late for you. You'll never be brave. You're pretending, that's all. Jack, Adam and everyone else will eventually see how pathetic and cowardly you are.'

The fear, which had abated since she'd come to Australia, had rediscovered its voice.

No wonder it was back. So many frightening things in just one day. The scene with Fila's father. How close she had come to having a full-blown panic attack afterwards. Then, already feeling vulnerable and off kilter, meeting Jessica and instantly recognising herself in the young girl.

Time to sleep. Let it go. Don't think about any of it. Nothing to be afraid of. Nothing at all. I'm okay, everyone's okay, we're all safe ... Breathe in ... Hold one, two, three ... Breathe out ...

Chapter 19

'What *on earth* are you doing?'

Laura startled at the sound of Esteban's voice. He had been home a few days now, a small respite before another spate of back-to-back trips. She wasn't used to him being in the house, materialising out of nowhere, and it could cause her to jump in fright, like now.

'I'm cleaning,' she replied, privately thinking that standing in the shower cubicle with a cloth and a spray-container of detergent should make it obvious enough.

'Yes, I can see that,' he nodded with feigned gravity. 'What I do not understand is why you have no clothes on? Is this how you clean, these days?'

She grinned rather sheepishly. He was exaggerating, of course. She did have some clothes on: her bra and knickers.

'Only when I'm doing the showers. I ruined my suit with bleach the last time.'

Esteban tilted his head to one side and looked his wife up and down appraisingly. 'I think I like it. Yes, if you must clean incessantly, this attire does make it easier for me to bear ...'

'Oh shut up.' She pointed the spray nozzle in his direction. 'Go away, you funny Spanish man, and let me work in peace.'

Laughing, Esteban retreated from the bathroom. Laura scoured the shower walls until they were gleaming. Then, still in her underwear, she moved onto the guest bathroom where she repeated the process. Though Kasia had offered to clean this bathroom, her efforts thus far had been unimpressive, and everything was in need of a thorough scrubbing.

Laura hummed while she worked. For once, Esteban was home and, in an unusual but very welcome alignment, Kasia happened to be out for the afternoon. This was how her household was meant to be. Laura felt happy and lighter in herself, but then she always felt like that when the Polish girl was not around.

* * * * *

'Esteban?'

'Mmm …' Her husband was engrossed, keeping one eye on the evening news while working on his laptop.

'Esteban, listen …'

He glanced up, his fingers poised over the keys. 'What?'

'Kasia has been taking things,' Laura declared solemnly.

His gaze sharpened. She had his full attention. 'Stealing?'

'Not exactly stealing.' Laura tried to be fair. 'More like helping herself.'

'For example?'

'She's been using my expensive perfume …'

'And how do you know this?'

'Because I put a mark on it, and when I was in the bathroom earlier I noticed that the level had *definitely* dropped.'

Esteban processed the information, his dark eyes narrowing as they always did when he was thinking through something difficult. 'Where was the perfume?' he enquired eventually. 'In the cabinet?'

'Yes.'

His eyes narrowed further. 'Is it not reasonable for her to assume that the perfume was hers to use?'

'No, I don't think so.'

'Cariño, she eats food from our pantry, and drinks juice from our fridge. Why is it unreasonable that she uses the perfume in our bathroom cabinet?'

'It just is,' Laura replied, hating how petulant she sounded.

'We have told her the spare bathroom is for her use, yes? Why would we leave something in there we *didn't* want her to use?'

'It's pretty obvious. Anything that's shut away in the cabinet is out of bounds.'

'Laura, she is from another country, maybe the distinctions are not as clear to her as they are to you. Please, do not be like this.' His tone was gentle, non-accusatory, but still somehow managed to be cutting. 'Kasia does not seem to have many clothes or possessions. Why begrudge her a spray of perfume? It is unlike you to be ungenerous.'

Ungenerous? Laura suddenly felt like crying. When she'd put that mark on the bottle of perfume, she'd been sure she was proving something significant – something that would make Esteban realise that Kasia was untrustworthy and did not belong in their house. But in his eyes, all she had been proving was her own pettiness.

Blinking back tears, Laura went in search of Olivia, needing to bask for a moment in her innocent, nonjudgmental love.

Olivia was in her room, surrounded by a circle of Barbie dolls.

'You've all been very naughty,' she addressed the Barbies sternly, unaware that her mother was watching. 'Carly, you're grounded. JoJo, you have to clean your room as punishment. Bella, you have been the worst! Go to the naughty corner right now.'

'Hello, Floss.' Laura hid a smile. 'What are you up to in here?'

'Playing,' Olivia replied simply, her small fingers dressing a naked Barbie in tennis whites.

'You sound very cross with your Barbies.'

'They've been testing my patience,' Olivia parroted in a tone that sounded very similar to Laura when she was cross.

'Are you their mummy?' Laura asked, kneeling down on the floor.

'No. I'm their auntie.'

'Where's their mummy?'

'She's dead,' Olivia stated sombrely.

'Oh, dear. The poor Barbies. I feel quite sad for them. Any chance of a hug?'

Abandoning her half-dressed doll, Olivia looped her arms around Laura's neck and pressed her small body close. The fact that her daughter didn't hesitate for one moment, that she was prepared to drop the game she had been playing so steadfastly all afternoon, filled Laura with both pride and the warmth she had so badly needed.

'You are a wonderful little girl,' she murmured, kissing Olivia's flyaway hair.

'And you are a wonderful mummy,' Olivia declared.

Laura ran her hand down Olivia's velvety cheek. 'Imagine, in a few weeks' time you'll be five. My baby will be *five years old*. And we're going to have a big party to celebrate.'

Olivia pulled away. 'I don't want a party,' she announced, looking Laura steadily in the eye, as though she were the mother and the one laying down the rules.

'Really?' Laura was taken aback. Didn't every little girl yearn for a birthday party? A day when she could feel special and a little bit spoilt, like a princess? 'Why not, Floss?'

Olivia shrugged, as though her reasons should have been obvious. 'I don't want to be five.'

'What's wrong with being five?' Laura enquired, bemused.

'I don't want to get older.'

'We all get older, Floss. It's part of life.'

'Well, I don't want to die and end up in heaven, like Joe. Nobody even knows if you have TV up there.'

Laura tried to hold back a smile. 'Oh, you don't have to worry about dying for a long, long time, Floss. You'll be very old when you die.'

'How old?'

'At least a hundred,' Laura improvised.

Olivia shrugged, clearly not convinced. 'And I don't want to end up bonkers like Auntie Moira either, and she's only sixty-seven.'

Laura shook her head in amazement. Not only was Olivia obsessed with mortality; she seemed to have formed opinions on mental heath, too. How did she even know Moira's exact age? Laura sighed. If this was Olivia at five, Laura shuddered to think what she'd be like as a teenager. Then again, maybe inertia would set in along with the hormones, and Laura would look back fondly on curious conversations like this one.

'Olivia, Auntie Moira has a disease in her mind, and she can't help being forgetful and a bit confused. Not everyone gets that disease.' Laura reached out and took her daughter's small hand in hers. 'Now, think about it. If you don't get older, then you'll never get married and have babies of your own …'

'I don't *ever* want to be a mummy,' Olivia countered rather fiercely.

Laura was beginning to feel exasperated. 'Why ever not?'

Olivia paused, and her reply seemed all the more clearly enunciated and harsh as result. 'Because I don't want to be busy and worried and tired all the time like *you* are, Mummy.'

With nothing left to say, and feeling ridiculously close to tears, Laura ruffled Olivia's hair before getting to her feet.

Ungenerous. Busy. Worried. Tired. Maybe she was being overly sensitive, but it felt as if Esteban and Olivia didn't even like her today, let alone love her.

Chapter 20

Mel plonked herself down on Erin's couch, swinging her legs, clad in navy skinny jeans, onto the plump cushions. 'Ah, comfort at last. I've been on my feet all day.'

Erin handed her a cup of coffee. 'Here you are, Madam.'

Mel accepted the coffee with a grateful smile. 'Bloody students. Our first day back after the holidays, and already I'm reduced to a headache-inflicted shell of my usual carefree self.'

With her blonde hair gathered in two perky pigtails and her nautical-inspired red and white striped top, Mel looked fresh and youthful, and not at all like the sufferer of a crippling headache. Her white canvas shoes had been left by the door, and Erin wondered idly if Mel had gone to school dressed like this, or if she'd changed after she'd got home.

'Like your jeans,' she remarked.

'Thanks. My Year 12s like them too. They even asked for the name of the online store where I bought them.'

'I didn't know that teachers at Macquarie Grammar School were permitted to wear skinny jeans,' Erin commented in a prim tone.

'It's the first day back after the holidays, and everyone's

trying to ease themselves in, me included,' Mel replied unrepentantly. 'I must say, Sir Jack appeared to be in a particularly good mood today. He was positively beaming from ear to ear.'

'Was he?' Erin couldn't help smiling.

'Yes, indeed he was.' Mel adopted an officious tone. 'So all went well with the offspring?'

'If you mean Jessica and Talia, yes, all went well.'

'So it's all systems go?'

Erin paused. It was scary, putting it like that, as though her and Jack's relationship was now set in stone.

Rather suddenly, she felt like changing the subject.

'I'm thinking of having a party,' she announced. The idea had been circling since she had moved in, but had only voiced itself now.

'Woo-hoo!' Mel swung her legs down off the couch, and sat forward eagerly. 'When, where, who, what ...'

Her excitement was infectious, and Erin laughed as she attempted to reply. 'Sometime in the next few weeks, depending on everyone's availability. Here. You and Jack and some people from work. Cocktails, finger food, that kind of thing.'

'Awesome.' Mel clapped her hands. 'You can put me in charge of cocktails.'

'Absolutely not. Everyone will end up with alcohol poisoning.'

'Music, then.'

'Okay,' Erin agreed, though she suspected that Mel's taste in music would be slightly too juvenile for the people she had in mind. 'Actually, the party will be a good opportunity for you to meet Adam,' she added in what she hoped was a casual tone.

Mel narrowed her baby-blue eyes. 'You're not trying to fix me up with that hyperactive boss of yours, are you?'

'Absolutely not,' Erin assured her, even though that was precisely what she had in mind.

Now that she knew Adam didn't have a girlfriend, she'd decided that he was the perfect man for Mel.

* * * * *

'Jesus, Moira,' Laura exclaimed, walking into a cloud of smoke. '*What* are you doing?'

'Having a ciggie,' Moira replied nonchalantly.

'You don't smoke!'

'Oh, yes, I do.'

'No. You don't.'

'Yes. I do,' Moira returned in the exact same tone as Laura.

They sounded like a two-part act in a pantomime. Laura almost giggled.

She threw open the window, then turned to Moira and held out her hand to help her up. 'If you're going to insist on smoking, I'd better take you outside.'

Moira's back garden had been overgrown and neglected the last time Laura had looked, but today the hedges were trim and the grass freshly mown.

'Someone's been hard at work, I see,' she said approvingly.

'Paddy,' Moira offered between puffs. 'He came around over the weekend with the boys. "Me Tarzan," he said when I opened the door. "Me here to tame jungle." I had to laugh. Fair dues, they worked like troopers. They had a truckload of clippings at the end of the day.'

Like many semi-detached houses of its age, the garden was big in relation to the size of the house. Laura remembered Moira and Joe talking over the years about extending the back kitchen, but it had never happened – presumably because there hadn't been enough money. It was nice, though, to emerge from the confines of the house to this relatively expansive garden. Paddy and the boys had done an impressive job clearing it out. It had indeed been like a jungle, and would have taken a lot of hard graft to restore it to this almost perfect state.

'I'll go in and get you a seat,' Laura said to Moira.

'Don't.' Moira shook her head. 'I'm sick of sitting down. All day long, I sit down. In that stupid room.'

Moira was in an odd, quite rebellious mood, Laura noted.

'Who got you those cigarettes?' she asked.

'The cleaner.' Moira stuck her hand in her cardigan pocket and extracted the smuggled packet, offering it to Laura. 'Want one?'

In university, Laura had been a smoker. Just a few cigarettes a day, little enough to make it relatively easy to give them up when she met Esteban and he told her how disgusting he found the habit.

'Okay, then. You've convinced me.'

Moira also had a lighter in her pocket. Laura would have to speak sternly to the cleaner. Giving a woman with Alzheimer's a lighter was giving her the means to burn down the house, and the cleaner should have known better. Laura slipped the lighter into her jeans pocket rather than returning it to Moira.

She inhaled, the smoke catching in her throat, the taste of it bringing forth a gush of memories from her university days.

'Where's the little one?' Moira tapped some ash onto the grass. 'I haven't seen her in a while.'

'Olivia was sick last week. And her daddy's home this week, a novelty for them both, so I left them curled up together on the couch, deeply enthralled in a princess movie.'

Laura had to give it to Esteban. When he was home, he was endlessly generous to Olivia with his time. Whether it be watching a movie, or taking her to the park, or playing soccer in the garden, he seemed to fit in much more quality time than Laura did.

'Esteban won't be impressed when he smells smoke on me.'

'Joe hates the habit too.' Moira slipped all too readily into the past. 'He thinks the cigarettes are the cause of all the problems.'

Laura took another, measured puff. 'What problems?'

Bitterness and smoke clogged Moira's voice. 'The baby problems.'

Baby problems? Did that mean Joe and Moira had trouble conceiving?

'Nobody told us it was wrong. Young mothers with babies in their bellies and cigarettes in their mouths, ignorant of the dangers … I listened to Joe, though, and I gave them up.' Moira allowed her cigarette to float to the ground, before she stamped on it with a surprising amount of resentment. 'I did everything I could … I stopped at nothing.'

Laura extinguished her own cigarette more gently. So Moira and Joe had had trouble getting pregnant. Funny how no one in the family had mentioned this. It certainly explained how much Moira adored Erin, an intense devotion that Laura remembered noticing even as a child. Moira had obviously suffered through a long, fraught wait for her baby. These flashbacks of hers were fascinating, to say the least, and Laura would love a long chat with her aunt about that time in her life, but the subject always seemed to evoke extreme emotions before Moira rapidly became drained and exhausted, as she was now.

'I think I need to sit down after all,' Moira said, her rebelliousness fizzling away before Laura's eyes.

Laura took her aunt's arm and helped her back inside. Nothing seemed to have any permanence: impulses to smoke, or clean out her wardrobe, or chats about the past or present, nothing lasted more than a few, fleeting minutes.

Back inside the house, Laura vacuumed and dusted the front room, eradicating the last vestiges of smoke.

'Sorry about this, Moira,' she held out her hand, sympathetic yet firm, 'but I'd better take those cigarettes with me …'

Wordlessly, Moira surrendered the packet.

Laura kissed her aunt's cheek. 'I promise I'll bring Olivia next time.'

In what seemed to be becoming a pattern, Laura left Moira's house feeling more effective and fundamentally more at peace than she'd felt when she arrived.

Chapter 21

To: *Erin* <Erin.Donovan@yahoo.com>

From: *Fila Azizi* <Fila.Azizi@gmail.com>

Dear Miss Erin,

I sincerely apologise for my father. I fear he has been very rude to you. He is very inconsistent. One minute, he wants me to be educated, have a job and be a modern woman, but then he gets scared by what that means (my independence from him) and goes back to his traditional views again. He knows that the traditional ways are wrong when it comes to how women are treated, yet when he is feeling insecure he seems to cling to them. It's fortunate that I understand him better than he understands himself. I know I'll be able to talk him around and that he'll eventually allow me to return to college. Until then, perhaps you could send some class notes to this email address, which I can access from the local public library.

In case you are wondering about the perfect English in this letter, a friend helped me write it (I didn't want my language limitations to compromise my apology in any way).

I am sorry again for my father. I hope you can understand that he is a good man at heart.

Yours sincerely,

Fila

181

To: *Laura* <Laura.Torres@globaltranslation.com>

From: *Erin* <Erin.Donovan@yahoo.com>

Hello stranger. Haven't heard from you in a while. I presume it's because you are as chaotically busy as ever? All is well here. Work is good, except for a small incident with the father of one of my students. Actually, it didn't feel like a small incident at the time – it was very upsetting. Of course, I handled it all the wrong way. Will I ever learn to speak up for myself? Things are still going remarkably well with Jack. I keep expecting it all to end, but somehow it hasn't. I've met his daughters, so I guess that means things are getting serious. Jessica and I already have a good rapport. Talia is more aloof, but I think that's just her personality (hopefully, it's not me!!!). How is Mum this week? I talked to her on the phone yesterday and she seemed very vague, as though I were some distant acquaintance and not her daughter. How has she been with you? I know you are busy, so I won't go on and on, but do let me know what you think about Mum when you have the chance to reply.

XX Erin

To: *Erin* <Erin.Donovan@yahoo.com>

From: *Laura* <Laura.Torres@globaltranslation.com>

Hi Erin. Sorry for the long silence. Yes, things are as chaotic as ever. Something obviously has to give – I just don't know what! Your mother has been more vague and disoriented the last few weeks. She has mistaken me for Cathy a few times now, and talks as though we're in Paris and not plain old Dublin. I caught her smoking, too. The cleaner gave her the cigarettes and – can you believe this? – a lighter. I wanted to sack her on the spot, but Gerry convinced me to give her a second chance.

Even though we take it in turns to bring Moira a cooked dinner in the evenings, she does occasionally get it into her head to cook herself, and I do worry that on one of these occasions she'll forget to turn off the pan when she's done. What can you do but just hope and pray that such a thing won't happen? She seems so happy and content in her own surroundings, it would be tragic to move her to a home where she'd have no memories of you or Joe. I think we all know that will have to happen eventually, but hopefully it's still a long way off.

Sorry, I have to fly. Savita is rapping on my window and looking very cross. Oh dear ... we must have had a meeting booked ...

Take care and talk soon,

Laura

Dear Erin,

Hello again from Lisha. I have found a job. It is not the kind of job I wanted, but Mother says it's the kind of job I can expect without a proper education (she is still very annoyed with me). Do you remember the butchers at the corner of Chapel Street, the one with the really fat owner? That's where I work now. The fat man is my boss. He is very nice to me and patient as I learn the ropes. I try not to stare at the blood in his nails and streaked across his white coat. When I am more settled in, I will advise him that white is not the best colour to wear in a place like this.

I hope you do not mind me keeping in contact. Perhaps you have moved on with your life and cannot even remember what I look like.

Yours faithfully,

Lisha

Hey Jessica,

Thanks for looking me up on Facebook. I'm glad that we're now friends. Have a good day at school.

Erin

183

Hi Erin,

There is no such thing as 'a good day at school'. I don't like my teacher, and most of the other kids think I'm a bit weird. Not that I care what they think. Not really.

Counting you and Mum and Dad, I now have a total of 23 friends on Facebook. Talia has 187.

XX Jessica

Dear Erin,

Thank you for the lovely letter, and all the photographs. Laura has put the snaps in an album for me, and when you see them one after the other they tell a story. Seeing how you have changed over the months reminds me of how I changed in Paris, the initial feeling of not belonging, and then gradually relaxing into the city. Some days I worry that you won't come home at all. I know that's how I felt. My concentration isn't good and so I can only write a few lines.

Love always,

Mum

Hi Erin,

Have some tickets for Rugby League on Saturday night. Should provide a fascinating insight into Australian culture. Are you interested?

Let me know,

Adam

Sorry, Adam. Always keen to learn about Australian culture, but already have plans for Saturday night. Make sure you keep the following Saturday free. I'm having a party. Further details to follow,

Cheers,

Erin

Chapter 22

As Erin uncorked a bottle of French champagne (Fizz had succeeded in making her believe that only the best would do when it came to bubbles), she heard Lady Gaga burst from the speakers. Whoa, that was a bit too loud. Emerging from the kitchen, she found Mel – the most obvious culprit – chatting to Thu, Zelda and Maria from the childcare centre. Adam and Jack were engaging in what appeared to be an on-off conversation, and Fizz and Lydia were floating around with trays of food. Nobody seemed the slightest bit fazed by the blaring music. Erin topped up everyone's glass, then positioned herself next to the men.

'Anything I can do to help?' Jack asked, leaning close so she could hear him.

'No thanks.' She smiled in Fizz's direction. 'I've hardly had to lift a finger myself.'

Adam followed her gaze and grinned. 'Once she stops force-feeding us those sausage rolls, I can see her dancing on the tables.'

Erin laughed. 'Well it takes one to know one, Adam.'

As she sipped her drink, she felt Jack's arm curl around her waist, and she looked up in time to catch the fleeting look of surprise on Adam's face. Of course he didn't know they were a couple; Jack's name hadn't come up in any of their conversations at work.

'Have you had the chance to speak to Lydia, Jack?'

'Not yet.'

She unfurled his arm. 'Come on.' She threw Adam a quick smile. 'Back in a minute.'

Jack and Lydia were both so passionate about literacy and education, Erin knew they would get along like a house on fire, which would leave Erin free to concentrate on getting Adam and Mel, currently on opposite sides of the room, together.

Lydia, having returned her tray of food to the kitchen, was now enjoying a glass of red wine. 'Jack,' she beamed. 'I was hoping to get the chance to talk to you.'

Within minutes, Jack and Lydia were engaged in a very detailed discussion about literacy impediments and the associated social and psychological consequences. The only problem was that Jack's arm was back around Erin's waist, making it difficult for her to slip away. By the time she felt she could politely extract herself, she discovered that Adam had found Mel off his own bat. They were talking. In fact, they looked as though they were having quite an animated discussion. Now they were laughing. Excellent. Erin smiled to herself. She'd been right in thinking that they were a good match. In a few years' time, gathered around a dinner table for some occasion or other, they would all fondly look back to this moment in time and say, 'Remember the night Adam and Mel met ...'

'I need to make a cameo appearance in the kitchen,' she announced to Lydia and Jack, and darted away before either of them took it into their heads to follow.

The kitchen was remarkably neat, with food platters washed, dried and stacked neatly on the counter: Fizz. Erin popped some chicken skewers in the oven, opened a second bottle of champagne and departed on another mission to top up drinks.

The next couple of hours passed in a whirl of laughter and loud music and, on Erin's part, a few too many glasses of bubbly. She surrendered fully to the warmth and noise around her, forgetting temporarily about the food – thankfully, Fizz rescued the chicken skewers from the oven.

At one point, Jack appeared by her side, looking apologetic. 'I have to go soon.'

'It's still early.' She frowned at him.

'I have a school commitment first thing in the morning.'

He was sober, she realised. While she had been drinking too much, Jack had hardly been drinking at all.

'Oh … You didn't say …'

'Sorry, I should have mentioned it.'

'Yes, you should have.'

Quite suddenly she felt very cross with him. So what if he had something on in the morning, something that obviously required him to be alert and not suffering the effects of a big night out. She'd told him about this party *weeks* ago: he should have tried to wheedle out of whatever commitment it was.

Jack said his goodbyes to everyone, and then Erin saw him to the door.

'I'll call you tomorrow.' He tried to kiss her. She turned her head away.

'I'm not happy with you,' she informed him.

'I know.' He pulled a face. 'I'm sorry. Have fun.'

Erin turned back to the party, which had lost some of its glow. She hadn't been expecting too much of Jack, only that he would get to know her work colleagues, enjoy himself, and *stay*. She was disappointed in him. And embarrassed, too. Her own boyfriend had been the first guest to leave her party!

'Have a caramel square, dear.' Fizz appeared, bearing yet another tray. She had been alternately serving and clearing up all night.

'Thank you.' Erin popped the bite-sized caramel and chocolate in her mouth, and the sugar hit restored some of her wellbeing. 'And thanks for everything you did tonight, Fizz. I feel quite guilty that you've had no time to relax and enjoy yourself.'

'This *is* me enjoying myself,' Fizz stressed. 'Being around people, feeding them, taking care of them, is what I enjoy the most. I'm so happy to be here – thank you *so much* for inviting me.'

Fizz's warmth and loveliness and sheer delight at being invited to the occasion helped Erin overcome her annoyance with Jack. She turned the music up another notch (had someone turned it down while she'd been arguing with Jack?), filled her glass again, and was dancing with Thu when Mel came over an indeterminable while later.

'Mel!' Erin turned excitedly towards her friend; she felt as though she'd hardly spoken to her all night. 'Well, how's Adam?' she asked in an urgent whisper. 'Do you like him?'

Mel shrugged. 'He's all right.'

'Only "all right"?' Erin queried.

'Yes.'

Erin felt stunned. 'Are you saying you don't like him?'

'I do like him. But not in that way.'

'God, Mel,' Erin spluttered. 'You are *impossible* to please. Adam is *lovely*. He's funny and kind and …' Noticing Mel glance in the direction of the door, Erin was suddenly suspicious. 'Don't tell me you're going home, too.'

Mel flashed a guilty smile. 'It's almost midnight.'

'Since when were you Cinderella?'

'Look, Erin, I've had enough to drink and I'm ready to go.'

'Then have some water and stay – I was counting on you being here until the sad and sorry end.'

'I don't want to stay!' Mel was beginning to sound like a rather truculent child.

'Why?' asked Erin exasperatedly.

'I feel awkward …'

'Awkward? Because of Adam?'

'Not just Adam … I don't have anything in common with the others.' Mel's eyes latched onto Lydia and Fizz, who were standing by the kitchen doorway and laughing about something. 'To be honest, the demographic is a bit old for me.'

Erin said nothing for a while, anger burgeoning and rendering her speechless. 'Go,' she managed, marching towards the door and opening it with a flourish. 'Go.'

'Sorry.' Mel attempted to apologise. 'That came out wrong –'

'Just go, Mel.'

Mel, looking extremely sheepish, did as she was told, and Erin shut the door after her a little too vigorously. Conversation stopped, the music sounding tinny without the underlying hum of voices. Conscious of everyone's eyes on her, she summoned a bright smile as she recovered her glass from where she'd left it, and took a long gulp. Jack had been a stick-in-the mud tonight, and Mel was being downright ageist. Erin was furious – no, furious was too mild a word – she was *livid* with them both.

Lydia came over and hooked her arm around Erin's waist. 'Okay, darling?'

Erin was a number of things at that precise moment – angry, disappointed, embarrassed – none of which qualified as 'okay'.

'Sorry, I shouldn't have slammed the door like that.'

'In my opinion, a slammed door adds a nice, dramatic touch to an occasion.'

'True.' Erin smiled ruefully.

Lydia squeezed her waist. 'And you're welcome to slam the door when I leave in the minute. In fact, I'd be disappointed now if you didn't!'

'Oh no, Lydia,' Erin wailed. 'Not you, too.'

'I'm afraid so. Thu is our designated driver. She has to get back to her babysitter, and I'm grateful for the lift.'

'Okay,' Erin sighed. Some party this was turning out to be. 'Permission reluctantly granted. You're all officially allowed to leave.'

'Good girl. Now, where did I put my jacket?'

'It's in the bedroom, I'll get it for you.'

In the semi-darkness of her room, Erin gathered up the jackets from where they lay on her bed, feeling utterly deflated. Midnight, and her party was over. Not one person to stay back and have a quiet drink with, no one to dissect the night and laugh over the funny parts with. Suddenly, out of nowhere, images from parties in her mother's house filled her head, images from a long, long time ago, before her father fell ill and her mother lost her grasp on reality: Cathy dancing unsteadily in high heels, Paddy singing ballads in the corner, Gerry collecting empty glasses. She remembered the time her mother and father gave up trying to wind up the party and retired to bed in the early hours of the morning, leaving a roomful of people downstairs. Ignoring a sudden, surprising surge of homesickness, Erin went back to where her guests were waiting to depart.

'Bye, Thu. Thanks for coming, drive carefully. See you on Monday, Fran ... Fizz, Lydia will walk you down on her way ... No, there's no more cleaning up to do, my kitchen is gleaming, thanks to you ...'

As they made their way noisily down the stairs, Erin turned to Adam, the last one left. 'Are you squashing into Thu's car, too?'

'Not unless Lydia is willing to sit me on her knee.' He grinned. 'Thu's car, or should I say minibus, is at full capacity. Anyway, I'd be dragging her out of her way.'

'Should I ...' Erin began to ask if he would like her to call him a cab, but for some reason she didn't finish the sentence. Instead, she heard herself ask, plead, 'Please don't go just yet, Adam. Stay a while.'

His eyes met hers, and for a few moments it felt as though he could see everything: her disappointment with Jack and Mel, that flash of homesickness in the bedroom, and all her other insecurities.

He closed the door. 'Sit down, Erin. I'll get you a drink.'

While he was in the kitchen, Erin changed the music to something softer. Then she slipped off her shoes, flexed her toes, and curled her legs beneath her on the couch. This was what she had envisaged at the start of the night, sitting down and having a last drink while musing over every small detail of the evening. But instead of Mel and Jack, it was Adam who had stayed back with her.

He emerged from the kitchen juggling a bottle of beer, a glass of wine, and a tumbler of water, handing the latter to her first.

'I'm thinking of your head in the morning,' he explained.

'Good point.' She smiled gratefully, and drank back most of the water in one go.

He leant back into the cushions. 'Ahh. This could get a bit too comfortable.'

For a while they were both silent. She sipped her wine, and he drank his beer. It struck Erin that she had never seen him so quiet, or so still. At work, he was always on the move, running from one place to the next. Even when sitting at his desk, he was prone to fidgeting and swinging on his chair. This stillness was something new to her. Was this what he was like at home, when he was alone?

She took another sip of wine, and then cast him a sideways glance. 'So, how did you and Mel get along?'

He blinked, as though surprised by the question. 'Fine. Why?'

Erin held back a smile. 'Oh, I thought you two might make a good couple.' She waited for him to respond. When he didn't, she was forced to prompt, 'So, did you like her?'

'Mel?' He sat forward a little. 'She's all right.'

Funny, that was exactly how Mel had described Adam: 'all right'. Maybe they were both being coy, covering up the fact that they did indeed like each other. Maybe, despite her assertions otherwise, a strong attraction to Adam had made Mel feel so awkward that she'd left early?

'Any chemistry at all?' Erin pressed, testing out this possibility. 'Not even the slightest frisson?'

'No, and no.' Adam was quite definite. 'I don't think I'm her type, and she's not mine.'

Erin grinned philosophically. 'Oh, well, so much for that … Incidentally, what is your type, Adam? Just for the record …'

He laughed. 'Well, if Jennifer Aniston were single …'

Erin shook her head. 'No movie stars allowed! Or supermodels.'

He laughed again, but didn't seem inclined to provide any further guidelines on his perfect woman.

'Well?' Erin prompted again.

'The quintessential girl next door,' he supplied eventually, along with a self-conscious shrug. 'Someone who is fun and kind, and not obsessed with clothes or how she looks. Someone who likes people and family, because that's what life is about for me. I'm a pretty simple bloke, really.'

Erin nodded approvingly. She liked his 'type'. 'That's very helpful. If I come across such a girl …'

He rolled his eyes, and they shared a smile before falling back into a comfortable silence.

'What about Jack?' he asked sometime later.

Now it was Erin's turn to be coy. 'What about Jack?'

'Are you two serious?'

'Yes. At least I thought so.' She sighed. 'As you probably noticed, I was pretty annoyed when he left tonight. Maybe this is the phase when we discover all the not-so-wonderful things about each other.'

Adam smiled wryly. 'In a few days' time you'll both be able to laugh about it and put it down as your first fight.'

Erin wasn't sure. Did it even qualify as a 'fight'? Perhaps it would have been more satisfying if they'd had a real shouting match. Then again, she wasn't the sort of person who went around having shouting matches, and she suspected Jack wasn't either.

Adam seemed to read her mind. 'You're not much of a fighter, are you?'

She smiled. 'No, I'm not. I'm terrible at any kind of confrontation . . . And I think I've already told you how easily frightened I am ... Anyway, we were talking about Jack ... I made a huge effort with his daughters, Adam. I don't want him thinking that our relationship is one-way, with his family and friends and work commitments being the main focus and mine a mere inconvenience.'

Erin was surprised at the vehemence in her voice.

Fearing that Jack's ears must have been burning as he slept, she changed the subject and spoke instead about her mother and the impossible situation at home. Then Adam told her about his mum, and his brothers and sisters and the army of nieces and nephews, all under her steely command.

'Mum swims and walks every day, and gardens in between all the grandchildren-related commitments: awards at assembly, reading groups in class, soccer and netball and rugby matches at the weekends, Mum is always there. Actually, she's very competitive, and can be embarrassingly loud on the sidelines.'

Listening to him, Erin felt an ache for her own mother, all the things she could and should have been, but wasn't. Walking, swimming, gardening, grandchildren: none of the above.

'I should go,' Adam yawned.

But as they both contemplated getting up from the couch, another conversation began, and then another. The sky outside began to change colour, grey infusing the black. Birds squawked, waking up in bursts of noise. The predawn cold infiltrated the warmth of their conversation. Erin shivered.

'I didn't realise this party was going to be an all night one,' Adam mumbled, and Erin realised that he was half-asleep.

'Neither did I.' Quite suddenly, tiredness had crept up on her, too. 'You can sleep here,' she decided. 'I'll get you a blanket.'

With a great deal of effort, she peeled herself off the couch. She gazed blankly into her linen cupboard for a few moments before realising she had no such 'blanket': her bed linen was minimal. She hadn't been in the apartment long enough to accumulate spares. Her head foggy with sleep, she stumbled into the bedroom and heaved the duvet from her bed. Stretching it across Adam, she surveyed him with bleary fondness, his ruffled fair hair, the stillness of him half-sitting, half-lying there, a stillness she would smile about on Monday as she watched him bounce around the college. Then, because it seemed like the only sensible option, she climbed under the duvet next to him, and promptly fell asleep.

Chapter 23

Laura hadn't been spying; she'd come across the message purely by accident. In fact, Kasia's carelessness had caused it: her carelessness in not switching off the computer, and her further negligence in leaving the message open, so that when Laura pressed ESCAPE to get rid of the screen saver and log off, there it was: a black and white testament to what Kasia thought of them all.

Hi Tomasz,

I have sent some money. It should be in your depleted bank account in a few days. I must be crazy, funding your social life like this. Please be sensible and keep some of the money for your textbooks. I regret to confirm that I am still captive to the Wicked Witch of the West (let's say WWW for short) ...

Laura had read to the end of the sentence before it dawned on her that *she* was the 'wicked witch' referred to in the message. Sucking in her breath, she rolled out the office chair so she could sit while she read the rest of the message.

She is very controlling, and wants to know exactly what Olivia and I are doing every minute of the day. When I eat in the kitchen, or when

I turn on the television or radio, she adopts this critical, distasteful expression. Really, Tomasz, that expression of hers makes me want to walk straight out the door ...

Laura completely forgot that she had been shutting down the house for the night, and that she still had to check that the doors were locked downstairs and the appliances switched off. She forgot everything but the message in front of her, a message that evoked so many strong feelings, she couldn't yet begin to categorise them.

Seriously, I will explode if she suggests one more time that I go to the park with Olivia. What is her obsession with the park? Does she not realise that most days it is too cold and wet to walk there, and that the play equipment is far too young for Olivia's age anyway? Olivia prefers to go to the shopping centre, or put on ballet shows for her dolls. Laura does not know her daughter, but then how could she? She spends all her time at work. Even when she is home, she is still working ... work, work, work ... It is no surprise that she is so uptight. It's funny, Tomasz, but this situation makes me appreciate Mama. She may fuss and nag and fuss and nag, but she has always been there for us ...

Amidst all of Laura's conflicting feelings, fury surged to the fore. How dare you, she muttered. *How dare you suggest that I don't know my own daughter and what's best for her. How dare you use my computer to slag me off like this.* Laura and Esteban mainly used their work laptops for their home computing needs, and the upstairs computer lay largely unused. Of course Laura had mentioned to Kasia that she was welcome to use it, as she was welcome to use everything else in the house. But to think that she was using it in this manner, to facilitate these attacking, degrading, unfair statements about Laura herself, made a mockery of their generosity.

She thinks that I am stupid, Tomasz, that I don't see how poorly she regards me, and how much she hates having me in her house. I have a degree in marketing and management. I am clever enough to tell what she is thinking, and much, much more ... Anyway, enough about

WWW. Too much negative energy, as Oprah says (I watch reruns of her show every day).

There is some good news. I have met a boy – a nice Polish boy – but you are not to tell Mama. I see him many nights of the week. If it wasn't for him, I would go totally insane …

Although Kasia's rant was clearly over, Laura nevertheless read to the end of the message, and then proceeded to read some of the other messages in the SENT box, which added to the overall picture: how much Kasia disliked her job, and detested Laura. Interestingly, she did have nice things to say about Olivia and Esteban, which made her hatred of Laura all the more personal and unjust.

Olivia, the little girl, is extremely polite and grown up. It's easy to mind such a sensible girl – to be honest, she doesn't need me very much. Esteban is very kind to me. Whenever he is home, he always takes time to chat, not just issue instructions. If it were just Olivia and Esteban in the house, I would not mind this job while I wait for something better. Esteban understands that this nanny role is a stepping stone for me, a start in these difficult economic conditions, but Laura regards it as my long-term career, and considers me unworthy of it, without even taking into account my education and qualifications. She is so self-centred, so unable to understand anything outside her own world. And she is such a control freak, everything has to be just so. I do not know how Esteban can stand her …

Laura switched off the computer. She locked the doors downstairs, checked the appliances, and got ready for bed. It was a good thing Kasia was out tonight, because if she'd been home Laura would not have been able to resist a confrontation. This way she had some time, and thinking space, to consider how best to remove the girl from their house and their lives. Good, too, that Esteban was away. He would try to mediate; it was how he was wired. Sadly, there was no way to mediate or resolve this situation. Kasia had to go. Tomorrow, after a night's sleep and the chance to rally herself, Laura would give the nanny her notice.

* * * * *

'Mummy, you're *here*.' There was wonder in Olivia's voice as she bounced on the bed.

Laura blinked her eyes, disoriented, before she realised that Olivia's presence meant she was late. Very late, in fact. She always left the house long before Olivia woke. Damn. She must have forgotten to set the alarm on her phone last night. Black, printed words flashed into her head, words from Kasia's messages, harsh, judgmental, jarring her from the last vestiges of sleep. She blinked again, wiping them out. She would process those words throughout the day. Right now, she urgently needed to get to work.

Work, work, work … Kasia's voice echoed mockingly in her head as she threw back the covers.

After kissing Olivia's brow, taking a record-fast shower and throwing on her most comfortable business suit, Laura went downstairs. She found Kasia in the kitchen, munching on toast topped with a mound of marmalade. Recalling last night's message once again, Laura consciously set her expression to neutral.

'Good morning.'

Kasia nodded in reply to Laura's greeting, her face contorting as she chewed.

'Are you expecting to be home tonight, Kasia?'

'I can be,' the Polish girl replied after swallowing a mouthful of toast. 'If you wish.'

'Yes, please …' Laura paused, still formulating in her head how much to say at this point. 'I'd like to talk to you alone, when Olivia has gone to bed … Well, I'm late now, so I'd better run. I'll try to get home early tonight. We'll talk then.'

Olivia trailed her mother to the door and Laura crouched down to give her a hurried hug.

'See you later, Floss. Have a lovely day.'

'Yes, Mum,' Olivia responded obediently.

Laura straightened and opened the front door. As an afterthought, she stopped to ask, 'Olivia, do you like going to the park?'

Olivia shook her head.

'Why not?'

'The slides are too small for me. Everything there is too babyish.'

Laura smiled sadly. 'Silly me. I didn't realise you had got too big for it.'

Olivia giggled. 'You're a silly billy mummy.'

Laura stooped to hug her again, before closing the door from the outside.

So Kasia had been right about one thing – the park – but that certainly didn't mean that all her other gripes and opinions had any basis. Far from it.

* * * * *

As usual, the demands of the working day wiped everything else from Laura's mind. Though she had fully intended to devote some thinking time to Kasia, it was only when she sat back in her car, some ten hours later, that she could begin to contemplate how their conversation might go. She would give Kasia three weeks' notice, she decided. More than enough time to find alternative accommodation and employment. If Laura had been a true 'witch', as Kasia so liked to describe her, she would give Kasia no notice at all, but even though she felt angry and betrayed, she would not be able to live with herself if she virtually threw Kasia out on the street.

Soft summer rain speckled the windscreen. Laura resisted the urge to flick on the wipers, playing a waiting game to see how long her vision could prevail over the gathering drops. On the whole, the summer had been wet and disappointing.

Schoolchildren, their summer holidays already half over, had nothing more than a handful of sunny days to look back on. Four weeks to go until Olivia started school. Less than two weeks to her birthday. Time was such a strange concept: sometimes it flew – your baby became a little girl in the blink of an eye, your business morphed from an amateurish start-up to a fully blown enterprise in a blur, one's life changed drastically without one even noticing. On the other hand, a simple half-hour commute, a tedious meeting, or even a pause in conversation, could seem endless. Even though she was hurtling towards Olivia's first day at school, which meant big decisions and changes to routine, Laura felt too bogged down to plan appropriately even for tomorrow. And the unpalatable truth was that firing Kasia would make Laura even more bogged down and helpless, limiting her options considerably.

Her phone rang. God, she never had a moment's peace, not even when she was driving. Irritably, she pressed the answer button.

'Laura? It's Gerry.' Her uncle's voice boomed through the speakers. Laura swiftly turned down the volume.

'Hello, Gerry.' Instantly, her mood lightened. Kind, obliging, contagiously cheerful, Gerry was the one person in Laura's life who didn't make demands of her. And so she was rather stunned when he said, 'Laura, I *hate* to ask, but I need a favour …'

'What is it?'

'Aidan has smashed my car, the eejit, and I've no wheels to get over to Moira this evening.'

'Is he all right?' Even though her youngest cousin was exasperating, unreliable and routinely irresponsible, Laura was fond of him, and would hate to think that he had hurt himself, or anyone else.

'Nothing injured but his pride,' Gerry replied dryly, 'and his bank balance by the time he's paid the excess on the insurance. Listen, Laura, I know you've probably had a long day, but would you be able to pick up my shift with Moira this evening?'

'Of course I can,' she assured him quickly. 'You know, Esteban's car is sitting in our garage, Gerry, and you're more than welcome to take it. I know Esteban would prefer it to have a run than be parked there all week while he's away.'

'I might take you up on that offer, love.'

Laura hung up from Gerry and put a call through to home. Kasia answered, sounding as hostile as ever.

'I have to drop over to see my aunt unexpectedly. Would you mind going ahead with Olivia's dinner and settling her down to bed?'

'I thought you were coming home early.'

'So did I.'

'You still want to talk to me?'

Laura sighed with frustration. She had really wanted to get their 'talk' over and done with, but now – having just asked a favour of Kasia – the timing no longer felt right. 'It can keep until another night.'

At the next intersection, Laura did a U-turn and headed in the direction of Moira's house. The rain fell faster and thicker, blurring the windscreen and her vision. Finally, she relented and flicked on the wipers.

* * * * *

'This is a poor excuse for a summer,' Laura stated, shaking the raindrops from her hair.

'It's always this way.' Moira smiled rather nostalgically, glancing towards the window as she spoke. 'I don't know why we expect any different.'

Laura shivered. Her top was damp, too.

Moira smiled again. 'Put on the kettle, love. That will warm you.'

Laura proceeded to the kitchen, where she filled the kettle and set two cups next to it.

'Aidan crashed the car,' she announced, standing in the doorway to the living room, the kettle humming behind her.

Moira looked confused. 'Which one is Aidan again?'

'He's Gerry's youngest. You know, the one who got suspended from school three times, and who was caught shoplifting on Grafton Street. Now he has a car crash to add to his list of accomplishments!'

'Was anyone hurt?'

'No.'

'Well, that's all that matters,' Moira said simply.

Laura went back to the kitchen, popping tea bags in the cups before filling them with boiling water.

'Here you are.' She set down Moira's cup on the small table next to her armchair. As Laura straightened, a photo on the mantelpiece caught her eye. It was unframed, and was propped against one of the other photo frames. The photo was of Erin, standing amidst a group of beaming people – work colleagues? – whom Laura didn't recognise. She picked it up for a closer look.

'This is new,' she said to Moira.

'What?' Moira had been gazing out the window at the rain.

Laura showed her the photo. 'It's new. I haven't seen it before. Isn't it strange not to know who these people are?'

Moira stared at the photo. In fact, she was staring so hard that Laura felt it would be rude to take it away. 'She's beautiful, isn't she?' she said finally, her voice so faint that Laura could barely hear.

'Yes, she is.' Erin *was* beautiful, Laura thought, now staring every bit as intently as Moira. She always moaned about her hair having no body, her face being too round, and her mouth too small. Her own worst critic, she never stepped back to see the overall effect. Her mouth, when it smiled, wasn't small at all. Her glossy, almost-black hair was a dramatic backdrop for her luminous eyes, which were such a stunning feature that all her other supposed shortcomings faded into nothing.

'She has Julien's eyes.'

Laura startled. 'Sorry?'

Moira looked up, her expression sombre. 'She has Julien's eyes,' she repeated with conviction.

Laura almost forgot to breathe. 'Who's Julien?'

Moira frowned at her. 'Don't act stupid, Cathy. It's annoying.'

'I'm not Cath –'

'Stop,' Moira raised her voice. 'Just stop.'

Moira was so agitated that Laura dropped the subject and returned the photo to the mantelpiece. Rather ironically, the frame it had been propped against held an old photo of Moira and Cathy, a photo that had been on Moira's mantelpiece for as long as Laura could recall, and one she had always particularly liked because it seemed such a happy snapshot. Two young women, sisters, heads touching, smiles lighting up their faces, a carefree breeze tousling their waist-length hair: Moira, clearly older, her clothes slightly more sensible, a few tiny crinkles at the corners of her eyes, but with a smile that transcended them; Cathy by her side, wearing a chic, loosely knitted hat and scarf, beaming with excitement; and in the background the Eiffel Tower, soaring into the pale blue sky, a towering testament to the fact that these women lived a different life – an exotic, foreign life – before they returned to the ordinary Dublin suburb that had remained their home ever since.

Who the hell was Julien, and how did he fit into that picture?

Chapter 24

The Monday morning after her party, Erin walked into her classroom and found her students clustered around Fila, welcoming her back with a flurry of hugs, smiles and exclamations in broken English.

'You're back!' Erin stated, coming forward to impart a heartfelt hug of her own.

'Yes.' Fila grinned delightedly. 'Here I am. Ready to learn and be top of your class once again.'

Everyone laughed at her cheekiness. Their laughter was a milestone, though nobody but Erin would have known it.

Until now, her students had lacked a sufficient grasp of the language to manage humour. It was the only thing she missed about her old job at St Patrick's: the droll remarks by Tristan, the giggling girls, the underlying humour even on the dreariest and most hopeless days.

Now Fila had not only managed to make a joke, but the entire class had understood it.

'Okay, everyone. Back to your seats, and let's see if Fila is as smart as she thinks she is.'

Erin's quip earned another round of laughter.

Erin then led a discussion about education and schools,

writing important words and phrases on the whiteboard. As usual, time flew by. In fact, Erin was startled when she heard the bell for recess. Was it that time already? The class departed en masse for the canteen, Erin following them after she had wiped the board clean and spent a few minutes unnecessarily tidying her desk. It was rather silly, but she felt mildly apprehensive about seeing Adam after Saturday night. Nothing had happened between them – it had been completely innocent – but had she not been so drunk she would have realised that it was not a good idea to sleep under the same duvet as one's boss. Midmorning on Sunday, the doorbell had woken them both. Disoriented and dishevelled, and still in yesterday's clothes, Erin had opened the door to a delivery boy thrusting an enormous bouquet of flowers under her nose.

'Delivery for Erin Donovan.'

Erin didn't need to read the sealed envelope to figure out who the flowers were from: Jack. She knew she was being churlish, but the ill-timed delivery was annoying. Jack should have known that she was still sleeping, and it was plain rude to wake someone up, even if it was to apologise for one's behaviour with an obnoxiously large bunch of flowers.

Adam, who had swung into an upright position while she was taking delivery of the flowers, seemed every bit as embarrassed and vulnerable as Erin.

'I'd better get going,' he mumbled, trying, in vain, to flatten his hair with his hand.

'Have a coffee first.' She moved to the kitchen before Adam could say no, dumping the bouquet in the sink.

At first, the smell from the flowers seemed to overpower any conversation. Adam drank his coffee and Erin went about her normal morning routine, which involved having a pint glass of cooled boiled water with her vitamins before allowing herself any caffeine.

'Why are you popping all those pills?' Adam asked, watching closely as she swallowed back one after another.

'To nourish my brain,' she replied between gulps.

'Really? How?'

'The Omega-3 stimulates brain function and increases memory,' Erin told him in a bouncy, informative tone. 'Vitamin E is an anti-oxidant and helps protect cells from damage. Ginkgo is good for the circulatory system and promoting alertness and clarity. The B vitamins are important for the overall health of the brain.' She sounded remarkably like a radio commercial.

He wasn't sold. 'That's a lot of pills you're taking. Are you sure you need all of them?'

'With my family history, yes.' Their eyes locked. 'I'm scared of many things, Adam – confrontation, change, certain social situations, to name but a few … But the thing I am the most *petrified* of is losing my memory and ending up like my mother.'

'I didn't know that Alzheimer's was hereditary …'

'Research indicates that early-onset can be.' She shrugged as though it was an off-chance only, when everything she'd read on the subject indicated that the statistics were higher than that.

'And you think these vitamins will help?' he asked carefully.

'Yes, along with a good diet and frequent brain workouts.'

He smiled briefly. 'Brain workouts?'

'Puzzles, crosswords, brainteasers,' she informed him. 'It's important to give the brain as much of a workout as you give your body.'

He didn't ask any further questions. A short while later, he stood up and said he needed to get going.

He kissed her affectionately on the cheek. 'Thanks for the party and the coffee and all the brain information.'

Now Erin scanned the overcrowded kitchen and sit-down area. No sign of Adam. It would have been good to see him, to banish any shreds of self-consciousness before Saturday night became bigger in her mind than it actually was. Never mind. No doubt she'd see him before the day was out.

As Erin made herself a strong cup of tea, Lydia appeared

by her side. 'There you are! How are you, my dear? Fully recovered from Saturday night?'

'Yes.' Erin grinned sheepishly. 'Sorry if I was a bit overzealous in trying to keep everyone from going home.'

'Don't worry. It was a lot of fun.'

Lydia made herself a coffee, and they sat down at the end of one of the long plastic tables.

'And everything's patched up with your friend Mel?' Lydia enquired with a concerned smile.

'Yes, all's okay. She called yesterday to apologise.'

Mel, unlike Jack, was smart enough to proffer her apologies later in the day, after Erin had had a chance to catch up on some sleep and was in a more receptive mood.

'It's the prodigal friend,' Mel had stated with a lopsided smile. 'Coming to beg forgiveness.'

Erin, frowning to let her know she wasn't automatically forgiven, had opened the door to let her in.

Fixing two glasses of icy-cold, hangover-soothing water, they sat on the couch and talked more honestly than ever before.

'What was up with you last night, Mel?'

'I didn't like being set up with Adam.'

'Really? You went home early just because of that?'

Mel sniffed. 'I *hate* matchmaking. Too many expectations from everyone involved. All those expectations make me feel defensive, and when I'm defensive I can get a tiny bit belligerent. Not to talk about how *inadequate* it makes me feel. Really, I prefer to go it alone when it comes to finding men.'

Erin was taken aback, by both the strength of Mel's feelings and the underlying lack of self-confidence she was revealing. Erin had always admired Mel's seemingly natural confidence, and it was something of a shock to realise that her friend felt inadequate in any area at all.

'I'll never do it again,' Erin promised, adding, with a smile, 'You're on your own.'

'And I'm sorry about that age demographic remark,' Mel

continued sombrely, 'that was really mean of me.'

Erin nodded. It *had* been a really mean remark, and she would have been mortified if Fizz or Lydia had overheard it. 'You need to broaden your horizons, Mel. Age isn't important when it comes to friendships, and you'll have a really limited existence if you deny everyone and everything that's supposedly old. You're thirty-four, not sixteen.'

'I know. I'm sorry, I really am.' Mel looked both sheepish and extremely contrite. 'You know, I'm not used to this side of you, Erin. I've never seen you so vocal about what you think.'

'You mean I'm usually a walkover?'

'You know you are.' Mel's smile was affectionate. 'But maybe you're finally showing your teeth.'

'That's something my mum used to say.'

'Mine too …'

A short, comfortable silence followed.

'I still can't believe that you didn't like Adam,' Erin mused aloud. 'I thought he'd be perfect for you.'

Mel shrugged. 'I did like him. He was nice, good company, really funny at times … but there was no chemistry.'

Erin emitted a short laugh. 'So you're expecting a big bang when you meet the right guy?'

Mel shook her head. 'Nah, I don't know what to expect, whether it's a mini explosion, or something that creeps up on me. Or, with the luck I'm having, whether I even meet anyone at all.'

'Of course you'll meet someone,' Erin insisted. 'And whoever it is will instantly know how incredibly lucky he is.'

'It's crystal-ball territory,' Mel sighed, not really listening to Erin's reassurances. 'How do you know you've met the love of your life? How can you trust that your feelings will last? Or, if it's one of those friendship-turns-into-love scenarios, how do you know the requisite feelings will *develop*? Really, it's all too vague and slippery for my liking.'

Erin didn't know the answer and so she just listened, inwardly resolving that from now on she would be a lot more sensitive about Mel's revolving-door love life.

'I'd better get going,' Mel said eventually, standing and stretching. 'I want to try out this new trampolining place. You're welcome to come along.'

Erin laughed. 'No, thanks. Not with a hangover. Probably not ever.'

Mel was her dearest friend, and when Erin had lectured her on growing up and acting her age, she didn't mean it entirely, because life would be very boring if Mel wasn't up with the latest trends, or dashing off to pop concerts every other weekend, or coming at life with such fresh, unconstrained enthusiasm.

Later on that night, Jack finally turned up in person, and after she informed him in no uncertain terms that she expected him to stay for the full duration of all future parties, and to make his best efforts to socialise with her friends and wholeheartedly enjoy himself in the process, they retired to the bedroom for the most wonderful make-up sex.

So everything was resolved. Everything but Adam.

Now, as Erin chatted away to Lydia she watched the door for him. She didn't need to speak to him; just seeing him and exchanging a smile would be enough to dispel any awkwardness. He didn't make an appearance. At the sound of the bell, Erin and Lydia drained their cups and went their separate ways. Back in the classroom, Erin found an envelope on her desk.

Dear Miss Donovan,

I deeply apologise for my aggressive, inappropriate behaviour in regard to you. It is difficult being a father in such changing times, and to know what is the right thing to do. Many days I feel afraid, and before I know it, my fear becomes anger. My daughter, Fila, is everything to me. She returns to your class with my blessing, and I hope you will continue to teach her English to the same high standard.

Kindest regards and my sincerest apologies,

Yasir Azizi

Erin looked up to meet Fila's gaze and nodded silently, accepting the apology and Fila's part in it.

Jack, Mel, Fila's father. So many apologies in the last two days, and each evoking its own set of conflicting feelings.

Chapter 25

Laura greeted her mother with a kiss on the cheek before sitting down at the small table smack in the middle of the bustling café, one of Cathy's favourites.

'What are you having?' her mother enquired.

'A plain white coffee, thanks, Mum.'

Cathy relayed the order to a waitress who had appeared at just the right moment, and knew her by name.

'Well, this is an unusual treat,' Cathy began when the waitress had left them alone. 'What's up?'

Laura felt herself bristling. 'Nothing.' Actually, something was 'up', as Cathy had put it, but Laura planned to ease gradually into the conversation, not blurt it right out. 'I thought this would be nice, that's all. Dad's always around at your house, Olivia is underfoot at mine. It's nice to be on our own for once. No one interrupting us for this or that.'

Cathy ran a hand through her freshly styled hair and her gleaming lips widened into a wry smile. Laura's own lipstick was faded – there had been no opportunity to reapply it since rushing out the door this morning – and her hair was faded too, badly in need of a colour and cut. She made a mental note to book in with the hairdresser.

'You're absolutely right.' Cathy leant forward and smiled again. 'This is a nice, civilised way to catch up, and we should make a habit of it. How's work? You must be having a quiet spell to say you can contemplate popping out like this.'

'I wish.' Laura grimaced. 'Work's crazier than ever. Esteban has signed two major contracts this week alone. We're going to have to hire some more staff.'

'It's better to be hiring than firing,' Cathy pointed out. 'So many companies are letting people go these days.'

'Yes, it *is* good, I know. It's just that more work and more staff mean more pressure for Esteban and me, and poor Olivia loses out.'

The waitress arrived with a coffee in each hand. She placed them carefully on the table and asked if there was anything else they wanted before she departed with a friendly smile.

'Olivia will be at school in a few weeks,' said Cathy, shaking some artificial sweetener into her cup. 'She'll be so taken up with her teacher and her new friends she won't feel like she's losing out at all.'

School. Laura hadn't intended to bring up that particular subject, but as Cathy had broached it herself, perhaps it was as good a time as any to ask for her help.

'Mum, is there any chance you could pick Olivia up from school one or two days a week?' Laura paused to check her mother's reaction. Her face looked closed, not at all receptive. Laura sighed inwardly. Well, she had started, so she might as well finish. 'Obviously, Esteban and I would get home from work as early as possible, so it wouldn't be for long, just a few hours ...'

'What's wrong with Kasia?' Cathy asked after a telling silence.

'Kasia will not be staying on. It's not working out with her.'

Cathy sipped her coffee, creating another deliberate silence. Eventually she asked, 'Isn't there an after-school service that collects children from the local schools?'

'Yes, there is, and we're planning to use it. But it would be ideal for Olivia to come home directly one or two days a week …'

Laura had already done a lot of research into after-school care, and though the carers and the facilities seemed perfectly nice, she worried that the day would be too long for Olivia.

'If you're worried about that, why don't you hire another Kasia who can take Olivia to and from school, and mind her in her own home?' Cathy was suggesting everything but her own involvement. How typical.

'We only need someone a few hours a day. It would be difficult to find someone willing to do such limited hours.'

'You don't know until you try,' Cathy replied tartly.

Laura smarted at her mother's tone. 'So that's a no?'

'It's too much of a commitment, Laura. I have my life too, you know. I've done my time with school runs and homework and all the rest. I'm meant to be enjoying myself at this stage of my life, not starting it all again.'

So that was that. Cathy would not help. Laura shouldn't have brought it up today. Now she felt angry, let down and totally unsupported. Was she wrong to expect Cathy to help out a little? Yes, her mother did have her own life to live, Laura fully understood this and agreed with her, but one or two afternoons a week were not a major imposition, surely? And it wasn't as though Olivia needed nappy changes or bottles of formula every few hours. She was at quite a self-sufficient age, and she was as good as gold, most of the time.

I would do it, Laura thought. *When – if – Olivia has children, I will help her out. I'll set boundaries, just like Mum has, but I'll still commit time to supporting my daughter and my grandchild.*

Laura drank the rest of her coffee. She should return to the office. Cathy reached for her bag on the floor. Apparently, she was also ready to call an end to their impromptu catch-up.

'Who's Julien, Mum?' The question came out sharp and accusing. So much for easing it into the conversation!

'What?' Cathy frowned, quite obviously confused by the sudden change of topic.

'Moira brought him up the other day. She knew him in Paris, I think, so I thought you would know who he was.' Laura could hear a certain degree of spite in her voice, but could not remove it.

'He was someone in our circle.' Cathy shrugged. 'Moira would have had a distant acquaintance with him.'

'Are you sure it wasn't more than that?'

'Absolutely sure.' Cathy stood up, slinging her bag onto her shoulder. 'You can't exactly rely on what Moira says these days, you know.'

Out on the street, Cathy gave Laura a perfunctory kiss on the cheek and walked away. Laura watched her mother, her hair bobbing with each stride in her high new-season sandals.

It was true that Moira often recalled events out of sequence and mixed up who was who, but as far as Laura knew her aunt didn't *invent* things. Something told Laura that Cathy was lying, and that she knew more about Julien than she was letting on. Then again, Laura mused as she walked briskly back to work, maybe she was so angry and disappointed with her mother that, quite simply, she wanted to think the worst of her.

* * * * *

A pounding noise filled the house. Laura and Olivia looked at each other quizzically.

'Someone is at the door,' Olivia announced in a theatrical whisper. Tucked in bed, she obviously found the prospect of an unexpected visitor a lot more exciting than the bedtime story Laura was in the process of reading to her.

'Mmm ... I wonder who it could be.' Laura put down the book and stood up. Maybe Kasia had forgotten her keys. Or maybe it was one of those door-to-door charity collectors. Olivia followed her downstairs and together they pulled back the curtain on the glass panel at the side of the door.

'It's Uncle Gerry!' Olivia yelped.

Laura should have guessed. Gerry knocked on doors every bit as enthusiastically as he approached all other aspects of life.

She opened the door and greeted him with a grin. 'Jesus, Gerry, there's no need to take the door down.'

'Just making sure you're all on your toes.' He laughed and hoisted Olivia up into his arms. 'Did I wake you up?'

'No.' Olivia shook her head, her hair tousled though Laura had only just brushed it. 'Mum was reading to me.'

'Thank God.' Gerry feigned relief. 'It's bad luck to wake a princess, you know.'

Olivia laughed delightedly.

Gerry regarded her with a deadpan expression. 'If I take you back to bed, will you promise me you'll go straight to sleep? A sleeping princess is good luck, you see, and I could really do with some good luck at the moment.'

'Okay.' Olivia giggled.

While they were upstairs, Laura located the keys to Esteban's BMW. She'd been playing phone tag with her husband since yesterday, and hadn't yet managed to ask him if Gerry could borrow the car. Esteban wouldn't have a problem with it. Unlike most men, he wasn't precious about his car, and he was particularly fond of Gerry and would want to help him out.

A few minutes later Gerry joined her in the kitchen. 'It's a lovely age she's at. Make sure you enjoy her, Laura. The years slip away – before you know it she'll be taller than you, and sulky and wanting nothing to do with you but for your credit card and your car, which she'll drive too fast and smash into stationary vehicles ...'

Laura smiled ruefully. 'You make it sound awful, Gerry.'

'It is,' he lamented. 'It is.' He took the keys from Laura's outstretched hand. 'Thanks for this. You've mentioned it to Esteban, haven't you?'

'Yes, of course,' she lied because Gerry wouldn't take the car if he knew that Esteban hadn't given his express permission.

The only thing Laura didn't like about her house was the garage. Built in an era when families were considered lucky to have any vehicle at all, it could only fit one car, and it didn't have direct access to the house. They had installed a modern door, though, and as Laura walked out the front door she clicked the remote to open it.

'It's a nice evening,' Gerry commented as they waited for the door to finish rolling up.

'Yes.'

The children next door, a few years older than Olivia, were playing tip-the-can, hiding in the lengthening shadows of their front garden. These long summer nights would be over in a few weeks, and the children would soon be indoors by this hour, doing their homework if not already in bed. School and its regimen would be reasserted, and these late nights, these games played in the semi-darkness, the fun and the freedom, would be a distant memory. Laura almost felt sorry for the children.

Gerry sat in the car and the engine hummed to life. Reversing out of the tight confines of the garage, he came to a halt next to where Laura stood waiting. Wearing a big grin, he rolled down the window.

'Now, this is a car I'll enjoy driving. Makes a nice change from my old banger.'

Laura laughed. Gerry twiddled with the controls on the dash, figuring out what was what.

'Gerry, do you ever remember hearing about Julien?' Again, the question seemed to come of its own accord. 'Apparently, he knew Mum and Cathy in Paris.'

The headlights came on, illuminating the dusky surrounds. Gerry also turned on the radio before he responded. 'Julien? If I remember correctly, he was your mother's boyfriend.' Her uncle refocused his gaze from the dash to her face, his expression as honest and earnest as ever, having no idea of the enormity of the words coming out of his mouth. 'That's right. I remember her telling me that Julien had broken her heart. It was a harsh lesson for our Cathy. She had broken many a heart herself before she fell for him.'

Gerry thanked her again and said goodnight, reversing carefully down the remainder of the driveway. Laura stayed outside until the car was out of sight.

Upstairs, she checked on Olivia before beginning her own bedtime routine. It was funny how she could calmly cleanse her face and brush her teeth as thoughts crashed so violently around her head. She needed to be logical, set out the facts clearly. Moira had said that Erin had Julien's eyes. What other way was there to interpret such a statement, other than conclude that Julien was Erin's father? Julien, Cathy's boyfriend. So Moira had an affair with her sister's boyfriend, and had a baby by him? Good Lord. Surely not!

I stopped at nothing, Moira had stated that night in the garden, her bitterness melding with the smoke from her cigarette, confiding, decades later, that there had been fertility problems.

I stopped at nothing.

What exactly did Moira mean by that? Was she implying that the affair had been a clinical, premeditated attempt to conceive a baby, rather than a passionate, damn-the-consequences fling?

Did Joe know about it? Had she confessed to him about the affair, about how far she was prepared to go?

Did Cathy know? Maybe she hadn't admitted to a deeper relationship with Julien because her heart had indeed been broken by him, and by her sister, and it was all – even now, so many years later – too painful to speak about.

You can't exactly rely on what Moira says these days, you know.

Maybe Laura was interpreting it all wrong. Maybe she was, as Cathy had suggested, putting too much reliance on Moira's ramblings.

Downstairs, she heard a key turn and the creak of the front door as it opened and shut. Kasia. Laura had intended to wait up for the nanny, to finally confront her, but now she could not recall a word of what she'd planned to say. All Laura could think about was Julien and if he was in fact Erin's father. Kasia paled into insignificance by comparison.

Laura shook her head, trying to clear it and reprocess the information, but the only fact that remained certain was that this was far too big and complicated for her to reason out alone. Her face pink and shiny with moisturiser, she sank onto the bed and called Esteban. The phone rang and rang. Esteban's voice finally came on, asking the caller to leave a message. Laura hung up. There was no way to summarise this into any kind of succinct message. She needed to talk it through in detail, and as usual Esteban wasn't here, not even at the end of the phone, when she needed him.

Chapter 26

Dear Mrs Torres,

Our records tell us that it's your daughter's birthday next week. At playschool, we celebrate birthdays very enthusiastically, so please send in some cake and we will sing Olivia Happy Birthday in our best singing voices.

Kindest regards,

Mrs Riordan

PS: We prefer cupcakes, if possible. No need for sharp knives and less mess. Thank you for your consideration.

To: Erin <Erin.Donovan@yahoo.com>

From: Laura <Laura.Torres@globaltranslation.com>

Hi Erin,

How are you? It feels like ages since we've spoken. Not much news to tell, only that I nearly got Gerry arrested! To cut a long story short, Gerry borrowed Esteban's car, I forgot to tell Esteban, and my dear husband, who got home tired and bleary after a long flight and needed the car to go straight into work, found that his BMW had vanished. In fairness, he did try to contact me before ringing the Guards, but I was tied up in a project meeting, and I never go anywhere near his car, so he assumed it had been stolen. For once, the Guards did their job and found the 'stolen' car, pulling Gerry over on Lucan Rd. Gerry explained that he was a relative, the Guards confirmed this fact with Esteban, and they let Gerry go. Both Esteban and I were mortified. Talk about nonexistent marital communication. Sadly, it highlights just how distant we are these days.

Your Mum is good, she's eating well enough and Paddy has been taking her to the park whenever the weather is fine. She does seem to be getting more muddled, though. Half the time she thinks she's in Paris. I enjoy hearing titbits about what it was like, but she has made one or two strange comments. Does the name Julien mean anything to you? It's nothing to worry about, just wondering if she's mentioned him before, that's all.

Well, that's it from me. How is Jack? Still in love? Report back with all the juicy details!

XX Laura

To: Erin <Erin.Donovan@yahoo.com>

From: Lisha.Mbah@stpatricks.ie

Dear Erin,

I have decided to return to school in September. Working at the butchers has been a valuable lesson. I do not want to work in a job like this for the rest of my life. I do not want blood in my fingernails, or to have to smile cheerfully at snooty customers. I want a job with responsibility, status and money. I am going to be a businesswoman, not a retail assistant. I will return to St Patrick's and get the best Leaving Certificate possible, and then I will go to university and do a Bachelor of

Commerce. The girls at St Patrick's no longer bother me. After two years, when I leave school, I will never set eyes on most of them again. I will make new friends at university, people with broader minds and who care about things other than clothes and make-up.

I know you were disappointed when I left school, and I think you will be happy to hear about this new development.

Kind regards from your old student,

Lisha

To: Lisha <Lisha.Mbah@stpatricks.ie>

From: Erin <Erin.Donovan@yahoo.com>

Dear Lisha,

I am delighted to hear your news. Well done for making such a mature, considered decision.

Good luck with the new school year. As you all get older and wiser, you may find that you have more things to like about the girls at St Patrick's. I think I've mentioned my friend Mel to you in my previous messages? Well, if Mel and I had known each other at school, we most definitely would not have been friends. I would have been too introverted for her, and she would have been too confident for me, or so we would have thought. As it happened, we didn't meet until university, by which time we had both matured enough to understand that friends don't have to be a mirror image of ourselves.

I look forward to hearing from you again soon,

All the best,

Erin

Hi Erin,

Mum and Peter are working in the bistro, Talia is at her friend's house, and I'm home alone for the afternoon. I'm not allowed to answer the door to strangers, or help myself to the chocolate biscuits in the fridge, or spend the whole afternoon on the computer. Mum phones every half hour to make sure I'm okay and keeping to the rules. I thought this would be exciting, but I'm actually VERY bored.

XX Jessica

PS: I now have 26 friends on Facebook. Talia has 195.

Hi Jessica,

I was so glad to see your message pop into my inbox. As a matter of fact, I'm having a boring Saturday afternoon, too. Your Dad is at some major sporting event at the school (yes, he teaches languages, not sport, my question too …). My friend Mel is at the same event, and I'm at a loose end. At least I don't have to keep to any rules!

On Monday, I will ask some of my students to like you on Facebook. It will be good for their communication skills (and some of them are not much older than you).

Cheers,

Erin

To: *Laura* <Laura.Torres@globaltranslation.com>

From: *Erin* <Erin.Donovan@yahoo.com>

Hi Laura,

I'm still laughing at the thought of Gerry being pulled over on Lucan Rd. I can just see his expression. Poor Gerry. Being in any kind of strife with the authorities would horrify him. I bet he'll never borrow a car again for the rest of his life.

I haven't heard Mum mention Julien. I wonder who he is? Thank you all again for taking such good care of her. It's hard to be so far away and so reliant on everyone else's generosity. This break was meant to make things simpler, to clear my head, but I'm only just realising that it has made everything so much more complicated. I imagined that I would cruise along for the year, float on the surface of life over here and recharge my batteries in the process. Instead, I've been sucked into a new job, new friends, apartment, boyfriend ... and the thought of leaving everything behind to return to Dublin fills me with panic and that terrible, all-too-familiar sense of being trapped.

I'm seeing a lot of Jack. We've had a milestone of sorts – our first argument – and our relationship feels closer, more real than ever. Jack knows all about Mum, but it hasn't occurred to him that I will eventually have to go back to her. See how complicated it is?

Thanks again, and please do let me know if Mum says or does anything else that worries you.

Love, Erin

PS: Please tell Olivia that one of the things I miss the most is hugging her. The postman should be knocking any day now with her birthday present.

Chapter 27

The canteen was the very essence of the college, and if she had the time, Erin could waste away hours in here. Delicious smells permeated the air, an eclectic mix of cuisines being enjoyed by an equally diverse mix of nationalities. Students were encouraged to speak English, but their different accents, skin tones and dress seemed only more pronounced against the uniform language. There was chatter, laughter, students bustling in and out of seats. The atmosphere never failed to stimulate Erin's senses and was particularly welcome after a difficult morning trying to distinguish past and present tenses with her baffled class.

Adam rushed into the canteen directly after her, and almost knocked her off her feet.

'Sorry.' He smiled a busy, distracted kind of smile as he steadied her by the shoulders.

She grinned at him. 'Slow down, Adam. What's the rush?'

He returned her grin with a sheepish one of his own. 'The Department of Immigration is chasing my approval on something I absolutely don't want to approve, Thu has a plumbing problem in the childcare centre and wants me to have a look at it before she calls in someone who actually knows what they're doing, and Lydia is hounding me for some paperwork ... I've come here to hide.'

As Erin laughed, Adam got two mugs and began to fill the first from the hot water dispenser.

'I can make my own,' she said when she realised one of the mugs was for her.

'It's as easy to make two as one,' he replied breezily. 'Tea or coffee?'

'Tea, please.' From Erin's previous experience, Adam's tea was marginally more palatable than his coffee. As he seemed so intent on making her hot drinks, maybe she could direct him a little. 'Just leave the teabag in another little while ... and a tiny bit more milk, please.'

Adam clearly didn't have the time to sit down, and so they stood to the side and sipped from their mugs.

'How was your weekend?' she asked conversationally.

'Hectic. Had a big family do on Saturday night. Went to the rugby on Sunday. How was yours?'

'Quiet.' By the time Jack had finished with the school sports on Saturday, it had been too late to do anything else. On Sunday, they'd gone to the cinema, the movie heavy and quite depressing and doing nothing at all to elevate Erin's weekend.

Adam groaned as Lydia walked into the canteen, spotting him immediately. 'Oh no, she's found me.'

'Adam ...' Erin began as Lydia weaved her way towards them.

'Yes?'

Erin hesitated. She wasn't about to complicate things between them, was she? No. After a disappointing weekend, she simply wanted to broaden her circle of friendships. That was all.

'If you happen to get tickets for the rugby again, I'd love to go,' she said in a rush.

Oh God, why was she going red?

Lydia reached them before Adam could reply. 'You've been avoiding me,' she stated in her most upper-class tone.

'Never,' Adam protested, adopting an air of boyish innocence.

She crossed her arms. 'I need those forms, Adam.'

'They're the very next thing on my agenda,' he assured her, before adding, rather flippantly, 'I'm putting them ahead of the toilet problems in the childcare centre. What more can you ask?'

Throwing the rest of his tea down the sink, he turned to smile at Erin, resting a hand briefly on her shoulder. Was that his way of saying yes to the rugby? Her face flared up again.

Adam rushed off, leaving Erin to deal with an assessing stare from Lydia. Though the older woman said not a word, there was no doubt that she was jumping to all the wrong conclusions.

* * * * *

It was a lovely restaurant, one of the best in Dublin, and though Laura was technically working, she was unreservedly enjoying the ambience, the food and the company. So many evenings she ate alone, and hardly heard the sound of her own voice but for a few surly exchanges with Kasia and her phone calls with Esteban, so late at night that they were both too tired to talk at any length.

'The project is only slightly behind schedule,' she assured the operations manager of the motor company, a heavyset man who looked more like a truck driver than senior management. 'We've had some delays with the Polish and Russian translations. Our usual contractors have been inundated and we've had to use people who aren't as familiar with our internal processes and our strict adherence to deadlines. Our expectations have been clarified now, and we don't expect any further delays. In fact, we hope that by the end of next week we'll have caught up fully. Isn't that right, Savita?'

Savita nodded gravely. 'Yes, that is correct. There is even a small chance we will finish ahead of schedule.'

While Laura was enjoying herself, Savita seemed to be having the opposite experience. Though professional and polite as ever, she was nothing like her usual warm, outgoing self. This project and its demands were clearly taking their toll.

Pete, the operations manager, nodded approvingly at the suggestion that the project might be ahead of schedule, and proceeded to top up their glasses with the expensive red wine Laura had ordered to complement the top-class meal. Savita covered her glass, indicating that she didn't want anything more to drink. Laura had had quite enough, too. In fact, Pete's face was becoming slightly blurry. She felt mellow, sleepy, and the thought of climbing into bed and sinking into a long, deep slumber was suddenly irresistible. But it would seem bad manners to turn Pete down and leave him to drink alone. She allowed him to fill her glass, deciding at the same time that she wouldn't drink it. Tomorrow was Olivia's birthday and she needed a clear head to get through everything at work so she could leave early and spend some time with her daughter.

'We've been extremely impressed with the transparency and overall commitment of your company.' Pete's beefy hand looked as though it could easily crush the wine glass he was holding to his lips. 'In fact, we've recommended Global Translations to our sister company. You should hear from them in the near future.'

More business. It seemed to be streaming in from all sides, and for once Laura enjoyed the feeling of accomplishment and success and didn't fret about how they were going to deliver all these new contracts when they were already stretched to capacity. She beamed at Savita, whose lips stretched into a faint reciprocal smile. The Indian woman was really off form tonight. Once Pete finished his drink, Laura would ask for the bill and then she and Savita could go home and collapse into their beds.

In the end, it was another hour before they left the restaurant. Pete had become more and more chatty, talking about his wife and kids at length, showing them photos on his phone, relaying sporting, academic and domestic anecdotes, apparently content to yap forever about his family rather than go home and see them in person. When Laura finally got away, it was after midnight, and she was drunk, definitely drunk – she had, without intending to, finished that glass of wine, and another one too – which did not bode well for the morning.

Kasia was still up, mesmerised in front of the TV, the front room in darkness save for the flickering screen.

'Thanks for babysitting,' said Laura from the door.

Kasia nodded imperceptibly.

It was as Laura turned around that she thought of them. The cupcakes. For playschool. For Olivia's birthday. Tomorrow. Fuck! How could she have forgotten? What kind of terrible mother was she? Now it was too late. Olivia would have to do without. Poor Olivia, she would be the only kid at playschool who didn't have cupcakes for her birthday. But what could Laura do? Maybe she could buy some in the morning, before she went to work. Where could she buy thirty-odd cup cakes at 7 am? Fuck! Fuck! Fuck!

There was nothing else for it. She had to make them, or bake them, or whatever, now, right now. Never mind that she was drunk and half-asleep. She had to make – bake – those cupcakes.

The pantry: flour, sugar. The fridge: butter, eggs, milk. A mixing bowl. Her faithful Nigella recipe book. Thirty-two kids. Three batches. She just needed to triple everything in the recipe. God, but it was hard to do maths when one was drunk! Some of the flour missed the bowl and dusted the counter and her top. Was it worth throwing in more to compensate? A splash of milk. Easier said than done when one's hand was so unsteady. Not to worry. It would be fine. Cake was cake to five-year-olds. They were hardly that discerning, were they? A quick blitz with the electric mixer. Fuck! Now she had cake mix on her top, too.

'What are you doing?' Kasia, lured from the TV by the commotion, regarded Laura from under that long fringe.

'I'm making cupcakes. For playschool.' Laura stuck a finger in the mix to test it. 'Mmm ... something isn't right.' She thrust the bowl at Kasia. 'You taste it.'

Kasia complied, sucking on her finger thoughtfully. 'It's too buttery.'

Laura frowned at the recipe, the words and figures blurring in front of her eyes. '125g of unsalted butter, that's 375g for three batches, so three slabs ... what am I doing wrong here?'

Kasia came closer, examining the recipe before turning her scrutinising gaze to one of the empty butter wrappings. 'Each slab is 250g, not 125. You need one and a half, not three!'

Of course. How stupid. Laura didn't know whether to laugh or cry. 'What am I going to do?' she wailed.

'You're going to have to double all the other ingredients,' Kasia replied plainly.

Just as Laura was thinking it was all too hard, and that she would somehow manage to source the cupcakes in the morning, Kasia stepped in and took control. Deftly she added more sugar, eggs and flour, the bowl almost overflowing with the extra ingredients.

Laura, looking on, had a strange attack of the giggles. 'If you use the electric mixer on that, it will explode all over us.'

Kasia twisted her thin lips into a smile. 'We'll mix it lightly by hand, and then transfer half to another bowl. Hopefully, the ingredients will be evenly spread.'

Laura found another bowl and Kasia divided the mix in two. They blitzed, taste-tested and began to lay out patty cases in preparation.

'We'll need seventy-two,' Kasia deduced, her maths a lot more snappy than Laura's in these early hours of the morning.

'We'll be here all night.' Laura yawned. 'Maybe we should just throw out the surplus mix.'

Kasia scowled at her.

'Okay,' Laura relented. 'Seventy-two it is.'

Finally, the first batch was ready for the oven, which Laura had at least thought to turn on in advance.

'What about the icing?' Kasia flicked her fringe out of her eyes with the back of her hand.

Laura shrugged guiltily. Her plans hadn't extended that far. The five-year-olds wouldn't expect icing, would they? Yes, now that she thought about it, of course they would.

In the meantime, Kasia had turned around and disappeared into the pantry. 'You don't appear to have any icing sugar,' her muffled voice announced a few moments later.

'No, I don't believe I do.' Laura felt another yawn rising from deep inside her. Would she ever get to bed tonight?

Kasia emerged. 'We could melt some chocolate.'

'I suppose we could,' Laura agreed unenthusiastically.

Finally, at two in the morning, all seventy-two cupcakes were baked and iced, and lay like brown polka dots across the white stone countertop. Laura, sober by now and past the stage of exhaustion, thanked Kasia for her help, to which Kasia nodded and said a brisk goodnight. Laura loitered in the kitchen. It was in quite a state: flour on the floor, cake mix on the splashback, bowls and utensils piled high in the sink. Sleep had to be her priority, though. Tomorrow was going to be a long, energy-draining day. She went as far as turning out the lights, but then just stood in the darkness trying to fathom how she could sleep knowing there was such a mess here. Walk away. Leave it. Sleep.

She couldn't. Despairing at this obsessive side of her personality, she flicked the lights back on and began to clean up. While Kasia and Olivia and the rest of the world slept, Laura scrubbed, wiped and swept.

Chapter 28

'Come on, sleepy head. It's time to make a move.'

Erin stretched her arms and toes and reluctantly opened her eyes. Jack was sitting on the bed, fully dressed in dark pants, blue shirt and a patterned tie, his work attire.

'It can't be that time already,' she protested.

He regarded her with feigned gravity. 'I'm afraid it is. I need to go to work. You need to go to work. The fun is over, my dear.' He kissed her forehead. 'I'll call you later, okay? We'll sort out something for the weekend.'

'Okay.'

Erin lay motionless after Jack left. Despite his assertions, she still had plenty of time to get ready for work, which was good, because she was finding it difficult to motivate herself this morning. Her head felt heavy and rather sore, as though she had a hangover, which was decidedly unfair since she hadn't even had a drink last night. She and Jack had stayed in and watched television. A sedate, alcohol-free evening that should have had her waking up bright and refreshed this morning.

Eventually, after a good ten minutes of contemplation, she slowly got out of bed, and promptly realised that she felt much worse upright than lying down. In the kitchen, she discovered a cup and plate on the draining board, evidence that Jack had had some breakfast. It was only right that he felt at home in her apartment, but for some reason the cup and plate – which had been thoughtfully rinsed and left to dry – immediately irritated her. She shook her head, puzzled by her reaction, her head too foggy to work out what it was she found so annoying.

Popping two Panadol in her mouth, she downed them with a glass of water. Then, not having the strength to do another thing, she sat down shakily at the kitchen table. Obviously, the Panadol needed some time to take effect. She would rest her head on her arms while she waited.

Twenty minutes later, most of which she spent drifting in and out of sleep, she realised that the Panadol was not going to get her over the line. Making it into work was an impossibility – she would be lucky to prise herself away from the table and make it back into bed. She needed to let Adam know.

Summoning the last of her energy, she reached weakly for her mobile phone, which was charging on the counter, and dialled his number.

'Good morning, Erin.' He sounded chirpy and bright, and on the move somewhere, as always. 'How are you?'

'I'm sick,' she announced in a very pitiful tone. 'I'm sorry to let you down, Adam, but I can't take this morning's class.'

'What's wrong? Have you been to the doctor? Don't worry, I'll take the class. Where were you at? No, don't tell me, I can skip ahead and cover something else on the syllabus. Make sure you take care of yourself, Erin. Lots of liquids and rest. Is anyone dropping in to check on you?'

Though she was feeling completely wretched, his over-the-top concern prompted her to smile.

'Jack,' she lied, because she didn't want Adam turning up to check for himself that she was alright. 'Jack will pop in after work.'

After assuring him again that she would be okay on her own until Jack called, and that all she wanted to do was sleep and there was no need for anyone to be there watching her do that, she finally put down the phone.

She sent Jack a text.

Feel terrible. Have just called in sick to work.

Less than a minute later a response beeped on her phone.

Poor you. Sleep lots. Will call you later.

It was a perfectly reasonable response, but after Adam's gushing concern, it felt overly civilised and somewhat detached.

Her eyes rested again on the cup and plate at the side of the sink, and she finally figured out what it was she had found so irritating earlier. If Adam had been here this morning, he would not just have made a coffee for himself, he'd have made one for her, too. It would have tasted awful, but that was beside the point.

That was all the thinking she could manage for now, and probably for the rest of the day. Bed beckoned.

* * * * *

The surplus cupcakes were an instant hit at work. Beaming with childish delight, Johan selected the largest one and proceeded to demolish it in one enthusiastic bite.

'This has made my day,' he pronounced, cupping his hand to catch some falling crumbs.

'I'm glad to be of service.' Laura grinned. 'François, would you like one?'

The Frenchman was more modest with the cake he selected. 'You made these?' he enquired, raising his dark brows.

'Yes.'

'I didn't know that you baked.'

'Neither did I. Not until the early hours of this morning.'

'This tastes very good.' François ate in a much more

restrained fashion than Johan. 'Worth the black bags under your eyes, eh?'

'Most definitely.' Laura smiled.

It had been 3am before the kitchen had been restored to its usual pristine state, and before she had allowed herself the luxury of finally going upstairs to bed. Even though her body had ached with tiredness and was ready to succumb to sleep, her mind had been frustratingly alert, insisting on going through her schedule for the next day over and over again, as though thinking alone would get the work done. Just as dawn began to tinge the darkness in the room, she finally drifted off, only to be woken what felt like moments later by the trilling of her alarm. Totally disoriented and tired to the point of feeling dizzy, she considered calling in sick. She could roll over and sleep for another few hours, then take Olivia to playschool and listen as her classmates sang her Happy Birthday. They could spend a lazy afternoon together at the park. No, on second thoughts, not the park, somewhere else. But the same irritating, dutiful side of her personality that had compelled her to clean the kitchen in the early hours of the morning forced her out of bed, into the shower and out to work.

Actually, she didn't feel so bad now. The tiredness felt rather pleasant, like a buffer from reality. She was floating through the day with the faint suspicion that she was neglecting to do many of the things she ought to be doing, but without the focus to really care about what wasn't getting done.

Johan helped himself to another cupcake. 'I miss Savita's cooking. Work has not been the same since she stopped cooking for us.'

'Cooking for you is not Savita's sole purpose in life, Johan,' Laura replied crossly. 'She is a talented project manager and translator. Not a mother figure.'

Johan looked duly chastised. 'I am sorry. I miss her cooking, that is all.'

Savita was onsite with the motor company this morning.

Laura found a container in the kitchen and put some cupcakes in it. She left the container on Savita's desk. All those meals Savita had lovingly made and shared. Had anyone in the office ever thought to return the gesture?

At four in the afternoon, when Laura caught herself catnapping at her desk, she decided to call it a day. Tomorrow she would catch up on everything she should have done. Tomorrow, after a solid night's sleep.

Olivia was thrilled when Laura walked through the door.

'Mummy,' she squealed, hurtling towards Laura at top speed and crashing into her legs.

Laura bent down to hug her. 'How is my special birthday girl?'

'Great, Mummy. I don't mind being five. I feel the same as I did when I was four.'

Laura smiled. 'See, there was nothing to worry about. I knew you'd like being a big girl ... Did Daddy call?'

Kasia, who was standing a few steps away, replied. 'Esteban called this morning, but we had already left for playschool. He left a message. We listened to it when we got back, didn't we, Olivia?'

Olivia nodded. 'He said he was very sad to miss my birthday, and that he owed me a hundred birthday kisses to make up for not being here. Imagine, Mummy, a hundred kisses ...'

'He'll have to kiss you for hours and hours.' Laura straightened and spots danced in front of her eyes. She was seriously tired now. 'How were the cupcakes, Floss? Did the other kids like them?'

'The cakes were *yummy*.' Olivia smacked her lips. 'I couldn't believe they had *chocolate* on them. I'm *so* lucky ...'

Laura glanced at Kasia and they smiled at each other cautiously. It had been very nice of her to step in and help last night. But it didn't change what Laura had read in those messages. She needed to remember that.

'Come on, Mummy.' Olivia tugged her hand. 'I've made a cubby house outside. Come and play with me.'

Laura allowed herself to be dragged out to the garden, and belatedly realised what a lovely afternoon it was: a patchy blue sky overhead, dappled sunshine on the lawn, the scent of freshly mown grass from a nearby garden.

Olivia's 'cubby house' was at the base of an overgrown hedge, an old sheet enclosing the hideout from the world.

'This looks lovely, Floss. Nice and cosy.'

'Come inside, Mum.'

Laura peered into the dark, tiny space. 'I don't think I'd fit. Why don't I get a chair and sit over there, where I can watch you play?'

'Okay.' Olivia took a moment to consider how this scenario could be worked into her game. 'You can be the mummy, and I can be the girl. You're really tired so you can't leave your chair ...'

Laura sank into one of the garden chairs, smiling as she raised her face to the sun. 'That's right. The mummy is really tired, and she falls asleep all the time. And the girl has to whisper when her mother is sleeping ...'

Olivia, her imagination caught, lowered her voice to a whisper, and Laura closed her eyes. Soon she drifted into a light sleep, relaxed by the warmth of the sun, soft murmurings from Olivia, and a rare feeling of contentedness.

She woke when the sun dropped behind the hedge. The spot where she was sitting was now enveloped in shade. Olivia pottered close by, dropping petals and leaves into a plastic bowl. Laura watched her through half-shut eyes, and with a tender smile. She felt mellow, as though she could sit here for hours drifting in and out of sleep, and reality.

'The sleepy mummy is awake,' she announced. 'What is the girl doing?'

'The girl is making dinner for the mummy.'

'Wonderful, the mummy is very hungry.'

After a few minutes, Olivia presented her with the plastic bowl. 'Your dinner, Mother.'

'Thank you, dearest, kindest daughter.' With gusto, Laura

pretended to eat. 'Delicious! You take such good care of me. Can I have a hug?'

Olivia didn't need to be asked twice, launching herself into Laura's arms.

'Mummy, do they have birthdays in heaven?'

The game seemed to be over, and the real Olivia was back, along with her morbid fascination with life after death.

'Yes,' Laura decided, picking a stray petal from her daughter's feathery hair. 'They definitely have birthdays in heaven. And they have every kind of cupcake you can imagine.'

Chapter 29

'How are you, dear?' Fizz looked Erin up and down, her small eyes full of concern.

'I'm good.' Erin smiled, and bent down to plant a kiss on her neighbour's soft, cool cheek. 'Come in.'

'You still look a bit peaky, if you ask me.' As always, Fizz made directly for the kitchen, putting the container she was carrying down on the counter, and lifting the kettle to test that it had enough water before flicking the switch. 'Are you eating?'

'Yes, and I see that you are intent on feeding me again.' Erin glanced at the container. 'What have you got in there?'

'Some savoury muffins.' Fizz's sigh sounded a touch exasperated. 'I tried to make chicken soup, but it came out awful, not the way I wanted at all. I don't know how it can be that I bake so well, yet I'm such an awful cook ...'

Erin smiled fondly. 'Oh, Fizz. I don't believe for a moment that you're a bad cook.'

'Don't argue with me, dear. I really am terrible.'

'I wouldn't dare argue, Fizz.'

They both laughed. Fizz made two cups of tea, put the muffins on a plate, and they sat companionably at the table.

'Maybe we could do a cooking class together,' Erin suggested, nibbling the muffin tentatively. Though she wouldn't admit it to Fizz, her appetite was still touch and go after the virus. She had missed almost a week of work, and while Adam and the other staff had attempted to fill in for her, there would be a lot of catching up to do when she returned tomorrow.

'A cooking class?' Fizz queried.

Erin shrugged. 'I've been thinking of enrolling in one. It would be great to have a friend to do it with.'

Fizz stared at her. 'You're a sweet, lovely girl, Erin, and I'm flattered that you think of me as a friend, and not a batty old woman.'

Erin smirked. 'You're only slightly batty, Fizz, and I'm quite used to it by now.'

'You cheeky thing.'

Though they were both laughing again, Erin could see that Fizz was visibly touched, and Erin found herself reflecting on the fact that the two closest friendships she'd formed since getting here were with women who were significantly older than her: Fizz and Lydia. Had she been subconsciously looking for a mother figure, yearning for maturity, wisdom and warmth?

Fizz was speaking again. 'Actually, Erin, as a friend, I'd like to ask your opinion on something.'

Erin wrenched her thoughts away from the difficult subject of her mother. 'Fire away.'

'At your party, Lydia mentioned something about tutors going to people's homes, helping them learn English, and ever since she mentioned it it's been playing on my mind ... Would it be awfully silly to think I could be one of those tutors?'

'I don't think it's the slightest bit silly, Fizz,' Erin replied solemnly. 'Quite the opposite, in fact. I can't think of a better tutor than you.'

'I've been bored the last few years,' Fizz admitted after taking a dainty sip of tea. 'I can't shake the feeling that I should be doing more with my life, getting out more. Maybe this is something that could be beneficial to everyone.'

'Absolutely.' Erin nodded emphatically. 'It's a fabulous idea, Fizz. Most tutors are retired, like you, and so have spare time that they can donate.'

Fizz laughed in a self-deprecating fashion. 'I'm not exactly newly retired, am I? I'm in phase two retirement, if not phase three. I'll be seventy-five next birthday!'

'Age has nothing to do with it. You're articulate, you have a nice manner with people … But you'll need some way of getting to their homes …'

'I could get the bus,' Fizz offered.

'Or we could find you a family close by.' Erin grinned. 'Do it, Fizz. Phone Lydia tomorrow.'

'I will.' Fizz seemed to be certain now, and grinned in return. 'Now what about those cooking classes?'

'Maybe we should attempt one major change at a time.'

'Good advice.'

After Fizz left, Erin's thoughts reverted once more to her mother. This past week, Moira had been on her mind more than usual. Memories of when she'd been sick as a child; her mother's cool hand against her burning forehead; flat lemonade, grapes and other treats to whet her appetite; despite feeling miserable, the warm, secure knowledge of being loved. God, she missed her mother. The astute, deeply caring, wise woman she used to be, and – just as much – the warm familiarity of the confused, often childlike shell that she was now.

What was she going to do? How long more could she live here and shirk her responsibilities at home? Going back was going to be harder than she'd ever imagined, but going back, and relinquishing this new life, was the harsh reality. So harsh it made her feel sick inside. There was no escaping it, though. She had no choice.

* * * * *

Lydia hugged Erin tightly at work the next morning. 'Welcome back, darling. How do you feel?'

'I'm fine.' Erin smiled as she released herself from Lydia's firm embrace. 'Fully recovered. Glad to be back.'

Erin *was* glad to be back at work. In fact, she'd been surprised by how much she missed her colleagues and her students. The college was like a second home, and she'd felt displaced and out of sorts not being able to come here every day.

'You've lost some weight,' Lydia commented gently.

'A little.' Erin shrugged. 'One of the few upsides.'

'And you had someone taking care of you?'

'Yes. Fizz was like a mother hen, and Mel was very sweet ...'

'And Jack?' Lydia prompted.

Erin hesitated. 'Yes, Jack was great, too.'

Great was being generous. Jack had been all right: he'd phoned every day, and called around to see her a few times, but Erin had felt that something was lacking. In his emotions, and her own. Then again, given how sick she'd been, her instincts were probably not that reliable.

'By the way, Fizz is interested in becoming a home tutor. She's going to call you.'

'Wonderful.' Lydia beamed. The home tutoring service was her passion, and new recruits were welcomed with open arms. She promptly pulled out a folder from one of the wall shelves. 'Here, give her this information pack for me.'

'Will do. Thanks.'

Erin took the folder and tucked it under her arm. It was quarter to nine, time to head to her classroom and prepare for her students. Something was holding her back. Something that had been bothering her all week. Something she would have talked through with Mel, had Mel not been too close to it.

Erin flopped into one of the seats around Lydia's meeting table and admitted, 'I'm confused about Jack.'

Slowly, Lydia sat down next to her. 'What's so confusing?'

Erin chewed on her lip. 'He's lovely. Good-looking, great conversationalist, committed to his job, committed to me ...'

'But?'

'But it feels as though something is missing.'

'And what is that?'

'That's the problem. I don't know.'

Lydia's faced creased into a smile. 'Ah, the elusive X factor.'

Erin emitted a short, self-deprecating laugh. 'Who do I think I am? Jack is lovely. His girls are lovely. The whole package is good. *He's* the one who should be doubting *me*, not the other way around. He's the one getting the bum deal.'

'I'm not going to grace that comment with a response.' Lydia sniffed.

'It's true.'

'It's rubbish ... Do you love him, Erin?'

'I like him. A lot.'

'I didn't ask that. I asked if you loved him.'

Erin shrugged. She had no idea. 'What's love anyway?'

'I'm the last person you should ask.' Lydia's sigh was tinged with bitterness. Erin had the impression that the older woman hadn't been in a relationship since her turbulent marriage. Though she was curious, there was no time to ask Lydia now and begin another conversation. It was ten minutes to nine.

'What should I do?' she asked in a last-ditch attempt to make sense of these niggling doubts she'd had all week.

Lydia clasped her hand in a grip that was uncomfortably tight. 'You should be brave. That's the only thing that any of us can do.'

Be brave. It sounded so simple. So pure. As though it were the answer to every dilemma in life, not just this one.

* * * * *

'Erin! Erin!'

Adam pelted towards her at full throttle. About to turn into the canteen for some lunch, Erin stopped in her tracks.

'I've been trying to get to you all morning,' he said, breathless by the time he reached her, 'but I've been foiled at every attempt. How are you?'

'I'm fine,' she assured him. 'Everyone has been so concerned. I'm really touched.'

'Let me know if you feel tired later on, if you want to leave work early.'

'I doubt I'll feel that way but, yes, I won't hesitate to let you know if I do,' she replied, tongue-in-cheek.

He smiled. 'We missed you.'

She smiled back. 'I missed you all, too.' Then, she jerked her head in the direction of the canteen. 'Are you stopping for lunch?'

'No. Places to go, people to see … Hey, before I go, I have some tickets for the weekend … for the rugby … if you feel well enough, of course …'

'Great. Count me in.'

'Okay.' Adam seemed genuinely pleased. 'Jack, too?'

Erin hesitated. Jack had no qualms about making his own plans every now and then, so why should she?

'I'm not sure it's Jack's thing. Why don't you ask Lydia?'

'Good idea. I'll catch her later.'

Then with an absent-minded smile he was gone.

Erin was halfway into the canteen when she heard his yelp. She ran back out to the corridor. Down at the end, by the sliding doors, Adam was bent over in two, clutching his face in his hands. She rushed towards him.

'What happened? What have you done?'

'I walked into the door.'

'Didn't you see that it was closed?'

'Evidently not.'

Lydia, whose office was close by, arrived at the scene with a new student in tow, a young bewildered-looking man.

'You've broken your nose, haven't you?' she stated accusingly.

'No, it's fine.' Adam tried to hide a wince.

'It's bleeding.'

'Just a small bit.'

'How do you know it's not broken?'

'I just do.' Adam, his fingers pinching his nose to cull the blood, looked from Lydia to Erin to the student. 'Now, if you'll excuse me, I'm already late for a meeting.'

He walked away, holding his head and shoulders straight, obviously trying to disguise his embarrassment and pain.

Lydia and Erin shared a look before bursting into laughter.

'I knew that would happen one day. I knew he'd do himself an injury.' Lydia turned to her open-mouthed student. 'That was Adam McKenna, the director of the college, a very self-possessed and talented man – when he's not walking into doors.'

Chapter 30

'How much longer?' Olivia piped up from the back seat.

'Five minutes,' Laura replied, though it was probably closer to ten. The traffic wasn't particularly heavy but it was turning out to be one of those annoying journeys where *every* set of lights was red. It wasn't as though Moira would be watching the clock while she waited – her thoughts were more likely to be lost somewhere in the abyss of time – but Laura still didn't like to be late.

'We can play snap again,' Olivia decided.

With one thing and another, it had been a few weeks since Olivia had seen Moira, and her excitement was both palpable and very sweet.

Laura smiled. 'My daughter, the card shark.'

'What's a card shark?'

'Someone who is clever at cards.'

Laura pulled up outside Moira's terrace more than ten minutes later. The outside of her aunt's house looked neat and well cared for. Paddy and his boys kept tabs on the garden, and Cathy had mentioned that she'd cleaned the windows last week. At the start of summer, Gerry had painted the trims. Taking care of Moira and her house was truly a family effort.

Laura turned her key, Olivia darting through as soon as the door was opened wide enough to accommodate her slight frame.

'Auntie Moira,' she called, skipping down the hallway and into the kitchen.

Her gasp carried in the silence of the house, and Laura, feeling a sharp, sudden dread, rushed after her daughter.

'Auntie Moira is on the floor.'

Laura knelt by her aunt's side and grasped her icy hand. 'Oh, Moira. What happened?'

'I fell,' she croaked, her eyes watery and scared. 'I can't seem to get myself up.'

'Do you think you've broken something?'

'I don't know … If you just could help me up …'

'I think I should call an ambulance.'

'No ambulance.'

'But Moira –'

'No ambulance.' Moira was clearly distressed. 'Please get me up. Please.'

Hoping that she wasn't about to exacerbate any injuries, Laura complied with her aunt's wishes and positioned her hands under her arms to lift her. But despite the fact that she seemed nothing but skin and bones these days, Moira was surprisingly leaden. Laura, realising that she didn't have the strength to lift her alone, gently eased her back down.

'I'll ring someone to help,' she promised in what she hoped was a calm, unruffled tone of voice.

'Phone Daddy,' Olivia suggested. 'He's really strong.'

Laura wished that she could phone Esteban rather than have Gerry or Paddy see their sister like this, so helpless and forlorn. 'Daddy won't be home until later tonight. Olivia, come and hold Moira's hand while I use my phone.'

Olivia knelt down next to her grand-aunt, and gently took her hand.

'You're going to be okay,' she said in a very grown-up voice.

Gerry wasn't answering his phone. It rang and rang and rang. His voicemail clicked through. Leave a message? No. Her fingers trembling, Laura called up Paddy's number. It was busy. She was having lousy luck. The red lights. Nobody answering their phone.

Because she was beginning to feel desperate, and rather illogical, she chanced Esteban. Of course, her call went straight to his message bank. If her memory served her correctly, he was in a plane somewhere over mainland Europe. Why, oh why, was he never around when she needed him?

What to do? Moira seemed to be dead set against an ambulance but it was looking like Laura's only option. She would have to bring her aunt into hospital for a check-up anyway.

Just as she was on the verge of dialling triple nine, Paddy phoned her back.

'I have a missed call from you ...'

Laura had never been so happy to hear his voice. 'Moira has had a fall ... I need your help, Paddy, to lift her up ... I'm not sure if she's hurt ... she doesn't seem to think so ... how soon can you get here?'

Paddy estimated that he was ten minutes away.

'Thank heavens,' she sighed.

As soon as she hung up, Laura went into the living room to recover the cashmere blanket which, regardless of the season, Moira liked to drape over her knees as she watched television. Back in the kitchen, she laid the blanket gently across her aunt's prostrate body.

'You're freezing. How long have you been here?'

'A long time,' Moira replied in a frail voice.

Laura mentally went through her aunt's schedule. The cleaner would have come in the morning, and as far as she could remember, Gerry had been rostered for lunchtime.

'You saw Gerry today?'

'Yes, I did.' Moira seemed relatively certain of this fact. At the mention of her brother's name, she sought the comfort of her usual mantra. 'Moira, Gerard, Patrick and baby Cathy.'

'How long after Gerry left did you fall? Can you remember?'

'No, I can't, but it feels like I've been here forever. I thought I'd die here on the floor.'

Gerry would have left around one. It was now after six, which meant her aunt could have been lying here helplessly for more than five hours. No wonder she looked so frightened. Laura had to hold back her tears.

'Don't worry. We'll have you up in no time. Paddy is on his way.'

'Moira, Gerard, Patrick and baby Cathy ... Moira, Gerard, Patrick and baby Cathy.'

Olivia extracted her hand from Moira's grip. 'I'll get you some water, Auntie Moira, and a biscuit, because you must be hungry.'

Olivia's gaze sought approval from her mother. Laura nodded, and as her extraordinarily practical five-year-old daughter clumsily filled a cup with water, she had never felt so proud of her.

Moira seemed to read her thoughts. 'Children are a gift,' she insisted, her voice suddenly strong and clear. 'A precious gift from God.'

* * * * *

Paddy arrived twenty minutes later.

'Sorry.' He rolled his eyes with exasperation. 'Every single light went against me.'

Laura smiled wryly. 'I know the feeling.'

Crouching next to his older sister, he joked, 'Were you on the bottle again, Moira?' His voice was uneven, evidence that he found this situation far from easy.

Moira smiled weakly. 'Oh, I was having a grand old party for one, I was.'

'All right, my lady, let me check you out before we lift you, okay?'

Moira granted permission with a slight nod of her head, and he proceeded to lift her arms and legs one by one, gently bending and rotating each joint.

'I'm not happy with your right arm, Moira,' he said. 'Does it hurt?'

'Yes, it does.' She looked surprised at the realisation. 'No wonder I couldn't get myself up.'

'Here's the deal,' Paddy said authoritatively. 'We'll sit you up, make you a nice cup of tea, and then we'll bring you into hospital to get that arm x-rayed. All right?'

'No ambulance,' Moira stated firmly.

'No ambulance,' Paddy promised. 'I'll be your personal chauffeur!'

'I don't like ambulances ...' Moira stared into the far distance, her mind suddenly somewhere else. 'The baby ... *all* the babies ... lost, gone forever ...'

Laura pulled Paddy aside. 'What does she mean?'

'I assume she's referring to the miscarriages she had before Erin was born,' he replied sotto voce.

So Moira and Joe hadn't had fertility issues, per se. They had managed to conceive – a number of times from the sounds of it – but poor Moira had miscarried at least one of her babies in the back of an ambulance. No wonder she thought children were so very precious, a gift from God that had eluded her until Erin had come along. But how and where did Julien fit in? Was it really possible that he was Erin's father, and that she had his eyes? Or was he just a name from another place and time, a name that Moira had randomly latched on to? It was a question for later, when Moira was x-rayed and safe.

Paddy instructed Moira to hook her good arm around his shoulder. He eased her into a sitting position.

'Now, my good assistant, Laura here, will stand behind you so that you don't lose your balance, and the beautiful Olivia will pull out that kitchen chair for your derrière.'

'What's a derrière?' Olivia asked.

'It's a bottom,' Paddy told her. 'It's a fancy word for Moira's bottom.'

They all laughed then. For some reason, Laura found Paddy genuinely amusing tonight.

As Paddy promised, they made Moira a cup of tea once they had her sitting on the chair. The tea had the desired effect – Moira was now much calmer. She declined anything to eat other than another sweet biscuit, which Olivia provided before devouring one herself.

'I forgot about your dinner, Floss,' Laura said wearily. 'You must be starving.'

'Why don't you take her home,' Paddy suggested, 'and I'll take Moira in. You can follow me once you're ready.'

'Thanks, Paddy.' Laura stood up. She kissed Moira's crinkly cheek. 'I'm leaving you with your chauffeur, and I'll see you in the hospital. Okay?'

'I don't like hospitals.'

'I know you don't. I understand, Moira, I really do.'

Laura had to turn her head so that none of them, not Moira, nor Paddy, and especially not Olivia, would see the tears welling in her eyes.

* * * * *

Kasia was home, which Laura had hoped would be the case, but with the way her luck had been going she hadn't dared to plan on it.

'Auntie Moira fell on the floor and needs an x-ray,' Olivia announced before Laura could explain the situation. 'Uncle Paddy is taking her to hospital because she doesn't like

256

ambulances. Mummy needs you to mind me because Daddy isn't here again.'

Well done, Olivia! What a succinct summation of the situation.

Laura grimaced. 'I'm sorry to drop this on you, Kasia. Do you have plans tonight?'

'I can change them,' Kasia said slowly.

'It should only be for a couple of hours. Esteban's flight is due to land at eight.'

'It is okay.'

'Thanks, Kasia. Olivia hasn't had any dinner …'

'I will make her a sandwich.'

Jam and bread? Did it matter? 'Perfect. Thanks.'

Laura changed into a more comfortable pair of shoes, ran a comb through her hair, which was in dire need of professional attention by now, and came back downstairs.

'Tell Esteban I'm at St James'.'

'I will.'

Laura rushed back out the door, ignoring her own hunger pangs, the image of a strangely appetising jam and bread sandwich lodging itself in her brain.

By the time she got to the hospital, Paddy had already negotiated the admissions procedure and Moira, looking even more frail and scared, was waiting for her x-ray.

'They're giving her priority,' Paddy told Laura when she asked how long they were likely to have to wait. 'Let's hope it won't be too long now.'

Laura was less hopeful. Her recent experience of hospitals consisted of the two occasions she'd taken Olivia to Accident and Emergency – a broken toe when she was three, and scarlet fever a few months later. Time was like a vortex in here, minutes and hours mysteriously sucked away.

Trying not to think of the calories, Laura got herself a bag of crisps and a bar of chocolate from the vending machine.

Sitting back down on the hard plastic seat, she offered the

bag to Moira, who shook her head.

'No, thank you. I'd love a cigarette, though.'

Laura grinned at her aunt. 'I'd love one too, but they aren't allowed in here.'

Moira looked surprised. 'Since when?'

'Oh, about the last thirty years,' Laura replied dryly.

Moira snorted. 'Good Lord, my memory is appalling.'

Once again, the three of them were laughing. Despite the upset and drama, there had been truly funny moments throughout the evening, and despite Moira being frightened and confused, it was reassuring to know that she was still in possession of her sense of humour.

An hour later – not bad by hospital standards – Moira was taken through to the x-ray department.

'Can you see if it's broken?' Laura asked the radiologist, peering over his shoulder at the image on the screen.

'I'm qualified to take the pictures, that's all.'

'But surely you can tell –'

'That's for orthopaedics.'

Afterwards they were shown to one of the consulting rooms, where they waited a further twenty minutes before a doctor, nurse and two medical students arrived.

'The elbow is fractured,' the doctor explained matter-of-factly, holding the black and white image of Moira's arm up to the light so that they could all see. 'There's the crack.'

'Paddy broke his arm once,' Moira stated. 'He fell backwards off the garden wall. Our mother said he was lucky he didn't break his head.'

Paddy shrugged sheepishly. 'I was nine years old at the time. I stay away from walls these days.'

'I was the eldest,' Moira informed the doctor. 'I was held responsible for all the others. It was very boring being the eldest.'

The doctor smiled. Though clearly rushed off his feet, he seemed to be making an effort to slow down for Moira's sake.

'I'm the eldest, too,' he told her. 'Of five. Do you remember the fall, Moira? Did you trip over something? Did you slip?'

Moira frowned as she tried to recollect what had happened. 'I don't remember anything. Nothing at all.'

'We want to keep you in for a few days,' he said, making some notes in her file.

'Oh, that won't be necessary,' she assured him.

'I'm afraid it is. Not only do we want to keep an eye on that elbow of yours, which is broken in a very tricky place, we also want to run a few tests and make sure that the fall wasn't caused by anything more sinister.'

Laura and Paddy exchanged alarmed looks. It hadn't occurred to either of them that the fall might be caused by anything other than Moira losing her balance.

'I don't like hospitals.' Moira folded her arms.

'We're very nice in here.' The doctor smiled pleasantly. 'I promise.'

He finished his notes, and imparted specific instructions to the nurse on how the elbow should be set.

Laura followed him and the medical students outside. Already, his long strides had the group a good distance down the corridor.

'Excuse me,' she called.

He turned. 'Yes?'

She took a few steps closer and so did he. The students hung back uncertainly.

'Exactly what did you mean when you said the fall could have been caused by something more sinister?'

'I was referring to the possibility that your aunt may have had a stroke.'

Laura felt the strength drain from her. '*A stroke?*'

'We don't always see outward signs of a stroke,' he replied kindly. 'In fact, silent strokes are a lot more prevalent than symptomatic ones. We'll do an MRI tomorrow and discuss what we find. Okay?'

Laura nodded numbly.

Back in the consulting room, the nurse had begun work on Moira's arm. Laura avoided Paddy's questioning gaze. She'd tell him later on. Right now, she was in serious danger of bursting into tears. Again.

* * * * *

More hours were sucked away before Moira was found a bed in one of the wards, and it was after midnight when Laura got home. She sat woodenly in the car and watched the digital clock turn over another few minutes. She might have stayed there, too emotionally and physically drained to move, had Esteban not opened the door of the house. He must have been listening for her car. Laura took a deep breath as she pulled the keys from the ignition. Esteban came halfway down the path to greet her.

'How is she?'

'They've kept her in ... She has a broken elbow, and they want to give her an MRI tomorrow ...' Laura heard the wobble in her voice. Was she finally going to cry? Or could she hold back her tears yet again? Which would it be?

'An MRI?'

'It's possible that the fall was caused by a stroke.'

'Oh, Laura.'

She was going to cry. Definitely. Her throat felt full. Her cheeks ached.

'You weren't there. I really needed you tonight, and you weren't there. You are *never* there for me ... Or for Olivia ... Never.'

'You're right,' he said gravely. 'I'm sorry.'

'Sorry isn't good enough,' she cried, aware that she was creating a scene out in the open, in the dead of night. 'We need you *here*. Not at the end of a phone, not on a plane somewhere. Right here, at home with your family. We need you for breakfast and dinner, for birthdays, for ballet and school concerts, for times when things go wrong. We *need* you. Do you understand? Do you?'

'Yes, I do.' His voice was broken. Was he crying too? 'I do.'

Laura allowed him to pull her close, and she tried to take strength from his arms, and to stop the tears that were gushing from her eyes. Deep breaths. She needed to pull herself together. Crawling straight into bed with the hope of feeling better in the morning wasn't an option. She had to call Erin as soon as she went inside. Slow, deep breaths. She needed to be as calm as possible. Because Erin would be beyond distraught.

Chapter 31

Erin made a concentrated effort not to gawk at Adam's nose at the staff meeting the next day, averting her eyes downwards to her notebook.

Her colleagues showed no such sensitivity.

'It's like a beacon ...' Thu exclaimed in a tone of wonderment.

'Once the swelling settles down, I think the bump will give my profile a nice ruggedness,' Adam countered.

'You're an occupational health and safety hazard!' said Fran, one of the teaching staff.

He bowed graciously. 'I do my best.'

Lydia sniffed with disapproval. 'This might encourage you to slow down, and to take time to look where you're going.'

'Thanks for the advice, Lydia. And I'll pretend I didn't hear you and Erin laughing behind my back yesterday.'

Erin, at hearing her name, looked up to meet his eyes. She smiled shamefacedly. 'Sorry, Adam. It *was* funny, though.'

After a few more heckles about his nose and the perils of being always in a rush, Adam began the meeting, which was about a new software system being piloted by the Department of Immigration.

'This system will measure migrant reach, student retention, education and settlement outcomes, childcare, counselling, home tutoring –' Adam listed, stopping midstream as someone's phone began to ring rather loudly. 'Who's forgotten to turn off their phone?'

It took Erin a few moments to realise that it was hers. 'Sorry.' She smiled once again at Adam, this time apologetically, while she fumbled in her bag to find her phone. Where was the stupid thing? Who was ringing her at this time of the morning? Had Jack left something behind in her apartment? Here it was. Erin switched it off, but not before noticing that the call was from Laura.

'The new system will track each student individually, and the results will be analysed and amalgamated to ensure that the college is meeting the key performance indicators in our contract with the government ...'

Erin was only half-listening to Adam. This was an odd time for Laura to call. It was after midnight in Ireland. What was she doing up so late? Really, that girl needed to slow down.

'The government's aim is to use the system all around the country, and to thereby gain consistency in its migrant program ...'

Erin tried to focus. New computer system ... Consistency ... Laura wasn't ringing with bad news, was she? No. That was being automatically negative. Laura could very well be calling with *good* news. Maybe she was going on a holiday, or she was pregnant, and so excited she hadn't stopped to think that Erin would be at work at this time of the morning. Erin would call her back immediately after the meeting. In half an hour. Whatever it was could wait until then. Unless it really was serious.

Erin stood up suddenly, realising she couldn't wait that long to put her mind at ease. 'Excuse me, Adam ... I just need to check something ... I'll be back in a minute.'

She left the meeting room quietly, clicking the door shut behind her. Once outside, she switched her mobile back on. It took a few long moments before it was functional again. Laura had left a voice message.

'Ring me as soon as you get this, Erin. It's about Moira.'

Oh God. Something had happened to her mother. Something bad, not good. Panic swelled inside her. Her chest began to feel tight.

Breathe. Breathe.

All the other upstairs meeting rooms were occupied. Adam's empty office was Erin's only chance of privacy. She rushed inside, hoping he wouldn't mind. Her fingers were shaking so much she could hardly hit the right keys on her phone to locate Laura's number. It took a few attempts. Breathe. Breathe. There. She had managed it. Now it was ringing. And Laura was saying hello.

'It's me,' Erin said breathlessly. 'You were looking for me?'

'Yes …' Laura sounded short of breath, too. In fact, she had tears in her voice. 'Your mother has had an accident …'

So intense was the rush of anxiety and guilt that Erin had to bend over.

'She fell and broke her elbow. More seriously, they're worried that the fall might have been caused by a stroke …'

As Erin listened, her chest constricted further and further. It hurt. Really hurt. She was having a heart attack. This time she really was.

* * * * *

'Z … Y … X … W…'

'Erin.' It was Adam. Stopped in the doorway of his office, she would have found his expression comical had she been feeling remotely humorous. 'What are you doing in here?'

'Cleaning,' she told him as matter-of-factly as she could.

'Your office is an absolute mess, Adam … V… U … T … S…'

'Okay, that's a fair call.' For a moment, he looked slightly abashed about the state of his work environment. 'But is there a particular reason why you're reciting the alphabet backwards?'

'Because my doctor told me to. To distract myself.'

His eyes swept across the straightened piles of paperwork on his desk. 'And you're cleaning my office for the same reason?'

'Yes. Cleaning is good. Very distracting.'

'And why, exactly, this sudden need to distract yourself?' he asked, coming further into the room and stopping disconcertingly close to her.

She dropped her eyes from the sudden scrutiny of his gaze. 'Because I'm panicking.'

He took a few moments to process this information. 'Do you need to lie down?'

'No, lying down is bad.'

'How about walking?'

She shrugged. 'I don't know.'

'Okay.' Though she could hear a smile in his voice, she didn't risk looking him in the eye again. 'Clean away, but maybe we can talk instead of doing the alphabet thing. Who was the phone call from?'

'My cousin Laura,' she replied, briskly wiping the limited surface space on his desk with a cloth she had found in the kitchen.

'Why was Laura calling you?'

'My mother.' Erin's voice broke. She wiped furiously at a ring mark on the desk before she could continue. 'Mum fell and broke her elbow … The doctor suspects she may have had a stroke.'

'I see. That is upsetting news. I think I would panic too if I were in your shoes.'

'No, you wouldn't, Adam,' she whispered, her hand stilling

on the soggy cloth. 'You'd feel sad and shaken … but you wouldn't feel as though you were about to die.'

'Is that how it feels?'

'Yes.'

'So, it's happened before?'

'I didn't know what it was the first time, what was happening to me. I thought I was having a heart attack – the school called an ambulance at my insistence – but it was nothing but panic, sheer and utter panic. I felt so *stupid* afterwards.'

His voice was gentle, with no evidence of its usual urgency. 'And you've been to the doctor and he's given you some techniques to deal with the panic?'

'Yes.' At last she looked at him. It was force of habit, something her mother had instilled in her: an apology didn't count unless you were looking the person you had offended in the eye. 'I'm sorry, Adam. I should have told you about this before taking the job … I should have told you that you had a nutcase on your hands.'

He dismissed her apology with a self-deprecating laugh. 'Hey, speaking of nutcases, didn't you see my nose today?'

She tried to laugh, too, but it came out sounding more like a sob. 'I'm a fraud … I should have told you about the panic attacks upfront, and I should have told you that I couldn't possibly stay in this country for longer than a year … that's what Laura convinced me to do … to take a year out …'

He took her free hand, encasing it with both of his, stroking it with his thumbs. 'So you're telling me you need to go back home?'

'Yes.' That massage thing he was doing to her hand was having an effect. The panic had subsided. In its place was resignation. 'Please believe me when I say I love my job and I love my life here. But I have to go back. I knew this from the outset. *There's no other way …*'

She was crying now, weary resigned tears. Poor Adam.

She'd cleaned his office only to fill it with her own neurotic, emotional mess. In fairness, he didn't seem at all fazed. Funny how he was so calm and still, as though he had all the time in the world to listen to her woes. The last time she had seen him like this was the night he'd slept on her couch. That seemed like a lifetime ago now.

One of his hands rose to her face and brushed away her tears. 'Go home. See how your mother is. Reassure yourself for the short term at least. The rest will work itself out.'

It sounded so simple, just like Lydia's advice yesterday. Be brave. Everything would work itself out.

If only.

Chapter 32

'Is this where I live now?'

It was the third time Moira had asked this question since Laura had come to visit an hour ago.

'No. This is a rehab centre. The doctor wants you to stay here while your arm gets better. The hospital needed your bed for someone else.'

'Oh.'

They lapsed into silence. The TV flickered in the background, the sound so low it was indiscernible.

'Do you want me to turn it up?' Laura asked after a while.

Moira shook her head. 'No – I've no interest in it.'

Moira seemed as keen as Laura to use the silence as an opportunity to think. The room had a pleasant view of the gardens and this was where the older woman trained her eyes while she thought. What was she thinking of? Another garden, another place and time? Or perhaps a day that was similar to this one, with its white sky and filtered sunshine?

Laura was thinking about Erin, who was arriving home later tonight. Emotional, guilt-laden phone calls had punctuated the few days it had taken Erin to organise her flight and to be away from her job and apartment for a couple of weeks. That first call when Erin had all but broken down on the phone, followed by the call when Laura had told her that the doctor's suspicions had been confirmed and a minor stroke had indeed been the root cause of the fall. Then a call to let her know that her mother was being moved to this rehab centre. At least the next time Laura spoke to Erin it would be face to face. She could comfort and reassure her in a way she couldn't on the phone.

Moira, gazing steadfastly out the window, seemed to be transfixed by the manicured lawns and the small trees that were tossing with the breeze. Or maybe it was the patients and their aides, walking with hooked arms along the paths, that she found so captivating.

'We should go outside,' Laura suggested. 'I could ask the nurses for a wheelchair.'

Moira looked as though she was about to dismiss the idea, suggesting that she was content to look at the garden and had no desire to experience it.

'Come on,' Laura urged. 'It's a lovely day.'

Moira's expression morphed from dismissive to undecided, before she nodded with a small measure of enthusiasm.

Laura spoke to one of the nurses, and secured a wheelchair and some assistance to help Moira into it: the cast on her arm seemed to have really affected her aunt's balance.

Outside it was as pleasant as it had promised to be from the inside, a hazy sun breaking through the thin layer of cloud, a mild breeze playing pleasantly against Laura's face. She pushed the heavy chair around two laps of the garden, the effort inducing a slight sweat. Moira said nothing for most of the time. She seemed to be in a very vague state of mind today.

'Erin's flight will be landing in Dublin in six hours,' Laura said conversationally, parking the chair next to a bench so she could sit down and catch her breath. 'I think she'll be very impressed with this place.' Laura had told Moira a number of times that Erin was flying home to see her. She had come to realise that repetition helped her aunt greatly when it came to retaining information. 'Won't it be wonderful to see her?'

Moira stared into the distance. 'You should have told her not to come. I don't want to get in the way of her new life. I'm fine.'

Laura smiled and shrugged. 'I think Erin needs to reassure herself of that. Nothing we say is good enough. She needs to see you for herself.'

Moira blinked. 'She's always been such a good girl. Caring and loyal to a fault … We made the right decision, Joe and I. We did the right thing.'

Laura's heart beat slightly faster. What decision had Joe and Moira made? To stay together even though Moira had had an affair? To raise Erin as Joe's child? Should she ask Moira outright about Julien?

Before she could articulate the right words in her head, Moira turned suddenly in the chair and grabbed Laura by the wrist.

'This secret is killing me, Cathy. Slowly but surely, I'm dying from it …'

'Moira –'

'When Joe was here I had someone to share it with, but since he's been gone I've had to carry it all alone. It's seizing my mind, destroying it cell by cell …'

So Joe knew. If what Moira was saying could be relied on – and that was the biggest question here – Joe had known from the outset that the baby wasn't his. That was something at least: Moira had been truthful with her husband. Their marriage hadn't been based on a lie. But their family had been, and Erin, who'd always had such identity issues, deserved to know the truth.

'Moira, you need to let Erin know who her father is,' Laura said, quietly but firmly. 'When you see her, you must tell her the truth.'

Moira looked at her strangely. Silence stretched between

them, a silence loaded with secrets and lies and decades of cover-ups. 'I think it's more important that I tell her who her mother is,' she responded eventually.

Laura frowned. 'You're her mother ...'

'Stop playing stupid, Cathy,' Moira snapped, her thin fingers digging into Laura's wrist. 'I've told you before that it isn't becoming of you.'

'But you're her mother. You raised her, and cared for her, and loved her ...'

Moira laughed bitterly and dropped Laura's hand. 'But I didn't give birth to her, did I? You did that, Cathy. You did that.'

Chapter 33

Paris,
July 1975

Dear Paddy,

Well Cathy has arrived, and Paris has been duly taken by storm! In the first few days, we took her around the city and showed her all the sights, but Cathy being Cathy, she soon made it clear that she was far more interested in the nightlife than the tourist attractions. She has taken up residence in our house, but she's been out enjoying herself so much that Joe and I have hardly seen her (more than once, Joe has encountered her in the hallway on his way to work, she on her way in from a night out …). Of course she has a boyfriend already. Have you ever known Cathy to be single for longer than a moment? I've warned her about the men here, how much more sophisticated and dangerous they are than the boys back home, but I think this is precisely what attracts her to this new man. He's a musician and plays in the city's most elite clubs, hence Cathy's late hours. I know she's twenty years old, an adult, but I still think of her as the baby of the family, and I feel responsible for her safety, for her happiness, for everything. Silly, isn't it? After all, I was the one who urged her to come here, and now I'm the one who wants to lock her in her room to keep her safe. These over-the-top mothering instincts must come from being pregnant. Four months now, Paddy, and I feel great – confident – and so does Joe. By Christmas we'll have a baby in the house and we'll be far too preoccupied to worry about Cathy's comings and goings and unsuitable boyfriends.

Hope all the family is well. Love to everyone.

Moira

August 1975

Dear Gerry,

It's happened again: poor Moira lost the baby. She woke in the night in terrible pain, and gave birth in the ambulance on the way to hospital. A tiny baby boy – absolutely perfect, if it weren't for the fact that he was dead. She named the baby Eamon, and we buried him yesterday in a cemetery on the outskirts of Paris. She's distraught, Gerry, consumed with grief. She let her guard down and allowed herself to believe this baby would make it, and so the loss has been more profound than ever before. She trails around the house, like a desperately unhappy ghost. (Anna, the maid, also has a habit of skulking around in the shadows and I have to be on alert these days not to have the life frightened out of me.) I'm the first to admit that I know nothing about babies, but I have to question this relentless urge Moira has to hold one in her arms. It's obviously not worth all the heartbreak. When will she see sense?

Despite the sadness of the last few days, Paris has been treating me wonderfully. I can do exactly as I want – live how I want to live – and the freedom feels like a drug. I've met a man, a French man. His name is Julien and he plays the saxophone in a blues band – he's talented AND handsome. I know you always joked that I would never fall in love because I was too much in love with having fun – but I think this might be it. Julien makes all those boys at home seem exactly that: boys, not men. Now I wish I'd come here sooner. There I was, wasting the last few years in Dublin, wallowing in ordinariness, when all the time I could have been experiencing Paris and how truly extraordinary it is.

In a few months, when Moira has recovered, I'll move in with Julien. I can hear your gasp of shock. No, we will not get married, or have children, or do anything so conventional. You don't realise, Gerry, how repressed and behind the times Ireland is. Seriously, I could have an affair, Julien could keep a mistress, and nobody here would raise an eyebrow. It's sometimes difficult to believe that Dublin and Paris are not that far apart in terms of geographical distance. In terms of everything else – life, attitudes, love – they're worlds apart.

Must sign off. Julien has a gig at a very exclusive club tonight and I must get my glad rags on. Try not to worry about Moira. I will keep an eye on her as best I can.

XX Cathy

Dear Mrs Donovan,

I am writing following your recent consultation in my office. I appreciate our conversation was distressing and that you found it hard to accept my diagnosis and recommendation, and so I feel compelled to put in writing what we discussed. From my examination of the aborted fetus, your recent miscarriage was caused by a variety of chromosomal abnormalities. It appears that you and your husband have an abnormal gene that is being repeatedly passed on, resulting in multiple pregnancy losses. Given your medical history, and the amount of blood loss and physical and mental distress of your recent miscarriage, I strongly recommend that you do not endeavour to conceive again. I have enclosed some information on adoption for you and your husband to consider.

Please come and see me if you have any further questions. I am sorry to be the bearer of bad news, and I sympathise deeply with your situation.

Yours faithfully,

Docteur Gynecologue Philippe Vivies

Dear Julien,

I am dropping this note in your post box because you seem to be out every time I call around. If I didn't know better, I would think that you were avoiding me. You're panicking, aren't you? You think I want to keep the baby. I know you so well, but you must not know me at all if you think this is what I want for my life. I meant what I said, and I have already seen a doctor and got a referral to a clinic. I've even booked in for the procedure, but there is a one-week cooling off period during which I must reflect and decide if I want to go ahead or not. I have assured the clinic that I will not change my mind, and I resent having to wait a week to have this ordeal over with. I have been feeling ill these last few days, once or twice I had to rush from the dinner table to the toilet bowl where I promptly ejected my meal. God, I hope Moira does not suspect anything. How ironic that she has been trying all this time to make a baby, while I, who could not think of anything worse, have ended up pregnant. Such are the ironies and cruelties of life.

I will write again when the procedure is over. We can resume where we left off, and this time we will be more scrupulous about birth control. I miss you terribly, and look forward to things going back to the way they were.

Ton amour,

Cathy

Dear Mama,

I am sorry that I have not written to you for a while. My days are a strange mix of tedious and busy, and I am coming to the conclusion that I will never make a good housemaid. It is very evident that Moira, the mistress of the house, finds me awkward and unengaging. Sometimes she looks right through me, as though I am not really here, and it amuses me that it does not occur to her how much I see, and how much I know. You will be shocked at the recent events in this house. Cathy, Moira's sister, is pregnant.

I figured this out on my own (after all, I was the unfortunate one who had to clean up stray pieces of vomit from the bathroom). I am also responsible for sorting through the mail, and the clinic's address was printed clearly on the envelope. Everyone in Paris knows what happens in that clinic. Of course the man involved has turned his back on her – don't they always? Now, I am about to admit to interference, or meddling, but I prefer to think of it as the former. I 'accidentally' put the clinic's letter in with Moira's mail and, as I'd hoped for, she opened it without realising it wasn't addressed to her. The two sisters have been having arguments since, behind closed doors, of course, but sound has an eerie way of travelling in this house. Moira's voice is pleading, Cathy's is obstinate. Joe has been called in to mediate. He sounds torn.

'Children are precious,' Moira keeps repeating over and over again. I agree with her, and this is why I did what I did. I know what will happen, how this dilemma will play out, though the three of them haven't quite figured out the obvious yet. There is a happy ending for everyone but me (it is inevitable that they will return to Dublin and I will be out of a job). Maybe this will be an incentive for me to get something better. A job in a bank or an office, perhaps? I think I am done with dusting, making beds and being invisible.

Your loving daughter,

Anna

Chapter 34

Erin found her seat, nestled between an overweight middle-aged man deeply engrossed in his newspaper, and a teenage boy with earphones plugged into his stick-out ears.

'Excuse me. Sorry to disturb you.'

The older man, with a slightly irritated expression, stood up and stepped into the aisle, allowing her barely enough space to manoeuvre past his jutting stomach.

This was the last leg: London to Dublin. She would be home in an hour. *Home.* The word evoked nothing, no sense of belonging or comfort, no feeling at all, just a strange void. Her eyes felt gritty and red. Sleep had eluded her. She had tried, of course, turning off her reading light, shutting her eyes, but there was no escaping the fact that she was alert in every way, conscious of the wrench of leaving Sydney, her job, her friends, and dreading the impossible situation that awaited her at 'home'.

As the plane began to move backwards, Erin checked her watch. The flight was departing on time. In fact, each leg of the journey had gone without a hitch. Like it or not, she was being spirited back to Dublin. She'd been travelling for over thirty hours, thirty hours without sleep, thirty hours without enlightenment. Her thoughts were becoming disjointed. The man next to her, who had selfishly commandeered both armrests, had his newspaper open at the sports section. The stewardess, trying to suppress the urge to giggle, was demonstrating how to inflate a life jacket. Erin suddenly recalled that she had left a carton of milk on her kitchen counter. She had been about to dispose of it. What had happened to distract her? Yes, Lydia had dropped by unexpectedly.

'I came to wish you a safe journey. And to give you a big hug.' Lydia's sinewy, ballerina arms had clasped Erin tightly to her. 'And to tell you to be brave.'

Erin had to laugh. 'Oh, Lydia, you tell me to be brave so often that I'm beginning to suspect you're very well aware of what a scaredy cat I am!'

Lydia didn't laugh. It seemed that bravery was a deadly serious matter. She looked Erin squarely in the eye.

'Bravery does not come naturally to some of us. There's no point in doing one brave thing and thinking that's all that's required. Every morning you get up, every single day of your life, you must take a moment to remind yourself to be brave.'

Shortly after Lydia left, Mel phoned to say her goodbyes.

'My students are being such a nightmare today,' she moaned. 'I feel like jumping in your suitcase and coming with you.'

'Jack is taking me to the airport. He'd oust you from the suitcase and order you back to work.'

'Drat. Must come up with another plan …' Mel's tone became wistful, nostalgic. 'I can't help being reminded of when you had to go home because your dad was ill.'

'I know. Me too.'

This was what worried Erin the most: the last time she had said goodbye to Mel. Both of them so innocent, without any exposure to life's hard knocks and cruel turns of fate, they'd fully believed that her father's illness was an upsetting yet temporary glitch. He would have treatment for his cancer, and once he was recovered – no other, less successful outcome had been contemplated – Erin would rejoin Mel in Australia. Such confidence they'd had. So little insight into real life.

Once she had hung up from Mel, Erin threw a few more things into her suitcase, zipped it up and rolled it to the hallway.

Jack arrived bang on time, as punctual as ever. However, he was unusually introspective on the journey to the airport. It was as though he, too, didn't trust this sudden departure and its supposedly temporary nature.

'You are coming back, aren't you?' he asked at one juncture.

'Of course I am.'

Despite the conviction in her tone, and the fact that both her apartment and job had been left in an unresolved state which demanded her return, she understood his mistrust. She felt exactly the same way, as though the very minute she stepped into her old life she would instantly realise that there was no turning back, and that she was trapped, this time for good.

Minutes from the airport, her phone beeped with a text. From Adam.

Hope it goes well. Keep in touch. Will be thinking of you.

She would be thinking of him, too. In fact, he'd been occupying more than his fair share of her thoughts these last few days. The warmth of his friendship, his irrepressible enthusiasm for life, the way that thinking of him was enough to make her lips twitch with a smile. She was going to miss him for the couple of weeks that she was away. If it turned out to be longer than that, if it was *permanent*, she would feel quite bereft. It was all very confusing and, she was the first to admit, not particularly fair on Jack.

The drop-off zone was experiencing a lull, and Jack had to compete with only a couple of other cars for kerb space. He pulled in, but just as Erin undid her belt, he changed his mind, pulling out again to take a spot further along. Jumpy, indecisive, introspective, he wasn't himself today.

'We need to talk when you get back,' he said, swinging her suitcase onto the pavement.

'We do?' she asked distractedly. 'What about?'

'Well, you know how much I care about you, and I want to take our relationship to the next level …'

The next level? Which was what, exactly? Moving in together? Getting engaged? Oh, dear. They *did* need to talk when she got back. Just not in the way he was expecting.

'Don't forget to call.' He leant down to kiss her goodbye, not realising that in many ways she was already gone from him.

Yes, it was all very confusing. Jack. Adam. Mel. Lydia and her obsession with bravery.

The confusion was weighing Erin down, immobilising her.

Finally, somewhere over the Irish Sea and much too late, she drifted off to sleep.

* * * * *

Laura pummelled the door with her fists. Never in her life had she felt so angry, and making noise like this was so satisfying; a quiet tap would simply not have done the situation justice. If she had been a man, she could have barged the door with her shoulder, crashing into the house. Now that would have been a statement: I am here, and look at how furious I am; and let me tell you that the damage to the door and your property is paltry next to the damage caused by your selfishness and deceit.

Through the frosted glass panel on the side of the door

she saw the outline of a figure advancing down the hall, and she hoped with all her might that it was her mother, not her father.

It was.

Cathy opened the door and blinked her blue eyes with surprise. Wearing a silk robe, she looked as though she was on her way to bed. 'What on *earth* is the matter?'

'You,' Laura screeched. 'You are the matter.'

'Good Lord. My grown-up daughter is apparently in the throes of a full-blown tantrum.'

'This is *not* a tantrum.' Blood rushed to Laura's face. How typical that her mother would be so dismissive and condescending. 'I *know* … I know *everything* … And I don't know how you can live with yourself.'

Cathy's face was the picture of innocence. 'You know *what*, exactly?'

She was a good liar, her mother, but then she'd had more than thirty years of practice, *thirty-four* years to be precise.

'I know what happened in Paris,' Laura hissed. 'I know the truth about *Erin*.'

Cathy's expression remained impassive. It was her tone, a slight breathlessness, that gave her away. 'Your father is watching telly upstairs. You'll have to keep your voice down …' She stood back from the door and gestured Laura inside.

In the kitchen, her mother extracted two wine glasses from one of the cabinets, and without checking with Laura if she wanted a drink, screwed the lid off a bottle of shiraz, filling each glass to the rim. Her hand shook ever so slightly. Laura noticed this only because she was staring at her mother as though she had never seen her before.

'Does Dad know?' she asked in a hard voice.

Cathy leant one hand on the counter while she gulped her wine. 'Nobody knows. Moira, Joe and me … it was strictly between the three of us. Though I always suspected that the maid knew something … Anna …'

Laura shook her head in disbelief. 'How could you all do this? How could you tell such a fundamental lie? How? Or, more importantly, *why*?'

Cathy shrugged. 'Because Moira desperately wanted a baby, and I, just as desperately, didn't want one … In fact, I'd planned to have an abortion … I wasn't ready to be a mother …'

Laura sipped her wine. It tasted sour in her mouth, but maybe that was the conversation rather than the wine. She tried to assemble what she knew.

'So Moira found out that you were going to have an abortion and talked you out of it?'

Cathy nodded, and took another long drink from her glass. 'She understood that I didn't want to be a mother. She said she would raise the baby, and nobody needed to know it was mine. That way the baby would be saved, and I would be saved – from hell, apparently.' Cathy's laugh was brittle. 'It was a win-win.'

Laura frowned. The deception hadn't been that simple, had it? 'But what about Erin's birth certificate? You must have been listed as the mother?'

Cathy shook her head. 'I used Moira's name at the hospital, so all the paperwork was in her name. Nobody asked for ID in those days. It was easier than you'd think.'

'And the father. Did you see him afterwards?'

'Julien?' Cathy sounded wistful. 'No, I never saw him again. He completely broke my heart … Your first love is always the most poignant, isn't it?'

Laura had to swallow a retort. 'And so you all came back to Dublin, and Moira and Joe passed the baby off as theirs, pretending that Moira had been pregnant in Paris?'

'Yes. There'd been so many miscarriages, nobody asked any questions, everyone was delighted for her. As I said, it was easier than you'd think.'

Cathy had finished her glass of wine while Laura had hardly touched hers. As her mother refilled her glass, to the rim again, she spilt some of the wine, a dark red blotch staining the white stone countertop. Immediately, before it left a stain, she found a cloth and wiped it away. Laura watched her every movement with growing disdain.

'I can't believe you didn't tell Erin this, that it never occurred to you that she had a right to know she was your daughter.'

'She's Moira's daughter,' Cathy replied in a light yet insistent tone. 'Moira was the one who wanted to keep her, not me.'

'How could you have watched what she went through last year, the panic attacks, feeling so torn over Moira, so trapped, how could you have stood by and not said anything? At the very least, you could have eased her guilt about going away, but you never said a word.'

'I am *not* her mother.' Cathy's voice was becoming as scratchy and repetitive as a broken record. '*Moira* is her mother.'

There was no question that Cathy meant what she said. She wasn't harbouring a secret longing to embrace Erin as her first-born daughter. She really did see Erin as Moira's child and not her own. How could she be so callous? So blinkered?

Suddenly *everything* made sense to Laura: Cathy's offhand mothering when she was little, her ongoing – almost dogged – avoidance of commitment and responsibility, right down to her reluctance to adopt a useful and meaningful role in Olivia's life. Motherhood, grandmother-hood, all of it was like a foreign country to Cathy. A place where she didn't feel comfortable and had no sense of belonging.

Laura pushed away her half-drunk glass of wine and hooked her thumb underneath the shoulder strap of her bag.

She addressed her mother in a steady, mature voice.

'The problem with you is that you're still not ready to be a proper mother, and I'm not sure that you ever will be.'

And with that, she walked out.

Chapter 35

Erin woke as the plane hit the runway. She felt both disoriented and deeply lethargic, her lips and the inside of her mouth dehydrated. As though to taunt her, the teenage boy on her left unscrewed a bottle of water and took a long, unselfconscious slug.

'Welcome to Dublin,' the captain said pleasantly over the intercom. 'It's fifteen degrees outside, and you'll all be happy to hear it's a mild, clear night. If you're visiting Dublin, please proceed to our tourist desk ...'

She wasn't a visitor. She didn't need a rental car or a hotel room for the night, or any help getting a bus or taxi. Esteban was going to meet her and take her home. Simple.

'If you're returning home after a holiday, then welcome back. We hope you had a lovely break ...' the captain went on.

No, that didn't apply to her either. Australia hadn't been a holiday, it had been her life.

She was in neither category of traveller referred to by the captain. No wonder she felt so out of place.

The plane came to a halt, and suddenly there was a race: belts were un-clicked, overhead lockers were sprung open, and carry-on bags were hoisted through the air. The overweight man on Erin's other side was surprisingly agile, and was one of the first to retrieve his bag. He stood with his newspaper tucked under one arm, his bag in the other, frowning at the queue in front of him until it slowly moved forward. Erin sat patiently, waiting for a break in the line of exiting passengers. The teenage boy next to her was getting twitchy – he clearly didn't like being trapped like this. This is nothing, she felt like telling him.

It took a few minutes. That was all. A few minutes for a gap to materialise in the line, to slide out of her seat, to yank her cabin bag from overhead, and to smile politely and say thanks to the crew on her way off the plane. Another few minutes to go through passport control.

'Where are you travelling from tonight?' the security officer enquired as he checked her passport.

'Australia.'

'Always wanted to go there myself,' he declared cheerfully.

So had Erin.

Now that she was officially in Ireland, it took another few minutes for her luggage to appear on the carousel, and no time at all to sail through the green channel in customs.

She was here. She was back. There was Esteban, waving and weaving his way through the crowd. He looked tired, she noticed. Jaded in both the physical and mental sense. Resigned. Unhappy.

Exactly how she felt herself.

* * * * *

Laura glanced out the window for the zillionth time. It was an unusually still night. There was very little traffic, not a sound from the neighbouring houses, not even a hint of a breeze. It felt as though the night was waiting for Esteban's car to turn into the driveway, and precisely from that moment the stillness would be shattered, confusion and turmoil would prevail, and nothing would ever be the same again. Laura would hear his car. There was really no need to keep watch like this, but still she felt compelled to do so. What a night it had been. What a day. What a week. Erin would be feeling overwhelmed, too, at the end of a long journey and an emotional few days. Maybe Laura should wait to tell her, allow her a night's sleep and the chance to get her bearings. Yes, she would wait until the morning. It was going to be difficult, she wouldn't sleep a wink herself, but dumping this news on Erin the minute she arrived simply wasn't fair. She would wait. She would *make herself* wait.

As she kept watch, a white flimsy-looking car slowed on the road and pulled in at the kerb. Erin hadn't somehow missed Esteban and got a lift with someone else, had she? The back door of the car opened and Kasia emerged, laughing at something, looking happier than Laura had ever seen her. A boy got out directly after her, leaving the car door open behind him. Technically, he wasn't a boy. He looked as though he was in his early twenties, which made him a man, but Laura felt so old these days that everyone else seemed childlike by comparison. They kissed, Kasia and her boyfriend, ignoring the jeers from the other occupants of the car, oblivious to the fact that Laura was spying on them. Young love. Once upon a time, Laura and Esteban would have done the same, undeterred by a car full of teasing friends, undeterred by where they were or what tasks they should have been doing. How did one recapture that bravado and all-consuming passion? How did one stop young love from slowly degenerating into old, unhappy love?

Kasia's boyfriend cupped her face and kissed her one last time before hopping back into the car. It took off with a screech of tyres. Kasia turned to unlatch the front gate, and Laura quickly moved away from the window.

'Did you have a nice night?' Laura enquired a few moments later, pretending to plump the cushions on the sofa.

'Yes.' Kasia's smile didn't seem as sly as usual. Maybe it had never been sly to start off with. Maybe Kasia was right and Laura was a control freak who always believed the worst of people. 'Yes, I did, thank you. Goodnight.'

Kasia turned and went upstairs, obviously eager to lock herself in her room to daydream – or night-dream, given the late hour – about her boyfriend. Laura found herself wondering if the relationship was serious, if it would end in marriage, children and a mortgage, or if it was one of those short, sweet, carefree romances that Kasia would reminisce over when she was older and tied down with someone else.

She heard the sound of an engine outside. The noise got louder, and headlights illuminated the lamp-lit front room. She had been waiting, keeping watch for the last half hour, yet now that the time had come she felt oddly surprised and off guard. She dropped the cushion in her hand, watched it tumble in slow motion to the floor.

Esteban was here.

Finally, her husband and her *sister* were outside.

* * * * *

Erin was shocked at how pale, tense and exhausted Laura looked. The ferocity of Laura's embrace was a further shock, and when she finally let go tears were rolling down her face, blotching her usually flawless skin. Erin, confronted by her cousin's obvious distress, felt her heart go into freefall. Something had happened. While she'd been in transit, obliviously watching movies and flicking through magazines, or maybe during that very brief time she'd been asleep, Moira had suffered another fall or, even worse, a second stroke.

'What's wrong?' Erin looked from Laura to Esteban for an

answer, but Esteban seemed as confused by Laura's emotional state as she was. 'What is it? Has Mum taken a turn for the worse?'

Laura swallowed and coughed, and wiped her face with her sleeve, a very un-Laura-like action. 'Moira is fine … Sorry, Erin … What a terrible way to greet you … Come inside.'

Esteban spoke, his voice muted. 'Where do you want the suitcase, Laura?'

Laura stopped in her tracks to answer him. 'Just put it on the landing for now … thank you.'

The exchange between husband and wife was civilised. Too civilised. Erin detected a formality, a coldness that caused her heart to drop for the second time in as many minutes. Things weren't good between Laura and Esteban. This explained why Laura was so emotional, and why both of them looked so awful. Laura had mentioned some issues in her emails – disagreements about the nanny, long work hours vying with responsibilities at home, Esteban's ever-increasing travel commitments – which Erin had blithely dismissed as normal marital and workplace stresses. Now that she was here and witness to the tension, the distant politeness, it was obvious that the problems were more significant than she'd thought.

With a sense of disquiet, Erin followed Laura inside. It felt odd to be coming home to Laura's house and not her own. The plan was to spend the night here, and to move home tomorrow, if she desired. Right now, she couldn't think that far ahead.

Laura's house was even more immaculate than she remembered: freshly polished wooden floors, the stone countertop gleaming under the kitchen lights, no stray shoes or toys or any other evidence of the little girl who lived here.

Erin sat on one of the stools. 'I guess Olivia has been asleep for hours.'

'Yes. Her bedtime is seven. Eight at the latest.'

Laura filled and put on the kettle, her movements jerky.

Next, she laid out cups, saucers and plates. Erin would have told her not to go to so much trouble – all she wanted was a cup of decent tea after the awful stuff on the flight – but Laura seemed intent on being the perfect hostess, whipping out a matching milk jug and sugar bowl, sandwiches cut into delicate triangles, a plate of sweet biscuits and a platter of fruit. She was doing an excellent impression of a Stepford wife.

'Thank you for going to so much trouble.'

'It's no trouble,' Laura insisted in a strangled voice.

Erin sipped her tea, and felt the caffeine take effect, reviving her. This was hardly the right time to have a heart-to-heart, not with Esteban upstairs and at risk of overhearing, but she simply couldn't ignore how deeply upset and off kilter Laura was tonight.

'You don't seem yourself,' she said, sotto voce. 'Is everything okay with Esteban?'

Laura put down her cup sharply, rattling the saucer.

'We're going through a bit of a rough patch,' she admitted, her voice not as low as it could have been. 'Actually, it's been more than just a "patch". But I don't want to talk about Esteban right now.' Laura was pushing the palms of her hands against the counter, as though resisting something. 'We need to talk about something else … I need to tell you something … I tried to wait until the morning, but I realise now that I can't keep it from you … you have a right to know …'

What on earth was Laura talking about? If she wasn't specifically anxious about Moira or Esteban, then what was bothering her? The nanny? But Erin wouldn't have 'a right to know' anything about Kasia. It wasn't like Laura to be overly dramatic, or to be anything but direct. She'd been very odd from the moment Erin had arrived.

'What is it?' Erin enquired, hoping the calmness of her tone would rub off on her cousin.

Laura hesitated. Her eyes locked with Erin's. Fresh tears welled in them.

'It's about our mothers ... and that time they were in Paris ... and when you were born ...'

* * * * *

Erin's first reaction was an urge to write down what Laura was saying to her. Not to burst into tears or gasp in disbelief, but to grab a pen and some paper and make bullet points. She detested lists, mistrusted the thought of not relying solely on the strength of her own memory, but what she wanted to write wasn't a list, per se. It was more a filling-in of gaps.

Fact: Cathy is my mother, not Moira.

Fact: Someone called Julien is my father, not Joe.

This changed everything, absolutely everything, but it also made an immediate, weird kind of sense. It was as though the axis of her world had shifted ninety degrees and parts of her that had never quite fitted in suddenly did.

Fact: I knew I was different. I looked different, for God's sake, with my olive skin, dark eyes and hair.

That sense of being different, of not quite fitting in, had been the root cause of many of her problems at school. It didn't matter how much Moira and Joe had loved her at home, because love – no matter how devoted – couldn't generate that innate sense of belonging that was missing in her, the same sense of belonging most people took for granted. But it wouldn't be right to attribute all her problems to being 'different'. Her self-esteem and confidence were naturally on the low side, and she was easily worried and frightened: this was her personality make-up, this was who she was. Feeling different from everyone else just hadn't helped.

Fact: I grew up thinking I was an only child, and so did Laura, and all the time we were sisters or, to be exact, half-sisters.

This was the only true surprise. She had a sister. Laura.

What would it have been like if they'd grown up in the same house? Would they have been close, like some sisters, or would they have fought constantly over toys and, later on, clothes and make-up?

Laura seemed to read her thoughts. 'I think I would have been a painful younger sister. I was a self-important little madam, remember?'

Maybe, but what about all those lost, lonely years Erin had yearned for a sibling, someone to talk to, to laugh and even argue with, someone with whom she could have developed her negotiating powers and thereby confidence. Surely, the positives would have far outweighed the negatives?

'We found each other eventually,' Laura was saying now.

Yes, they had found each other as adults, become close, encouraged and relied on each other like true sisters. If she had been feeling flippant, Erin could have said 'better later than never'.

'I want to talk to Cathy,' she said instead, and the forcefulness of her tone took her aback.

'It's late.' Laura was placating in contrast, the voice of reason. 'We'll go to see her in the morning. Together.'

It seemed too long to wait. Erin had questions for Cathy. Lots and lots of questions. And she *deserved* answers and as much information as Cathy could provide. That was all she wanted from her. Information. Nothing else.

Laura was right, though. It was too late. Nearly midnight. Not that there was any chance either of them would sleep tonight.

Chapter 36

Evidently, Cathy hadn't slept much either. Lipstick, full make-up, coiffed hair, she was as immaculately turned out as ever. Her eyes let her down, though, and heavily applied mascara and eye shadow only served to highlight their bleariness.

Both Erin and Laura declined when Cathy offered tea. Niceties seemed superficial in the circumstances. The three of them sat in the spacious, high-ceilinged front room, light flowing generously through the large bay window. As a child, Erin used to love this room. In fact, she had been in awe of the whole house, its airiness and sense of space, its effortless style. Her own home had always felt dowdy and slightly embarrassing by comparison.

As Cathy didn't seem inclined to say anything, other than make a repeated offer of refreshments, Erin took the lead.

'What was he like?'

Cathy visibly startled.

'He was a musician,' she replied tersely, as though this sliver of information was all that Erin should need to know.

'What kind of musician?'

'He played in a jazz band.' Cathy stopped again. Seconds ticked by. Finally, she elaborated further. 'He played the saxophone mainly, but he could turn his hand to a number of instruments. He was very talented.'

So he was a gifted musician. Erin almost laughed. If she had been looking for an instant link to him, an obvious inherited trait, then she would have been bitterly disappointed. Thankfully, she found it more hilarious than discouraging that she, his daughter, was tone deaf and completely devoid of rhythm. Did he have a sense of irony, too?

'Do you have a photo of him?'

'Not to hand.'

'You'll find one, won't you?' she insisted. 'I want to see if I look like him.'

'You have his eyes,' Laura interjected, speaking for the first time. 'Moira said so.'

Cathy took a sharp intake of air. 'I'll go and look for a photo.'

As Cathy made her way up the stairs, her steps sounding heavy and reluctant, Laura turned to Erin. 'Our mother is not enjoying this.'

'Well, I'm not having a whale of a time either,' Erin replied darkly.

'You know,' Laura continued, looking pensive, 'I've read about mothers who were devastated to give up their children, who regretted the decision for the rest of their lives, but Mum isn't like that at all. She gave you up, handed you over to Moira, and completely shut off the fact that you were hers.'

Erin shrugged. 'She wanted an abortion, remember, so I expect she didn't feel any emotional connection to me.'

'She said last night that Julien broke her heart,' Laura mused. 'Maybe she blamed the baby – you – for causing them to break up.'

'Maybe ...' Footsteps sounded on the stairs, and there was no time to confer any further. A photograph must have been closer to hand than Cathy had expected. Or perhaps she was returning empty-handed.

Her mother – would she ever get used to thinking of Cathy

as such? – re-entered the room, and she did indeed have a photograph in her possession. Wordlessly, she handed it over.

With a detached curiosity, Erin studied the man in the photo. She saw her shade of hair, her skin tone, and, yes, her eyes.

'He looks more Italian than French.'

'His grandmother was Italian, I believe,' Cathy supplied, sitting back down.

The photo's background was muted lighting and shadowy faces, a bar or a nightclub, maybe in the aftermath of one of his gigs. His arms were folded – was that a look of mild irritation on his face? – and he wore a black shirt and pants. He was tall, or at least seemed to be. Photographs could be deceiving.

'He looks a bit older than you were at the time,' Erin commented.

'He was eight years older,' Cathy revealed, and paused before adding, 'I thought I was sophisticated and worldly, but I was, in reality, a very inexperienced twenty-year-old and no match for him.'

So Cathy had been out of her depth?

'How do you mean?' Erin probed.

'He was confident and outgoing and liked to be centre stage. He was easily bored, Julien. And I found that side of his personality engaging and fun ... until he got bored with me.'

Musical. Confident. Outgoing. Evidently, looks were the only thing Erin had in common with her biological father.

'Did you ever hear from him again?'

'No.' Hurt flitted across Cathy's face. 'I saw his name on the inside cover of a CD once – he was one of the musicians credited – and even that was terribly disconcerting.'

'You should have told me,' Erin stated, handing the photo to Cathy, who seemed surprised to receive it back. 'It wouldn't have changed how I felt about Moira, and I wouldn't have gone all clingy or sentimental, but I would have appreciated knowing this before now.'

Cathy, defiant rather than apologetic, met Erin's gaze. 'We made a pact, Moira, Joe and me. We would never tell *anyone*, not a soul, no matter what. We would take the secret to our graves. I threatened to go through with the abortion if they didn't promise. I didn't want a baby, Erin. I'm sorry to be harsh, but that's the truth of it. I was twenty, I had my whole life ahead of me ...'

'You had me not that long later,' Laura pointed out.

'Three years later, and I grew up a lot in that time,' Cathy countered. 'I got married and promptly got pregnant, as was expected at the time. In today's world I would have held off, perhaps waited until I had the maternal urge or, if that didn't occur, until my biological clock demanded a decision one way or the other.'

'Thanks, Mum.' Laura was sardonic. 'I'm feeling really wanted here.'

'I'm being as truthful as I can be,' Cathy replied brusquely before training her eyes back on Erin. 'You're Moira's, Erin. You wouldn't *exist* if she hadn't intervened. She reared you and loved you. You *unequivocally* belong to her. Do you understand?'

Erin nodded. She fully agreed.

A short while later, with nothing left to say, she and Laura left. On the street outside, before getting into Laura's car, Erin paused. As her eyes swept over the house, her sense of irony once again came to the fore. She had gravitated to this house and to Cathy as a child. Craving her aunt's company, she used to badger Moira to visit, and then didn't want to go home once she was here. Her heart used to beat faster in Cathy's presence. Everything seemed more vivid, more exciting, more fun. Yet much as she had adored Cathy and sought to be noticed by her, her aunt had maintained a dispassionate distance. No sleepovers in her house. No outings to the zoo or theatre. Nothing special. Just the odd piece of cast-off jewellery and half-empty bottles of nail polish.

It felt like an insult now, that nail polish.

Erin yanked open the passenger door.

'Moira next,' Laura stated, her expression grim as she put the car into gear.

* * * * *

Erin walked into the rehabilitation centre, her emotions in turmoil. She was concerned for Moira, yes. Disillusioned with Cathy, yes. Excited that Laura was her *sister*, definitely. All these feelings plus a constant yet surprisingly low-level disbelief that this was even happening.

'Your mother's room is down here,' said Laura, leading the way.

Technically, Moira was not her mother, Cathy was. Moira was her aunt. But the technicalities of the situation did not help control her emotions. They crashed inside her like bumper cars. Disillusionment bumped concern out of the way. Disbelief was sneaking up the inside.

The centre looked like a nice place, scrupulously clean inside and with beautifully maintained gardens semi-circling the sides and back of the building. The staff they met along the way smiled and said hello. Erin caught a glimpse of the recreation room on passing – a large flat-screen TV, residents playing cards, reading newspapers and enjoying morning tea. This added to her positive first impressions.

'It's this one.' Laura stopped outside a door that was half-ajar.

Right at that moment, with the door in front of her, waiting for her to push it fully open, fear crashed forward, aggressively bumping all her other emotions out of its way. Fear that Moira wouldn't recognise her, wouldn't instantly know who she was. Fear that she herself would feel detached from Moira, that the fact that Moira wasn't her mother – that horrible yet undeniable technicality – had created an instant chasm between them, and that their love, closeness and history had disappeared down the chasm, lost forever. The fear was so strong that Erin couldn't move, couldn't walk through the doorway.

Laura pushed her forward. 'Come on.'

Moira had her back to the door. Her chair was positioned in front of the window, and she gazed out at the gardens with the same intentness with which she used to gaze at the television in the front room at home.

'Moira,' Laura exclaimed. 'Look who's here.'

Moira turned her head, and her face lit up instantly. 'Oh my goodness.' She emitted a girlish squeak. '*Look at you.* My darling girl. Aren't you a beautiful sight?'

As soon as she saw her mother's face, Erin felt no doubt, no distance or sense of detachment or fear. She felt love. She felt relief that the love was still there. She felt protective and a little sad. Moira's hair had whitened, she'd grown thinner, and her sling and cast looked a sorry sight. Erin leant down to hug her frail body, to breathe in her scent. This was her mother. Older, weaker, but still, unquestionably, her mother. As Cathy herself had put it, Erin wouldn't exist if it weren't for Moira. And Moira, despite her deteriorating mind, knew that she was a mother. She had not forgotten who Erin was, or what she looked like. She might have forgotten other things, mixed up people and times and places, but she had not forgotten her daughter.

'I had a fall,' Moira revealed in a confidential tone when Erin loosened her embrace. 'I have to live here for a while, until my elbow mends.'

Laura pushed a seat towards Erin and Erin smiled gratefully at her as she sat down. 'Laura has been keeping me updated, Mum. That's why I came back, to make sure you're okay. Do you mind staying here?'

Moira's eyes glanced briefly to the window, and the

tranquil view of the gardens. 'It's not as bad as I thought it would be.'

Erin hid a smile. 'Well, that's good at least.'

Moira took Erin's hand and enclosed it in her own. Her fingers felt dry and cold. 'Are you back to stay?'

'Just for a few weeks,' Erin replied, and hated that she sounded so unconvincing.

'Of course.' Moira nodded, her face creasing in concentration. 'You need to go back to your boyfriend … Jack … the teacher.'

'Good recollection, Mum.' Strange that Moira had retained Jack's name and profession when she had forgotten so many other things. She had obviously attached an importance to him.

Moira squeezed her hand. 'He sounds lovely. Perfect for you. I'm happy that you've found someone, even though it means you'll be so far away from me.'

This endorsement of Jack, this blessing, as it were, to live with him in Australia, caught Erin unawares. She glanced helplessly at Laura, which was pointless, because Laura didn't know that she was planning to break up with Jack. In the meantime, Moira was looking at her closely and clearly waiting on a response.

'I don't want it to be a choice between you and Jack, Mum,' Erin mumbled.

'There is no choice,' Moira stated emphatically. 'You must follow your heart, Erin. I don't want to hold you back. I'll be happy once you are happy.'

Oh dear. Erin really didn't want to get into the details of her feelings, or lack thereof, for Jack, but this obviously meant a lot to Moira and impacted on her peace of mind. It wasn't fair to lie to her, or leave her with the impression that Jack was the love of Erin's life.

'Actually, Mum, I don't think Jack's the one for me …'

Her mother looked so crestfallen and Laura so stunned that Erin felt compelled to explain herself further.

'He is perfect, and lovely, as you put it, but he's not what I want. Actually, he's kind of like his school, Macquarie Grammar. Remember I turned down a job there? Well, there's nothing wrong with either Jack *or* his school. Both tick all the boxes, so to speak.' She shrugged to emphasise her point. 'I just want something different, something more exciting than having boxes ticked.'

'Oh,' Moira and Laura exclaimed simultaneously.

Should she confess that she had feelings for Adam? No. Definitely not. The last thing she wanted was Moira latching onto another name, only to feel let down if or when she found out that relationship had no future. Anyway, Adam himself was completely unaware that she had feelings for him, and she had no idea how *he* felt about *her*. Really, she was overloaded with feelings and emotions these days. It would be nice to feel absolutely *nothing*, to have some respite from it all.

There was a knock on the door, and a staff member popped her head inside. 'Morning tea,' she announced cheerfully, and wheeled in a trolley laden with cups, and plates of shortbread and chocolate biscuits.

She poured Moira a cup, and offered some to Erin and Laura, too.

'Thank you.' Erin accepted the tea, grateful for both the distraction and the caffeine.

Laura also accepted the offer.

The tea lady left them a plate of biscuits to share. Silence blanketed the room as soon as she departed. Moira sipped from her cup. Laura nibbled on a biscuit. Erin used the time to come to a decision.

'We went to see Cathy this morning, Mum,' she said quietly. 'Before we came here.'

Laura choked on her biscuit and stared at her in askance.

'She should know.' Erin lifted her eyes to meet Laura's stare. 'This secret has been killing her.' She turned her eyes back to Moira. 'Mum, Cathy told us –'

'Moira, Gerard, Patrick and baby Cathy,' her mother interjected.

That mantra again. How many times had Erin heard it over the years? Hundreds? Thousands? She used to believe that it soothed Moira, that reciting the names of her siblings symbolised security and familial love, a stronghold in her life. But now she realised the mantra wasn't prompted by a need for comfort, it was prompted by anxiety, anxiety at the very mention of her baby sister's name, anxiety that their secret, their pact, might become known.

'We know the secret, Mum. Laura and I know about Julien and Cathy.'

Moira's mouth fell open.

'We know about the abortion she planned,' Erin continued calmly, 'and how you talked her out of it, and the cover-up.'

'How do you know?' Moira looked frantically from one of them to the other. 'Who told you? *Cathy will be furious.*'

'Cathy is absolutely fine,' Erin stated authoritatively, though this was stretching the truth. 'Don't worry about Cathy, and don't worry about me. Everyone is fine. You must let go of the secret.'

'But I –'

'No buts.' Erin shook her head firmly. 'Let it go, Mum. It's been eating away at you for far too long now.'

Doctors and medical scientists would maintain that the cause of Moira's early-onset Alzheimer's was partly genetic and partly unknown, but over the last twenty-four hours Erin had formed her own theory. This secret, this cover-up, had been like a tumour in Moira's mind, growing and growing and growing until it had overtaken everything else – her memory, her logic, her sense of self. Just as motherhood was essentially foreign to Cathy, secrecy was foreign to Moira, fundamentally at odds with her open personality, gnawing away at her until she had become exiled from her own mind. She had never reconciled to its existence, or become used to it in the way one might become used to a strange city or place. It was clearly too late to undo all the damage it had done, but Erin hoped it was not too late for Moira to enjoy some relief from its domination of her every waking moment.

But for now Moira was still distressed. The secret was too deeply ingrained to let go its hold just like that. It would take time. Maybe days or weeks of persuasion. Erin hugged her mother, held her fragile, wavering body close.

'You don't need to worry anymore, Mum,' she whispered. 'Stop thinking about it. Let it go … Let it go …'

Chapter 37

The house smelt musty and disused, which was odd considering that it was less than a week since Moira had been sleeping and eating and living in it. Erin deposited her suitcase in her old bedroom and set about opening all the windows. The fresh air did nothing to abate the slightly sour smell, or the sense of claustrophobia that had overcome her on walking in the front door.

She would make a cup of tea, have something light to eat, and then go to bed. It had been a long, draining day. After seeing Moira, she and Laura had gone for a drive in the country. Together they had raked over the details of their combined childhoods, but had found nothing at all – other than Erin's inexplicable yet persistent sense of displacement – that so much as hinted at the true circumstances of her birth. First Communion, Confirmation, birthday parties, at each milestone Cathy had retained the poise of an aunt as Moira, unwaveringly, fulfilled the role of mother. They drove all the way to Wicklow and back, reliving every family get-together, sharing shards of memories from when they were young all the way through to the present day, trawling for clues. Nothing. If it hadn't been for Moira's illness, the secret would have never surfaced, never rocked the foundations of Erin and Laura's existence, the very essence of who they each were. Sisters. At every pause in their conversation, no matter how brief, this word rushed in to fill the gap. *Sisters.*

Enough thinking. Tea. Eat. Bed. Erin boiled the kettle and popped a tea bag in a mug, but as she stared at the darkening water she realised she'd forgotten something at Cathy's. She needed to go back. Now. *Right now.* If she didn't, she wouldn't sleep tonight.

Ten minutes later, the taxi she'd flagged down was speeding off in search of its next fare, and she was standing on Cathy's front step for the second time that day.

The Cathy who opened the door looked even more haggard, her eyes red – she'd obviously been crying.

Erin had to harden herself. 'I've come for the photo.'

Throughout the day she had come to the realisation that she needed to have *something*, some form of evidence to prove who she was, where she had come from, and to which she could refer occasionally, if nothing else.

Cathy nodded, and stood back to let her in.

'Go in and sit down.' Cathy gestured towards the front room. 'You look exhausted.'

It was true. Erin felt utterly shattered. Maybe coming here hadn't been so imperative after all. Right now, she could sleep standing up. Jet lag and emotional turmoil, a potent mix.

Cathy reappeared, holding a large square box. Sitting next to Erin, she opened the box and lifted out a leather-bound photo album.

'This is everything I have.' She relinquished it, setting it across Erin's lap.

With sudden, acute trepidation, Erin opened it up. There was Cathy, dressed in a shimmering off-the-shoulder gown, next to Julien, who was decked out in black-tie.

'That was us at a charity ball …' Cathy supplied.

Erin turned the page to another smiling, more casually dressed couple.

'And that's us down at the river one day …'

As she assessed each photo, Erin found herself studying Cathy more than Julien. Young, vivacious, clearly in love with Paris and with the man by her side, it was difficult to feel angry with her. Had she deserved to fall pregnant, putting an abrupt end to those heady, carefree times? Of course not. Had she deserved to have her heart broken by Julien, to be abandoned by him and never see or hear from him again? Absolutely not. Cathy's unguarded happiness in the photos quantified the extent of the hurt and heartbreak that had followed.

No, it wasn't the *young* Cathy Erin was mad at, it was the one sitting next to her. Surely it would have been a better strategy to tell Laura and Erin the truth rather than chance them finding out the way they had. How had Cathy kept silent while witnessing Erin's panic attacks that stemmed from the fear of being forever trapped, unable to leave her mother, unable to live her own life? Not to mention Erin's fear that she would end up like Moira. Why hadn't Cathy taken her aside, assured her that she wasn't at any greater risk of getting Alzheimer's than anyone else in the family because she wasn't, in fact, Moira's daughter?

'I love you dearly, Erin,' Cathy murmured, covering Erin's hand with her own. 'I've always loved being your aunt … I –'

A loud knocking on the door cut off whatever else Cathy had planned to say.

* * * * *

Laura had read to Olivia and tucked her into bed. Then she'd gone downstairs with the intention of doing a quick tidy-up before collapsing into bed herself. The decision to go around to her mother's came out of the blue. One minute she was wiping down the countertop, the next she was clutching her car keys and sticking her head inside the study to inform Esteban that she was going out.

She drove faster than usual, so fast that her tyres screeched as she rounded one particularly sharp corner. It was only when she heard the screech that she realised what had spurred her out of the house: a resurrection of last night's lividness. All day she'd been so focused on Erin and what she was feeling that she'd all but smothered her own emotions.

I got married and promptly got pregnant, as was expected at the time. In today's world I would have held off ...'

Cathy's words had been simmering away in her head, and it was only now, at the very end of this interminably long day, that they'd bubbled over, leaving an overflow of hurt and rejection that simply had to be dealt with.

Unlike last night, Laura didn't bang down the door, but she did knock hard enough to hurt her knuckles.

'You didn't want me either,' she cried when Cathy opened the door. 'If it hadn't been expected of you, you wouldn't have –'

'Erin's here,' Cathy spoke over her. 'Come in.'

'I'm fine *right here!*' At that moment, standing her ground seemed every bit as physical as it was metaphorical to Laura. 'I always *knew* you didn't want me.'

'Of course I wanted you,' Cathy replied, her voice rising a few notches.

Laura saw Erin emerge from the front room, but the extra audience did not in any way temper her fury. 'I always felt I was an *imposition* on your lifestyle, and that I had to prove I was worthy of all the extra trouble I caused.'

Cathy, after a backward glance to Erin, adopted a more conciliatory tone. 'Look, I'm the first to admit I found it tremendously difficult. Back then, there were no how-to books, and no internet to look up. My own mother was ill, Moira was preoccupied with Erin, and I was pretty much on my own. There were times when I was quite simply *terrified.'*

'Well, I'm sorry if I was so damn *scary!'*

'Some of us are not natural mothers, Laura.'

'You're telling me!'

'When I see you and Olivia together, that ease you have with her, I feel sad because I never felt ...'

Cathy trailed off, frowning into the darkness behind Laura. Was that the sound of a car? Laura swung around. Yes, a car had pulled in at the kerb, and she had just registered that it was Gerry's car when she saw him emerge, followed by Paddy from the passenger side. *What the hell?*

'Have you told them?' Laura looked from Cathy to Erin, but both of them looked as surprised to see the brothers as she was. Maybe Gerry and Paddy had come for another reason altogether.

'What's going on?' was Paddy's greeting.

'You tell us,' Cathy replied cagily.

Paddy shifted uneasily from one foot to the other. 'Well, on my end, I went to see Moira this evening and she was saying things that made no sense ... So I called around to Gerry ...' He looked to his brother to supply the remainder of the story.

Gerry's voice was unusually quiet, his gaze aimed solely at Cathy. 'And I'm here because your husband arrived on my doorstep and asked to stay for a few days.'

'*Dad has moved out?*' Laura shrieked.

Fresh tears welled in Cathy's eyes. 'This has all been a huge shock to him, too.'

'Jesus. This just gets worse and worse.' Laura fumbled in her bag to find her phone. The urge to speak to her father took precedence over everything else, and she felt enormously guilty that she hadn't thought of calling him earlier. Of course this affected him too. It affected *everyone*. It was a mess, a terrible, terrible mess.

Finally, she located her phone in the depths of her bag. On seeing it, Cathy held onto her arm, restraining her with surprising force.

'Your father just needs some space, that's all. *Leave him be.*'

Laura shook herself free of Cathy's grip. Tears smarted her eyes. Was this it? The end of her parents' marriage? A marriage that had been a perfectly happy one (despite her mother's mammoth deceit) until now?

'It's only temporary,' said Cathy, somehow sounding certain of this fact.

Laura blinked, trying to clear her brimming eyes. 'This isn't fair on Dad ... He must feel that he doesn't know you at all.'

Gerry nodded, obviously on Ian's side, too. 'He can't believe you kept this from him, Cathy. And to be perfectly honest, I can't believe it myself. I thought we were a close family ... This makes a mockery of that.'

Gerry's words hung in the dark, cool air. Seconds ticked away as moths bashed against the outside light, a spurt of traffic passed on the road, and each person tried to grapple with what this meant for them, individually as well as collectively.

It was Paddy who broke the silence. 'What about poor Erin? Isn't she our main concern here?'

Suddenly, all eyes were trained on Erin, who was standing slightly back from everyone else.

'I'm all right,' Erin said clearly, and was surprised to realise that she meant it. Her gaze flicked from Gerry to Paddy to Laura to Cathy. They were far from perfect, all of them, but they weren't a mockery either. Standing there, she could feel the love, the caring, the good intentions of everyone. Even Cathy, because with her red, puffy eyes, and with her disapproving brothers and indignant daughter, and with her husband who had just walked out on her, she didn't make a very convincing villain. Obviously, there was much to be resolved, but not right now. Erin felt herself sway, fatigue closing in rapidly; it had been three days since she'd had a proper night's sleep. 'Look, could we stop standing here in the dark and cold, and can one of you drive me home? I could fall down with exhaustion.'

Chapter 38

'Laura, there's a call for you on line two.'

'Thanks, Polly.'

Laura picked up the call and had a fifteen-minute discussion with the caller, an existing client, almost none of which she could remember by the time she hung up.

God, she was finding it hard to concentrate. *She was so far behind with everything.* Her inbox was rejecting new emails because it had reached its quota. Documents requiring her signoff were stacked high on her desk (just looking at them was enough to give her a rather alarming sense of vertigo). Phone messages, little yellow slips filled out in Polly's schoolgirlish handwriting (most of them requiring action of some description), were lined up for her attention. To be honest, it felt a little bewildering to be back at her desk after three days off, and to have to deal with things like deadlines, software glitches and contractor hire agreements. Rather like her email system, she felt as though she had reached her quota – her mental quota – and any further information or requests for action would be rejected out of hand.

Focus, she told herself sternly. *Focus.*

Her mind, it seemed, was prepared to focus all right – just not on work. What was Erin doing right now? Had she gone to see Moira this morning? Or maybe, as Laura had suggested, Erin had taken a break from family matters and looked up some old friends instead. Laura had the crazy urge to pick up the phone and check Erin's exact whereabouts. This is what came from spending the best part of three days together.

'My sister is out this morning,' Laura announced aloud to no one in particular. 'I will phone *my sister* later today. Now, I will stop thinking about her and get some bloody work done.'

Following that, she managed to clear some emails with large, space-consuming attachments so that her inbox was functional again. She signed some documents, returned some calls, but just as she was getting into the swing of things and making some progress, someone knocked on her door.

'Savita!' Laura smiled automatically when she saw who it was. 'Come in. Sit down. It feels like ages …'

'Hello, Laura.' Savita smiled in return, but Laura instantly noticed that it was a restrained smile. 'It's good to see you back.'

Laura pulled a face. 'I wish I could say it's good to be back. I feel *overwhelmed* by my backlog, as though I've been away three weeks rather than three measly days … Anyway, enough about me, how can I help you this morning?'

Savita leant forward and placed an envelope on Laura's desk. 'I have come to give you my resignation,' she said softly.

Laura left the envelope where it was. If she didn't open it, then the resignation wasn't in writing (at least not in writing that had been *read* by anyone), and she had a better chance of persuading Savita to reconsider.

'I know you've been extraordinarily busy,' she began, 'and I know your family life has suffered …'

Savita shifted in her chair. Her bangles jingled as she clasped her hands together. 'My family life hasn't just suffered, it has been *non-existent* these last few months. My husband is distant and my son is wary of me – I'm like a visitor in my own house. I've had no time to cook meals, to take care of my herb garden, to catch up with my friends, or do anything else that makes me happy. I thank you for the opportunity, Laura, for entrusting me with Project Chariot and for believing in me. And I will stay until the project finishes in another four weeks or so, because I am proud of what I have achieved and want to see it through until the end … and because I don't want to let you down. But I will leave Global Translations when the project is complete. I love my job, but I love my family more. It is not hard for me to make a choice … I choose my family…'

Laura closed her mouth, deciding against all the responses that had come into her head while Savita had been delivering her speech. There was nothing she could say. Nothing worthy, at least. Savita had made up her mind, and she had the courage of her convictions. Laura felt both humble and a little bit in awe.

'I'll be extremely sorry to see you go,' she said eventually.

The office would not be the same without Savita. She had been the mother figure, nurturing and feeding everyone and creating a sense of family amongst all the nationalities and personalities. In fact, the office hadn't been the same since the day she'd started working on Project Chariot and become instantly consumed by its demands. Johan and a few of the others had lamented her absence more than once.

But wasn't this the very point that Savita was making? If the 'mother' wasn't around, or was too preoccupied and busy to provide any nurturing, then the family fell apart at the seams. The mother was the lynchpin.

Laura wished that she had Savita's courage.

Imagine quitting, walking out, saying enough's enough.

Imagine saying to Esteban and Olivia that she was *choosing* them over her work, putting them first.

Once Savita left and Laura was alone, she tutted aloud at the direction her thoughts had taken. It wasn't quite the same when one was both the boss and the overstressed worker.

Imagine writing a resignation letter to herself! Well, that was just plain ridiculous.

Or was it?

* * * * *

Erin's old bedroom was like a time warp. She'd been nine or ten – she couldn't exactly remember which – when she'd begged to have the walls painted pink. Her poor eager-to-please dad had spent a whole week of his holidays stripping the old wallpaper, sanding back the walls, and diligently applying an undercoat before three layers of pastel pink. A few years later, when she'd grown out of love with the colour, she simply hadn't the heart to tell him. The pinkness was cloying, suffocating. How had she put up with it for all those years? Soft toys – fluffy bears, floppy-eared rabbits, an enormous gorilla – were lined up on a shelf, another throwback to her childhood, dusty now and every bit as suffocating as the walls. Tomorrow she would take down all the toys, and those that survived the washing machine would be despatched to the closest charity shop.

She sat cross-legged on the bed. There was so much to contemplate, so much information to process, that for now she couldn't begin the clean-up or do anything else at all but think. Her thoughts kept flitting from one thing to the next. She needed to focus, deal with one matter at a time. Cathy first. Now that a few days had elapsed, Erin could feel her initial resentment and hurt receding. In some ways, she could understand Cathy's position. A young, relatively naive woman in Paris in the seventies, finding herself pregnant to a man who didn't want to know about it: of course she wouldn't want to keep the baby. Her sister steps in, talks her out of the abortion she had already arranged, and promises to rear the baby as her own. In essence, it had been a surrogacy agreement between the sisters. Cathy had agreed to carry the baby for Moira, to hand it over to her when it was born, and not to think of the baby as her own at any point. Erin's empathy faltered, however, when it came to the events of the last few years and Moira's deteriorating mental health. Cathy should have pre-empted Moira letting the secret slip, and long before that she should have reassured Erin about her own health concerns. Cathy had handled things badly, there was no doubting it.

'I've always loved being your aunt ...' she'd said.

The truth was that Erin, in return, had always loved being Cathy's niece, and simply couldn't imagine life without her aunt's effervescent presence. Despite everything, that underlying attraction to Cathy was still there, and always would be. Slowly, Erin was gaining clarity on what outcomes she wanted, and one of them – perhaps the most important – was to remain on good terms with Cathy. With that specific purpose in mind, she would go to see her aunt again, and again ... however many visits it took to find a way forward.

That was Cathy. To be continued. Who next? Jack? Was she *really* going to break up with him? In the cold light of day streaming through the small, square bedroom window, it seemed more than a little bit insane. Attractive, accomplished, decent, Jack was everything she'd wanted, everything she'd dreamed of on the nights she used to lie in this very bed, hugging a pillow to her chest and wishing that her life was vastly different from what it was. There was nothing wrong with Jack, nothing at all, and right now she couldn't think of a single solid reason to break up with him. She would have to use that hackneyed break-up line: *It's me, not you.* But it *was* her, not him. She wanted something different from Jack, or rather *someone* different. Someone more spontaneous, someone who would stay all night at a party regardless of a commitment early the next morning, someone prepared to abandon work and rush to her side if she were ill, someone who did silly things like walking into doors because he was in such a perpetual hurry, and someone who made her laugh each and every day … Adam. Should she test the waters with Adam before breaking up with Jack? No, that was wrong and not fair on either of them. Did breaking up with Jack automatically mean that she had to break up with Jessica, too? Dear, vulnerable Jessica, whom Erin desperately wanted to protect rather than upset in any way. But Jessica wasn't a valid reason to stay with Jack. Erin knew this. Maybe if she remained friends with Jack – which she hoped would be the case – she could still keep an eye on Jessica from afar.

God, all this thinking was downright exhausting. Erin decided that she had done enough of it for now. She would drop into St Patrick's, as Laura had suggested, and see Ted (still wearing his threadbare grey cardigan, no doubt), the formidable Madame Gallas, and maybe even Tristan Keary, who would indubitably be taller and cheekier than ever. If she got her timing right, she might be able to have lunch with Lisha. If Lisha wasn't available for lunch, Erin would organise to see her some other time. Lisha was rather like Jessica. Erin didn't want to let Lisha go from her life until she was sure that Lisha had weathered those awful, uncertain teenage years when being different or shy was enough to undermine the rest of your life.

As Erin swung her legs off the bed, her gaze fell on a photograph tucked well behind the cosmetics and other photo frames that lay atop the chest of drawers. She picked it up, and wiped off the dust with the cuff of her sleeve. Her secondary school graduation class. There she was, back row, tall, awkward, blatantly different. And there was Rachel Murphy, her chief tormentor, directly in front of her. But then Rachel had never been far away, her derision and unfathomable hatred ever-present, if not in the classroom itself, then around that corner, at the end of that corridor, or waiting ominously in the playground. Where was Rachel

Murphy now? Maybe she had a high-flying, arse-kicking corporate job where she was equally admired and feared. Maybe she was a stay-at-home mum who bullied and harassed her children to tidy up after themselves and do their homework. Maybe she had mellowed and turned into someone Erin could potentially be friends with, if they ever ran into each other again. Unlikely.

Downstairs, Erin opened the back door and proceeded to put the photo, frame and all, into the rubbish bin.

The lingering question was not why she had left the walls of her room that sickening shade of pink, or why she hadn't disposed of those soft toys years and years ago; it was why she had ever tolerated that photograph in her room. Her mother had given it to her a few months after graduation, without any inkling of how truly miserable Erin's school years had been. Erin should have told her mother the full truth, should have begged to move schools rather than begged to have her walls painted pink, should have been brave and fought her corner (that's what Lydia would have counselled, had they been friends back then).

Never mind. What was done was done. And Rachel Murphy was finally gone – out of her life and into the rubbish bin, where she belonged.

Chapter 39

The house was a mess. Laura didn't know where to start: the overflowing laundry basket, the dirty floors, the kitchen, the bathrooms ... She felt rusty and somewhat bewildered, just as she'd felt at work this morning. The trick was to roll up her sleeves and get stuck into it, the way she'd done at work – eventually. Dividing the dirty clothes into whites and colours, she gathered the whites and deposited them into the machine. After tossing in some detergent and choosing the wash cycle, Laura extracted the vacuum cleaner from where it was stored under the stairs. She vacuumed the living area, the kitchen and the hall, feeling a sense of satisfaction as she sucked up all the stray food particles and flecks of dirt. How did the place get so dirty so quickly? Olivia wasn't a particular messy child, and none of the adults in the house were that way inclined either. They all wiped their feet on the way in, ate food at the dinner table only, and cleaned up after themselves as they went. So how had all this dirt accumulated? Maybe the world was essentially a grubby, filthy place. Maybe the act of cleaning was going against nature, and could offer nothing more than temporary respite from the grime. Nevertheless, it always gave Laura a sense of achievement that seemed to surpass the fact that the effects were short-lived.

Laura had started on the stairs when the front door opened. Her heart leapt in fright and she almost lost her footing on the stairs. The noise of the vacuum must have drowned out the sound of the garage door and Esteban's car. She exchanged a wary nod with her husband. After that scene in the garden, when she'd screamed and ranted at him and caused them both to cry, he had been doing his best to be supportive. Something had shifted between them since. Things were different, but Laura hadn't had the opportunity to analyse the difference and establish if it was good or bad. She'd been too absorbed with Erin and Moira and Cathy, not to mention her father, who had spent two nights at Gerry's place before moving back home. She continued vacuuming, paying a great deal of attention to each step on the stairwell. Out of the corner of her eye, she saw Esteban proceed from the hall to the kitchen. Right now, he would be in the process of unloading his pockets of his phone, wallet and keys – she didn't need to be there to know this – and leaving them on the counter where they would stay until she came along later on and moved them to the top drawer of the buffet: their rightful place.

At the top of the stairs, Laura switched off the vacuum; she didn't want to risk waking Olivia. Now, time for a quick job on the upstairs bathrooms. Slipping on some rubber gloves and clutching a damp cloth, she began the task, whizzing from toilet to bath to shower, spraying, wiping, scrubbing. She began to perspire from the effort. Esteban reappeared when she had progressed from the main bathroom to the en-suite.

'I'll be finished in about ten minutes if you want a shower,' she stated to his reflection in the mirror, before looking down to scowl at a mark on the vanity that was proving particularly stubborn.

'I don't want a shower,' he replied in a flat tone of voice. 'I want you to stop.'

Laura scrubbed at the mark, using as much force as she

could muster. It wasn't budging. Damn it. A permanent stain on their beautiful stone-top vanity. Damn it. Damn it. Damn it.

'Stop,' Esteban repeated from behind her. 'Stop all this cleaning. It's driving me crazy.'

She froze, the cloth in her hand suspended over the stain that would not go away.

'We need to talk,' he stated.

'Yes, we do,' she replied, the words stinging her throat as though they were shards of broken glass.

They both needed to apply the brakes, stop everything else they were doing and talk to each other, honestly. This talk was long overdue, and absolutely necessary, but she found the prospect of it truly daunting. She already knew he wasn't happy, and wasn't that the summation of everything else? Their marriage, their business, their life together, *everything* was compromised by his unhappiness. It was like that stain on the vanity, blighting everything else around it.

'Look at me, Laura.' He came closer, lifted her chin with his hand. His touch felt warm and a little bit strange. 'I can't talk to you if you won't look at me.'

Laura raised her eyes to meet his. Deep brown, thick lashes, once upon a time she used to lose herself in his eyes.

'I feel torn down the middle,' she admitted hoarsely. 'You, Olivia, work … some nights my limbs actually ache, as though they've been pulled in different directions …'

Esteban let go of her chin. 'It might be easier to conduct this discussion somewhere other than the bathroom,' he suggested wryly.

Laura actually smiled, and followed him from the en-suite to their bedroom. They sat on the edge of the queen bed and turned to face each other.

'I've been thinking about Global Translations,' she began, deciding to focus on the business first because it was so much easier to broach than his unhappiness, 'and how it has taken over our lives. I want to step back, Esteban. I want a shorter working week, four days to start with, with a view to eventually going down to three. I'm not yet sure how to achieve this, how I'll manage to get my work done in less time, but I know the balance is all wrong as it is and I have to do something to address it before the damage to our personal lives becomes irreparable.'

The idea had been percolating since Savita's resignation earlier today. Beautiful, brave Savita who wasn't afraid to make a choice between her family and her career. The choice wasn't so clear-cut for Laura, when the business was her own and she derived so much pleasure and satisfaction from it. No, Laura couldn't simply walk away, as Savita had done, but she could *step back*. She would hire an assistant to pick up the slack. If she found someone extremely competent, it might work. Correction: she would *make* it work, no matter what.

Esteban nodded, some of the tightness easing from his face. 'That would be a good change, Laura, and it's a reflection of my own thoughts, too. I've also been thinking about our business, and planning for how we can handle this growth spurt without working ourselves into the ground ...'

'And?'

'I want to promote François. I want to make him our sales director.'

Laura frowned. This was unexpected. François was great at his job, but she was at a loss to comprehend how promoting him into what sounded like a brand-new role could be the answer to *any* of their problems.

'François? *Sales director?*'

'Yes.' Esteban sounded quite certain. 'I know it's a new role and means additional cost, but I think the business is big enough now to justify a more hierarchical structure. François is ideal for the job: competent, reliable and excellent with clients. As an added bonus, he doesn't have a wife or family and so he's in the perfect position to travel as extensively as the role will require.'

Ah, so travel, or rather the availability to travel, was at the crux of Esteban's proposal. No doubt this new business structure was the result of weeks of planning, and knowing Esteban, he would have already sought financial advice to ensure that the company could afford the changes.

'But where does that leave *you*?' she asked him.

'I'll take on more of an executive role,' he replied, 'focusing on strategy, partnerships and policy, and with a lot less travel.'

It was a brilliant solution. François would jump at the opportunity, Esteban's focus on strategy could only be a positive thing for the long-term direction of the business, plus – and this was the major selling point for Laura – her husband would be based in Dublin, on call for school pick-ups and drop-offs, unexpected sicknesses and myriad other things his family needed him for.

'Actually, I'd like to travel more than I currently do,' she blurted, and was instantly surprised at herself. Why had she said that? Did she really want to travel? Did she want to stay away from home at night, negotiate her way through foreign cities and business etiquette, and be at the mercy of erratic airline schedules? *Really?* Yes, well, a little bit. Every now and then she would like to jet off to somewhere new, sample the local cuisine and culture, and top off the experience by staying in a luxurious hotel, waking the next morning with just herself for company. Not every week. Just every now and then. 'Just the occasional trip,' she qualified, to stop Esteban from forming the wrong conclusion.

'Okay.' His smile held a hint of mischief. 'That amendment can certainly be accommodated in The Plan. Now, part of my executive role will also involve working from home one day a week, so I can spend quality time with my daughter. Olivia and I will have pancakes for breakfast, chocolate biscuits for afternoon tea, and work on our soccer skills at every available opportunity … '

Laura couldn't help grinning. 'This executive role of yours is beginning to sound a little bit cushy.'

He shrugged disarmingly. 'With both of us working a four-day week, it will help solve some of the logistical problems when Olivia starts school.'

That reminded Laura. School was intricately linked to Kasia. God, she had so many things she needed to discuss with her husband, things that should have been discussed weeks ago. But there simply hadn't been enough time, or energy.

'Esteban, we need to let Kasia go. She doesn't enjoy this kind of work, and we can't justify a full-time nanny with Olivia at school.'

He nodded. 'Yes, I agree ... actually, Kasia is part of my plan ...'

Laura scowled at him. Kasia didn't warrant being part of their family or business strategies. She had done *nothing* to earn that status.

'She lives under our roof,' Esteban countered before Laura could air her misgivings. 'Of course, she must be part of the plan ... And I am of the opinion that we should offer her one of the new junior roles at the office ...'

'Esteban, I really don't think –'

Once again, he cut her off before she could gather any steam. 'Give her a chance, cariño. Give her the opportunity to do something she really wants to do. Be generous. We have dozens of new roles for which we are recruiting. What's wrong with giving one of those roles to Kasia?'

What was wrong was that Kasia despised Laura. Kasia thought she was *self-centred and unable to understand anything outside her own world*. Kasia thought she was *a control freak, and that everything had to be just so*. Not forgetting that Kasia had scathingly referred to her as The Wicked Witch of the West, which would have been amusing if it weren't so hurtful. So why should Laura be generous to Kasia? To prove that she was *not* self-centred or a control freak, to prove that she was simply stressed and too enmeshed in the overwhelming demands of her life to be like the person, the girl, she truly was. The girl who used to be such fun, and so intrinsically impulsive and generous. The girl who used to pride herself on her ability to understand and get along with people from other cultures.

Laura would say yes to Esteban's proposal because she wanted to prove Kasia wrong, and because she wanted a second chance to show Kasia who she truly was.

With that decided, Laura looked up and met Esteban's unwavering gaze. 'Will this plan make you happy?'

'Will it make *you* happy, cariño?' he replied cryptically.

'What do you mean?'

'What I mean is that I don't think you realise how much of my happiness is tied up in how you are feeling.'

Though English was not his first language, her husband had an undeniable talent with words. He was more succinct than anyone else she knew, more forthright and, in this case, breathtakingly accurate. It was true that she'd been just as unhappy as him, and in all this time it had never occurred to her that if she gave some thought and time to her own happiness, his happiness would also improve.

'Yes, it will make me happy.' She flung her arms around his neck, kissed him enthusiastically, and laughed – more loudly and extravagantly than she had in months – when she realised that she still wearing her canary-yellow rubber gloves.

Chapter 40

The next day dawned with watery blue skies, winds that gusted leaves and litter along the street, and the distinct feeling of autumn. It was another day for getting things done and Erin, using the blustery weather to her advantage, stripped the beds in her mother's house and hung a number of loads of wet washing on the line.

Coming inside from one of her trips to the garden, the empty clothes basket hitched on her hip, she was astonished to find Gerry on his way into the kitchen from the other direction.

'Jesus, Gerry! Where did you pop up from?'

He grinned apologetically. 'I rang the doorbell, and nearly belted the door down with my fist, but to no avail. I guessed that you must be out the back, so I took the liberty of letting myself in …' He held up his key as proof before shoving it deep into his trouser pocket.

'Fancy a cuppa?' she asked as she set down the basket.

'I'd kill for a coffee.'

Erin filled the kettle, and surveyed the pantry for some biscuits to cater for Gerry's infamous sweet tooth. The pantry was well stocked – a weekly grocery shop was one of the many things that Laura did for Moira – and Erin soon found what she was looking for.

'There.' She slid a steaming mug of coffee and a plate of shortbread biscuits in front of her uncle. 'Now you won't need to kill me.'

He chuckled at her little joke, took a long appreciative drink from his mug, and swallowed down a biscuit in two enthusiastic bites.

'Actually, Erin, the coffee and biscuits are lovely, but I'm really here for a chat. I want to run something by you.'

Erin stopped stirring her own coffee and gave him her full attention. 'Fire away.'

'Well, you know how Aidan and I haven't been getting along very well,' Gerry began.

'Yes.' Erin grimaced. 'The crash …'

Gerry sighed, took another rather loud sip from his mug, and then sighed again. 'It's not just the crash, or the car … I wish that was all it was. We're at loggerheads about *everything*. Some days it's all I can do not to give him a good smack, like I used to when he was a young lad, but of course he's an adult now and unfortunately a smack is out of the question. Anne-Marie says we need some space from each other, and that's what I wanted to speak to you about.'

Anne-Marie was Gerry's warm, loving, and infinitely wise wife. If Anne-Marie was of the opinion her husband and son needed some breathing space, Erin agreed.

'So how do I come into it?' she asked curiously.

Gerry looked up. 'We thought that maybe Aidan could move in here.'

'Here?' Her eyes widened in surprise. 'Are you serious?'

He nodded. 'If you think about it, it's not such a daft idea. It would give him space from me, which everyone agrees is a good thing, but more importantly, it would enable Moira to return to her own house to live. We've all been nervous since the fall, and you know only too well that your mother isn't yet willing to give up her home and her independence for some kind of institutionalised care. This is a way for her to return here to live, and to be safer. The rest of the family would still keep a roster, as Aidan would be at college most days. But he'd be here at night when the risk is the greatest. If something went wrong, if she fell again, he'd either be on hand to help or he wouldn't be far away, and she wouldn't have to lie there waiting for whoever to call and find her hours later. It's a way of giving him some freedom and some responsibility at the same time. It was Anne-Marie's idea.'

It was a good idea, and solved a number of family dilemmas at once. Erin saw only one major impediment: Aidan himself.

'I can't see Aidan wanting to do this, Gerry. Tell me why a twenty-year-old student would want to live with an aunt suffering from Alzheimer's? What's in it for him? Really, I don't think he wants to get away from you that badly!'

Gerry snorted. 'Oh, but he does.'

'Seriously, Gerry,' Erin tutted.

Gerry downed the rest of his coffee. 'There are other benefits. This place is a lot closer to the college than ours is, so he could walk there every day and save the bus money. And Anne-Marie says that he's seeing some girl who lives close to here. Obviously, we'd have to set some very clear rules around the girlfriend.'

Erin took a while to think. She tried to imagine her young, deviant cousin living in the house, making Moira cups of tea, chatting to her of an evening while they watched television. 'How do you think Aidan and Mum would get along?'

Gerry grinned. 'I think they'd get along famously. Aidan might always be in trouble, but he has a good heart, he really does. I've no doubt at all that he'd be kind to Moira, and I think she'd get a great kick out of him. Moira rather enjoys naughty people. She used to be so tolerant of Cathy, no matter what she got up to ...'

Gerry's voice trailed away. Since the big family fracas on Cathy's doorstep, Erin hadn't had the opportunity to speak to Gerry, or Paddy, on their own; there had always been someone else around when she'd run into them at the rehab centre. Reading Gerry's expression, she realised that he had dropped Cathy's name into the conversation deliberately. He wanted to talk.

Erin smiled awkwardly. 'Well, regardless of who my mother is, you're still my uncle.'

'And you're still my favourite niece.'

'I bet you say the exact same to Laura.'

'Ah, I can't pull the wool over your eyes …' He smiled fondly, and then became solemn. 'How do you feel now? Are you still okay about this?'

'Yes, surprisingly so.'

'Really?' He didn't look convinced.

'Yes, really,' she assured him. 'It answered a lot of questions, and somehow – though logically it should have had the opposite effect – I fit better into this family now. Moira will always be my mother, but at the same time I've realised that the responsibility for her is not all mine, and that I'm not in this alone.'

Erin, Laura, Paddy, Cathy, Gerry, and now Aidan, they were all in it together. Between them all, Moira would be well taken care of. This arrangement with Aidan would tide them over for a year or two until he left college and got a job, and then they would have to go back to the drawing board and possibly have another look at institutionalised care. But the future wasn't just Erin's problem. In her absence, the family had pulled closer together. Or maybe they had always been close but she'd felt so much on the outer that she hadn't noticed. Now, knowing the full truth about herself, she was finally able to settle into her own unique niche.

In fact, she felt so bolstered by her family's love and support that she had no qualms at all in picking up the phone as soon as Gerry left.

'Hello,' she said in a happy voice to the customer service representative at the other end of the line. 'I want to make a change to my return flight, please. Can I bring it forward by a week? … Yes, Sydney … Yes, it's a great place to live … Thank you so much.'

Dearest Gerry and Anne-Marie. Not only had they found a solution for Aidan and Moira, they'd come up with a solution for Erin too, and her uncle had known this well before he'd let himself into the house and startled her so. In essence, he had come to tell her that it was okay for her to leave, that he had it covered.

Moira, too, had given her blessing. *I'll be happy once you are happy.*

The simple fact was that Erin was happy in Sydney.

Chapter 41

Esteban hoisted their suitcase clear of the baggage carousel, and winced at how heavy it was. 'You have the kitchen sink in here!'

Laura smiled sheepishly. 'Everything but ...'

He rolled his eyes. 'It's only four days, you know.'

Yes, she knew, but she wanted it to feel as though it was much, much longer than that. When they went out at night, she wanted to spend time getting ready, and she wanted more than one outfit and pair of shoes to choose from. She wanted to try out her hair straightener – the one she'd bought last Christmas, the one that was still in its box – and to use the body and hand lotions she never had the time to apply at home. When she finished the book she was currently reading, she wanted to immediately start another, and then, if there was time, another. Hence all the baggage.

Rolling the suitcase along on its wheels, they negotiated their way through the crowds. Barcelona airport was always a busy hub, Friday evening perhaps its busiest slot. Men and women in business suits, families, the elderly, students, backpackers, every demographic was represented in the throng. A little girl about Olivia's age flitted past, nonchalantly pulling along a small hot pink suitcase, already the consummate traveller despite her youth. Esteban noticed her too.

He smiled indulgently. 'Olivia would love a suitcase like that.'

Laura frowned. 'Do you think she'll be okay with Mum and Dad?'

Laura had agonised over whether to bring Olivia or not. No doubt her daughter would have been thrilled with the plane – she'd been too young to retain any memory of the last time she'd been on one – and she would have loved having her mum and dad exclusively to herself for four whole days. But much as Laura would've enjoyed having Olivia along, she recognised that she and Esteban badly needed some time to themselves, and that the lifestyle changes they'd promised each other would mean nothing if they didn't rediscover themselves as a couple.

'She'll be grand,' Esteban replied.

It never failed to amuse Laura when Esteban used words like 'grand'.

'You're sounding more Irish by the day,' she teased him, and he shot her a grin.

Regardless of his turn of phrase, her husband was right. Olivia would be fine, and hopefully this time together would cement a closer, more practical relationship between grandmother and granddaughter. In fact, Cathy had surprised everyone, maybe even herself, by offering to mind Olivia while Laura and Esteban were away.

'I know I'm not the perfect mother or grandmother,' she had confessed when she called at the house with her offer to babysit. 'It doesn't come naturally to me, and never has. But that doesn't mean I don't love you or Olivia, and I promise that I will try harder ...'

After everything that had happened, Laura felt that she understood her mother better, and she'd finally stopped wanting Cathy to be something that she wasn't. Cathy would never be a stay-at-home, apron-wearing, warm and homely mother. Now that Laura had accepted this, she felt that she and Cathy would have a more mature and much less disappointing relationship. When Laura needed help, she would ask for it, and though Cathy's response would never be gushing, Laura felt sure she would step up to the plate.

Finally, Laura and Esteban were outside. People milled, taxis honked, and a warm breeze caressed Laura's face. She closed her eyes and breathed in the heat and its smell, the babble of Spanish voices around her, and the poignant feelings automatically evoked. They had come here to rediscover themselves as a couple, and Laura also aimed to uncover the girl she used to be. The carefree, fun-loving, live-for-the-moment girl. In truth, she would have preferred to go to Granada rather than Barcelona, because Granada held all their precious memories and was where that girl used to live. But Granada would have involved dropping in on Esteban's family. Fond as Laura was of her in-laws, seeing them would have stripped away the romance they were both seeking with this trip.

'Taxi queue this way,' Esteban declared, making a start in that direction.

The young Laura would not have got a taxi; saving time was not something she cared about.

'Wait.' She caught Esteban's arm. 'Let's get the bus.'

A smile broke slowly across his face. As students, they used to get the bus everywhere. He understood what it was she was trying to recapture.

He stepped close, and whispered a warning in her ear. 'If we get the bus, it is imperative that we sit on the back seat, and you must hold my hand, and kiss me in front of strangers …'

She giggled. 'Exactly. Lead the way.'

Chapter 42

'Knock on,' Adam yelled, jumping to his feet in a flurry of indignation. 'Come on, ref, open your eyes,' he added when it became apparent that the referee had not spotted the alleged infringement.

As he plonked back down on his seat, Erin refrained from pointing out that the referee was a lot closer to the action than they were. Their seats were behind the goal, tucked under the eaves, and given that the ball seemed to be spending most of its time down the other end, she was astounded that Adam could see enough to make any judgment at all. This was the third rugby league match he'd taken her to, and though she was still fuzzy on the rules, she was surprised by how much she enjoyed the games. Each time they had come with a large group of Adam's friends. Essentially the same group of people who were here today, but as the tickets for this semi-final had been hard to procure, everyone was spread out across the stadium in clusters of twos and threes.

'Down the wing,' Adam urged next to her. 'Look around, see the gap ...'

In the month that Erin had been back in Sydney, she had

also gone for after-work drinks with Adam, and once for an impromptu meal. She'd lost no time in letting him know that she'd broken up with Jack, but sadly Adam didn't seem interested in pursuing anything further than a friendship with her. Her feelings had only grown deeper and more consuming. At work, she constantly wondered where he was around the college, what he was doing, and when she would see him next. At night in bed, she stayed awake concocting imaginary scenes where he would suddenly realise how much she meant to him. It was hard sitting next to him like this, hard not to reach out and take his hand, hard not to lean in close and momentarily quieten him by kissing him on the lips.

Secrets kill the mind. Tell him. Tell him.

But what if he didn't feel the same way? How *excruciating* that would be! She could just imagine how it would be at work.

Good morning, Adam. What did you want to discuss at today's meeting? The new software pilot? No problem. By the way, please don't be put off by the fact I threw myself at you ...

On the other hand, what if he *did*, by some wondrous alignment of the stars, have feelings for her, but – same as her – was afraid that those feelings may not be reciprocated, and didn't want to jeopardise their working relationship.

And what if she never told him how she felt, never took the risk, and some other girl found out how wonderful he was? What if Erin was forever relegated to being his friend, and had to stand by and witness him meeting and marrying someone else?

Make the first move, Mel – who was no shrinking violet when it came to men and who was, to everyone's astonishment, currently dating a man significantly her senior – would advise.

Follow your heart, would be Laura's input.

Be brave, Lydia would say.

Speaking of bravery, Erin already deserved a medal of some sort because breaking up with Jack had been one of the most courageous things she'd ever done. Dear straightforward Jack, who had done nothing wrong other than be his reliable, un-spontaneous self. Ready to take their relationship to the 'next level', he had been hurt and bewildered by her apparent change of heart. She'd done her best to explain how the last seven months had been a journey of immense self-discovery, how much their relationship had taught her about herself and what she wanted in a partner, and how much she cared for him and wanted to keep him as a friend. It had been an emotional, deeply upsetting scene for them both, but they were both sincere about a future friendship, and with every text and phone call since, and even a quick catch-up for drinks last week, it was getting easier.

Suddenly, the crowd began to roar. A player had found a gap – the same gap Adam had been going on about earlier? – and was flying down the wing. The opposing team was giving chase and closing in. Would he make it? Everyone, including Erin, was on their feet, screaming and shouting, at the player, the slow-to-react defence, or the referee.

Just shy of the try line, two burly defenders finally caught up with the player, grabbing at his waist and swinging him viciously towards the ground. As he went down, his hand, with the ball still miraculously in its clutch, reached out and landed decisively on the other side of the line.

TRY!

Adam lifted her up in the air and they squealed excitedly at each other.

It was now or never.

Drawing on every ounce of bravery she possessed, every last morsel of fortitude, audacity and nerve, she clasped her hands on either side of his face.

'I love you, Adam,' she yelled.

She'd done it. Never mind that she was shaking like a leaf. Or that blood had rushed to her face and it now felt a radiant shade of red.

He seemed startled, lost for words. Oh God. What had she done? He was embarrassed. She'd ruined their lovely friendship. Why had she opened her big mouth? Oh, no, no, no.

Wait, he was smiling. Grinning from ear to ear. Looking as if he'd won something. Maybe it was okay after all.

'Adam?'

He answered in the most astounding and perfect way: he kissed her. Not a friendly kiss. A *real* kiss. A kiss that made her whole body buzz. A kiss that made her legs woozy and suddenly incapable of supporting her weight. A kiss that strangely made the noise and crowds recede until it felt as though it were just the two of them alone together. If this was her reward for being brave, she could be the most fearless person in the universe.

Now he was saying something. Something about her being his type. 'Party ... you ...' What party? Did he mean the one at her apartment? The night he'd slept on her couch? Yes, now that she thought about it, she remembered asking him what his type was. Was he saying that he'd had feelings for her back then? 'Family ... caring ... fun ...'

She could only catch a word here and there: it was impossible to hear clearly amid the bellowing crowd and booming speakers. Then there was a sudden lull and she *distinctly* heard him say, 'I love you too.'

Chapter 43

To: *Erin* <Erin.Donovan@yahoo.com>

From: *Laura* <Laura.Torres@globaltranslation.com>

Sent: Thursday 26/6/2012

Hi Erin,

I am sitting here in the most hideous mess, toys, shoes, socks and tissues (Lucia had the most delightful fifty seconds of contentment as she plucked them out one by one) strewn everywhere. In my constant bid to remain relaxed and focused on the important things in life, I am sitting smack in the middle of the aforementioned mess and composing an email to my dearest sister. Resist. Resist. Do not give into the urge to clean up. Someone, anyone, hand me some blinkers. Lucia is like a tornado, leaving a trail of destruction wherever she goes. We are all a little terrified of her, to be honest. I look at her, and then look at the other orderly members of my family, and I wonder where on earth she came from. Yes, I understand the biology side of things, and how a romantic getaway to Barcelona can result in a new addition to the family exactly nine months later. It's her personality that flummoxes me. Was this pocket-rocket sent down from heaven to force me to let go and be more chilled out? Or was she sent so that I would lose the last shreds of control over my life? I'm assuming it's the former, because the latter seems to be a foregone conclusion anyway.

Olivia, I am happy to report, is continuing to do excellently well at school. She enjoys writing and maths, but her favourite subject is religion (God, heaven, angels and the intricacies of the afterlife continue to be an obsession!). She's a good big sister to Lucia, very tolerant and understanding – even when Lucia scribbled in ink all over her favourite doll (Olivia may be growing out of her Barbies, which could explain why she was so philosophical about Lucia's artwork).

Esteban is also doing excellently well. He enjoys being a stay-at-home dad once a week, and brings Lucia to the park and indoor play centres in vain attempts to use up some of her endless energy. I, too, enjoy my day at home, and appreciate my time at the office all the more (oh, the wonderful order, and the compliancy of the staff who actually listen to me when I speak, and do what I say …). The business is continuing to expand, and now Esteban is hiring a human resources manager to help with the endless recruiting and training. Mum takes Lucia on Tuesdays. She finds her very challenging (an observation I cannot argue with), but I think she can see that the more time she spends with her granddaughters, the greater rewards she will reap as they get older (she and Olivia are the best of friends now). Kasia's cousin, Eva, helps out on the other days of the week, and she is fortunately much more child and domestically oriented than Kasia. Speaking of our infamous former nanny, Esteban has promoted her again. Actually, I'm glad he talked me into giving her a second chance – she has proved to be a hard worker and a dedicated employee, and much more suited to working in an office than with children. Her brittle personality has its advantages when it comes to getting things done (she holds quite some clout with the other staff).

Moira has settled into the nursing home remarkably well. The staff are very friendly, and seem to be committed to making the atmosphere as homely and non-hospital-like as possible. I think we chose well, you and me. All that research we did when you were here last year paid off. Moira genuinely enjoys the company, the organised outings and even the food. 'This is where I live now,' she keeps telling me, in case it might slip my mind.

And has Gerry already told you that Aidan got engaged? It seems our wild young cousin has finally acquired some sense and maturity. Not only has he managed to hang onto a job (a whole year without getting fired!), but he's going to be married too (at some vague date in the future … they don't seem to know exactly when the wedding might occur!). You know, he visits Moira regularly at the home, and this pleases her no end. His fiancée visits too, though Moira can never remember her name. Aidan says that a young family has moved into Moira's house (he's seen children playing ball in the front garden). It was sad selling the house, but that's life, isn't it?

Old habits die hard. I simply cannot sit in the middle of this massacred room. In fact, it is testament to how much of a changed woman I am that I have lasted this long. Big kiss for Adam. Please let him know that Paddy continues to sing his praises, so won over was he when he finally met him last year.

XX Laura

PS: Next week I am going to Milan for two delicious nights. All on my own. I will send you a postcard … Ciao!

To: Erin <Erin.Donovan@yahoo.com>

From: Fila Azizi <Fila.Azizi@gmail.com>

Hello Erin,

I hope you are well, and I am sorry that it has been a while since I've been in contact. The reason I have been so busy is my new job. A few months ago, I started as a call centre operator in a bank. I answer phone calls, dealing with customer queries and complaints, and updating information as necessary on the computer system. Even though some of the customers are cranky because they have been inconvenienced in some way, I absolutely adore my job. Dealing with difficult people has dramatically improved my English, and I enjoy proving that I can help them, proving them wrong, as it were. Sometimes they refuse to believe that I am based in Sydney (there is a perception that all call centres must be located somewhere in Asia). The cynicism and verbal abuse upset many of my colleagues, but not me. I brace myself for the difficult customers, and I very much enjoy the nice, polite ones that come along too. Every time I take a call, I wonder how this one will go. Each one is unique, and I enjoy the variety. When people ask what I do for a living, I tell them I am a 'call girl'. It is amusing to see their expressions. I do eventually explain that I work in a call centre, not a brothel.

I love my job mainly because I know how lucky I am. Do you remember Abdullah? Well, he stacks shelves in a supermarket while the rest of us sleep at night. And Padma is a Stop-Go girl for a road construction company. She has to stand for hours on end at road works and turn her sign one way and the other. That is all she does. Stop, go, stop, go, all day long. So I am lucky, you see?

I hope you are well and enjoying your marriage to Adam. I do not have a boyfriend at the moment. This worries my father as he thinks I am becoming old and far too independent. I think there is no such thing as being too independent, and at nineteen I object to being called old!

Maybe one day when you call your bank you will hear my voice at the end of the line. Wouldn't that be funny?

Love,

Fila

Dear Tomasz,

Good news. I have been promoted again. I am now a Translation Consultant. With this role, I have more frequent meetings to attend, more responsibility, and a junior staff member assigned to me. I like being a boss. I try to put myself in the shoes of the junior, and I always treat her with respect. But I am firm too, and I expect high-quality work. I know that Esteban and Laura are impressed with my developing managerial skills. I think they can see a different side to me now, just like I see a different side to them. It is odd – but very good – how things have turned out.

I have broken up with my boyfriend. He wants to get married and start a family and I want something else. I have a good career path here in Global Translations, and I want to take every advantage of the opportunities available to me. I am not sad about the break up. It has been coming for a long time.

I must go. In the morning I have a meeting with an important new client. I will wear one of my new suits (I have invested some of my salary increase in a new wardrobe). I know you do not care for clothes, but you must realise that how you dress is an important part of how you are perceived in business. Recently I came across the cheap black suit I wore when Laura first interviewed me. The suit is now in the charity bin outside the church. Hopefully, it will be of use to someone else, perhaps another immigrant girl looking for a stepping stone job as I was.

Give my love to Mama, and can you please make sure that she is investing the money I send and not allowing it to sit idle in her bank account?

Your loving and VERY SUCCESSFUL sister,

Kasia

Dear Erin,

Yippee. I am finished my Leaving Cert, and at long last I am finished with school. I thought this day would never come. Music was my final paper, and it was weird walking out of the dark exam hall into the sunshine outside. It felt like a very significant moment in my life, as if everything from now on would be brighter and better than before.

Quite a few people finished on the same day as me, and we did something crazy to celebrate: we set light to our text books in the rubbish bin outside the school. Courtney Lynch used her cigarette lighter to start the fire, and as the flames took hold and rose up from the bin, another strange thing happened: my eyes met Courtney's eyes. All those years in the same class, all those taunts and snide remarks, yet I cannot ever remember looking her in the eye. It was only for a few seconds, through the flickering flames, but I realised that Courtney and I actually had something in common: we were both ecstatic to leave school.

I am going to be working in the butcher's again over the holidays. As you know, it is not my favourite job (all that blood — yuck!), but the money will keep me afloat at university. I am so looking forward to starting my business degree. I remember you told me that university is a lot more accepting and diverse, and I look forward to learning in that kind of environment. This will be a new start, and I will make every effort to form friendships. Of course, I will be in touch again before then.

Yours sincerely,

Lisha

Dear Laura,

I am writing regarding your recent advertisement for a Human Resources Manager. I would like to apply for this role. Since leaving Global Translations in 2010, I have acquired some skills and qualifications in Human Resources (including a postgraduate diploma and eighteen months relevant work experience). Working in HR has suited my personality as well as my family commitments at home (I'm afraid that the constant urgency of project management was not suited to me or my family). I would love to return to Global Translations with my new skills. I have missed you all, and I hope you will consider this application favourably. My updated CV is enclosed.

Your former employee,

Savita

Hi Erin,

Major news: Dad has a new girlfriend. She's a nurse, and we're going to meet her during the holidays. Talia is not so keen (as you are aware, she is less friendly than me), but I am very excited. You know, I prayed every night that Dad would get back with you. Then when you got married and there was no hope of that happening, I prayed he'd find someone just like you. God must have been listening because Dad seems really happy again.

Please reply to tell me what you know about Dad's new girlfriend. And when you're speaking to him next, can you please drop the hint that Talia and I are sick of ten pin bowling? We'd rather spend these holidays re-exploring the city, seeing the sights and doing some shopping (correction, lots and lots of shopping).

See you over the holidays,

XX Jessica

To: Laura <Laura.Torres@globaltranslation.com>

From: Erin <Erin.Donovan@yahoo.com>

Sent: *Tuesday 30/6/2012*

Hello baby sister (aren't I lucky that you don't find it annoying when I call you that?) How are you? And how are Esteban and Olivia and gorgeous little Lucia? I miss you all, and it feels like six years and not a mere six months since I was last home.

Adam and I are settling into our new house, and beginning to realise the enormity of what we've taken on. These old terraces are all charm when you fall in love with them, but we have now exited the honeymoon period and all the flaws and leaks and essential repairs have become depressingly apparent. I've discovered Adam's only fear in life: DIY. I am as inept as he is, but we have not lost our sense of humour, and while despairing about the work that needs to be done we regularly collapse into fits of therapeutic – though not very productive – giggles.

I have some news, Laura, really good news, but you must promise not to tell anyone just yet. I'm pregnant! Isn't that wonderful? Moving to Sydney was clearly the right thing to do, and it has worked out for the best in every possible way. I think the baby is a boy. In fact, I've already picked out a name. Something Irish, of course, but I'm not going to tell you what it is, not until I'm holding the baby in my arms (I'm rather old-fashioned that way). I can't help wondering who this baby will look like? Adam? Me? Cathy? Julien? I've been looking at my father's photograph more often, searching for features which my baby might share. Don't worry, I'm not hatching a plot to track Julien down and drop a bombshell on him. I'm quite certain that this increased curiosity is hormonal and will abate as soon as the baby is born. Still, I can't help wondering if Julien ever thinks about Cathy's baby and what happened to it. Did he ever find out that she didn't go through with the abortion? And I've been trying to imagine myself in Cathy's shoes — a baby on the way, so much younger and more naive than I am now, and without a supportive husband or partner. I can understand how scared she was. I would be terrified if I didn't have Adam (who, I might add, is as giddy as a teenage girl at the thought of being a dad!). Speaking of Adam, I hope more than anything that the baby will be like him. I hope our child will make people laugh, and be brave and kind and passionate. On a more frivolous note, I hope this child can dance (with the same enthusiasm but ideally more skill than Adam). On my doctor's advice, I've ditched all my vitamins and now the only supplement I take is folic acid (which is recommended for the first twelve weeks of pregnancy). Adam is particularly happy that my pill-popping days are over (you'd swear I was some kind of drug addict!). I'm ravenously hungry and eating everything I can get my hands on, so hopefully there are enough vitamins C, B, E and all the rest going into my body and my brain.

I'm writing this letter glancing across at a lovely antique dresser that Adam and I paid far too much money for. There's a photograph of you and me on the dresser, taken the night of my going away party. Remember that night? Of course you do, you organised it all. I hate saying this, but our smiles look forced, and our eyes seem to mirror the sadness and struggles we were both experiencing at the time. The photograph is only a couple of years old, but it feels as though it could be from a completely different era. You know, leaving Mum was the hardest thing I've ever done, and the fear and guilt and panic took a long time to subside. But I can finally say it was worth it. I've found my place, in my family, in society, and in the world. Adam makes me choke with laughter every day. This house, though a renovating nightmare, truly feels like home. My job could not make me feel more fulfilled or happier than it does. And, the most wondrous thing of all, I am going to be a mum. A glance at that photograph is enough to establish how far I've come. The girl with those sad, fearful eyes and the woman I am today are worlds apart.

Just one closing thought. Our house, when it's eventually renovated, will have two small but hopefully pleasant spare bedrooms. Please think about coming over and staying with us. Maybe in the New Year? We won't mind Lucia running wild if you don't mind a newborn wailing for hours on end (of course, there's always the possibility my newborn will be one of the placid babies that sleeps for hours on end ... unlikely, though, when you consider his father's hyperactivity ...). Regardless, we would dearly love to see you all, and for all your jet-setting and globetrotting, baby sister, you have never been to Sydney.

XX Erin

Acknowledgements

Worlds Apart took a relatively short time to write yet a frustratingly long time to publish, so sorry to all the readers who have been waiting so patiently while I've been trying to grapple with the recent changes in the publishing industry. It's here – at last! – and I have many people to thank for this.

Thank you, Tracey Ellem, for allowing me to sit in on your French class, and for correcting all the mistakes I made from using that online translation site!

Thanks to Damian Scattergood for telling me about your job in translations, and to Andy Pyke for showing me around your wonderful college and answering my many questions. (Err, I hope you don't mind that Adam is loosely based on you? Bit late to be asking, I know …).

Thanks to my early readers: Ann Riordan, Amanda Longmore, Erin Downey and Rob. I would be lost without all of you.

Similarly, the editing suggestions of Julia Stiles and Sarah Shrubb have significantly moulded this novel, so a big heartfelt thanks to the both of you.

Thank you, Isabel Alfonso, for helping me with Esteban's character, and Suzanne Magill for your help with Moira, and Monique McDonell, for generously sharing the intricacies of your own publishing journey.

Thanks to Tamara Phelps and Donna Heagney, for introducing me to the right people, and to Caroline Ross for her endless supply of hilarious anecdotes.

Okay, I am nearly at the end ...

Thank you, Liane Moriarty, for reading *Worlds Apart* and for providing such a glowing quote. Thank you, Dianne Blacklock, for being such a great sounding board. It's been such a pleasure working with you both. Our library talks, our road trips, our shared newsletter (Book Chat), our 'office' get-togethers, have all been such enormous fun and have kept me going when I might have otherwise given up.

Thanks to Rob and Conor and Ash. You inspire me every day, and sorry that everything that happens to our family ends up in one of my books. I love you all very much!

A massive thank you to Brian Cook. For reading all the drafts of all my novels, for constantly doing things that are not strictly in his job description, for helping me to forge on. It's been quite a journey (we could even write a book about it!).

Finally, thank you to all my readers, for your patience, for your ongoing support, and for those lovely encouraging messages you send to me (which always seem to arrive on days when I need some serious encouragement!). Thank you!

ALSO BY BER CARROLL

Less Than Perfect

Can we ever really leave our past behind?

From an early age, Caitlin O'Reilly was taught by her father to strive for nothing short of perfection. Growing up in a small town in the North of Ireland, she tries to live up to his expectations, and when she goes to university and falls in love for the first time, she thinks everything really is perfect. Until one day when the town, her love and her family, are completely destroyed.

Ten years later, Caitlin has created a new life for herself in Melbourne, leaving her past and her family firmly behind. But when she meets Matthew and finds herself falling in love again, what happened in Ireland is suddenly closer and more relevant than ever, unearthing all the hurts and betrayals and secrets she has tried so hard to bury. As Caitlin's life reaches another crisis point, it seems that there is nothing she can do to keep her past and her present from colliding …

This is an emotionally gripping story about love, forgiveness and less-than-perfect families.

The Better Woman

Sarah Ryan grows up in her grandmother's house in a small Irish village. Sarah is clever and ambitious and eager to move away from the sleepy village. She fully believes that John Delaney, the boy-next-door and her first love, will be right by her side … until he breaks her heart.

Jodi Tyler is raised on Sydney's northern beaches amidst a close and loving family. But Jodi has a secret, a tragic secret which leaves her determined to make a success of her life. Like Sarah, Jodi's grandmother ends up providing her with a home. And when Jodi falls head over heels in love, she too ends up with a broken heart.

This is a story of two remarkable women who face all life's challenges head on – and those they love and lose on their journey. Set in Ireland, Australia, London and New York, Sarah and Jodi make their way in the world unaware that their lives are running in parallel. It is only when they both want the same thing that their paths will finally cross …

High Potential

Katie Horgan is going places: soon she'll be a partner in the prestigious law firm where she works. But her love life is going nowhere – until she meets Jim Donnelly. Jim is brilliant, handsome and, like her parents, Irish. The only problem is that he already has a girlfriend.

When Katie is sent to Ireland as part of her training, she happily settles into life in Dublin where she works in a clinic that provides free legal advice to the homeless. She befriends Mags, who makes it her business to initiate Katie into Dublin's social scene. Then Jim Donnelly comes home on a visit, their relationship deepens, but everything begins to unravel ...

Bit by bit, the truth comes out, about Jim, Mags, and the reason that Katie's parents left Ireland – and Katie learns that life and love are not as black and white as she always thought.

Executive Affair

Claire Quinlan is unlucky in love and fed up with her life in Dublin. So when an opportunity arises to transfer to the Sydney office of her company, she grabs it. She sets up house in Bondi with her old friend Fiona, finds a new boyfriend Paul, and is sure that her life has changed for the better.

But her new job and boyfriend are more challenging than she imagined. She finds herself falling for the handsome American vice-president, Robert Pozos. Robert is sophisticated and charming and very complicated. He spells another broken heart, but she just can't seem to stop herself ...

Then Claire uncovers a corporate fraud and she suddenly doesn't know who she can trust. Everyone has something to lose: Robert, Fiona, Paul. But Claire, who always played it safe, is risking the most.

Just Business

Niamh Lynch appears to have it all: a high-flying career, a handsome, successful husband and a loving family. But looks can be deceiving.

From the moment she has to deliver the terrible news that there will be heavy redundancies at her workplace, her marriage crumbles and her life falls apart.

Certain cracks have been there for a long time, since her family left Ireland. Others are new. Who will catch her as she falls? Her mother whom she can't forgive? Her father from his grave? Or Scott, a man who has just lost his job, but who seems to understand her in a way nobody else does?

Ber Carroll was born in Blarney, County Cork, and moved to Australia in 1995. Her first novel, *Executive Affair*, was inspired by her initial impressions of Sydney, and her exciting, dynamic work environment at the time. Ber now lives in Sydney's northern beaches with her husband and two children. *Worlds Apart* is her sixth novel. Incidentally, Ber is short for Bernadette, but please don't call her Bernadette: this is what her mother calls her when she is in trouble for something.

Ber's novels have been published in five countries, including Ireland. If you would like to know more about Ber and her novels, you can visit her website at www.bercarroll.com, or you can subscribe to her newsletter (Book Chat) with fellow authors Dianne Blacklock and Liane Moriarty (see Ber's website for a link to the newsletter).